Praise for Tanya Huff's previous short story collection, *What Ho, Magic!*

"Ms. Huff is a marvelous talent whose vibrant characterizations and intelligent plotting make each new book a very special reading experience."—*Romantic Times*

"I love the way Huff writes. She creates rich, complex fantasy worlds, populates them with likable characters, includes lots of humor and action, bright, lively dialogue."—*VOYA*

"Tanya Huff delivers great action and the perfect mix of reality and mystery."—*Sense of Wonder*

"Readers will stay on the edge of their seats..."—*Romantic Times*

"This is fantasy at its finest."—*Rave Reviews*

Relative Magic

by

Tanya Huff

Meisha Merlin Publishing, Inc.
Atlanta, GA

"Burning Bright" Copyright © 1999 by Tanya Huff. Originally published in *Earth, Air, Fire, Water*, DAW Nov 1999

"When The Student Is Ready" Copyright © 2002 by Tanya Huff. Originally published in *Apprentice Fantastic*, DAW Nov 2002

"Nanite, Star Bright" Copyright © 2002 by Tanya Huff. Originally published in *Once Upon A Galaxy*, DAW Sept 2002

"All Things Being Relative" Copyright © 2001 by Tanya Huff. Originally published in *Villians Victorious*, DAW April 2001

"Now Entering The Ring" Copyright © 1999 by Tanya Huff. Originally published in *On Spec*, Winter 1999

"Death Rites" Copyright © 2001 by Tanya Huff. Originally published in *Assassin Fantastic*, DAW 2001

"Someone To Share The Night" Copyright © 2001 by Tanya Huff. Originally published in *Single White Vampire Seeks Same*, DAW Jan 2001

"Oh Glorious Sight" Copyright © 2001 by Tanya Huff. Originally published in *Oceans Of Magic*, DAW Feb 2001. Reprinted in *Years Best Fantasy And Horror*

"Sugar And Spice And Everything Nice" Copyright © 2001 by Tanya Huff. Originally published in *The Mutant Files*, DAW Aug 2001

"Another Fine Nest" Copyright © 2002 by Tanya Huff. Originally published in *The Bakka Anthology*, Dec 2002

"To Each His Own Kind" Copyright © 2001 by Tanya Huff. Originally published in *Dracula In London*, Ace Nov 2001

"Nights Of The Round Table" Copyright © 2002 by Tanya Huff. Originally published in *Knight Fantastic*, DAW April 2002

"Succession" Copyright © 2002 by Tanya Huff. Originally published in *Pharaoh Fantastic*, DAW Dec 2002

"Swan's Braid" Copyright © 1996 by Tanya Huff. First published in *Swords Of The Rainbow*, April 1996. Collected in *Stealing Magic*, Tesseract Books 1999

RELATIVE MAGIC

Published by Meisha Merlin Publishing, Inc.
PO Box 7
Decatur, GA 30031

Editing Stephen Pagel
Interior layout by Lynn Swetz
Copyediting & proofreading by Rachelle S. Udell
Cover art by Keith Birdsong
Cover design by Kevin Murphy

ISBN: Soft Cover   1-59222-014-2

http//www.MeishaMerlin.com

First MM Publishing edition: September 2003

Printed in the United States of America
0 9 8 7 6 5 4 3 2 1

Table Of Contents

It took me a couple of false starts to get going with this story. Eventually, I found a book called Fire *by Hazel Rossotti, a Fellow and Tutor in chemistry at St. Anne's College Oxford. It was a great help and pretty much proved to me once and for all that people will write books about anything. Although—besides myself and her mother—I'm still not sure who's buying them.*

BURNING BRIGHT

"MOM?"

Beth Aswith opened her eyes and stared up at the young woman bending over her. "Good, you made it. Did you come alone?"

"No, Alynne gave me a lift."

"Alynne?" Beth glanced suspiciously around the small room as if she expected to see her daughter's oldest friend hiding behind the curtains or under one of the ugly, orange plastic chairs. "Where is she?"

"She's waiting for me down in her car. She wouldn't come in."

"Why not?"

"I think it has something to do with a guy she was dating."

Silver brows dipped down. "She put a date in the hospital?"

Beginning to feel like part of a Three Stooges routine, Carlene dragged a chair over to the bed. "I think he works here, Mom."

"Well, I wouldn't be surprised if she *had* put a date in the hospital." Thin fingers clutched at the blanket. "She's an eccentric little person."

Circumstances helped Carlene resist the urge to announce "it takes one to know one". As a child her mother's eccentricities had been fun, as a teenager they'd been embarrassing, and as an adult, well, they put Alynne's in perspective. "I don't want to argue with you, Mom. Not here, not now." She caught up her mother's hands in both of hers. "Tell me what's happening?"

"Didn't they tell you? I'm dying."

"Mom, you're *not* dying." Elbows braced on the mattress, Carlene leaned forward until she could capture her mother's pale gaze with her own. She knew it was a mistake the moment she did it—no argument could stand against that pale stare. When shaking her head failed to dislodge the unwelcome truth, she leaned back. "Oh my god. You really are."

"I really am. We all have our allotted time and mine has run out. I meant to end this properly but I thought I had another year. Such a pity because I was so looking forward to seeing how the experiment came out. Let this be a lesson to you." Her fingers returned the pressure of Carlene's grip. "Always check your math."

"Mom, what are you *talking* about?"

"What do you think?"

"Mother!"

"Sorry, force of habit. That whole answering a question with a question thing; we're all trained to do it." Beth frowned slightly. "It's supposed to make us seem mysterious. Can't see how."

Silently vowing not to lose her temper at her mother's deathbed no matter how surreal things got, Carlene fought to keep from grinding her teeth. "Mysterious, no. Annoying, yes."

"Thought so." She snorted. "Make them work it out for themselves, they told us. Once you *start* solving their problems they'll expect you to solve all their problems."

"Mom…"

"But enough about me, I'm dying…"

"Stop saying that!"

"…we need to talk about you."

"I'll be fine."

"No, you won't."

Releasing her mother's hand, Carlene pushed back the chair, walked over to the window, counted to ten, and returned. Only her mother could turn what should be a touching moment of resolution into a petty argument. "Yes, I will. I'll miss you very much, but, after a while, I'm sure I'll be fine."

"Fine is a relative term."

"Mother…"

"I've enjoyed being your mother." Sagging back against the pillow, Beth seemed faintly surprised by the revelation. "Watching you grow and learn was the most fun I ever had."

"Even when I got suspended for pounding Terry McDonnell's head against the playground?"

"The little snitch deserved what he got."

Carlene returned the smile. "Thank you. I've enjoyed being your daughter."

"You're not human, you know."

"What?"

Her free hand raised to forestall further protest, Beth suddenly struggled to draw a breath. "What time is it?" she gasped as she released it.

"Ten thirty."

"Oh, bloody hell." The eyes that locked on Carlene's might have been the eyes of a dying woman, but they were also the eyes of a woman who expected to be obeyed. "Stay away from the oxygen tanks."

Carlene waited for the next breath.

There was no next breath.

Barely breathing herself, Carlene slowly stood and backed away from the bed. The too conditioned hospital air had picked up a shimmer and she could hear nothing through the sudden roaring in her ears.

Her mother was dead.

Beth Aswith was dead.

Bindings began to unwind.

Carlene remembered.

"Oh crap..."

She barely had time to move away from the curtains before she returned to her true form.

The flesh she'd worn for twenty four years turned to ash so quickly there wasn't smoke enough to register on the alarm over the door. The flooring got a little scorched and the ambient temperature of the room went up about fifteen degrees but she managed to regain control before she set the whole hospital on fire.

It wasn't easy and had there been an oxygen tank handy, she wouldn't have been able to resist but there wasn't and she did and eventually, she calmed down.

Burning only enough oxygen to maintain a brilliant white flame barely an inch high, she danced over to the bed and, leaving a scorched line along the blanket, settled in the air above the dead wizard's nose. "See," she said, unable to stop herself from flickering, "I told you I'd be fine."

They'd been together for over a hundred years before the final experiment. Even measured in combustion rates, that amount of time, that kind of companionship, couldn't be burned away as quickly as flesh. Her flame dimmed and she dipped down close enough to temporarily warm cold lips.

"And I miss you very much."

A change in air currents warned her that the door was opening.

"Ms. Aswith?"

She sped past the nurse and out into the hospital corridor. Staying close to the ceiling, where the glare of the fluorescent lights rendered her virtually invisible, she followed the blue line to the elevator, took the elevator to the ground floor with a pair of grumbling orderlies, and finally flew out the front doors.

The sense of freedom was intoxicating. She ignited a dead leaf just because she could then sped off to rediscover the joys of a world with no boundaries.

A nickel smelter in Sudbury.

Fifteen hundred acres of spruce forest in Siberia.

The marshmallow on the end of a boy scout's stick.

A lava flow on Maui.

She was everywhere fire burned and everything burned if the fire was hot enough.

There was only one, small problem. She couldn't burn away Carlene. She'd gotten into the habit of being human and burning bored her.

"Tell me again; you're a what?"

"A fire elemental."

"Cool." Feet up on the trunk that served her for a coffee table, Alynne took another swallow of beer. "And Beth wasn't really your mother she was a wizard who gave you a body so you could see what it was like to be human?"

Resting on the wick of a meditation candle, Carlene flared. "That's right."

"And you liked being human and now you want my help to get you another body."

"Yes."

"I don't know." Alynne's eyes narrowed as she studied the flame. "You needed my help yesterday afternoon and then you ditched me in a hospital parking lot."

"I *said* I was sorry!"

"Easy to say." Setting the empty bottle carefully on the frayed arm of the couch, she stood and shrugged a Toronto Maple Leafs hockey jacket on over a faded Grateful Dead T-shirt. "Well, let's go."

"That's it?"

"That's what?"

"You're going to do it?"

"You thought I wouldn't?" One hand beat dramatically at her chest. "You cut to the quick."

"Sorry." Carlene carefully disengaged herself from the wick and followed her friend out into the hall. "I have to say, you're taking this whole thing a lot better than I expected."

"How long have we been best friends?"

"Ever since you bit me in second grade."

"And I should throw all that away?" There were five locks on her door but only one of them worked. "What kind of best friend would that make me? Besides, that whole voice out of a burning bush thing is historically kind of hard to argue with, not that a pot of winter savory counts as much of a bush." She lifted the gate on the freight elevator just high enough to duck under. "Although the next time you show up to tell me you've turned into something weird, you could wait until I'm not holding something breakable." Using the hammer left in the elevator for just such an occasion, she wacked the button for the first floor. "You owe me a Princess Leia, Star Wars glass."

"Sorry."

"Actually, you're a lot more interesting now than you used to be."

"Thanks a lot," Carlene muttered, lightly charring the two by six bracing the back wall.

Given the gasoline fumes leaking out of Alynne's car, Carlene thought it might be safest if she made her own way home.

To the wizard's house.

It looked different, dark and empty. She'd lived there as human for twenty-four years and for almost fifty years in her true form before that—had, in fact, helped the wizard decide to buy it—but she felt no more connection to the house now than she did to any other building on the street. Burning a little copper out of the air pollution, the brief blue flare the elemental equivalent of a human sigh, she wondered if everyone who discovered they were adopted felt as disconnected to their past.

The distinctive sound of Alynne parking by Braille pulled her out of her funk and she swooped down to windshield level.

"Swamp gas ahoy." Alynne stepped out onto the sidewalk and hipchecked the driver's side door closed. "You look like one of those will'o the wisp things."

"Sometimes I was."

"Yeah? You ever lure men into swamps to drown them?"

"Once or twice in the old days to protect the wizard." She lead the way up the path. "It's not something I could do now."

"Not even to a really bad man?"

"Well, I guess…"

"Not even to some guy who like broke your best friend's heart and ripped off her favorite pair of motorcycle boots when he left?"

"I'm *not* luring Richard into a swamp to drown him."

"Bummer."

"Now be quiet until we get inside. Ever since he retired, Mr. Chou has taken it on himself to be a one man neighborhood watch."

"Was he the guy who found your mom passed out in the garden?"

"Beth *wasn't* my mother." It was more of a sizzle than a snarl.

"Oh yeah. Sorry."

The spare key to the side door was inside the hollow body of the hedgehog boot scraper. Alynne fished it out, unlocked the door, and the two of them slipped into the house.

"Don't turn on the lights," Carlene cautioned.

Moving carefully down the basement stairs in the dim glow from her friend, Alynne snorted. "This is your house now. There's no law against breaking into your own house."

"If I don't have a body, I can't have a house."

"But we're here to get you another body."

"And until we do, we shouldn't be here."

Alynne paused and shook her head hard. "Whoa. Paradox. I hate it when this happens."

Carlene decided it might be safest not to ask how often Alynne had found herself in similar situations although she was beginning to realize how much of their friendship seemed to be built on a willing suspension of disbelief.

The workshop door was locked as well but this time, there was no spare key.

"It's a wooden door, can't you burn through it?"

"I can burn one molecule of oxygen at a time and slip through the key hole but I need *you* in the room with me."

"So burn the whole door down."

"The heat would ignite the rest of the house."

"Not good." Alynne boosted herself up onto the washing machine and sat swinging her legs. "Well, you've always been the smart one."

Carlene settled into the recycling box and absently started burning old newspapers a sheet at a time. She'd always done her best thinking on organics.

"I thought you quit smoking?"

"Ha. Ha." Extending herself a little, she burned the smoke as well.

"So how come you're not igniting the rest of the house now?" Alynne wondered unwrapping a stick of gum.

"Paper burns so quickly it's easy to control."

"You think your mom's cable's still hooked up? 'Cause if we're not accomplishing anything down here, I'd like to go upstairs and watch bullriding."

"Beth wasn't my mother." Rising off the paper, Carlene moved toward the door. "There *has* to be a way in."

"Fire's not out."

"What?" Adjusting her point of view back the way she'd come, Carlene flared briefly orange. "Crap. Could you throw some water on that…"

"What's the magic word?"

"Water!"

Alynne shrugged and blew a bubble. "Close enough."

Burning around the lock did, indeed, set the door on fire but after Carlene had moved up by the ceiling and safely out of the way, a bucket of water put it out again.

"Could I put you out with this?"

"No. I'd just burn the oxygen in the water. I'm not *a* fire, I *am* fire."

Alynne shoved the bucket back under the laundry room sink. "Then why'd I have to wait until you moved out of the way?"

"Carlene didn't want to get wet."

"But you're Carlene."

"I know."

" "Girlfriend, you need help."

"That's why we're here."

"Right." Shoving the door open with the toe of her boot, Alynne moved cautiously into the workshop.

"You can turn on the light. This room has no windows."

The four banks of florescence temporarily blinded human eyes but had no effect on Carlene. She swooped slowly around the cluttered room, lightly touching down on the worn chair pulled up close to the furnace vent, on a coffee mug still holding an inch of cold liquid, and on an old, stained apron.

"You miss your mom, don't you?" Alynne asked softly from the threshold.

"Yeah." This time she didn't protest the relationship. "It's funny but in spite of all the junk in here, this room seems empty without Beth puttering about, or sitting reading, or blowing something up. She summoned me back in 1859, when she needed a really hot and precise burn and we got to talking, you know the way you do, about combustion rates and stuff and then the next time she summoned me, it was just to talk. I think she was lonely. I was her only companion for over a hundred years before she gave me flesh."

"Why? Was she was the last of her kind?"

"No, there's other wizards. They just don't get along." Carlene snorted, a tiny tendril of flame flicking in and out. "A group of wizards together is called an argument."

"Like a flock of geese?"

"Amazingly similar."

Carefully picking her way around stacks of ancient tomes, worn copies of Reader's Digest, and piles of boxes labeled, *National Geographic—heavy!* Alynne made her way to the stained wooden table in the center of the room. Unlike every other horizontal surface in the workshop, it held only two things; an enormous crystal ball on a gleaming brass base and a bulging loose leaf binder. "It looks like Beth wrote everything down," she said, flipping the binder open. "Hey, in 1968 you could buy a loaf of bread for twenty-seven cents and you could exchange six ounces of virgin's blood for a quarter pound of dragon's liver. Probably not at the same store..."

Picking up one of the loose pages, she squinted at the crabbed handwriting. "So what do you want me to do? Find her original recipe and follow it again?"

"I don't think it's going to be that easy." Discovering that the old steel brazier had been set up for use, Carlene settled into it.

"Why not?"

"First of all, you couldn't follow a recipe unless it lead you to Chinese take-out. Secondly, you're not a wizard and these things are a lot more complicated than they seem."

"Well, duh." Tapping the edges more or less square, Alynne closed the binder and turned to face the pale flame slowly consuming charcoal briquettes. "So why am I here?"

"I need you to summon the other wizards."

"Cool." She grinned and reached for the crystal ball. "I always wanted to take one of these babies out for a spin."

"Not with that." Carlene flared briefly blue again. "We have to find her address book."

The metal utility shelves along one wall of the workshop weren't as much crowded as they were stuffed. Old margarine tubs of troll parings were pressed up against tubs of gooseberry jam were pressed up against tubs of...

"Whoa! This is not oregano." Pulling a surgical glove from her pocket, Alynne filled it, tied off the wrist and stuffed it back out of sight. "I always wondered why your mother was so mellow."

"I think it may be more pertinent to wonder why you're wandering around with a pair of surgical gloves."

"Not a pair, just one."

"Oh, well, that's different." Wishing she still had eyes to roll, Carlene continued with her own search.

"Hey, can I have this unicorn horn?"

"If you promise not to use it on Richard."

"Cross my heart."

"Or David, or Amend, or Bruce."

Pouting, Alynne tossed the two foot long, spiraled horn back onto the shelf. "Are you even sure the address book is here?"

"It was in 1972."

"That's the last time you saw it?"

"I was never allowed in here as a human child."

"Hate to break it to you, girlfriend, by you haven't been a child for a while now. How'd she keep you out as an adult?"

"She was a wizard."

"Oh, yeah."

Fire saw the world as variations on a fuel source. Magical items, being both highly flammable and completely inflammable gave off a unique signature. In any other room, Carlene could have found the address book in less time than it would take her to initiate pyrolysis. In this room, it could take hours.

Hours passed.

"I am *so* bored." Sitting on the floor, surrounded by unboxed magazines, Alynne listlessly dumped a slinky from hand to hand. "You know *my* mother kept *her* address book by the telephone."

"Beth wasn't my mother and she certainly wasn't yours." Irritated enough to be burning almost orange, Carlene blistered paint across the front of a shelf as she tried to work out where the book could be. It had to be in the workshop because there was nothing magical in the rest of the house but it wasn't on the shelves and it wasn't in the boxes. "Wizards know when they're going to die. She should've been prepared!"

"Anger." Alynne nodded wisely. "Comes after denial, then there's grief, acceptance and something else."

"Sneezy, Grumpy, or Doc?"

"Just trying to help."

"Then find the address book!"

"Fine." Rolling up onto her feet, Alynne stretched to the limits of the Grateful Dead T-shirt and ambled over toward the armchair. "Why do you want to have a body again anyway? You're fire. You rock!"

"No, that would be earth." Carlene settled back down into the brazier. "And while being fire doesn't totally suck, I'd never be able to eat ice cream again, or have sex, or watch television."

"Sequentially or simultaneously?"

"Does it matter?"

Alynne shrugged. "Just curious."

"I want to be able to walk in the rain, feel clean sheets against my skin, keep doing all the things I took for granted for so long."

"You hated walking in the rain. You said it made your hair frizzy." Kneeling in the armchair, Alynne lifted a tangled pile of dried herbs off the phone, lifted up one end of the old black rotary machine, and pulled a small leather bound book out from under it. "Is this what we've been looking for?"

The steel bowl of the brazier pinged as it expanded in the sudden heat. "You know, you're a really irritating person."

Alynne's smile could only be described as smug. "I'll accept that as the compliment you intended it to be."

The address book updated automatically. All but one of the eight wizards listed had a phone number, six had email accounts, and three had fax numbers. The eighth had only a three word address— New York City.

"Sometimes wizards have trouble fitting in," Carlene explained, hovering over the book and trying not to set her friend's hair on fire. "They can't cope with being so incredibly different and finally they snap."

"We're talking a street wizard here? Eating out of dumpsters, sleeping on vents, freaking out the tourists?" Her lip curled. "That sucks. You've got unimaginable powers and you're eating someone else's spit off used pizza crusts."

"And thank you for that image. Just dial the first number."

"There's no name."

"Of course not. Names have power. Wizards don't give them out to just anyone."

"The number's in Sweden. What if this wizard doesn't speak English?"

"It's a wizard, just dial."

Dialing involved rather a great many numbers, including a few Carlene hadn't seen for the last twenty-four years. Alynne either didn't notice, or didn't care that there were suddenly numbers between eight and nine. But then, in all the years they'd known each other, Carlene could only remember Alynne actually taken aback once—after a grade eight track meet when Tommy Elliot, had stripped off his sweaty T-shirt and spontaneously…

"Rude bastard didn't even say hello." Alynne's announcement dragged Carlene's attention back to the present. "He's demanding to know who I am and why I'm using this phone. Sexy accent though." She turned her mouth back to the phone. "Hey, say that you knew our passion was doomed from the start. Why? Because

I've always wanted to hear that from a man with a sexy Swedish accent." Her fingers tightened around the receiver. "Yeah? Same to you and your mother!"

"Alynne!"

"Should you be burning that color?"

Carlene got herself under control just as a number of magazine pages began to curl. "Tell him Beth Aswith is dead."

"He says he knows."

"Tell him that while she was alive she gave a fire elemental a body."

"He says he knows, when she died it returned to fire."

"Tell him its still around and it wants another body."

"He says that's impossible and that you don't exist and then he called me something that probably wasn't an endearment and he hung up." Holding down the button with one finger, she pointed the receiver at the smoldering edge of the worktable. "Should I put that out before I call the next number?"

Six of the other seven wizards were even less inclined to believe or help. The seventh's line was busy.

Carlene thought over everything she knew about wizards and, had she a mouth, she would have smiled. As it was, she burned a bundle of lavender. "They must be calling each other."

"And that's good?" Alynne asked, waving the heavily scented smoke away.

"Oh yeah. They know someone's in Beth's workshop."

"That's bad?"

"Well, they can't just leave you here, there's dangerous stuff lying around."

"Oh yeah, I could really give someone a major hernia with those boxes of *National Geographic*. So one of them's going to show up?"

"No, *all* of them. They can't leave you here but they don't trust each other not to try and rip off Beth's spellbook, making the rippee significantly more powerful than the others 'cause he or she would have access to all Beth's spells as well as their own. Wizards maintain a very delicate balance of power."

"And once they're all here, they'll give you a body?"

Carlene burned brighter. "They may not want to but I'm sure we'll figure out a way to light a fire under them."

The only uncluttered area in the room was on top of the work-bench so that's where all seven wizards appeared—four women and three men of various races. The crowded conditions resulted in a lot of pushing and shoving and the whole experience didn't seem to put them in a better mood.

Carlene finally ended the bickering by moving just a little too close to a flask of mentholated essence.

The magical resonance of the explosion faded into a stunned silence broken by Alynne's impressed observation. "Cool. Cough drops."

Seven jaws dropped. Seven right hands rose and traced the sign of banishment.

Carlene felt herself flicker, felt the pull of pure burning, and suddenly remembered that in spite of syndication on three networks, she'd still never seen the episode of "Friends" where Rachel moves into Monica's apartment and loses the big hair and she wasn't going anywhere until she had.

Seven sets of silver brows drew down.

"That should have worked," a small Asian woman muttered, staring down at her hand in confusion.

Burning a little more oxygen, Carlene danced forward. "You have to know something before you can banish it."

"We *know* fire."

"Yeah, but you don't know me."

A tall man in a turban sniffed disdainfully. "It is clear you have been corrupted by human thoughts and feelings."

"Well, duh."

"You should never have been given a body," declared a blond man hiding most of his face behind impressive whiskers. "In creating you, Beth Aswith created a perversion."

"Perversion!?"

Alynne leaned away from the sudden heat. "Have you, like, really considered the consequences of making her angry?"

One hand clutching the smoking edges of his beard, the blond man added weakly, "And, quite frankly, we have no idea how she did it."

"We have found the spell." The tall man in the turban moved out of the clump, spellbook open across his hands. "But we still do not understand it."

"No, no, no." the Asian woman snatched the book from him. "We understand it. We just can't repeat it."

"Oh, you understand it, yah?" asked the bearded wizard, grabbing the book in turn. He snapped it shut. "There is nothing to understand, she is leaving out whole sections."

"She leave out only basics," someone back in the pack announced. "If you study basics..."

"Basically, you're an idiot!"

It degenerated into a seven part shouting match fairly quickly after that.

"If you're going to have to blow something up again," Alynne said, tossing another piece of charcoal into the brazier, "could you wait until I cover my pudding cup? The last time you got their attention, you dusted ash over my sandwich."

"We have decided..." An indeterminate noise caused the bearded wizard to pause and glance back at the six arranged in a semi-circle behind him. "We have *all* decided," he began again, "that since we can not banish you, we had best might do as you wish and contain you. We have figured out the spell but there is a problem, yah?"

"Yah what?"

"We have no—What do you call them?—raw materials. Usually, we would use straw, or leaves, or other organics. But the wizard you called Beth Aswith used..." He looked a little embarrassed. "...herself."

"Say what?"

"You were the spark of life added to an inert ovum. Flesh of her flesh, contained by her magical force."

"Wait." Carlene flared, the wizards stepped back in unison, and Alynne covered the mouth of her glass. "Are you saying she really was my mother?"

"In all essential particulars, yah. Your mother. But unless you want to be an infant again, we can not repeat the spell."

"We?" the Asian wizard muttered, her eyes boring holes in the reindeer knit into the back of his sweater.

He ignored her. "We know how to build a body from organic matter and even we know how to animate it, creating a golem of flesh as it were, but none of us..." One hand waved in the general direction of the wizards behind him. "...know how to keep it

together more than a few days. It would not hold the magic necessary to hold you and to truly live."

"She really was my mother." Burning couldn't express what she was
feeling. Grief. Joy. Loss. Confusion. Overwhelmed, Carlene burned up
a bundle of sage, Alynne's two sugar cookies, and Beth's old apron.

"Fire should not have emotion," the bearded wizard observed as
Alynne smothered a spark that had fallen from the apron into the chair.

"So give her a body."

"I have explained why…"

"Use Beth's."

Carlene flickered and nearly went out before she remembered
to begin combustion again. "What?"

Alynne settled back into the chair and took a deep breath. "Look,
she died two days ago right? But Carlene disappeared so they don't
know where to send the body so it's still in the hospital morgue.
Beth isn't using it any more so you guys use it as the organic matter
to build another body. Wizards hold magic so this new body made
out of an old wizard will hold the magic needed to contain Carlene
who does that whole spark of life thing again and voila! That's
French for Bride of Frankenstein lives," she added when all seven
wizards reacted by staring at her in confusion.

Seven pairs of eyes blinked.

"But I don't want to be the Bride of Frankenstein," Carlene
protested as the wizards went into a huddle.

"You won't be, they'll make you a new body."

"Out of a dead body! That's just gross! How can you even
think of something like that!"

"Oh, yeah, that's fine talk from someone who crispy crittered
the body she was in."

"That was different! I am *fire!*"

"Yeah. And you don't want to be!"

Carlene could see herself reflected in Alynne's eyes—a yellow
white flame, four inches high. Magical. Elemental. She turned away
first. "You're right. I don't want to be."

"All right. It might work." Once again the bearded wizard spoke
for the group. "But how do we get the body out of the morgue?"

Alynne snorted. "Well you all poofed in here without any trouble."

"This is a wizard's workshop. We cannot poof in, as you say,
anywhere."

"Figures. If I can get you into the morgue, can you poof the body out?"

"It will need two of us."

"Whatever." She checked her watch. "Oh look, Mickey's little hand is almost on the seven. Day shift'll be on in an hour. I'm heading upstairs to shower and borrow some clothes from Carlene's closet and that ought to give you time to decide which two are going with."

Fitting actions to words, she pushed past the wizards who watched her go, open mouthed. Except for the bearded wizard who moved back out of her reach.

"But how she into morgue?" asked one of the less fluent English speakers.

"She used to date one of the morgue attendants."

"Somehow, I am not surprised," the bearded wizard muttered.

Carlene burned blue. "Look, if she keeps pinching you, just tell her to stop."

"Was that Mr. Chou you were talking to?"

Alynne sat down on the bottom step and watched Carlene burn slowly up a broom handle. "Yeah. I told him you were crashing at my place and I just came by for some of your stuff. He says if you need anything let him know. He's a sweet old guy. Those two turkeys get back with the body okay?"

"Yeah. I just didn't want to watch. I mean, it's just organic matter to them but it used to be my mother." She sped up a strip of varnish to the top then back down another strip to bare wood. "Doesn't it just weird you right out?"

"After my best friend turned out to be fire and I gave a wizard a wedgie? No, not really. Besides, dead bodies are cool. You know what Gordon told me? If you catch them at the right time, you can pose them and they'll stay that way."

"That didn't help."

Alynne shrugged. "Sorry."

"So, how was Gordon?"

"I lead him on, I left him hanging. Same old, same old."

The workshop door opened. Unable to maintain a steady combustion, Carlene flared.

"We are ready now, yah?"

"You go ahead," Alynne told her. "I'll put out the broom."

The organic matter no longer looked anything like Beth Aswith. That helped. The seven wizards had taken it down to its component molecules and totally rebuilt it. It didn't look like she remembered Carlene Aswith as looking either—probably because she'd never looked at herself from a fire's point of view. The hair seemed a little dry and she had to remind herself that wasn't necessarily a good thing.

"We will use the spell that inserts the spark of life, which is you," the turbaned wizard told her. "When you are conscious of it picking you up, do not resist."

"I'm ready."

The words of the spell were eerily familiar—seven voices with seven accents overlaid a memory of a single voice and a single pair of hands holding her cupped in power.

"I've enjoyed being your mother. Watching you grow and learn was the most fun I ever had."

"I've enjoyed being your daughter."

It was happening. She could feel it happening. Feel herself settling into the body. Arms. Legs. Head. Heart.

"You're not human, you know."

Doubt.

The chanting grew louder. A little frantic.

Not human.

She could smell something burning. A horrible, final, smell.

Then cool fingers slipped into hers.

"You're not going nowhere, girlfriend. You never gave them two weeks notice at work, you have a dentist appointment next Tuesday, your winter coats' still at the dry cleaners, *and* you still owe me a Princess Leia Star Wars glass."

You couldn't get much more human than that.

"Alynne?" Carlene opened her eyes. "Where'd all the smoke come from?"

"You burned your hair off. Looks like hell. But don't worry, we'll tell people it's some weird mourning ritual."

"We have done it, yah?"

Cautiously, not wanting to shake herself loose, she moved all the bits that were supposed to move. "You have done it. Yeah."

As Alynne helped her to sit up, the wizards cheered. By the time she was standing, the mutual admiration they'd built by rebuilding her had begun to fade. By the time she'd walked carefully over to the chair and sat down, they begun fighting again.

The small explosion took them totally by surprise. Shocked into silence, they turned to face Carlene who blew out the match and tossed the rest of the firecrackers back on the shelf. "Thank you for what you've done. With your help, my mother has given birth to me twice. It's been a long night, you're probably all very tired. Go home and rest."

"That is all then?"

She looked down at her hands then up at seven identical expressions. "Unless you want to stay for breakfast."

They had to fight about which time zone left which wizard the most tired but eventually they left—simultaneously as they'd come, unwilling to allow any one of them to have the last word.

When the workshop was quiet, Alynne sat down and picked up the slinky. "Can I ask you a question? What happens when this new body grows old and dies? Do you become fire again?"

"I don't know," Carlene admitted running her fingers through the ragged remains of her hair. "But then, you don't know what happens to you when your body grows old and dies either. No one does."

"*...I was so looking forward to seeing how the experiment came out.*"

The slinky whispered from hand to hand. "I'm having myself frozen so I can come back to a better world."

"Better?"

"Well, George Lucus'll have the Star Wars movies done anyway."

Which reminded her. "You know, the wizards didn't bring me back you did."

Alynne looked up and grinned. "Yeah, I know, but let them have their moment."

"You've been great right from the beginning of this."

"Why not? Your whole problem was that in spite of being fire, you were still Carlene."

"Well, yeah but..."

"If you were still Carlene then the only thing that changed was your appearance."

"True but…"

"You were still you and I was still me and I'd be pretty small if I dumped you because you looked different. If I was going to do that, I'd do it now. At least until your hair grows back in."

"I guess if you put it that way, it's elementary."

The slinky stilled. "You've been waiting to say that all night, haven't you?"

Carlene grinned. "Hey, I'm only human."

I really enjoyed the wizards I wrote in "Burning Bright" so I decided to reuse them—or at least their mythos—for this story.

WHEN THE STUDENT IS READY

THE FIRST TIME Isabel saw him, he was rummaging in the garbage can out in front of The Second Cup at Bloor and Brunswick. He was wearing a filthy "I love New York" T-shirt, a pair of truly disgusting khaki dockers barely hanging from skinny hips, and what looked like brand new, high top black canvas sneakers of a kind that hadn't been made since the sixties—at least not according to her father who moaned about it every time he had to buy trainers. His dirty blond hair and full beard were streaked with gray, as well as real dirt, and both skinny arms were elbow deep in cardboard coffee cups and half eaten snack food.

She couldn't take her eyes off of him, which was just *too* weird. Having lived her entire life—almost seventeen years—in downtown Toronto she'd seen street people before. Seen them, avoided them, given them her loose change if she was feeling flush and they weren't too smelly or too old. This guy was nothing special.

Thumbs hooked under her backpack straps, she took a step closer. Considering the heavy, after-school foot traffic, he had rather a large open area around him. Which wasn't at all surprising when the breeze shifted.

Did she know him? Was he like some old friend of her dad's who'd fallen on hard times? Breathing shallowly through her mouth, Isabel tried to recognize a familiar feature under all the dirt.

As if drawn by her regard, he rose up out of the garbage and turned, what she could see of his face wearing an expression of extreme puzzlement.

"Half a Starbuck's apricot square will last forty-six hours and seven minutes without going moldy," he said. "A muffin…" Glanced into the garbage, he shook his head. Then he looked up again, locking blood-shot gray eyes on hers. "There isn't much time."

Isabel could actually feel the hair rise on the back of her neck. It was a totally gross feeling. Pulling a handful of change out of her pocket, she thrust it toward him. "Here, buy a *fresh* muffin."

The two dollar coin caught his attention. He plucked it off her palm, closed his right eye, and held it up to his left. "Twonie or not twonie. That is the question."

The coin disappeared.

She'd been watching the coin. Had almost seen it slide sideways into nothing. Had almost *recognized* the movement. She thought she heard something growl. A quick look around—no dogs. When she turned back to her streeter, he was in exactly the same position he'd been in when she'd turned away. "So, do you want the rest of this money or not?"

He shrugged and held out his hand.

Isabel dropped the change in his palm, careful not to touch anything, and hurried away. *Maybe Dad's right. Maybe I should start taking taxies home from school.*

"Dad? You home?" She didn't expect him to be home, not at four thirty on a Tuesday, not on a day that Mrs. Gerfinleo was in, but it never hurt to ask.

Shrugging out of backpack and blazer, she dropped them on the floor, kicked off her sensible black school shoes, picked up her backpack, and headed for her bedroom. By the time she got out of the shower, her blazer was hanging brushed and pressed on the door to the walk-in closet and her newly shined shoes were aligned neatly in their cubby.

Grinning, she threw on jeans and a T-shirt and made her way to the kitchen for her bi-weekly lecture on how clothing didn't pick itself up.

The kitchen was as empty as the rest of the condo.

"Mrs. G.?"

A noise on the terrace, the sound of furniture being moved, caught her attention.

Well, duh. Mrs. G. was out watering the plants.

"Mrs…." Her greeting trailed off, leaving her standing silently in the open doorway staring at the biggest crow she'd ever seen. Perched on the back of a rattan chair, head cocked, it stared intently at her out of a brilliant yellow eye. And it was staring at *her* not just in her general direction the way most birds did.

"What?"

In reply, it dropped the biggest streak of bird shit she'd ever seen down the back of the chair.

"Too gross! Go on, get out of here!" Flapping a hand at it, she added an emphatic, "Scram!"

Instead of flying away, it dropped down onto the terrace and hopped toward her.

"I don't think so bird." Stepping back, she slammed the door in its face.

It stopped, glared up at her, ruffled its feathers into place, and said…well, it didn't say anything exactly, it cawed like crows did but for a moment, Isabel was certain—almost certain—it had called her a stuck-up bitch.

"Okay. Low blood sugar. Definitely time for a snack."

Wherever she'd been, Mrs. G. had to be back in the kitchen by now.

She wasn't. But this time, Isabel saw the note.

Bella: Mr. Gerfinleo called from the emergency so I have to leave early. There was an accident with the forklift. Don't worry, he's okay if you don't count the broken leg. Your supper is in the refrigerator in the stone casserole. Ninety minutes at 350 degrees then grate some of the parmesan on top. Tell your father, I'll call him later when I know.

Well, that explained why the condo seemed so empty. It was.

About to peer into the casserole, Isabel paused. If Mrs. G. had left early, who'd picked up her clothes?

Clothing didn't pick itself up.

She saw him the second time on her way to Gregg's Ice Cream. Seven o'clock, her dad still wasn't home and half a dozen questions kept chasing themselves around in her head. If anything could take the place of answers, it was sweet cream on a sugar cone with sprinkles.

Her streeter was standing outside the Royal Ontario Museum, inside the security fence, inside the garden for that matter, both hands pressed flat against a floor to ceiling window, staring in at the Asian temple. His wardrobe had grown by the addition of a mostly shiny black jacket with the logo for Andrew Lloyd Webber's CATS embroidered across the back. Nobody but her seemed to have noticed him but then he did have the whole poor-and-homeless cloak of invisibility thing going.

About to cross to the southwest side Queen's Park—the museum's corner—Isabel stepped back up onto the curb and crossed to the north side of Bloor instead. When she then crossed west, four lanes of Bloor Street were between them.

It didn't matter.

As she drew level with him, her streeter turned and looked directly at her.

"Time is not an illusion, no matter what they say. Spare some change for a cup of coffee, miss. We need to start soon." He didn't shout, he didn't bellow, he just made his declaration in a quiet conversational voice.

She shouldn't have been able to hear him.

Then a transport drove between them. Caught by the red light, the trailor, decorated with a hundred paintings of closed eyes, completely blocked her view of the other side of the street. Isabel crouched down but a pair of sedans the next lane over blocked that view too. When she stood, the painted eyes were open, the irises a deep, blood red. As the transport pulled away, she thought she saw them blink.

The lawn at the ROM was empty except for half a dozen pigeons milling about like they'd lost something.

"Extra sprinkles," she decided, picking up her pace.

The best ice cream in the city was of less comfort than usual. She still needed answers. The light was on in her father's den when she got home.

"Hey, Dad?"

He pushed his laptop away and turned to face her, waiting expectantly.

"Have you..."

He was a good dad, the best dad—even if he did have a tendency to date men who weren't ready for commitment—but Isabel knew with a cold hard certainty, that he couldn't help her now.

"...heard from Mrs. G?"

If he realized that wasn't the question she'd begun, he didn't let on. "As a matter of fact, I have. She won't be in until Monday; Mr. Gerfinleo is going to need her at home. Will you be all right?"

"Me?" Did the weirdness show on her face? "Why?"

His brows dipped. "Because I've still got to leave for New York tomorrow morning and I'll be gone until Friday afternoon."

Oh yeah. New York. "Right. I forgot."

"You'll be on your own." He sounded less than convinced that it was a good idea.

"For less than three whole days." Isabel rolled her eyes. "I don't drink, I don't smoke, I don't have a boyfriend to bring over, I'm almost seventeen—even if I eat nothing but crap—which I won't— I'll survive and, as long as I avoid Mrs. Harris, no one's going to call The Children's Aid Society on you."

"I don't know. Perhaps you should go stay with your Uncle Joe."

"Uncle Joe thinks I should be allowed to get my belly button pierced."

He winced. "On second thought, you'll be safer here."

Four long strides took her to where she could bend and kiss her father's cheek, patting him on the shoulder in what she hoped was a comforting manner. "Have a good trip. I'll be fine."

She had no close friends amongst the girls at school, no one she could call and say, "Do you feel like something weird's about to happen?"

That left only one person. Isabel reached out for the phone. It slapped into her palm and she actually had her finger poised above the numbers before she managed to stop herself. No. Things would have to get a whole lot worse before she called her mother.

Which was when she realized that the phone had been across the room on the bed.

Her fingers tightened around the red plastic. That was not normal. Hearing crows talk was not normal. Normal people's clothes didn't hang themselves up. Normal people didn't have street people talk to them across four lanes of traffic.

"Normal people," she told her reflection, "would be way more freaked about this but I'm not. Does that make me not normal people?"

Her *reflection* looked normal enough.

She saw him the third time through the window of Dr. Chou's chemistry class. He was shuffling up and down on the sidewalk in front of the school. She was supposed to be studying ionization constants.

"Ms. Peterson?"

Isabel jerked her attention in off the street to find Dr. Chou and most of the class staring at her expectantly.

"Le Chatelier's principle, Ms. Peterson."

The blackboard rippled and she was staring at the back of Mrs. Bowen teaching Classical Literature next door. And then it *wasn't* Mrs. Bowen. And then she realized it was about to turn around.

That would be bad.

Very bad.

Its eyes would be a deep blood red.

I'm so *going to die.*

The blackboard reappeared so quickly, the front of the classroom picked up a faint fog of chalk dust.

For a moment, she couldn't breathe and then the moment passed and Dr. Chou was still waiting for an answer she didn't have. "Um, I'm guessing it's not the nice old man who was head of the school where Le Chatelier went as a boy?"

The class broke into appreciative giggles.

"Good guess. Loss of three points for being clever. Can anyone tell me the correct answer?"

Someone could. Isabel paid no attention to who. Her streeter was sitting cross-legged on the sidewalk, shoulders slumped in apparent exhaustion.

He was still there, fifty-five minutes later when the final bell rang. Pushing past a small clump of fellow seniors, she hurried toward him.

"Hey, Peterson."

It was an Ashley. Or maybe a Britney. One of the highlights and high hems crowd, anyway. Experience having taught her that ignoring them did no good, she turned.

"I'm so glad to see you finally got yourself a boyfriend." A toss of long, blonde hair behind one slender shoulder. "What *is* that aftershave he's wearing? Or is it Eau de *toilet?*"

Isabel's lip curled. "Up yours."

Ashley—or maybe Britney—jerked, eyes wide. "You're such a total loser," she sneered, but the insult didn't have the usual vicious energy behind it. Tugging at her kilt, she turned her attention back to her friends.

Isabel had to stand directly in front of him before he noticed her. "You did that. Stopped that…thing."

He nodded.

"You were waiting for it. How did you know it was going to be there?"

"It was drawn to your power."

"My power?"

He smiled then, showing incongruously white teeth. "The youngest is always the most powerful."

"The youngest?"

"Youngest wizard."

She wasn't even surprised by how little surprise she felt. "You keep saying there isn't time. Time for what?"

"To teach you before the test."

Uh huh. A test. "Is that what that…thing is? Was?"

"Spare some change?"

Isabel slapped her hands together an inch in front of his nose. "Hey! Let's maintain focus here!" He jerked back, his eyes clearing. "Is that…thing, the test?"

"No. It just wants your power."

"Great." A hundred new questions joined the earlier half dozen. She settled on the most mundane. "What's your name?"

His brow furrowed. "I have names."

"Good. Pick one."

"Leonardo."

"di Caprio or da Vinci?"

"What?"

"Pick another."

"Fred."

"There used to be one here but now there isn't and so I came. The others are all still arguing over which one of them it should be but there isn't time." Fred tapped his chest lightly with a grimy fist. "I know."

Under normal circumstances, Isabel wouldn't have believed a word he'd said but normal circumstances had been a little skint of late. The elevator chimed and she held up a hand as the door began to open. "Wait here until I check the hall. I'm *so* not explaining you to anyone."

The coast was clear. She got him out and moving fast; hopefully fast enough that no one—specifically Mrs. Harris—could trace the nearly visible scent trail to the door. She didn't breath until it closed behind them. Then she learned that breathing in an enclosed space with Fred was not a good idea.

By the time she stopped coughing, Fred had left the foyer and was standing in the middle of the living room.

Isabel hurried in beside him. "Look, my father is going to kill me if this place ends up smelling like the inside of a hot dumpster. You need a shower and some clean clothes."

"Clean." His tone suggested he was searching for a definition of the word. "Okay."

All at once, he *was* clean—hair, clothes, probably breath if she wanted to get that close, which she didn't.

"How did you do that?"

"Godfry!"

"What?"

Ignoring her, Fred headed for the terrace door and tried to push it open. On the other side, a big crow hopped from foot to foot and shouted, "Pull, you idiot." When he finally pulled the door open and went through, the crow fluttered up to the top of a rattan chair.

"Well?" it croaked. "Did you tell her?"

"He said he's here to teach me," Isabel answered before Fred had the chance. "That there'll be a test. He said I'm the youngest wizard and the nasty thing with red eyes is after my power—which rather redefined the rather shaky definition of normal I'd been working with. He didn't tell me what he is, it is, or *you* are."

"Him?" The crow turned to glare at her. "He's one of the nine—same as you."

"Nine?"

"Nine wizards. There's always nine. Don't ask why, I don't know. When one finally pops—and one popped early last year—the power finds a new conduit—that's you. It's been gathering in you since Beth Aswith died, which is why you're taking this so well in case you're thinking it has anything to do with you as a person."

Isabel curled her lip but the bird ignored her, swiveling his head to face Fred.

"Him, he's an old conduit."

"I'm a piece of O-pipe."

"Sure you are." And back to Isabel. "My name's Godfry, I'm with him. The big thing with red eyes, is a bad guy—sort of an anti-wizard. You've got no control right now so you're lit up like a Christmas tree. The bad guys want your power—well, they want everyone's power but you're the only one they can find."

"Great." She picked savagely at a thread on her blazer for a moment. The crow's explanation, although it covered the main points, had been a little light on detail. First things first. "So, if there's seven other wizards, how come I rate the dumpster diver?"

This time, Fred answered for himself. "No one else would come in time. A wizard with an apprentice gains power. They're arguing over who should get to teach you and so they'll argue and stop each other from coming to you until it's too late." He peered nervously around the terrace, hands wrapped in the bottom of his T-shirt. "I've seen it before."

"Haven't they?"

"Yes. But it's their own places in the web of power they're concerned with, not yours."

"Wizards, as a rule, aren't very nice people," Godfry snorted. "You should fit right in."

"Yeah, you'd fit in a roasting pan so, if I were you, I'd be careful."

"Oh, I'm so scared." Wings flapping, he hopped along the back of the chair. "Help, help, cranky teenager!"

"Stop it!" Fred's voice rang out with surprising force. "We haven't time."

"Oh, like you care," Isabel snapped. "'A wizard with an apprentice gains power', remember? You're in it for yourself like everyone else."

He frowned, confused. "What would I do with more power?"

She opened her mouth and closed it again. Even clean, he still had the frayed-at-the-edges look of the street. "Okay. Good poi..." Her eyes widened involuntarily—another physical sensation she could have happily done without—and she jabbed a finger toward the sky. "Look!"

Fred and Godfry turned just as the clouds drifted into new formations.

"I see a horsy," the crow mocked.

"There were eyes," Isabel insisted. "Blood red eyes in the clouds."

"It was the sunset through a couple of clear spots."

"It was not." Fred's hands were rolled so high in his T-shirt she could see the hollow curve under the edge of his ribs. "The first lesson is to trust what you actually see not what you think you should see."

"Or what I *want* should be there," Godfry muttered. "If you two want to see blood red eyes in the clouds, be my guest, I don't."

Unwinding a hand, Fred rested it lightly on the crow's back. "What you want doesn't change anything. But what *you* want..." He turned to Isabel. "...does. You have to agree to become my apprentice. Your choice."

"Your what?"

"My student."

"I have to agree to learn to be a wizard from a skinny dumpster diver and a smart ass bird or I wait around for the teeth and claws to catch up with the eyes?"

"Yes."

"Great choice."

"Not really. But you might survive either way. Some people do."

Except for the nervous mannerisms, Fred looked and sounded like he knew what he was talking about. And she had to admit that given giant red eyes, nervous mannerisms weren't unreasonable. "Okay. Why don't you get something to eat while I get changed. On second thought..." She had a sudden vision of the two of them in the kitchen. "...wait here and I'll bring something out."

When Isabel returned to the terrace in street clothes, Fred had eaten a deli-pack of sliced roast beef, half a loaf of bread, and was just licking the last of the mustard off a tablespoon. "Don't put that back in the...Eww. Tell you what." She pushed the jar toward him. "Why don't you just *keep* the mustard."

Smiling, he shoved the spoon down until he could get the lid on, screwed it tight and dropped the jar over his left shoulder. It never hit the terrace.

"What happened to...?"

"Pocket universe," Godfry told her, hopping down onto the table and poking around in the deli wrapping. "Very handy."

"I'm sure." It would certainly solve the forty-pound backpack problem. "So what's next?"

Fred stood and wiped his hands on his pants, leaving bright yellow smears against the green. "Next we go to my workshop and I teach you how to control your power."

"Okay, where's your workshop?"

"This is your workshop?"

A short walk from Isabel's building had brought them to the alley between the Sutton Place Hotel and the insurance headquarters next to it. Given the caliber of tenants in both buildings it was a pretty clean alley, but still...

"The world is my workshop."

"Cliché," Godfry put in from the top of a dumpster. "But true."

"Okay." She folded her arms. "So teach me."

Fred patted the air beside her shoulder. "Learn where your skin is."

"It's on my body."

"Can you feel it?" He headed for the dumpster.

Could she feel her skin? How stupid was that. Of course she could. She could feel her socks hug her ankles, the waistband of her jeans cutting in just a bit, how warm it was under her watch...

"From the inside." Fred's voice echoed about the dumpster and then floated up, eerily disconnected from his body. "Oh wow. It's a good thing I kept the mustard."

"You can't feel your skin from the inside," Isabel snorted at last. They were walking along College Street, heading toward Spadina.

"I can't?"

She glanced over at Fred but he was watching where he was putting his feet with single-minded intensity. "Okay. *I* can't."

"When you try, what do you feel?"

"I don't know." A pause while he crouched and picked something off the sidewalk—she didn't want to know what. "A sort of a sizzle."

"Good. You found the power." He straightened, putting the something in his pocket. "That's what I wanted you to find."

"Yeah? Then why didn't you just tell me to look for the power?"

"Did you know what to look for?"

"No, but..."

"Now you do. Get to know it."

Isabel sighed. What a waste of time. "Is that lesson two?"

Fred started. "There was a lesson one?"

"Yeah: trust what you actually see, not what you think you should see." They'd reached the lights and, as they seemed to have been wandering without purpose, Isabel crossed north with the green.

"Good lesson." He stepped off the curb after her. "Wish I'd had a fish."

"Right." And as far as she was concerned, that was it for the night. Godfry, by far the more consistently articulate of the two, had long since disappeared. "Look, I gave it a shot but it's getting late and I promised my dad I'd be in bed by midnight."

"You agreed to be my apprentice."

"Fine." She rolled her eyes and picked up the pace back toward Bay Street. "I'll be your apprentice tomor…"

The shadows moved in the way shadows didn't, drawing closer, growling softly, tiny red lights flickering in pairs. They were all around her, cutting her off.

"Find the sizzle! Grasp it. Throw it at them!"

Fred sounded kilometers away although she knew he couldn't have been more than a meter behind her. Propelled by the pounding of her heart, the sizzle raced around just under her skin. No way she could catch it. And what the hell did *grasp* mean anyway?

A louder growl. Isabel spun around to face it. Her elbow brushed shadow. Sparks flew. She wanted to scream but she couldn't find her voice. Wrapping her arms around her body, she tried to make herself as small as possible. Which seemed to contain the sizzle.

So she'd found it. Was grasping it. How did she throw it?

As a second shadow brushed icy terror against her.

The night exploded in light.

When she could see again, Isabel stared at the image of an elongated arm burned into the bricks of the building beside her, the talons nearly touching the shadow of her throat.

She peered through the white spots dancing through her vision. "Did I do that?"

"The youngest is the most powerful."

"So you said." There were other images burned beyond the closest one. "Cool. So, if I can do this, why do I need you?"

"Do you know how you did it?"

"Uh…" Icy terror. Light. "…no."

"Can you do it again?"

The sizzle had faded to a tingle—and in some places not even that. "Not right now."

"What if you had to? What if they attacked again?"

"More of them?" When he nodded, she moved a little closer to the streetlight. "Okay, okay, I need you. Still, can't I have a moment to enjoy my victory?"

"No." His voice dropped an octave and he held out his hand. "Teenager sets off explosion in street. Film at eleven."

"That's so retro but I take your point." The wail of police sirens were growing closer. His hand was still basically clean. She reluctantly put hers in it.

And they were standing outside her building.

Fighting the urge to puke, Isabel staggered back until her shoulder blades were pressed against the brick. Waiting for the world to stop rocking, she sucked in deep lungfuls of air.

"Downside to everything," Fred murmured philosophically. "Can you spare some change?"

Although Isabel offered him the use of the spare room, Fred spent the night on the terrace, wrapped in a disgusting sleeping bag he pulled from his pocket universe.

"I have to be where the sky people can contact me. And you have to sleep with your head at the foot of the bed."

"Why? Will it, like, scramble my power signature or something?"

"I have Liza Minnelli's signature on my arm."

Safe within her room, Isabel checked her messages and called her father back at his hotel. Conference was going great, blah, blah, blah. New York antique dealers had a few pieces he could use, yadda, yadda, yadda.

"Izzy, are listening to me?"

"Sure, Dad. I'm just tired. I'll see you Friday. Love you. Bye." She hung up before he could answer and glared at her bed. Wondering why she was listening to someone who ate pizza crusts covered in someone else's spit, she yanked up the sheets and moved the pillows down against the footboard.

The first time she woke, gasping for breath, she turned on every light in her bedroom before going back to sleep. The second time, she stuffed a pair of jeans along the crack under the door. The third time, she shoved her mattress off the boxspring and onto the floor so they couldn't come up at her from below.

At least I don't have to worry about Dad.

Hands rolled in the sheet, she stared at the ceiling and counted backwards from a hundred in French.

"You look like crap."

"You look like you'd go with cranberry sauce." Stepping past the crow, Isabel swept a searching glare around the terrace. "Where's Fred?"

"He left about sunrise."

"Contacted by the sky people?"

"Not likely," Godfry snorted. "They're just a figment of old Fred's imagination—his reason for why he goes completely buggy if he sleeps inside."

"Great."

"Hey, be glad he's not wearing the tinfoil helmet any more."

"I'm just glad he's gone." Feeling nothing but relief—the thought of getting Fred out of the building unseen had tied her stomach in knots—she headed for the terrace door. "Tell him I'll see him after school."

"He's expecting you to join him."

That stopped her cold. Turning, she frowned down at Godfry. "What now? Are you nuts. No way I'm cutting. My dad would kill me."

"And the shadows will what? Lecture you on responsibility?" He preened immaculate breast feathers. "Still, it's your choice, you can learn to be a wizard or you can put on that little fetish outfit and learn to be a productive member of society for as long as you manage to survive."

"Fine. I'll join Fred. But he'd better teach me the spell that makes lame excuses sound convincing."

It was too much to ask that the elevator be empty.

"Mrs. Harris."

"You're not going to school today?"

Isabel glanced down at her jeans. "Casual Friday."

"It's Thursday."

"Okay, casual Thursday then."

"I heard men's voices on your terrace last night *and* this morning. I thought your father was in New York."

"He is. You probably heard one of my CD's."

"No." A thin lip curled. "I know what *they* sound like."

"Can't think what it might have been then."

"Can't you?"

The elevator door whispered open. "Have a nice day, Mrs. Harris." Isabel charged through and across the lobby.

Half a block away, Godfry dropped out of a tree and landed on her left shoulder. He weighed a ton and his claws hurt even through her jean jacket and he was still the most obnoxious creature she'd ever met but it was so cool to be walking around with a crow on her shoulder Isabel didn't care.

"Who's the old broad with the pickle up her butt watching us from the door?"

"Mrs. Harris. She's always *watching*. She's totally bent out of shape that my dad's gay."

"Yeah? I'm usually pretty cheerful myself."

They found Fred back at the Second Cup at Bloor and Bay. He rose up out of the garbage as they approached, holding two half eaten blueberry muffins. "Good morning, apprentice. Breakfast?"

"No thanks." She flexed her shoulder as Godfry dove for one of the muffins. "I'll get my own. Then can we go somewhere less noticeable? My school's just north of here."

They ended up sitting in the concrete doorway of the TransAc Club, half a block south on Brunswick, Fred assuring her that they'd be undisturbed for a while. A while lasted two and a half hours by Isabel's watch. Two and a half hours spent chasing the sizzle under her skin while Fred gave lectures to passing ants.

They moved on just before the lunch shift showed up, heading south, then east along Dundas. Fred walked slowly, hitting up almost everyone they passed for change. When they got to Dundas and Yonge, he dropped what he'd collected in the battered old box sitting in front of an equally battered old man playing the harmonica.

"I don't need money," he explained. "And the world needs music."

"Even bad music," Isabel winced. Behind them, the harmonica wailed painfully.

"Yes."

"Is that the third lesson?"

"Sure. Why not."

"Do you have *any* idea of what you're doing?"

"Put your sizzle in your hands."

"Now?"

"The shadows don't ask so many questions."

It was hard to concentrate with the traffic and the people. "Okay."

"Put your palms together and pull them apart slowly."

Isabel rolled her eyes but did as she was told. For a heart beat, three pale lines of light connected her palms then they were gone.

Fred held up his hands. Even in sunlight, the multiple lines were a brilliant white. "This is control. This is what you need to be able to do before you can learn what to do *with* it. So, to answer your question…" The lines disappeared as he whirled to face a passing suit, grimy hand out stretched. "Spare some change, mister?"

Godfry caught up with them in the small park behind the Eaton's Center. Isabel vetoed a garbage can lunch and bought the three of them takeout. After they finished eating, she lounged back, the crow on the grass by her head, while Fred talked loudly to one of the spindly trees.

"He's got special sauce all over himself."

"Saving it for later."

"Gross."

"Hey, you're seeing him at very nearly his best. He's really into this whole master/apprentice thing."

"Master," she snorted. "As if. Godfry, how…"

"Did one of the nine end up a loony who sleeps on subway grates and talks to trees? Well, the other wizards think he couldn't cope with being so different, but me, I think he couldn't cope with not being able to change things."

"What do you mean?"

Godfy studied her with his left eye then his right. "When you get control of your power, what are you going to do?"

"I don't know; I haven't really had time to think about it." Plucking a few pieces of grass, she dropped them onto the wind. "Travel, I guess. Find that matching Queen Anne vase my dad's been looking for his whole life."

"Fred wanted to make the world a better place but you can't do that with power, you can only do it one person at a time. Even if you change the outside crap, easing droughts, ending wars that sort of stuff, you can't change the way people behave and that's where the problems really come from. After a while, the frustration just got to him."

"So he's too good to be a wizard?"

"Essentially."

"And I'm not?"

"Apparently."

"I'd be more upset about that but…" She waved a hand at the topic of the conversation who was methodically sliding lengths of folded newspaper down his pants.

They spent the afternoon down by Lake Ontario, freaking out a scattering of tourists and condo owners. Isabel kept expecting someone to call the cops but apparently these buildings had no Mrs. Harris. Lucky them.

Toward sunset, one of the waves rose higher than the others and half turned toward them, a translucent but nearly human face momentarily under the crest.

"Water elemental," Fred told her when Isabel squeaked out an incoherent question. "Don't trust them—most of the time, they work with the under-toad. But good eyes on your part. You saw what was really there."

"Rule one."

He nodded. "If that's your toaster."

Another fast food meal and an evening wandering slowly through alleys and access roads back toward Bloor. By the time they reached her building, Isabel could hold a single string of light between her palms for almost fifteen seconds. It wasn't much but for those fifteen seconds she knew what she was doing and she knew *that* was the feeling she had to capture and keep.

She'd have been happier about it had a previous attempt not arced up and plunged three city blocks into temporary darkness.

"No shadows tonight?" she asked as Fred dragged out his sleeping bag and unfolded it under the table.

"Now they know how much power they need to use to take yours so they're building it. Tricky for them. If they wait too long, you'll know what you're doing. They'll be back sooner than later." Hanging his *Cats* jacket neatly over the back of a chair, Fred smiled up at her. "But that's why *I'm* here."

Isabel was surprised to find that comforting. It was the only thing that had surprised her in days.

"One of the reasons I'm here," Fred ammended thoughtfully. "Because you're my apprentice. That's the other reason. Not that I wouldn't protect you if you were. Or weren't."

"Good night, Fred."

"Okay."

There was no way the clock in her bedroom was right. Except that it was the same time as her watch. And the microwave. And the VCR. And her computer. One oh five. AM. An hour and five minutes too late to call her dad—who'd left three messages.

He didn't sound happy.

Until five in the afternoon, Friday was pretty much a carbon copy of Thursday. At five, Isabel managed two lines of light for twenty seconds and was so close to *knowing* what she was doing that not being able to do it was driving her crazy.

She wanted to yell and curse and throw things.

"Why are we hanging around here?" she demanded, leaping off the concrete retaining wall that separated the parking lot from the alley. "What is he *doing?!*"

"What's it look like he's doing?"

"Sorting through a dumpster!"

Godfry spread his wings and methodically folded them again. "Good girl."

"He's not teaching me anything! I'm learning all by myself!"

"Hey, a few less exclamation marks and a little more remembering who taught you what you were supposed to learn in the first place."

"And has he taught me anything since? No." A snicker pulled her attention off the crow to two boys about her age crossing the parking lot. "What?"

"Weirdo," said one.

"Brain fried," snorted the other.

"Oh yeah, like you two are going to rule the world some day. You know, I don't need him to teach me how to be unpopular," she pointed out when the boys were gone. "I can do that on my own. I'm done for today. When he gets out of the dumpster…"

"It's time."

The crow and the wizard's apprentice turned to see Fred holding an empty laser printer drum and staring north.

"Time for what?" Isabel asked, searching the gathering shadows for flecks of red.

"Chinese food. There's great garbage behind the noodle shop."

"Forget it," she sighed. "I'll pay."

By the time they finished eating, it was dark. Godfry had devoured half a bowl of noodles and left while he could still see to fly. They were walking through the tiny park on Bellevue Avenue, arguing the merits of egg rolls over spring rolls when the shadows attacked.

"Fred!"

Darkness wrapped around him, reached for him. He screamed and Isabel echoed it although none of the shadows had gone for her.

"*...they want everyone's power but you're the only one they can find.*"

And Fred was with her.

So they could find Fred.

She could barely see him inside the shifting darkness. A dozen or more glowing red eyes swirled around him. He was confused. He'd expected her to be attacked and Fred didn't change gears quickly. By the time he did, it would be too late.

She was his only chance.

And when they finished with him, they'd be after her.

Hands ten centimeters apart, Isabel fought to control her breathing. *Find the sizzle. Find the sweet spot. Find where it works.*

Two strings of light stretched from palm to palm.

Oh, that's a lot of help.

How did Fred do it? He never concentrated on *anything* this hard. *Duh.*

Power snapped into place with an almost audible click. Half the shadows turned as a hundred strands of light formed between her palms.

Too late.

She smacked her hands together.

It was still nothing more than a crude release of power but this time she was doing it on purpose. With a purpose.

"Fred!" Blinking away after images, she dropped to her knees by his side. "Are you okay?"

After a short struggle, he focused on her face. "The rain in Spain falls mainly on the plain."

Isabel grinned. Suddenly her dad's interest in musical theater was actually useful. "Could you possibly mean, 'by Jove, I think she's got it?'"

"Okay."

"We rule. We rock. At the risk of sounding like the end of every bad sports movie ever made, we are the champions and champions deserve ice cream. There's a pint of Cherry Garcia in the freezer." She flashed a smile at a still wobbly Fred and reached for the condo door. "Technically, it's Dad's but he's not.... Dad!"

"Isabel."

Hurrying into the foyer behind her father were Mrs. Harris, a police officer, and two large men dressed like ambulance attendants. Isabel was suddenly very aware that behind *her* stood a skinny, grimy man who looked like he'd just been bounced across a park and who still had folded newspaper down his pants.

Anger and worry showed about equally on her dad's face. No, wait, anger seemed to be winning.

"I didn't want to believe what Mrs. Harris was telling me, Isabel, but when you weren't home last night and then I got the message from the school about you not being in class, and then you wander in... Do you even know what time it is?"

"Uh, ten?"

"Three."

She checked her watch. Three. AM.

"Time flies when you're having shadows."

"Thanks, Fred. You might have told me that!"

Fred shrugged. "Iceberg."

Which was either an enigmatic Titanic reference or he was gone again.

"He's probably her dealer," Mrs. Harris snorted.

Isabel ignored her, stepping between Fred and her father. "Dad, I know this looks bad, but Fred's my..." Quick, a word for what Fred was that her father would understand. "...friend. Okay, I cut school and I let him sleep on the terrace but he needs me."

"Needs you?"

"Yes! And he's teaching me so much."

Mrs. Harris pursed her lips disdainfully. "I can't imagine what."

"Try compassion," Isabel snapped. "And I'm sure you can't imagine it!"

"Isabel…" Her dad sighed and began again. It looked as though worry had won the final round. "Izzy, your friend has run away from a facility in Scarborough. The police have been searching for him for weeks. They recognized him the moment Mrs. Harris gave them a description. These men are going to take him to the facility and see that he gets back on his medication."

"Dad, he's not crazy."

"All right, but look at him, he's skin and bones, if he stays on the street he'll die. I don't know why you've suddenly decided to adopt him—and believe me, we're going to talk about this—but he's a person, not a puppy or a kitten, and you can't know what's best for him." Grabbing hold of Isabel's shoulder, he moved them both to one side. Pressed up against him, she could feel the fear rolling off him like smoke.

Afraid for her? Or of something?

The ambulance attendants, advanced.

"Fred! Do something!"

He stared wide-eyed at the approaching attendants. "I can macramé a plant hanger."

"Not helpful!" She had to do something. But what? All she knew how to do was make a bright light which was great at chasing shadows away but these were flesh and blood men. Big men. Big scary men. Even if she temporarily blinded them, Fred would probably just stand there blinking.

But what else could she do? What else had Fred taught her?

Trust what you actually see not what you think you see.

They'd already gone after Fred once.

What will you do if they come after you again?

No wonder the ambulance attendants were so terrifying. Their eyes were a deep, blood red.

As she pulled her hands apart creating a cat's cradle of light, the closer shadow turned to face her. She froze.

"They should take all these sorts of people off the streets and put them in institutions where they belong."

Thank you, Mrs. Harris. Shadows held no terror for her, she spent her life surrounded by shadows of her own making.

For the second time that night, Isabel slapped her palms together.

When she could see again, the shadows were gone and Fred was gone—was safe, she knew that for a certainty without knowing how she knew. Unfortunately, Mrs. Harris and the cop remained.

"Well, you have your daughter home safe and sound, Mr. Peterson. I'll leave you to handle it." From the look the constable shot her, he clearly thought rather too much had been made about a sixteen year old who stayed out late on a Friday night.

Her father looked like he had every intention of making even more about it. "I'm sorry to trouble you, officer."

"No. This isn't right." Mrs. Harris stared wide-eyed around the foyer. "Where are the others? There were other men here. A filthy one and two strong men to carry him away."

"Uh, ma'am, there was only the three of us until the young lady came home."

"No. That's wrong!"

The constable exhaled once, through his nose, and moved behind Mrs. Harris. "Just the three of us, ma'am. It's late, I'll escort you safely home."

She could walk out the door or she could be pushed. She chose to walk.

Isabel turned to face her father. "So. How was your trip, Dad? Have a good time?"

"Apparently not as good as you did."

Isabel was out on the terrace at dawn, holding a three day old salmon steak.

With a poof of displaced air, a broad shouldered blond in a cable-knit sweater appeared by the table. Throwing the piece of fish at him seemed like a perfectly reasonable reaction.

He frowned and deflected it with a glance. As it hit the floor, he turned his bright blue gaze back to Isabel. "Congratulations, you am passing your test."

"Am passing?"

"Are passed?"

"Let me guess. English as a second… Are there going to be many more of you?" she asked as a small Asian woman and a tall, distinguished looking man in a turban appeared as well.

All three of them ignored her, turning instead on each other.

"What are you doing here?"

"I came to inform her..."

"No, we agreed I would tell her..."

"I are telling her, yah."

"Oh no, not you. Me."

Shouting simultaneously, they disappeared.

"Well, you can see how much help they'd have been to you," Godfry muttered, dropping out of the sky beside the salmon. "Is that for me?"

"Yes. Let me guess; three more of the nine?"

"Who else. Do you know what they call a group of wizards? An argument."

Made sense. She shifted her weight to one hip and waited until the crow finished eating. "They said I passed my test."

"Yep." He flew up to his regular perch on the chair. "Last night, when you didn't immediately try to save your own ass and saved Fred."

"The first time or the second time?"

"The second time. The first time you were thinking that once they finished with him, they'd come after you." Wings folded, he cocked his head up at her. "As Fred would say, the world doesn't need wizards that taste good, they need wizards with good taste. You have to be worthy of the power."

"So Fred wasn't teaching me how to pass the test?"

"Wasn't he?"

Try compassion.

Isabel sighed. "Where *is* Fred?"

"Having breakfast."

"At the Second Cup garbage bin?"

"Nah. Not on a Saturday. Saturdays it's the dumpster behind the Royal York. You get in much trouble with your old man?"

She shrugged and, greatly daring, stretched out one finger to stroke an ebony shoulder. "I've been grounded for a month with no TV, but Dad says he understands teenage rebellion—as if—and I can probably pay my scholastic dept with a thousand word essay on responsibility. It could have been worse."

"You could have been swallowed by shadow. Not a problem now," Godfry continued before Isabel could respond. "You got control so you're in no immediate danger. The rest of the lessons can wait for a month."

"The rest of the lessons?"

"Oh yeah. A wizard's apprenticeship lasts seven years."

"What?" Stepping back, she kicked the chair leg, sending Godfry flying. "I am *not* spending the next seven years looking into dumpsters!"

"Hey, you agreed; don't take it out on the bird! Besides, there's a lot more than dumpsters—there's garbage cans, landfill sites, soup kitchens, overpasses, winters in cardboard boxes, summers in stormdrains, roadkill…"

Isabel slammed the terrace door, cutting off the crow's litany.

It was going to be a *long* seven years.

The premise for this story was to take a fairy tale and rewrite it as science fiction. My first choice, Sleeping Beauty, went immediately so I turned to the lesser known, The Shoemaker and the Elves. *I really like the gritty, working-class world-building I did for this story and used it in a story called* I Knew A Guy Once *that's not in this collection. (Or at this exact moment, even out yet.) I expect, I'll return to the mining station again.*

NANITE, STAR BRIGHT

LOST IN THE intricate depths of a sub-atomic filter, Ely Shoemaker remained oblivious to the dark shadow that fell suddenly over her workbench. Then something clamped down hard on her left shoulder.

"God damn it, Christine, I'm working!" Grabbing for the edge of the counter with one hand and shoving up her face plate with the other, she whirled around and came face to face with absolutely the last person she wanted to see.

"Where the hell's my tachometer?"

Unable to stop herself, Ely glanced toward one of the repair shop's crowded shelves.

Jean Perault followed her gaze. His lip curled. "Yesterday, you said it'd be fixed no later than 1730 today! It's later, Shoemaker. It's a whole half hour later and my tach still isn't fixed!"

"It's just the backup..."

"Yeah, it's the backup, but that's not the point. Point is, you said you'd have it fixed. And you don't."

"I meant to." She shook free of his grip and resisted the urge to jump off the stool onto his foot. Unfortunately, Perault was a shift boss at the fuel station and she couldn't afford to piss him off. Or at least piss him off any more than he was already. "I was going to do it this morning; I got it apart but I had an idea of how to fix my scrubber."

"Your scrubber?" He leaned around her and stared at the piece of machinery on the counter. "You're not still working on that piece of junk are you?"

"It's not a piece of junk. If we can get the contaminants out of the gas at source..."

"…we won't need to refine on station, we won't have to handle the waste gases, and we won't run the risk of another Red Tuesday. I've heard it all before, Shoemaker, but that doesn't change the fact that both the mag field and the electrical activity are too bloody strong to overcome with something small enough to fit into the pipe lines."

Ely opened her mouth but Perault cut her off before she could actually say anything.

"And yeah, if you could get it to work the company'd pay you a small fortune for it but you're missing the point."

"Which is?"

"Which is, my tach was supposed to be fixed today!"

"Look, Jean, I'm really sorry." Hands spread, she tried a conciliatory smile. "You're right. I shouldn't be messing around with this and ignoring paying customers. I'll fix your tach this evening and you can pick it up tomorrow on your way in to work. You weren't going to install it until tomorrow morning anyway."

"That's not the point…"

"I know."

Perault stared at her for a long moment. "Well, only because I don't have a choice…First thing, tomorrow though—0600. We've got a ship in at 0630 and I want to be there, with my backup tachometer, when they arrive."

"You will be."

"I'd better be." He stomped toward the hatch, paused with one foot out in the corridor, and turned. "If I'm not, and my crew ends up sitting around with their thumbs up their collective ass because we've had a breakdown with no backup part, you're covering the costs even if that means you have to sell every piece of junk in here for scrap."

"Switch to decaf," Ely muttered as the hatch slammed shut behind him. "It's just a god damned backup tachometer."

"Which you promised to have fixed this afternoon."

She pivoted slowly on the stool as Christine came through the hatch that connected their living quarters to the shop. "How long were you there?"

"Long enough. I was on my way in to get you for supper when Perault arrived. He has a point, Ely."

"I know." Slipping off the scope, she laid it on the counter beside the scrubber. "I really did mean to fix it."

"So I heard." Christine slid her arms around Ely's waist and rubbed her cheek against her shoulder. "Fix it after dinner."

"Please tell me it's not textured protein patties again."

"All right."

"Oh god, it is, isn't it?"

"It is, but looking at the bright side, there's not very many of them."

"Christine."

"We can't afford anything else. We still owe the company for those three weeks I was sick."

"Damned blood suckers…"

"Blood we could pay them." Leaning back, Christine rubbed thumb and forefinger together and added with a resigned sigh, "It's cash we're short of."

"Who isn't?" Ely snorted. "If I could just get this scrubber working we'd be so far ahead you could get sick every month if you wanted."

"Sick every month?" One corner of her mouth curled up. "You really know how to sweet talk a girl. Now, come to…"

The hatch into the shop swung open and both women turned to watch as an old man carrying a battered plastic crate stumbled over the lip. He staggered forward three steps, sideways one, and would have toppled had Ely not raced around the counter and grabbed his arm.

"Careful, Joe. Here, let me take the box. It looks heavy." It was heavy. She managed to get it to the counter but only just. "Damn, Joe. What've you got in here, rocks?"

The old rockhound cackled at the joke—either not caring or not remembering it was the same joke every time he showed up. "Got good stuff in there, Ely. Good stuff."

"You think so? Well, let me have a look then…"

Dr. Joseph Grim, PhD, had once been one of the company's best geologists. He'd been responsible for three top finds and a number of smaller ones—skipping around the edge of the asteroid belt from ore to ore, from bonus to bonus. When his luck ran out, it ran out in a big way. Certain he was on the way to his next big find, he ordered his pilot deeper into the belt than anyone had ever gone. No one knew why his pilot had agreed; no one would ever know. The ship crashed on one of the bigger rocks, the four man crew died instantly leaving only Dr. Grim. When his air ran out, unable to remove the tanks, he hooked himself up to each corpse in turn. When that air ran out, he used the equipment he had on board to pull oxygen from the ice on the rock. By the time the company found him, he was pretty much insane.

He used his savings to buy a small ship and go back to the belt. He wouldn't tell anyone what he was looking for.

When his savings were gone, he began selling the things he found.

Mostly, he found debris swept up by the belt. The flotsam and jetsam of five centuries of space travel.

Mostly he found junk.

This trip was no different.

Piece of nozzle and hose from an hydroponics setup. Chunk of burned and broken tube lining. Ely set them down on the growing pile. *Something that looks like an old distributor cap.* The last thing in the crate was about thirty centimeters long and maybe half that around in the center. The ends tapered to blunt points and it looked as if a number of things had been broken off it over the years. *And I have no idea what this is. Or what it's made of.* It was the color of old brass and the metal felt greasy. Hefting it, she was willing to bet it was probably hollow, or honeycombed. Not solid, anyway.

She set it on the top of the pile and looked up to find both Joe and Christine staring at her.

The old man rubbed his hands together. "Good stuff, eh?"

"Same as always, Joe."

Christine rolled her eyes.

When Ely made her first offer, Joe's lower lip went out. Translation; he didn't have enough to pay his docking fee. At her second offer, his lip went in but his brows drew down. He was calculating what he'd have to do without. When she made her third offer, he smiled.

And a damn good thing too. Ely thumb-printed the transfer on his grubby disc. *'Cause that's already ten times what this crap is worth.* But she couldn't leave him sucking vacuum and once or twice he'd actually had something she could use.

"When was the last time you ate, Joe?"

He turned to peer up at Christine. "Ate?"

"You've been forgetting again, haven't you?"

He shrugged, clearly having already forgotten the question. "Maybe?"

"Come on." She slipped his arm through hers. "You might as well join us for dinner although it's just textured protein."

His smile had all the pure joy of a child promised a treat. "I like textured protein."

"You would," Ely muttered taking his other arm.

"Because I'm crazy?"

"That'd be my best guess."

Ely returned to the shop after dinner, pulled the pieces of Perault's tachometer out of the mess on the shelf, and set them on the counter. She could fix it in an hour, maybe less, and then she could spend the time until power-down working on her scrubber. Fixing odds and ends was *not* going to get them out of the hole they were in.

Reaching past the pile of Joe's junk—her junk now—her elbow hit the oval *thing*. Steadying it turned into lifting it, turned into examining it, turned into discovering no more about it than she'd seen earlier. Intrigued, she slipped on her scope and dropped the face plate.

At high resolution, it became quite obvious that the thing had been damaged. Stubby ends, no more than three or four molecules wide and a dozen high stuck up along opposite sides of the long axis.

Which gave her an idea...

Power-down caught her deep within her scrubber.

Perault's tachometer was still in pieces.

"It's all right. Don't panic." In the dim light of the emergency exit sign over the shop door, she set the scope carefully aside. "I set the alarm for five. It's fixed when he's here at six. No problem."

Pulled from a dream where she was attempting to open a jammed door with a heavy drill, Ely woke to find Christine's head on her pillow and Christine snoring into her ear. By the time she got her to roll over, she was wide awake.

It feels like it's the middle of the night.

Heaving herself up onto one elbow, she peered at the clock. 0552.

"Oh crap!"

"What is it?" Christine muttered sleepily.

"The alarm didn't go off."

"Shoemaker's wives go barefoot."

"What? Never mind." She dragged a pair of overalls on, combed her hands through her hair, and ran for the shop. Maybe Perault would be late.

He arrived seconds after she did.

"Look, Jean, I can explain…"

"I don't want explanations, I want my tachometer." A long arm snaked out and snatched it off the counter. "Looks okay," he grunted, reluctantly.

It looked better than okay. It looked new.

Frowning, Ely replayed the previous evening in her head. No question about it, she had definitely left the tachometer in pieces on the counter.

"Hey, you even filled in the gouge that moron McGregor put in it during the disconnect. Now, you didn't have to do that."

"I, uh…" Ely shrugged. "You know."

"You do good work, Shoemaker. When you finally get your head out of your ass long enough to do it." His brows dipped in and he held out his free hand. "Your disc. I haven't got all morning."

"Right." She passed it over, watched as he thumb-printed the transfer, and took it back all without saying another word. There didn't seem to be anything she could say.

"It was fixed?"

"Yes."

"And you didn't fix it?"

"That's right."

Christine stared at the place on the workbench where the tachometer had spent the night and shook her head. "It had to be one of your friends playing a joke on you. Maybe Dave. That's the kind of thing he'd think was funny."

"Yeah, but Dave's nightshift this week. He couldn't have gotten away to do it. And no one wanders around this part of the station after power-down. No one with half a brain anyway."

"Which doesn't exclude a number of your friends from the maintenance crews. I suggest you make some calls." Kissing her quickly, Christine headed for the door. "I'll be done by 1630. It's your turn to make dinner."

Ely waved absently in the general direction of her wife's back. "Yeah, sure. Whatever." She pulled a vacuum pump off the shelf, disassembled it, and stared at the pieces. They remained pieces.

Suddenly restless, she went back into their tiny kitchenette, stared at the empty coffee canister, tried to remember the last time there'd been anything in it, and couldn't. It had been ages since they could afford even the chicory stuff and since they grew the chicory on station, that was saying something.

Fixing odds and ends wouldn't clear their debts, but it would, at least, buy them some coffee.

Back in the repair shop the vacuum pump still hadn't fixed itself.

"Okay. Fine. Be that way."

The seals were shot but then it was always the seals on vacuum pumps. She had another four on the shelves with the same problem. By 1530 that afternoon, she'd fixed all but one of them. The fifth, and largest pump, had been left running even after the pressure had begun to fall and the whole thing had seized into one solid mass.

"Replacing the seals is the least of your problems," Ely muttered, pushing it aside. Fixing it would mean a tidy bit of change to cover parts and labor but gods, where to start. She'd have to drill out two of the heat sink boots and one gasket cover would have to be cut off. She had the gasket cover in stock but the boots, she'd have to make.

"So I might just as well deliver the pumps that *are* fixed and leave this until tomorrow." Besides, she'd never gotten around to making those calls and at this hour most of her friends off the old maintenance crew would be at Sam's Bar.

"You were supposed to make dinner."

"Sorry." Ely crossed the shop with one hand behind her back trying to judge Christine's mood from her expression. Twenty years of practise had made her no better at it than she'd been when they first met. As usual, Christine wasn't giving anything away. "For what it's worth, no one was anywhere near here last night after power-down. I asked around then I stopped by security on the way back and had Janet check the logs."

"Did you tell her why?"

Curiousity had overcome any earlier pique over the uncooked dinner. Ely breathed a mostly metaphorical sigh of relief. "Did I tell her that someone snuck in and fixed a tachometer? Not likely. She'd think I was drunk. I told her I thought I heard someone trying to jimmy the hatch."

Christine frowned and unfolded her arms. "What kind of idiot would try to rob us?"

"Funny, that's what Janet said. I bought us something."

"Ely."

"No, it's okay. Perault's transfer covered what I paid Joe and I fixed those four small pumps today so…" She brought her hand out, the small bag balanced on the palm. The smell was unmistakable.

"That's real coffee."

"Yes, it is."

"Ely, that stuff costs five times what the chicory costs!"

"But it's ten times better."

"Our debt…"

"Won't looks so intimidating once we're highly cafinated."

"You think?" Christine sighed again but this time she smiled as she did it. "Come on, I'll reheat your protein patty."

Next morning, Ely hooked her stool up to the workbench, set her mug down, and discovered the big vacuum pump had been re-paired during the night. Not only repaired; it tested at a higher efficiency than it had been originally rated for. Stranger still, a chunk of Joe's broken tube lining was missing.

"What do you mean, missing?" Christine demanded.

"I mean, not here." Ely held up the remaining chunk. "Look at that clean edge. Something's cut a piece of it off."

"Something?"

"Probably the same something that fixed the pump."

"Let's hope."

"You're taking this very calmly."

Christine shrugged. "Why shouldn't I? So far, the *something* has been very helpful."

"Well, yeah, but…"

"Look, I'm going to be late for work. If you want to have security go over the shop, be my guest, but I personally don't think we should look a gift..." She paused, searching for a word and surrendering without finding one. "...gift in the mouth. Or am I wrong in assuming the transfer for the pump will be a sizable one?"

"Relatively," Ely admitted, turning the pump on its side and staring at the bottom.

"Glad to hear it."

When Ely looked up, Christine was smiling. "We're dumping and cleaning the D-bank yeast tanks today so I'll be home when I get here."

"Right. Bye." The smile hadn't been because she liked the thought of clean tanks. She'd been smiling because of the transfer for the pump. She hadn't smiled like that because of Ely for a long time. Not even the coffee had made her smile like that.

"Okay, fine. If that's the way you want it."

Twisting her hair up and securing it with a bit of wire, Ely pulled down a broken grappling arm removed from one of the exterior cleaning bots and, shoving her scrubber to the far end of the bench, she went to work replacing a joint. When she stopped for lunch, she threw a rag over the scrubber because even at the end of the bench it was too great a temptation.

By power-down, she'd received three more transfers for repairs and could barely keep her eyes open. Leaving the parts of a compressor scattered over the bench, she went to bed.

When she stumbled into the shop at 0630 the parts had been reassembled and the casing shone.

"Okay, now you're just showing off."

But the payment, added to all the others, meant they might actually have enough in the account to pay their bills at the end of the month.

And because she refused to be shown up by an invisible mechanic, she spent the day fixing a rotor that had been sitting forgotten on an upper shelf for nearly four months.

That night, she left three sprinkler heads from hydroponics sitting on the workbench in a row.

They were fixed by morning. Another piece had been taken out of the tube lining.

"Ely, what are you doing?"

"I'm building a sort of curtain."

"A what?"

"Something to hide behind that'll keep me from reading on standard sensors."

"Okay." Christine rubbed her forehead wearily and sighed. "Why?"

Ely ran power into the thermal screen, frowned, and disconnected the coupling. "So I can find out who's been sneaking in here at night."

"Station security…"

"Can be gotten around; you know that as well as I do. No, if we want to catch whoever's doing this, we'll have to do it ourselves."

"Do we want to catch them?"

She'd been thinking about that all afternoon. "Yeah. We do. Whoever's doing this has their own agenda and I'm not going to keep following it blindly."

Shaking her head, Christine walked past and into their quarters, throwing back a tired, "Maybe they're helping out of the kindness of their hearts."

"Right," Ely snorted. "Or maybe it's elves."

Half a dozen elves in greasy overalls danced across the top of the workbench. They were singing, in a jolly sort of way, although the words made no sense. Just as Ely knew she was about to understand, and knowing it was vitally important she understand, she woke up.

Wondering where she was, she lifted her head out of a puddle of drool, and peered around. *Oh right. I'm behind the 'curtain'.* And then, redundantly. *I must've fallen asleep.*

The emergency exit light over the hatch lit the area enough for eyes adapted to the darkness to see the workbench and the broken temperature gauge lying on it. There was no one in the shop.

Ely checked her watch. Two thirteen. Three hours and thirteen minutes since power-down and there was no one in the shop. Had they been keeping her under surveillance? Did they know she was there? Maybe the temperature gauge wasn't enough of a challenge. *Whatever. At three, I'm packing it in and…*

The click was just on the edge of audible.

Ely froze. The sound had come from much closer than the hatch. Another click. A little louder.

The temperature gauge began to sparkle. At first Ely thought her eyes were playing tricks on her, that the sparkle was no more than the random specks of color and light everyone saw when staring into the dark, but the specks weren't random or colored. They were white and making definite patterns on the gauge, and the more she looked, the easier they were to see.

Then a small clump moved off to the pile of Joe's junk still on the end of the bench and settled on a coil of corroded copper wire. They brightened, flashed blue for an instant, and returned to the gauge.

No more than ten minutes later, the whole sparkling mass rose up into the air and moved back to the pile of junk, landing on the oval sphere, thinning and finally disappearing.

"So you're saying, tiny lights came out of this...thing and fixed the temperature gauge."

"Not only fixed it, they fabricated a new piece for it out of this old copper wire." Ely was so excited she almost bounced. Waiting until power-up at five when she could actually see what had been done had been the longest three and a half hours of her life. "See the shiny bit?"

"I see it."

"And here, in the gauge."

Christine stared at the shiny copper amidst the incomprehensible bits. "Okay." She looked up and managed to catch her wife's eye. "So what are they?"

"They've got to be some kind of nanotech."

"You can't see nanotech, El. I mean, isn't that kind of what the nano part means?"

Ely grinned. "You can't see carbon molecules either but get enough of them together and you can see the lump of coal."

"Okay, granted, but nanotech's been illegal since the meltdown of '37 when those ore processors went out of control."

"I know." Ely lifted the oval sphere, one hand stroking it possessively. "But what if someone just tossed this bunch into space instead of destroying them?"

"Then they broke the law," Christine reminded her. "You have to turn them in."

"What? No. First, do you know what the penalty is for getting caught using nanotech—which I've been doing for almost a week now—and second, these have clearly been programmed to do repairs and I'm not giving them up."

Arms folded, Christine exhaled wearily. "Ely..."

"I said, no. Think about it for a minute Chris, this is our chance to get out of debt. It's like being able to hire a precision mechanic to do all the crappy, time consuming stuff and not only not having to pay *them* but not having to pay for the energy they use either."

"Which is?"

"I don't know, but probably hydrogen just like the big boys use, only they pull theirs out of the atmosphere instead of your friendly neighborhood gas giant." She set down the oval and caught up both of Christine's hands. "They fixed three sprinkler heads in one night and on two of them they had to fabricate a new actuator nut. Do you know how long that would take me on the lathe? Those things are so damned old no two are the same size. So forget about the debt for a minute, think of how it'll feel to pay off all of our bills at the end of the month and have enough left over to stock up on real food."

Still not entirely convinced, Christine shook her head. "We can't forget the debt."

"Okay, so we throw in a box of patties every month and put what we save on the debt. We'll be free and clear by the end of the year. Sweetie, you know the company hates to spend money on this station—bunch of cheap, suit-wearing bastards—so I can get as much repair work as I can do and with these little guys helping, I can do three times as much."

"The problem isn't getting the work. There's always been lots of work, *that's* why you decided to go into business for yourself. The problem is not getting it done." Turning her head, Christine looked pointedly at the scrubber still under the rag at the end of the bench. "You have a tendency to get distracted."

It took a major effort of will but Ely stopped herself from mirroring Christine's movement. "I worked on the scrubber so much because I knew I could work my ass off doing repairs and it wouldn't make any difference. But that's changed."

"Changed?"

"By the nanites."

"If we get caught with them…" But her tone had become speculation rather than protest and Ely knew she'd won.

"We won't."

"Promise me."

"I promise."

"Okay."

The second week after Joe's visit—which was how Ely had begun to think of time passing—was pretty much a repeat of the first. Pretty much. Word got around that Ely Shoemaker had finally got her head back together and was doing the kind of work everyone knew she *could* do. As a result, for every repair that went out, two or three came in.

There didn't seem to be anything the nanites couldn't fix or fabricate as long as they had the raw materials close at hand. They never left the bench and although Ely used her scope on the oval almost daily, she couldn't find the way they went in and out.

"What's that?"

Ely flipped up her faceplate and took the mug of coffee with a smile of thanks. "That, my darling, is part of the broken guts of a proximity buoy."

"The satellites that help guide ships into the fueling bays?"

"None other."

"Okay, call me an alarmist but shouldn't it be out there guiding ships?"

"And it will be tomorrow morning." Ely grinned. "I mean, I could work on it for the next two or three days but I think I'll fix a couple of vacuum pumps and leave it for the staff."

Next morning, not only was the buoy still in pieces but two small titanium components were missing.

"What the hell are you guys up to?" Moving the oval to the center of the bench, Ely flipped down her face plate. It looked much the same as it had except the tiny stubs along both sides of the long axis were definitely longer. The first two had in fact been joined by an intricate lacework of metal.

Well, it doesn't take a rocket scientist...

She was looking at the missing titanium.

Instead of fixing the buoy, they'd found what they needed and had begun making repairs.

"Which they've been programmed to do. Make repairs..."

Except that suggested the oval sphere was more than just a container for nanotech.

Was it a home?

A ship?

A ship, Ely decided. Her instincts were usually bang on about mechanical things.

So. Once they completed the repairs; what then? Would they be willing to stick around as unpaid labor? Probably not. The easiest solution? Keep them away from anymore titanium 6/6/2 and nothing had to change.

Ely pulled off her scope and sat staring down at her hands. Using illegal nanotech to get out of debt was one thing but to know what they needed and then to keep them from it. To essentially force them to work for her against their will. Granted, they could be nothing more than a bunch of very smart, very small, power tools but the whole thing stank of slavery

"How much!?"

"Aerospace grade titanium doesn't grow on trees."

Ely frowned. The only trees she'd ever seen were the fruit trees espadrilled in hydroponics. "What the hell does that mean?"

"It means, you ignorant vacuum sucker, that it's not just lying around to be picked up by all and sundry. It's difficult to extract, it's hard to work, it's..."

"...a part of every satellite, in most of the gas mining equipment and all of the heat exchangers. There's a lot of it around!"

"And there's a lot of uses for it." The company acquisitions clerk, looked blandly up at her over steepled fingers. "More uses than available alloy. Which makes it very, very expensive."

"I only need a hundred grams," Ely snarled. She'd extrapolated the amount needed for total repairs from the amount already covered by the satellite components. "'I don't want to sheathe the whole fucking station in it!"

"Good. Because I can get you a hundred grams; it's just going to cost you."

It was just going to cost her everything she'd made over the last two weeks.

"You've got to be kidding." Christine took four jerky steps away, and four back, her hands cutting words out of the air. "You break the law using this nanotech to get us out of debt and now you want us to go further into debt so it—they—can repair their ship and fly away?"

"Yes."

"Why?"

Ely sighed. This hadn't been going at all well. "I'm not positive they're nanotech."

"You were positive when you convinced me it would be a good idea to break the law." She leaned forward, brows drawn in. "You *convinced* me, Ely. And *now* you've changed your mind?"

"Well, yeah, sort of. I still don't want to turn them in. I want to let them go free."

"Because they might not be nanotech?"

"Yeah…"

"But they still might be?"

"Yeah, but…"

"So what are they if they aren't nanotech?"

"I don't know." Ely rubbed her thumb over the end of the sphere. "We'll probably never know."

"Well, we certainly won't know if you spend everything we have on a going away present for them."

"Your salary…"

"Won't cover the bills."

"I'll work harder, I promise."

Christine stared at her for a long moment. "Fine. Here, in case you've forgotten…" Lips pressed into a thin line, she wound her wedding ring up off her finger. "Titanium. Only Common alloy but they might as well have this too." Tossing it down onto the workbench where it rolled into Joe's pile of junk, she spun on one heel and stomped into the living quarters.

"Chris…"

The hatch slammed.

"Oh yeah, that went well."

Power-down found Ely behind her curtain, a hundred grams of titanium 6/6/2 sitting beside the oval sphere on the bench. This time, when she heard the first click, she was staring at the sphere. She couldn't see a hatch...

You know, a smart woman would be wearing her scope.

...but she could see a sparkling line arc out of the upper curve and descend to the titanium. The tiny lights froze for a moment, the first time she'd seen them motionless, and then they exploded outward, weaving wild patterns above the bench. It was silly to extrapolate emotion from a thousand points of light but Ely thought she'd never seen anything look so happy.

No, not happy. Happy didn't have the intensity.

Joyous.

She fell asleep around three and woke up when the power came back on.

The oval sphere, two bands of slate gray lacework along each side, hovered about fifteen centimeters above the workbench. As Ely approached, it settled slowly down to the scarred surface.

Old friends in the maintenance crew were curious about why she needed to space something out one of the small bot airlocks. She had to exchange a promise to tell the full story for the new codes. They wouldn't believe the story but it would be safe enough to tell as soon as the little guys got away.

They show up when you're down on your luck, I mean really down on your luck, and they make things better. Why? Well, they were programmed to fix things, weren't they?

She didn't need to be told which security camera was currently off line; fixing it was on the day's to-do list.

Once she got the airlock's inner hatch open, Ely carefully lifted the sphere out of her toolbox. She thought she could feel it vibrating against her fingers but it was probably imagination. When she set it in the lock, it rose and pivoted along its center axis.

She'd clearly put it in backwards. "Sorry."

"So am I."

When her heart started beating, when she could move again, Ely turned, wide eyed, toward Christine.

"You're doing the right thing...and don't say, *I know* because that's really irritating when someone's trying to apologize."

"Okay. How did you find me?"

"I went to the bar. Dave told me." Christine leaned forward and peered into the lock. "It's pretty."

They closed the inner hatch together, dogged it down, waited for the pressure to equalize then, holding Christine's hand, Ely opened the outer hatch.

The ship, if ship it was, hovered for a moment longer, sparkled briefly, and was gone.

The repair shop felt empty when they returned to it.

Dropping onto her stool, Ely shoved the piece of buoy out of the way and laid her head on her arms. Then she lifted her head and turned the buoy back toward her. "Okay, I guess they only needed ninety-four grams. They've replaced the titanium components."

"Did they finish the repair?"

"Looks like it."

"Nice they showed a *little* gratitude," Christine muttered, rummaging around in the junk for her wedding ring.

"Yeah, nice." Which was when it hit her. Slowly, barely breathing, Ely turned toward the scrubber and pulled off the rag.

It looked exactly the way it had when she'd stopped working on it. Virtue, it appeared, was its own reward.

"Thank god. They didn't use my ring."

The ring sparkled in the light as Christine held it up and Ely frowned. The ring had a matt finish. It shouldn't be sparkling. "Let me see that." Settling the scope on her head, she flipped down the face plate. Under high magnification it became obvious that the micronic oxide layer of the titanium had been electronically thickened to create different refractive effects. All the colors of the rainbow danced across both the inner and the outer curve of the band.

"What's wrong with my ring?"

"Nothing's wrong. They left us a message."

"A message? What does it say?"

All the colors of the rainbow...

...forming a complete set of schematic diagrams.

If they'd built the scrubber for her, how could she have built a second? Or a third? Or sold the patent to the company for the small fortune it would bring?

"It says, *and they lived happily ever after.*"

This story was originally written for an anthology called Villians Victorious. *Now, if the villains are going to be victorious the story has to be
either facetious or dark. Raise your hand everyone who thinks I went
dark. Okay, you two with your hands in the air, you clearly haven't read
my backlist. Off you go, we'll wait for you to catch up.*

I had such a good time writing this I almost felt guilty cashing the cheque.

ALL THINGS BEING RELATIVE

"MAJESTY, THIS IS Cornelius Dickcissel, the scribe."

Dropping to his knees, the short, plump man tried to remember everything he'd been told as the queen turned her head
toward him.

*"Never look her in the eye. Keep your hands out where she can see
them. Don't speak until she gives you leave. Don't wear black, she
doesn't find imitation flattering. And whatever you do, don't remind her
of her age.*

"You are Cornelius Dickcissel?"

"Yes, Majesty." Her voice saying his name made all the hair
on his body stand on end. He tried, unsuccessfully, not to sweat.
His own voice quavered a bit. As he couldn't hope she hadn't
noticed, he could only hope she wouldn't mind.

"You are the author of *Sir Harold, His Brave Battle With the
Great Pernicious Worm and His Subsequent Death and Devourment?*"

"Yes, Majesty."

"Good book; I was impressed that you took the time to
consider the dragon's point of view. Title needs work, though."

"It was my editor's title, Majesty."

"Baxter!"

"Majesty?"

"Have his editor killed."

"Yes, Majesty."

"Cornelius Dickcissel, look at me."

Over one hundred and seventy years old, the queen had left
behind the edged, ethereal beauty of her youth but not without one
heck of a fight. Only a blind fool could fail to notice the magical
enhancements. Only a suicidal fool would give any indication. Her

eyes *were* amber as the songs insisted although the tiny flecks of darkness in the golden depths were probably not the trapped souls of the men who'd loved her and lost.

Probably not.

Don't look her in the eye.

He hurriedly dropped his gaze and raised it again considerably faster; the tight black bodice being rather remarkably low cut.

"Do you know why you're here, Cornelius?"

He'd been making a conscious effort not to think about that. For lack of a better answer, he fell back on the catechism of his school days. "I serve at the pleasure of your Majesty."

"Yes, you do and, right at this moment, it pleases me to have you write the story of my life."

"Me, Majesty?"

"Do you see another Cornelius Dickcissel in the room?"

"No, Majesty."

He would write the story of the queen.

Him.

Cornelius Dickcissel.

He'd spent his whole life as far from the center of the empire as it was possible to get and still be in the empire, scratching out a literary career by rewriting local legends. And now this. This would... He swallowed, hard, as he realized. This would make his fortune!

The Dark Queen: My Story as told to Cornelius Dickcissel. He could see it now: a tasteful woodcut of the queen on a plain white cover. Every bookseller in the empire would move hundreds of them. And not just the booksellers—the mercers, the drapers, even the apocotharies!—everyone would be falling over themselves to buy a copy. There'd be sales of subrights to the players and possibly foreign sales as well—although there wasn't anything very foreign very close, not anymore.

Pity I spent that money having my will made up. Still, he couldn't have known and it was the traditional response to a personal summons from the queen.

"Baxter will find you rooms in the palace and provide you with the necessary supplies. We'll start tomorrow in my solar. I'd like to start today but one of the royal accountants has made a total mess of the tax rolls and I have to torture him to death."

"I was an only child; my sisters were jealous of my talent and beauty."

"Majesty?" Cornelius wet lips gone suddenly dry as the queen stopped pacing and turned a basilisk stare on him. Her solar was the top room in the palace's tallest tower. From it, she could see her kingdom spread out all around her, the verdant forests, the well-tended fields, the prosperous villages, the line of dark smoke where a rogue proletarian was being burned at the stake. "You told me to interrupt if I didn't understand. Don't you mean you were a *lonely* child? An only child can't have sisters."

The queen smiled. "My point exactly..."

I was five when I realized something would have to be done. Bella, who was twelve and as full of herself as only a twelve year old can be, was under the mistaken impression she would grow up to be the most powerful mage in the kingdom. And at nine, Celeste was the acknowledged beauty of the family. Bella would taunt me because I could only do baby magics and Celeste had a nasty habit of calling me carrots.

Early one morning in the nursery, Bella used a broadly theatrical and totally unnecessary gesture to light a candle on the other side of the room.

"Even I can do that," I told her, and lit the candle beside it. The implication that she too could do only baby magic made her very angry and instead of attempting something simple she jumped right to the most difficult magic she knew—transformation, becoming in quick succession a lion and then a bear.

I convincingly cowered in fear and, when she was herself again, I clapped my dimpled hands and cried, "Do more."

"What shall I become?" she asked me breathing heavily from the exertion but so very pleased I was impressed by her.

"Can you be a mouse?"

"Just watch me!"

And she was.

Which was, of course, when I let the cat in.

Our nurse had been excessively fond of "Puss in Boots"—although I can't remember her ever telling the story again.

Later that day, as Celeste was staring at her reflection in the smooth, dark water of an old abandoned well, the boards, solid enough to hold a five year old, gave way and she plummeted into the depths. Fortunately, she'd never learned to swim. Well, not fortunately for her, perhaps.

It was at about this time I discovered I looked magnificent in black.

So suddenly bereft of two of their three children, my parents doted on me until their untimely deaths just before my eighteenth birthday.

"Untimely, Majesty?"

"Untimely," the queen repeated a little sadly. "The poison worked quicker than it was supposed to and I actually had to have a legal guardian for the remaining months of my minority."

Cornelius searched for something to say and settled at last on, "I'm sorry."

"It wasn't pleasant, but I was young, I survived."

As he dipped his pen, Cornelius decided not to ask the obvious.

"Alone at last, I used my family's money to travel and learn—merchants, mages, assassins, politicians, I left no stone unturned in my search for knowledge. In fact, that's where I found a number of the politicians..."

It wasn't until he heard the soft *phut, phut* of her foot tapping against the carpet that Cornelius realized the queen was waiting for a response. He looked up from his notes to find her staring at him. "Majesty?"

"Stone unturned...politicians..."

He checked his notes. "Yes, Majesty, I got that."

She sighed. "Never mind. My teachers taught me that knowledge is power but only a fool would deny that power is also power..."

The prince, heir to a small kingdom, was handsome and charming but honestly, not too bright. For that matter, neither were his parents. Royal marriages should be considered state contracts and given as much attention as declarations of war and the resultant peace treaties. Which they often were. But when this particular prince couldn't decide on a bride, what did his parents do? They threw a grand ball at the palace to which they invited every young woman in the kingdom and told the prince to choose.

I wore gold, the exact same shade as my eyes. My hair cascaded down my back like falling flames. The prince couldn't take his eyes off me.

Until *she* arrived.

The perfect princess: blonde hair, blue eyes, her dress a frothy sweet concoction of white and blue, and on her feet the most ridiculous pair of glass slippers.

"Glass slippers, Majesty? Wouldn't they be... I don't know, breakable?"
"Yes."

She stank of magic. And destiny.

I, personally, have always felt you make your own destiny.

Too charming to leave the woman he was currently partnered with, the prince was making a fool of himself trying to keep this vision of loveliness in sight. To give credit where credit is due, she was aware of her effect on him and, smiling sweetly, went out into the garden so that he could finish his dance.

When the prince and I were married, some weeks later, we decided to hold the reception in that same garden. The summer flowers were beautiful and it seemed such a shame for our guests to have to stay inside.

Cleaning up behind the Dwarf Euonymus, the gardeners found the body of a urchin girl wearing the remains of ragged clothing covered in cinders and ash. Most of her blonde hair had been taken by small animals to make nests and it was no longer possible to tell what color her eyes had been. No one connected her to the mysterious princess who'd made such a brief appearance at the ball although had they bothered to check they might have found shards of glass in the ruins of her throat.

The king and queen died that fall. She had a little trouble with an undergarment—it quite took her breath away—and as he was running to her aid, he choked on a bit of apple. After a lavish double funeral, my husband and I took the throne.

"As it happens, I took it considerably further than he did but that is a story for another day. From the looks of your notes..." The queen nodded toward the piles of ink blotted paper lying like drifts of leaves on the table—her life from childhood to throne. "...you'll have quite enough to do for a while. I have given you the bare bones of a story, Cornelius Dickcissel. It is up to you to clothe it in the extras that people seem to require. Adjectives. Adverbs. Semi colons. Tomorrow morning, I shall read what you have done to my words."

"Tomorrow morning, Majesty?" He would have been appalled at the way his voice emerged as a terrified squeak had he not been so terrified at the appalling fate he'd meet in the morning. Even had his right hand not been cramping painfully, there was no possible way he could turn two jars of scribbled ink into the first section of a book by morning.

"Is there a problem with that?"

"Majesty, the proper writing of a book takes more time than the telling of it. There are, as you say, adjectives, adverbs..."

"Semicolons?"

"Yes, Majesty. Semicolons. And other punctuation."

"*Other* punctuation?" She raised a hand to forestall an answer and frowned thoughtfully. "I did quite like what you did with the dragon."

"Thank you, Majesty."

"Tomorrow morning bring me as many pages as you have completed and, if I approve of your *punctuations*, we will continue."

"And if not, Majesty."

"Then you won't continue."

"The book?"

The queen smiled. "Also the book. What is it, Baxter?"

"I beg your indulgence for the interruption, Majesty." The queen's personal assistant bowed deeply. "The dwarves have arrived."

"Yes, thank you, Baxter. You wouldn't think it to look at them," the queen told Cornelius as she stood and shook out her skirts, "but dwarves make the most amazing coffins. I've done quite a bit of business with them over the years."

Cornelius slid off the stool to his knees as she swept by him, skirts whispering suggestions for mayhem against the carpeting.

"This is good. You've really captured the way I worked to gain power, how nothing was handed to me. *What most amazes, gentle reader, is that such a delicate beauty could have the persistence and strength necessary to climb over eight bodies of those dear to her in order to reach the place at the pinnacle her destiny demanded she fill...* This is the sort of writing that made the story of Sir Harold such a hit."

"Thank you, Majesty."

"But there were nine."

"Nine, Majesty?"

"Bodies."

"My apologies, Majesty." Taking a deep breath, Cornelius very nearly squared his shoulders. "Majesty, there are places where more detail..."

"Would slow things down."

"Yes, Majesty."

"Are you ready to continue?"

"Yes, Majesty." While any other answer would have come with a low survival rate, he found he was more than ready—he was fascinated.

It was the tradition in my husband's kingdom for the queen to have her own small guard, their function mostly ceremonial. By the end of my first year as queen, I had provided employment for a number of young men who had previously been considered unemployable and added to our manufacturing base. Metalwork mostly. The man with the rivet concession made a small fortune.

After my husband.... died, his council wasn't entirely certain that my slender shoulders were up to the weight of government.

"Majesty, how did your husband die?"

She turned from the window. "It was a tragic accident during an inspection of the kitchens." Crossing the room, the queen pulled an ornate wooden box off the high curved shelf that circled the solar. "He was leaning over too far and fell into one of the ovens."

When opened, the box played a sweet, melancholy tune. "Baked instantly." She held the box toward Cornelius. "Gingerbread?"

"No, thank you, Majesty."

"Just as well, there's not much left."

I dealt with the council in the traditional way, replaced the carpets, and set about consolidating power. By the time I finished, the entire system had been admirably stream-lined. I gave the orders and my knights saw that they were carried out. With no more hereditary nobility, the common people were closer to the throne than they'd ever been and were able to rise in position based on merit rather than birth. With the understanding that ultimately the land was mine, I divided the grand estates amongst the people who worked them and, after the quiet, midnight executions of a few malcontents, the country prospered.

My largest problem turned out to be my knights. Granted, a certain amount of burning and pillaging was necessary in the beginning but they were getting out of hand. Some men are just like that, give them an inch and they'll want to be the ruler...

"Oh, very clever, Majesty!"

The queen sighed. "A polite chuckle would have been more believable and it wouldn't have spilled the ink."

"Sorry, Majesty."

"I'm not re-telling that bit. You can write it up tonight from memory."

I was prepared for the coup attempt. Large men in black plate mail with red cloaks and plumes don't sneak worth a damn. They clanked into the throne room one afternoon, absolutely destroying the parquet flooring with their spurs. I was extremely annoyed, the old chancellor had been washing that floor with his tongue since the change in power and it looked wonderful.

The captain could see I was upset. He pulled off his helm and his cruel mouth twisted up in a rather attractive smile. Somehow, he'd managed to keep all his teeth. "A pity to kill one so beautiful," he said, pulling his sword, "but I'm not so stupid that I'd let you stay around. I'd be dead before..."

He was dead before he hit the floor and the others were only half a heartbeat behind. The impact of all that steel was deafening.

"Do you remember my parents?"

Cornelius looked up from his notes, more than a little confused by the non sequitur. "Your parents, Majesty?

"Yes. This time, I got the dosage right. From the moment I discovered what my less than faithful knights were planning, I started poisoning them. After that, it was all in the timing. I haven't had a moment's trouble from them since."

A drop of ink fell from his quill and obliterated the queen's last words. "Majesty, are you saying that the knights, the knights who ride today, are the same knights who were with you back a hun...."

And whatever you do, don't remind her of her age.

Outside the solar, gray-green clouds rolled over the sun.

"...back when you first came to power?"

"Of course." Russet brows drew in. "You didn't know?"

"No, Majesty."

"Do your friends and neighbours know?"

"I don't think so, Majesty."

Visibly upset, the queen took up her favorite position at the window. "This is *exactly* why I need my story told. Some of my greatest work, forgotten in my own lifetime. With dark necromancies, I create a cadre of dead men to enforce my will and provide continuous policing at a cost other governments only dream of and barely six generations later what have they become? Literal shadows of their former selves. It's too depressing. I can't go on today. Write up what I have told you. And Cornelius..." She paused at the door, delicate features stamped with sorrow. "...make it terrifying."

"That won't be difficult, Majesty."

The queen had cheered up by the next morning. "I have sent word to the knights that they're to lift their visors when dealing with individuals—it's not necessary for mass slaughter of course but there's

absolutely no point in having created a tool and then never using it.
Thank you, Cornelius, without you, who knows how long this sorry
state of affairs would have continued."

"I live to serve, Majesty."

"Yes…"

He really, really didn't like the speculative expression on her face—
not now he knew living wasn't an actual requirement for serving.

Once I got my own small kingdom in order, I did what any
conscientious ruler would do: I looked about for economic opportunities. The kingdom to the north was in a shocking state of
anarchy when I arrived, the people without direction for almost
a hundred years while their royal family was trapped, sound
asleep in their palace, behind a barricade of thorns.

I'd never seen such a mess. Brambles grew over, under,
and around each other, twisting, tangling, and trapping approximately sixteen young men on their eight inch spikes. Princes all,
you'd think one of them would have had the brains to bring an
ax instead of a sword.

In almost one hundred years the barrier had grown to be
three times the height of a tall man. It had clearly never been
pruned. Have you any idea how much dead wood a hedge
accumulates in only *one* year?

When I was five, I could light a candle.

I backed my army a safe distance away.

"Smells like pork," someone said after a while.

"The fire has reached the palace," I told him.

The new map, drawn in the ashes, doubled my borders.

My new subjects had gotten out of the habit of paying
taxes but once they were convinced of the benefits a cen-
tralized government could provide—maintained roads, stan-
dardized schooling, access to foreign markets, enough man-
power to wipe out the entire family of any opposition up
to and including second cousins, in-laws, and pets—they
came around fairly quickly.

With my northern border secure, I led my army
windershins around the perimeter.

The surrounding royals had interbred past the point of
stupidity. And chins.

To the west, the ruling prince was looking for a bride by sticking a pea under a pile of mattresses. The result; a list of minor injuries and broken bones as one after another the young women rose in the night to use the commode. He'd have been significantly better off putting more money in defense and less in bedding.

To the south, the king had stuck his only daughter up on a glass hill and promised her hand and the kingdom to whoever could reach her. If you'll remember, we previously discussed how glass...breaks.

To the east, three princes had been sent out on quests by an ailing king unable to chose which should be his heir. Maybe he honestly didn't know which one had been born first, I didn't stop to ask. I set up roadblocks and when the princes returned, they were given state funerals. I still use the telescope but the apple rotted and the flying carpet was a cheap knock-off for the tourist trade.

"Majesty, did no one ever oppose you?"

"Not in the early days. People who put their daughters on glass hills in order to give away their kingdom to the first idiot with a sledge hammer aren't exactly masters of strategy and tactics. And the less said about that moron with the pea the better."

"But later...?"

"Later, there were heroes." To Cornelius' surprise the corners of her full mouth curved up into an abstracted smile. "We'll talk of them tomorrow."

The thing I loved best about heroes is that they were larger than life. In the beginning, they were almost indistinguishable—big, honorable men in plate mail on big white horses. As long as they behaved themselves, the knights had orders to let them reach me. I had a great deal of work to do in those early years but nothing broke up the monotony of governing like dealing with one of those silly paladins.

They usually arrived with three misconceptions.

That my army of thugs and cutthroats had been afraid to face them.

That I was an evil queen because I had conquered the surrounding countries and slaughtered the nobility.

That because their cause was just, they would prevail.

My army was extremely well disciplined and would face anything I told them to. Military victories made me an effective general not an evil queen and no one seemed to miss the dead nobility except the live nobility outside my borders. And they never did prevail…

"Seven paladins died, right down there in that courtyard believing until the end that their righteousness made them invincible although two through seven also wore powerful charms that kept me from using my magic against them."

Did she want him to look? Before Cornelius could decide, the queen turned from the window.

"Did you know they actually used to issue challenges? Well, there's no reason why you should, I suppose. They died long before your grandfather was born." Seven closed helms sat on the shelf next to the wooden box of gingerbread. Reaching up, she tapped a scarlet nail against the first.

"I, Sir Gerald de Faunae, do challenge the champion of the Dark Queen to single combat. When he is defeated, she will surrender herself to…Ribbit!"

The croaking continued as the next helm, then the next, offered its challenge, identical to the first except for name and final exclamation—two arghs, three gurgles, a shriek, and a whimper. Cornelius couldn't help thinking that two through seven would have been off without the charms.

As the final ribbit faded, the queen fought to bring her laughter under control. "Oh mercy," she sighed, wiping her eyes. "I'd forgotten how funny they were. Anyway…" She dropped back into her chair. "…after this lot, the paladins stopped coming. Maybe they ran out of big, honorable men. Maybe they ran out of white horses. I never knew."

"Is that when they started calling you the Dark Queen, Majesty?"

The queen smiled. "No." After a moment, she continued, as though Cornelius had never interrupted. "Further expansion was as much political as military and the heroes became…What is it Baxter?"

"It's getting late, Majesty, and before you can prepare for tonight's reception for the Gambanize ambassador, you have to meet the winner of the school essay contest."

"School essay contest?"

"Yes, Majesty. Five hundred words or less explaining why you allow the Beltains to live in peace to the north."

"Because they make an admirable buffer against the frost giants."

"And that *was* the winning essay, Majesty."

"Excellent. Cornelius."

Cornelius, who'd been trying to rub feeling back into his right hand, jumped.

"I want you to attend the reception tonight."

"Majesty, I don't..."

Her eyes narrowed as she stood. Baxter visibly braced himself.

"...know how to behave at such a function. I don't want to embarrass you."

"You won't." It wasn't so much reassurance as a command. "You'll be able to observe me interacting with foreign dignitaries and add it to the book. Besides, there'll be free food and alcohol— I hear writers like that sort of thing."

Cornelius smiled weakly. "Doesn't everyone, Majesty?"

"Not around here. Baxter will find you suitable clothing."

"If this is the small throne room," Cornelius breathed, staring wide-eyed at the nine gigantic chandeliers hanging from the mirrored ceiling, "what must the large throne room look like."

"Actually, it's fairly utilitarian," Baxter told him. "This one is used to impress, the other is for business which means everything has to be washable. A word of advice; if you're having sea food, stick to the white wine."

"Why?"

"The queen dislikes it when people drink the wrong wine."

"Oh." Then he got it. "Oh! Doesn't that whittle away at the guest list?"

"Not any more."

The queen and the Gambanize ambassador entered together. The queen looked magnificent. The ambassador, nervous.

With the exception of the ambassador's party, all the guests were self-made men and women who'd been able to take advantage of the queen's policies and rise to the top. In the Empire, everyone was equal under the queen and no one had red wine with the crab cakes. Cornelius, a mid-list scribe from the outer provinces, had never dreamed of finding himself in such company—or at least, he'd never dreamed of finding himself in such company and surviving it.

He sidled close to the queen in time to hear her say, "Actually, it's been years since much of my GNP went to the military. I find it much more efficient to put the money into teachers."

The ambassador shook his head, the beads woven into his beard swaying gently. "I do not understand."

"Every child in the Empire, regardless of wealth or social standing receives the same excellent education until they're ten. I control that education."

"It can not be so simple."

"Really?" The queen graciously accepted an offered canape. "How many kingdoms has Gambania conquered?"

"Three!"

"And held?"

As the ambassador shrugged sheepishly, the queen smiled.

Which was when it happened.

One of the guests ripped open the wide orange leg of his trousers, yanked out a small crossbow that had been strapped to his thigh, and pulled the trigger screaming "Death to the Dark Queen!"

Aiming first might have been an idea.

Cornelius' world constricted to the point of the crossbow quarrel speeding toward his throat. Impossibly slowly, he saw the queen pull the ambassador in front of him with her left hand while she drew a throwing dagger from a cleavage sheath with her right. The would-be assassin would have hit the floor a heart beat after the ambassador had either heart still been beating.

Then the world sped up again, and Cornelius tried to remember how to breathe.

In a silence complete but for the sound of bladders emptying, the queen crossed the room.

"You call that a hero?" She poked the cooling corpse with the pointed toe of one black leather boot. "I wouldn't call him a hero if you made him into a sandwich." She gave the silence a generous count of three then swept the room with an edged gaze. "Sandwich…. hero sandwich…. oh, never mind," she muttered, as appreciative laughter finally swept the crowd. "Not one of you got it first time around so there's no point pretending." Bending, she retrieved her throwing dagger, stepped over the body, and swept out the nearest door.

Unfortunately, it was the servants' entrance.

Hear pounding, Cornelius followed, pushing past the trio of panicked sheep in the suddenly far too tight red and black livery. He caught up when the queen allowed it, in the solar.

She was standing at her favorite window overlooking the courtyard, leaning on the window sill, desultorily feeding bits of raw meat to a raven.

"Majesty!" Dramatically dropping to his knees, he threw open his arms. "You saved my life!"

"Yes, I did. I'd say that made your life mine but it always was." She sighed deeply. "I'm feeling old, Cornelius Dickcissel. Where was the rush? Where the excitement?"

"Here!"

The sound of his fist sinking into the layer of fat on his chest brought a questioning gaze around toward him.

"Majesty, up until tonight your story has been just that to me, a story. But now!" He heaved himself up onto his feet. "Now, tonight, it has been brought to life." With adrenaline courage, he stepped to her side. "Allow me to bring it to life for others. Majesty, you are beautiful, and dangerous—deadly even. You are an archetype, Majesty, and an archetype deserves more than one mere book!"

"What are you talking about?" Queen and raven watched him with much the same expression.

He wet his lips and leaned toward her. "I'm talking trilogy, Majesty! A big, fat trilogy!"

"A trilogy?"

"Yes!"

The queen smiled.

"MagesTEEEEEEEEEEEEEEEEEEEEEEEEEEEEE…"

She shook her head and dropped down onto the window seat. Dark necromancies and dead heroes were one thing, but a trilogy? What could possibly have possessed Cornelius Dickcissel to suggest such a thing?

He should have known it wouldn't fly.

The body hit the flagstones below the window with a wet melon kind of splat.

At least not more than sixty feet.

"Baxter?"

"Majesty?"

"I'll be needing a new scribe."

I actually wrote this for an anthology about gargoyles but as it was so incredibly different from every other story that came in, the editor couldn't use it. You know what I like best about this story? It's different.

NOW ENTERING THE RING

KEVIN CHISOLM STOOD at the door to the gym—*No, training facility*, he amended—and wished there was someone he could tell about his unexpected good fortune.

Maybe he should have made more of an effort to keep in contact with his family after his parents died but they'd been so disapproving at the funeral. His Aunty May had gone so far as to say he'd killed his mother in all but physical fact when he'd gone out west after college to become an actor. His mother had always wanted him to become a priest, although, as she wasn't particularly devout, he wasn't sure why.

He had nothing against the priesthood, it just wasn't what he'd wanted. From the moment he'd made his first run for a touchdown in junior high, shoulder pads bouncing under the too large jersey and the crowd had risen to its collective feet cheering, he'd known. He wanted the crowd to keep cheering for him. So he'd disappointed his mother and gone to a small Midwestern college where he'd be assured of a place on the team. Dreams of being a star runningback had ended when he hadn't been quite good enough to go pro.

A throwaway credit in theater arts had suggested a new way, and he'd disappointed his mother again.

He wasn't a bad actor, but although he tried and tried again, he just wasn't quite good enough to go pro. Death had allowed him to keep that disappointment to himself.

When the elderly woman had first approached him on the street, he'd assumed she was fronting for the porn industry. Too polite to run her down, he'd jogged on the spot and listened to her pitch. Not porn, not this time. Wrestling.

"They're always looking for blondes," she'd told him. *"Big, pretty boys to play the hero. I've seen them come and go for forty years…"* Washed out gray eyes had narrowed. *"…and I think you've got that special something."*

He'd turned her down, politely, and started to run by.

"I know, I know, you're an actor." Her sigh had been as dramatic as anything he'd ever done. *"But I can name three wrestlers off the top of my head who've done movies."*

So could he.

The old woman's name was Trixie Hobble...

"Name I was born with, swear to God."

...and she was an agent. Of sorts.

Three weeks later, Kevin found himself under a pile of sweaty midgets in a scrubby arena out in the valley listening to people scream out the name Trixie had given him. It wasn't the feeling he'd been looking for, but it was a start.

Wrestling lost him the few friends he'd made. He didn't understand why, given how popular it was. Okay, maybe the country fair circuit he'd found himself in wasn't all that popular but everyone knew that it could lead to other things.

In only seven months, it had lead him here.

To this *training facility*.

Third time lucky.

Given the flamboyant image of the sport, the three letters on the door were almost classically subdued. In the wrestling world, this was varsity—not only because of the letters that showed up on everything from jackets to boxers but because this was as good as it got.

Shifting his gym bag to his left hand, Kevin rubbed a suddenly damp palm against his thigh and pushed open the door.

"All right kid, let him up."

Kevin rolled onto his knees and stood, reaching down a helping hand to Washington "The Titan" Jones still lying on the canvass.

"Thanks, man." Massive fingers wrapped around Kevin's wrist. "I gotta say, that was a textbook reverse atomic."

"You all right?"

"Just knocked the breath out me, that's all." The older man clapped Kevin on the shoulder and dragged his towel off the ropes. "I think he's ready, JT. He has the moves down cold."

"I think you're right." Beckoning Kevin out of the ring, the trainer lead the way across the gym to a set of metal risers against one wall and climbed to the top. "Can see everything from up here," he said, sitting heavily. "Come on." A three fingered hand patted the space beside him. "Sit."

Kevin sat.

"You gotta knack for this sort of thing, kid. It takes a better athlete than most people'll credit to keep from getting seriously hurt up there and enough of an actor to keep the whole thing from degenerating into farce." Scanning the wrestlers practicing below, JT sighed. "Although, lately, I think we're way over that second line. Even five, six years ago wrestling still had a little dignity. Now…" Straightening, he waved the end of the sentence away. "Anyhow, Trixie, bless her black heart, has a good eye. You think you're ready for a real fight?"

He'd been watching the practice rounds, taking mental notes, but this snapped his head around. "In front of people?"

"I sure as shit hope so." JT scratched at his arm through his sleeve. "Damn patch. Doc never mentioned it'd itch. Crowds make you nervous, kid?"

"No. They make me feel…"

"Stronger?"

"Not exactly." He'd been going to say "whole" but something in JT's face changed his mind.

"Not exactly?"

"I like it when they like me, it gives me a buzz."

"You want a buzz, suck back an expresso. You need approval, you get it from me or you get it from your peers. You can't connect to a wrestling crowd, kid, it's not safe. You have no idea what kind of crap you'd be forced to deal with. Now," he continued before Kevin could speak, "what'll we call you?" A long look brought both eyebrows down. "Too bad we retired Golden Boy."

"My mother wanted me to be a priest. Maybe we could…" He wasn't surprised to see JT shake his head but he'd needed to make the gesture.

"Forget it, kid. We don't tangle with the church. You think the Mounties got nasty, wait'll you have to deal with a group of pissed off nuns."

"Nuns?"

"Don't ask."

"Trixie called me her White Knight."

"Yeah? Well, given what we paid her for you, I'm not surprised." A few moments of scratching later, he sighed. "Okay,

White Knight it is. It's old fashioned but it'll give the pussies in the office an image to work with plus it might bring in any fans you impressed on the cornfield circuit."

Fans. People who came to see him. Kevin stared out at the half dozen men practicing mayhem and drew in a deep breath of the warm, sweat scented air. "Who will I fight? Gargoyle?"

Gargoyle was the only wrestler who practiced in full costume—from the body stocking and the fingerless gloves, right down to the fright mask with the double row of little ivory horns arcing back from his brow. He came after the others finished and worked with JT alone. Kevin had stayed to watch one afternoon and, after being pinned by an amazingly penetrating red stare, had been told in no uncertain terms to bugger off. Unlike the rest of the team, who only wore their over-the-top wrestler personae when the cameras were running, Gargoyle wore his all the time.

Kevin got the impression Gargoyle was probably the only wrestler in the entire industry who took it seriously. *This isn't what I do,* he told the world, *this is what I am.* If he fought Gargoyle, people would know who he was. They'd be cheering for him, not the name he'd been given.

"Gargoyle?" JT laughed loudly enough that The Axe Man, distracted by the sound, got closelined. "Gargoyle's out of your league kid."

"For now."

It was the trainer's turn to snap his head around. "Yeah," he said after a moment, "for now."

Satisfied, Kevin leaned back on his elbows. "I think I remember watching Gargoyle wrestle when I was in public school."

"Trust me kid, that was a different Gargoyle."

Kevin felt his ears burn. "Well, yeah. But you didn't retire the name."

"No. That's a name we never retire." The trainer sighed and dug at his arm. "There's always a Gargoyle wrestling somewhere."

"Now entering the ring, weighing 270 pounds and ready to rip the heart out of his upstart challenger—TITAN!

And coming down the aisle, having sworn to make his mark on Titan's broken body, to take his fight for right to the bad boys of the ring, WHITE KNIGHT!"

Kevin didn't remember much of the fight. Distracted by the noise in the packed arena he took an elbow in the face a lot harder than was intended and bled all over his new white tights. The crowd loved it. When he finally pinned Titan to the canvass in a prearranged finish, there were as many boos as cheers but the cheers were enough to get under his skin and start the buzz.

Three months later, after JT had vetoed his entering with a drawn sword—"We don't wanna to give the fans any ideas, kid."—he was leaping into unfair fights, evening the odds, and just generally being on the side of the good guys. It was hokey as hell but the fans ate it up and he began getting bags of mail.

But he wasn't any closer to fighting Gargoyle.

"Why not?"

JT pinched off his butt and tossed it in the garbage, shaking another out of the pack in almost the same motion. "Just because you're the flavor of the month, it don't mean you're up to Gargoyle."

"Yet."

The pause lasted longer than it took to light the cigarette and draw in the first, slow, lungful. "Yet," JT admitted at last. "You might, and I say might, have what it takes to make it to the top in this business. *If* you learn to distance yourself from the crowds."

"At least I'm not dragging guys out of the audience and shaking them."

"Ah, that's just part of Train Wreck's schtick. Point is, kid, he knows where he stops and they start and I'm not sure you do. I watch you out there and I see how the screaming pumps you up. That buzz you used to get, is it stronger?"

"No."

"You'd think it would be, wouldn't you? More screaming, more buzz, but it don't work like that. The more you get, the more you need to pump you up."

"I guess if they're pumping me up, that explains why my clothes don't fit anymore," he said with a laugh. When JT didn't answer, he stopped struggling with a knot in his bootlace and turned. The trainer had sucked the cigarette down to the filter and his face was almost as gray as the falling ash. "JT?"

"You're just…" He coughed, tossed the pinched butt away, and began again. "You're just putting on some muscle mass."

"But…"

"Leave it."

Kevin didn't know what he'd said to cause such a reaction but he left it. Because he hated the thought of carrying JT's anger with him when he went out to the ring, he attempted to change the subject. "Do you think they know?"

Knowing, only, ever, and always referred to one thing.

"Who? Your ever-loving fans? Of course, they know. Well, most of them know when they stop to think about it. Which is why we give them no time to think. They're here for the spectacle, they don't care how real it is. They're here to take all their petty problems and all their unrealized aggression and throw it in the ring with you."

Straightening, Kevin carefully closed his locker door. "I heard someone say on the radio that wrestling makes people more violent."

"People? I don't know about people, but when the fans leave here, they're too God damned tired for violence. If we don't wring 'em out and hang 'em to dry, we're not doing our jobs. Now then," he jumped off the massage table and gestured to the door with the glowing end of his cigarette, "get out there and do yours."

"Those things'll kill you, you know."

"Not soon enough, kid. Not soon enough."

Spectacle.

Except for Gargoyle, they all indulged in it.

Except for Gargoyle, they all did the dumb-ass posturing, the fake feuds, any and everything to whip the fans up into a frenzy.

The fans didn't seem to mind that Gargoyle only walked to the ring, slid under the lower rope, stood, and waited. They'd sit, almost quiet, expectant, until the second wrestler stepped into the ring when, as one they'd scream preapproval to the fight.

Gargoyle seemed like an empty form until the screams from a thousand mouths filled him. Completed him. Then, massive hunched shoulders came up, lips drew back off a mouthful of crooked teeth, and red contact lenses gleamed as he raked the air with blunt black nails and howled.

Astonishingly, not one fan ever claimed him as a favorite. That puzzled Kevin until he realized that favoritism was transitory and Gargoyle was something more.

Not spectacle.

Symbolism.

Kevin started cutting back on the one, hoping it might lead to the other. He watched all of Gargoyle's fights. On tape if he couldn't be there in person. He analyzed every move, began incorporating them into his practices. He no longer only wanted to fight Gargoyle, he wanted what Gargoyle had, a real connection to the fans.

"What the fuck was that?!"

"Just something I saw Gargoyle do. You all right, Titan?"

"The name's Washington." The older wrestler batted aside the offered hand and stood alone. "Titan's for the ring."

"I know. I'm sorry."

"Good. And when you're practicing with me, you stick to the script. Your Gargoyle might not care about having his ugly mug smashed into the canvass, but I do."

He was angry but more than that, he was afraid. "In fact, you can stop that whole Gargoyle crap right now, you hear. You do your job, you collect your check, and hopefully you retire with both ears still on your head."

"There's more to it than that for me."

Eyes narrowed, Washington searched his face and deflated so completely, it seemed as though someone had let the air out of a blowup doll of a man. "Yeah. I can see that." He sighed deeply. "Just be careful. You let the crowd in and you can't never let it out again."

"I just want to be the best."

"No, you don't. The best learn to keep their distance. The very best learn to do it before too much damage is done."

"Gargoyle doesn't keep his distance."

"You're making my point," Washington told him sadly and never got in the ring with him again.

Gargoyle died on national television as part of a Saturday afternoon network sports program with millions watching. The millions didn't know he was dead, of course. They saw him raise both hands in triumph after winning his bout, saw him open his mouth to give his trade mark howl—although the noise from the crowd drowned out any sound he may have made—and then they saw him collapse. He was dead before he hit the canvass but the network kept him cheerfully alive and recovering at an undisclosed location for the sake of their younger viewers.

To Kevin, who'd been watching in the dressing room, his own match long over, it almost seemed as though Gargoyle had collapsed under an enormous weight.

The funeral was private and no television cameras meant that only those wrestlers who hadn't been fast enough to avoid JT attended. Not many of the mourners actually mourned. Gargoyle had no family, no close friends, and, it seemed, no name.

It was a closed coffin, soon to be cremated so there would be no graveside service.

To Kevin's surprise, there was a priest.

"Anglican," JT muttered. "Gargoyle wanted one. Now, shut the fuck up, he's trying to pray."

"Almighty God, we commit to you the soul of our dear brother, in sure and certain hope of the Resurrection to eternal life, through our Lord Jesus Christ; who shall change our vile body that it might be like unto his glorious body whereby he is able to subdue all things unto himself..."

The place emptied quickly. Too quickly for anyone to notice that Kevin had stayed behind. The coffin sat alone at the front of the big empty room and as he walked toward it, he tried not to think too hard of what he was about to do.

The lid hadn't been secured.

In case one of the relatives had wanted to say a last farewell.

Lifting the lid, Kevin supposed he was as close to a relative as Gargoyle had.

He'd never understood why people said the dead looked as though they were only sleeping. His mother, her face remarkably unblemished by the accident that had left her both a widow and a corpse, had looked dead. Lifeless. He hadn't known where she was—Heaven, Hell, or going around again—but he'd known, without a doubt, she wasn't there.

Gargoyle, his great bulky body filling every available space inside the extra large coffin had been laid to rest in a suit and tie that looked ludicrously out of place. The gnarled hands with their blunt black nails had been crossed demurely over a charcoal pinstripe.

He was wearing his mask.

Kevin, who'd wanted to, needed to see the face under the mask, reached out a trembling hand.

When the leather peeled back, the double row of ivory horns remained. So did the protruding brow ridge and the deformed cheekbones. The dead wrestler had looked more human with the mask than without.

After a long moment, Kevin realized he wasn't surprised by what he'd found. He felt more as if he were waiting for something.

"They had to break his legs to fit him into the coffin." JT's voice was too matter of fact to be startling even while standing over a coffin staring down at a corpse.

"If I pried open an eye?"

"Red. People thought they were contacts." The trainer snorted. "Well, what else would they think?"

"What was he?"

"He was just a wrestler, kid."

Studying the deformities, Kevin felt as though he were close enough to understanding to reach out and touch it—but something kept him from making that final move. He had a thousand questions but he very much doubted he'd get the chance to ask more than one.

A thousand questions.

"What was his name?"

Ignoring a half dozen signs thanking him for not smoking, JT shook cigarette up into his mouth. "Gargoyle."

"No." Bracketing tensed shoulders, the seams of his jacket threatened to give way. "His real name."

JT exhaled and for a moment Kevin thought the smoke was the only answer he was going to get. Then as the older man reached out and closed the coffin he said, "Michael Hamilton. Now two of us know it. And I don't want you mentioning this to the others."

Staring down at his own reflection in the polished wood, Kevin shrugged. "What would I say?"

Without Gargoyle on the bill, the crowds changed. The screams for blood got louder, the ugliness moved front and center. The fights grew more vicious as time and time again the careful choreography fell apart under the onslaught.

Waiting to go on, Kevin stepped aside as The Axeman left the building on a stretcher.

"Is he going to be all right?"

JT shrugged. "Doc wants X-rays—who knows."

"What happened?"

"Again, who knows. We can go on like this for a while, spreading it out over the entire team, but eventually something's gotta give." He ran a nicotine stained hand up through thinning hair and sagged against the wall.

Kevin had the feeling he'd been forgotten. "JT?"

When the trainer looked up, his eyes were bloodshot and ringed with shadow. "Something's got to give," he repeated.

"What?"

For a moment, Kevin thought he was actually going to get an answer but then JT started groping in his pockets for his cigarettes and the moment passed.

"You're up next, kid."

He kept his eyes on the ring as he walked to the aisle. Usually, he could ignore the way his boots stuck to the concrete, every step pulling free of the mess with a sound like ripping velcro but tonight it almost seemed as though the floor was actually trying to hold him back. Usually his handlers kept the fans away but tonight a woman, with breasts almost as pneumatic as his own pecs, threw herself at him and stuffed her tongue in past his teeth. She tasted like popcorn. Usually he loved the sound of the crowd calling out for him. Tonight, although he still got the buzz, he heard the threat.

The match started badly and got worse.

The noise was like another wrestler in the ring. Or another thousand wrestlers since nothing held the miriad voices together. Nothing completed them.

Driven into an adrenaline frenzy, Train Wreck missed cues and very nearly did some actual damage. For the first time since he started wrestling, Kevin found himself really fighting. The ref, as much of an actor as any of them, suddenly discovered enough good sense to stay out of their way.

One eye had swollen shut and pain, gouging a signal from hand to shoulder, suggested a broken bone. Up against the ropes, twisting frantically to avoid a knee in the groin, Kevin saw only one way out.

Wether the crowd recognized one of Gargoyle's old moves or they just liked the sight of Train Wreak bleeding face down in the canvass, Kevin had no idea but they rose as one and howled.

He could feel the building vibrate.

The roar of approval lifted him onto his feet and turned him to each of the four corners arms spread wide. When Train Wreak dove at him from behind, he skipped nimbly out of the way and laughed at the sight of his enemy sprawled half out of the ring. The crowd laughed with him.

For the first time, he had a *real* connection with the crowd.

They were his.

He was theirs and they poured themselves into him.

He'd never felt so powerful.

So whole.

They told him what to do and he did it.

Anything was possible. The buzz built until it filled his head. It took over his body. It began looking for new territory to conquer.

It all ended in a blazing white light of pain.

He woke up in a hospital bed but not in a hospital. It still smelled like the gym. And cigarette smoke.

"JT?"

The trainer stepped out of the shadows. "I'm here."

"What happened?"

"What had to happen." He reached up and pulled down a shaving mirror attached to the wall on folding metal brackets.

Kevin stared at the unfamiliar face. Red eyes stared back at him. "I broke some blood vessels."

"No."

A padded mask with a double row of small ivory horns landed on the bed.

Kevin picked it up and turned it around in hands no longer quite his.

"The changes don't happen all at once," JT explained. "I'm not even sure the crowds would notice but the television cameras might so I got a series of them to help you look like you're going to."

"Gargoyle rises from the dead?"

JT sighed. "In a manner of speaking, he never really dies."

"Did you always know?"

"That it'd be you? No. Only that it *could* be you."

He could hear the lie. "Why didn't you try and stop me?"

"I told you not to let the crowds in. I heard Washington tell you. Hell, even Trixie told you. You chose."

Trixie. Who'd seen something special in him right from the beginning. "What if I won't?"

"Won't what? Won't go back in the ring? It's up to you. Can you give it up?"

A thousand people screamed his name inside his head. It wasn't enough. He needed…

JT read the answer off his face, nodded once, and turned to leave. At the door he paused, looked back toward the bed, and answered the question Kevin hadn't asked. "The ugliness has to go somewhere, kid."

"Ladies and gentlemen, he's back! The moment you've been waiting for! The moment every other wrestler's been dreading! Now in the ring, 282 pounds of red-eyed fury, GARGOYLE!"

They were screaming his name. The only name he had. He straightened massive shoulders and howled. They howled with him.

"We want blood!"

"Grind him into the canvass!"

"Knee the bastard!"

"Hurt him! Hurt him bad!"

And underneath it all, along the real connection he had with the fans, *"Bless me Father for I have sinned…"*

He wished he could tell his mother. She'd have been so proud.

*Now, if you'd written two books about assassins (*Fifth Quarter *and* No Quarter*) and then an editor asked you to write a story for an assassins anthology, what would you do? I really enjoyed working in the Quarters mythos again.*

DEATH RITES

AS THE SUN rose and the Seventh Army rose with it, the assassin's body appeared, lifted up over the top of the fortress wall by unseen hands.

"Marshal Arnon!"

Holding his kilt, the marshal stepped out of his tent in time to hear the soft melon crack of the assassin's head hitting stone as the body reached the end of its arc. "Sound carries in these hills," he said thoughtfully threading straps through buckles and cinching them tight. Kilt secured, he glanced up first at the wall and then at the senior of the two soldiers on guard. "Was that what you wanted me to see?"

"Yes, sir."

The marshal nodded and turned on one bare heel back toward the tent. "Tell Commander Zayit I want to see her immediately. You have my permission to leave your post."

"Sir, if Orban is dead…"

Marshal Arnon glanced up from his breakfast. "I think we can safely say that Orban is dead, Commander."

"Yes, sir. Orban's death—added to Visolela's and Ganit's— leaves the Seventh Army with only two assassins. Both are very young and wouldn't stand a chance against Commander Jolan— ex-Commander Jolan," she corrected hurriedly as the marshal's expression darkened.

"Especially as Jolan has already dealt with Orban, Visolela and Ganit?"

Commander Zayit winced at the question clearly not intended to be answered. The failure of the three assassins was, in a sense, the marshal's failure and he wasn't the sort of man who'd appreciate the reminder.

They'd effortlessly regained the three villages that had fallen under the ex-commander's control, but First and Second Divisions
together had not yet been able to come up with a way to pry her out
of her hilltop fortress—which wasn't surprising since the place had
fallen to Imperial expansion originally by betrayal from within. All
three dead assassins had managed to get inside the walls but with
Jolan expecting them...

A coin hit the table in front of her. Startled, she looked up to
see the marshal's amber eyes locked on her face.

"Crescent for your thoughts, Commander?"

"I was just thinking about the situation, sir."

"Yes, the situation." His lip curled. "It's beginning to look as
though a siege is my only choice. So much for a quick and glorious
end to Jolan's treason."

"Yes, sir." A siege had been his only choice from the moment he'd
allowed the ex-commander's small army to reach the hill fort. Too bad
it had taken the lives of so many good soldiers to prove it to him.

"You're thinking again. How long was the siege in '64?" he
continued before she could work out the response he required.

Zayit waited until he finished wiping his face with a damp cloth
and said, "Almost two years, sir."

"Seventeen years ago." He indicated to his body servant that
the table could be cleared. "And Jolan was there."

"Yes, sir."

"How long do you think she was planning this...rebellion."

Probably from the moment some pissant third cousin of the
Emperor was promoted over officers who actually knew what they
were doing. "I don't know, sir."

"No. Of course not."

Zayit stepped out of the way as Arnon stood and strode purposefully from his tent, falling into step behind his left shoulder as he
passed. When he stopped at his customary place and stared toward
the fortress, she wondered if he was thinking about the men and
women who, by his command, had charged the narrow approach
and died. Not once, but twice.

"I think we can safely say she's stocked up on arrows, rocks, and oil," had
been the marshal's only comment at the time.

His tent should have been in the center of the encampment but
he'd ordered it placed so Jolan could see him from the walls.

"I want her to know I'm here."

"I doubt she cares," Commander Baird had muttered a little too loudly and now Zayit was the only senior officer the marshal saw.

"The raven's back, sir."

"Are you certain it's the same bird, Commander?"

She was actually. Something set this raven apart. It was larger than most, and it had a way of staring into the camp that lifted all the hair on the back of her neck. Today it had drifted silently down to land beside the crumpled black figure outside the fortress walls. "Yes sir. I'm certain."

Then a second raven landed like a shadow beside the first.

"It seems to have found a companion."

"Yes, sir. Shall I send a squad out to collect the body?"

"No. Let him lie, as Visolela and Ganit lie."

"Sir, Visolela and Ganit went off the cliff. Orban is on the road."

"I see where the body is, Commander. Why do you think Jolan had it thrown onto the road? Precisely so we would send a squad to reclaim it." He squared broad shoulders and folded his arms. "But I give the orders here, not her."

Zayit couldn't see his face but she could hear the edged smile in his voice. Her right hand clutched at the silver and onyx ring she wore on the smallest finger of her left. The ring, given to officers with their commission, marked her as a priest of Jiir, Goddess of Battles. The marshal's ring held a ruby, the color of fresh blood. As he commanded the Seventh Army, he was high-priest of its goddess as well. He'd accepted the position as his due and had performed the necessary rituals with pomp and circumstance.

To challenge his belief would be to challenge his authority as a marshal of the Seven Armies and destroy her career.

At least five soldiers —as well as the two on guard—were close enough to have overheard. By mid-day, everyone would know Marshal Arnon had refused rites to one of the dead.

"Sir, we weren't able to do the rites for the others but Orban..."

"Will have to do without them as well. I have brought two divisions here for Jolan, burned a village, and lost three assassins. Now, I will have to maintain a division at her feet indefinitely. I think she has dictated quite enough." He nodded toward the road. "Besides, Jiir has sent her ravens. I'd say it was Visolela and Ganit come for their friend but assassins have no friends, even among

themselves. Have a courier prepare and I'll send my decision to
the Capital this morning."

Eyes locked on the ravens, Zayit started. "Your decision sir?"

"About the siege, Commander." Turning, he smiled down on
her. "I doubt the Emperor, my cousin, needs to be kept abreast
of carrion."

"Yes, sir." She remained where she was until she heard the tent
flap fall, and then she stayed a moment longer as the senior of the
soldiers standing guard murmured, "Why aren't the ravens feeding?"

They were standing, one at each end of the body, looking toward the camp.

The marshal of the Seventh Army was the Emperor's cousin and that
brought his message directly to the Emperor. His Imperial Majesty
read the report and asked to speak personally with the courier.

"Meaning no disrespect, Majesty," Marshal Usef of the First
Army protested, "but why?"

"Why indeed?" the emperor asked dryly. "Given that Arnon
allowed the traitor to reach the hill fort in the first place, I find it
difficult to believe things are going as well as he suggests."

"You think he lies to you, Majesty?"

"I think he omits detail, Usef."

Face flushed, the emperor slid forward to the edge of his throne.
"Do I understand you to say that Marshal Arnon refused death rites
to a blade of Jiir?"

"Yes, Majesty."

"When he could have recovered the body?"

"Yes, Majesty."

"And this is known?"

"Yes, Majesty."

The Emperor lifted his gaze from the kneeling courier, met Marshal Usef's eye, and jerked his head toward the door. When the courier was gone and the two men were alone, he growled, "Didn't we
send our cousin to the South Province to keep him out of trouble?"

"Yes, Majesty. You'd observed he was neither stupid nor without ambition."

"I've changed my mind about the stupid part." He slapped
the rolled report against his thigh. "He'll send both divisions over

to that traitor if he keeps this up. He'll turn a small rebellion into a civil war."

"That is possible, Majesty." The current border of the Seventh Province had been secure for barely a generation.

"I want this taken care of. Now. Send a message immediately—Second Division can go back to the garrison but Arnon's to remain with the siege."

"Punishment, Majesty?"

"Let's just say I'm not happy with him." The Emperor's smile was tight. "If I'm to fix this, I can't have him wandering all over Jiir's battlefield."

"Shall I..."

"No." A raised hand cut Usef's question short. "He's family. I'll deal with it myself.

Marshal Chela of the Sixth Army read the message handed directly into her care by an Imperial Courier for the third time. His Imperial Majesty wanted to borrow her best assassin. Unfortunately, her best assassin would be under the authority of the garrison's healers for another few weeks...

"If his...Imper...i...al Majes...ty com...mands..."

"Lie down, Neegan." Chela pushed him back onto the bed with her voice. Not even she would touch an assassin uninvited. "Even if the healers would let you go, I'm not sure I would. Jolan's already destroyed three blades—I'm not saying you wouldn't be able to deal with her under normal circumstances but you've got a hole in your throat you've barely recovered from."

His lips pressed into a thin line and one brow rose.

Chela, who'd known him for twenty years, translated easily. "Then why am I here? I want to know what you think about my sending Vree and Bannon instead. Granted they're young but they're good—they should be, with you overseeing their training—and they'll be unexpected. Jolan resigned her commission before they were posted and as far as I know there has never been a team of assassins in the Seven Armies before." Her smile nearly buried her eyes in curves of flesh. "Also, it's considerably more politic to send the Emperor an option rather than a refusal."

Neegan held out a thin hand. "Or...ders..."

"Sorry, my eyes only. And theirs if you think they can handle the job."

This expression a stranger could have translated.

"How can you decide if you don't know what you're sending them into?" She lowered her bulk onto the stool beside the bed. "This much is common knowledge: Commander Jolan's treason has allowed Arnon, that pompous ass, to put himself into a bad situation. The fortress is impossible to take down from without but there's a way in Jolan hasn't been able to find or she'd have closed it down. It isn't like her to make a point by killing assassins as they come through."

"Ar...un?"

She smiled again at the missing rank. An assassin had no family but the army. For Neegan to deliberately insult a superior officer... "They'll be taking no orders from Marshal Arnon. The Emperor is taking care of this, they go in under his orders alone."

He forced a lungful of air through the ruin of his throat. "Send...them."

Bannon dug a finger into one of the grain bags they rode with and ground the kernels together. "I'm not sure I like being loaned out like a waterskin or a whetstone."

"Orders are orders," Vree shrugged without looking over at her brother. She didn't have to look, she knew what she'd see. He'd be lying back, wearing only kilt and sandals and a petulant expression. "These orders just happen to come directly from the Emperor."

"Yeah? And that's another thing, since when does the Emperor get directly involved in this sort of shit?"

"When it involves *family*," she said with pointed emphasis on the last word.

"An assassin has no family but the army," Bannon reminded her poking her hard in the ribs.

The carter glanced back at the wrestling match, shaking her head. Easy to believe these two had trained together all their lives—they fit together like moving puzzle pieces. Less easy to believe they were brother and sister, in spite of an obvious physical resemblance. There was a sexuality in the way he moved that teased and provoked at the same time and a tension in her responses indicated she was well aware of it.

None of my business, the carter reminded herself. All assassins were a little bit crazy and rumors in the Sixth Army said these two were crazier than most.

Just before noon, they passed the ruin of Saburo. The buildings and most of the surrounding olive groves had been burned. In the months since, very little had been rebuilt.

"After Commander Jolan pulled back, Marshal Arnon turned the Seventh Army loose on it," the carter explained when Bannon asked why.

Which was all the explanation necessary.

If Marshal Arnon had turned the army loose, there wasn't anything to rebuild with.

"The people of Saburo probably thought that sort of thing never happened to Imperial citizens," Vree observed dryly.

"That'll teach them to harbor traitors," her brother agreed in the same almost sarcastic tone.

The carter heard double, even triple meanings, and decided not to ask.

They stopped in the heat of the day, feeding, watering and resting the oxen, then continued in the relative cool of the evening. Just before dark, the carter looped the reins and swiveled around on the seat. They were getting close, an army encampment left a distinct signature on the breeze, and she wanted to let her passengers know they should start thinking about slipping away unseen.

They'd already slipped.

Both assassins and their kit had vanished. They'd even shuffled the indentations of their bodies out of the bags of grain.

Impressed, in spite of her pique, for the only sounds they'd had to cover their departure had been made by the wagon itself, she'd barely turned back to her oxen when she heard a horse approaching. A moment after that an Imperial Courier appeared out of the dusk, the single golden starburst on his banner catching the last light of the setting sun.

"You've got to admire their sense of timing," she muttered, but whether she was speaking of the assassins or the courier she wasn't entirely sure.

"The Emperor has taken care of it."

"Sir?"

Marshal Arnon waved the message with its broken imperial seal under the commander's nose. "First, he keeps me here and now he has sent his own assassin into the fortress. I am to have *my* people in position so that when the gates are opened they can take advantage of the opportunity his Imperial Majesty has provided."

Commander Zayit frowned. "There are no assassins in the First Army."

"You think the Emperor can't get assassins if he needs them?"

"No, sir."

"No, sir indeed," the marshal mocked, throwing the message down onto his map table with enough force that its passage caused the lamp hanging from the centerpole to swing violently back and forth, painting dark shadows on the inside walls of the tent.

"When will the gates be opened, sir?" Zayit asked, trying not to think of how much the shadows looked like raven's wings. The longer the army spent looking at the dried and desiccated bundle Orban had become, the longer they spent speculating about the birds—three of them now—that came every morning to perch between them and the fortress, the longer they had to mutter about rites denied, the less like an army they were and the more like a mob. So far discipline had held but it was becoming harder and harder for the officers to hold things together. If something didn't happen soon...

"The gate opens tomorrow morning. My Imperial cousin tells me to ready the division without warning the sentries on the wall. Does he think I'm a complete idiot? This is *my* army!"

Actually, it was the Emperor's army but that was another thing the marshal didn't like to be reminded of.

"Well don't just stand there, Commander! Ready a company!" Lip curled, the marshal turned on her, arms spread sarcastically wide. "Didn't you hear: The Emperor has taken care of it."

The easiest way to avoid being given orders by Marshal Arnon, was to avoid Marshal Arnon—their orders had been quite clear about that. They'd been a lot less clear about other aspects of the job.

The original courier had known little about how the three dead assassins had gotten into the city. He knew there was a stream. It wasn't much, but since Orban, called from Third Division after the deaths of the other two assassins, had found it with the same information, Vree and Bannon weren't concerned. They'd all survived the same training and an access to a target that one of their peers could find, they could find faster.

The stream was easy to find. As dusk turned to true darkness and the sky over the hills turned from sapphire to onyx, they reached the place where it poured out of the earth. Knee deep in the icy water, Bannon ran a hand under the rock lip as far as he could. "It's doable," he said at last, stepping out. "But only just. If you had anything in the way of tits, sister-mine, you'd never make it."

Vree snorted and began stripping off her uniform. "Then you'd better keep your sling on, I'd hate for you to scrape anything that dangled off against a rock."

His smile flashed white in the darkness. "That water's so cold, it won't much matter."

They kept their voices low, the essess softened, although they were too far from either camp or fortress to be heard. Caution had kept them alive for the last two years—unlike most seventeen and eighteen year olds, they had a clear knowledge of their own mortality.

Prepared for the stream and the sort of swim it had likely meant, they separated the necessities out of their kit and wrapped them in waxed linen, careful to keep the bundles compact.

"Who goes first?"

"It'd better be me," Bannon sighed stepping back into the water wearing his sling and a throwing knife strapped to his left forearm. "I'm bigger and if get stuck I want you behind me where you can shove."

"Makes sense." Wearing only an identical throwing knife, Vree followed him, sucking air through her teeth at the first icy caress against her thighs. At the rock, she tied a silk rope around Bannon's waist. There was a small danger it could get hung up but taking out this particular target without their kit was more of a challenge than she'd accept—although during their journey, Bannon had expressed interest in trying. She watched her brother fill his lungs—once, twice, three times—and tried not to grin at his expression as he submerged. It'd be her turn soon enough.

The dark water was shallow and the moon nearly full. Vree watched the glimmer of Bannon's shoulders disappear, his back, his legs, his feet. The rope played out smoothly through her fingers.

She'd counted slowly to a hundred and fifteen when the rope stilled. Four feet, maybe five followed Bannon into the hill all at once, then three short tugs. He'd reached the other side.

Moving quickly, working her fingers to keep them from going numb in the cold, she tied off both kits, one behind each other. One breath. Two. A sound from the shore. Drawing in the third breath, she turned.

The unmistakable silhouette of three ravens watched her from the dead branches of a skeletal tree.

One hand rose to touch the onyx amulet of Jiir she wore on a leather thong around her neck, the other pulled twice at the rope. Releasing the third breath, she dropped her gaze to the water but, even as she followed the two packets in under the rock, she could feel the ravens watching.

The cold made it hard to think about anything but the cold. There wasn't room enough to swim against the current, nor was it smooth enough to allow Bannon to drag her along with their supplies. Arms outstretched, she pulled herself forward, counting slowly once again.

At 71, her reaching hand felt waxed linen. It wasn't moving. Pulling herself up as close as she could, she stretched out an arm beneath it, along the bottom. The stream bed narrowed suddenly, went from a horizontal slice through the hill to a vertical one and the first kit had jammed.

...72...

...73...

...74...

...75...

The rear kit pressed hard against her shoulder, she punched the bottom of the first as hard as she could.

...76...

...77...

All at once it jerked free and through. She guided the second as well as she was able and followed, turning sideways and up, the rock scraping almost gently against belly and front of thighs. A six count delay would have meant nothing in warmer water but her lungs were already aching and she had a thirty-eight count to go.

The current weakened as the passage widened and by a hundred she had the rope wrapped around one hand while the other kept her head clear of protrusions on the tunnel roof.

At 117 she surged out into open water. At 119 she surfaced and sucked in a lungful of air that had so much water in it, it was barely breathable. The noise told her she'd surfaced in the spray of a waterfall. Then her feet touched sand, a questing hand touched rock and she pulled herself up onto a ledge.

"Remind me to thank his Imperial Majesty for that experience," Bannon muttered in the darkness. "My balls climbed up so high they're sitting on my shoulders."

"Teach them to ask for crackers and I'd pay to see it." His voice told her he was standing so she stood as well.

They spent the next few moments warming up. Fingers stuffed into her armpits, she ran on the spot and heard Bannon doing the same. Had they not just come out of the water, the air underground would have been a cool relief after the scorching heat outside. As it was, it was almost warm and without a layer of wet cloth against skin, exercise was enough to chase the cold. When her feet no longer felt like blocks of wood and dexterity had returned, Vree reached out and lightly touched her brother's shoulder. "I vote we risk a light," she said when he stilled.

The waxed linen had done it's job. A moment later, they were studying the dimensions of the cave.

"Looks like we climb up beside the waterfall." Bannon's sigh blew out the candle.

They didn't bother dressing, the climb would leave them almost as wet as the swim although considerably warmer. Vree climbed with her eyes closed—it kept her from straining to see through impenetrable darkness. At the top, they walked against the stream through another passage just high enough to keep their heads and hands out of the water. When the passage opened up, a rising shelf of sand lead them to a beach and the silence told them they could safely light the candle again.

The beach lead them to a cleft.

A climb.

Another passage.

Another pool.

Flood waters had carved only a single path. They couldn't have gotten lost. The three assassins who'd taken this way before them had died in the fortress so there had to be a way in.

"Your turn to go first, sister-mine."

It took three dives before Vree felt the opening in the rock and then one more to fill her lungs and go through it. She'd counted to 70 and had almost decided to go back, when the rock opened up above her. Another thirty count and she surfaced. Her fingers brushed dressed stone.

"About time," Bannon muttered when she returned. "Too much slaughtering water down here for us not to end up in a well."

"Commander Jolan has to know that's how the others came into the fortress but she can't cut off her water supply." Running on the spot, Vree was thinking out loud as she warmed. "She's known from the moment Ganit missed his target. He died the same night he went in and it had to have been pretty obvious he came out of water. Visolela had to know she was climbing into a trap. Orban too."

Bannon shrugged. "When you know there's a trap, you avoid it."

"True. It's been..." She counted back. "...fifteen days since Orban. Commander Jolan had to know how many blades Marshal Arnon had with him and that he won't ask one of the other armies for help—he wouldn't want look weak. She knows the only thing he can do is settle in for a siege so she won't be expecting us. But she won't have totally let down her guard. She won't have someone staring down the well, but she's not the type to leave an access unguarded."

Marshal Chela had seen they were as well briefed on their target as time allowed.

"So we can get to the lip of the well without trouble but after that we'll have to be careful?"

"Yeah."

"Why didn't you just slaughtering say so?"

Vree sighed. "I was thinking out loud."

"You think too much, sister-mine."

Unwrapping their kit, they ate the dried meat and honeyed date bars while strapping on their weapons. They'd kept leather and steel dry as long as possible but climbing into a trap, they'd need them at hand. Their clothing they re-rolled in the waxed linen and strapped it to their backs—wet clothing would leave a trail, they'd dress once they were safely inside.

Three quarters of the way up the well, Vree stretched out an arm and touched Bannon's cheek. When he stilled, she signed *inside* against his skin. He nodded. The well was not only within the fortress wall, but within the fortress itself.

Just below the rim, they stopped. Listened.

Nothing.

Vree straightened her knees until her eyes cleared the edge. The well room was so dark, they might as well have still been in the caves under the hill. No guards hid in the darkness. Soundlessly, she slipped up and over the side, felt Bannon standing beside her, and moved off to the right. A moment later, each having determined half the dimensions of the room, they met again.

Commander Jolan had secured the well room by simply filling in most of an open arch and putting a door where there'd never been a door. The inconvenience for anyone drawing water had clearly been out-weighed by the alternative—throats slit.

"Guard outside?" Bannon breathed against her ear.

Vree nodded, pointing to the tiny line of light.

The only reason to have light was so that someone could see.

"One or two?"

Vree pressed her head to the crack and waited. Two soldiers— and all Jolan's traitors were ex-Seven Armies—guarding a locked cellar leading nowhere fifteen days after anything had happened, would be talking.

After a while, she laid one finger against Bannon's cheek.

They'd have to convince the guard to open the door without calling for help.

It had been fifteen days.

Fifteen slaughtering days.

And yet here he was taking his turn in the bowels of the fortress—the shitty bowels of the fortress, he amended—waiting for Marshal Moronic-Cousin-to-the-Emperor Arnon to try something stupid. Arnon would if anyone would but still...

It had been *fifteen* days.

Legs crossed, back against the rough wood of the door, he picked at his teeth with the point of his dagger. He'd never been so tempted to fall asleep on duty.

Bored, bored, slaughtering bored...

The sudden scrape of stone against stone inside the well room jerked him erect. A muffled curse spun him around. The distant splash brought both brows in under the rim of his helm.

Something had fallen into the well.

Something big.

There were more distant splashes. Smaller ones. As if someone had fallen and was struggling in the water.

Marshal Arnon was scraping the bottom of the barrel as far as assassins were concerned. According to Commander Jolan, there were two fifteen year olds left in the entire Seventh Army.

Sword drawn, he opened the door.

The lantern light spilled into the room and over the well. One of the capstones was missing and the one next to pulled out of line, the elongated print of wet fingers showing where the assassin had lost a precarious grip. Grinning, he lifted the lantern and moved in for a closer look but the well was too deep for his light to reach the water and the splashing had stopped.

A pair of shadows dropped silently down from the ledge of the old arch and disappeared into the fortress.

The Emperor wanted the situation resolved and his orders had been explicit.

But they had to find the commander before they could kill her.

The bureaucracy in the Capital had spit forth a plan of the fortress. It hadn't included the well-room but by the time Vree and Bannon reached the kitchens, they'd filled in the blanks. Skirting a pair of snoring bodies, they made their way to a patch of deep shadow at one edge of the open wall and stared across the courtyard. The Commander would be somewhere in the central tower.

While they'd been moving through the hill, the nearly full moon had dropped low in the sky, creating bars of light and dark between the buildings. Assassins paths.

Useful. But they'd still have to waste time searching the tower. The search had likely killed Ganit. The longer it took to reach a target, the greater the odds of discovery.

Together? Bannon signed, looking annoyed.

Vree nodded. They'd lose most of the advantage they had over the previous three assassins if they separated.

They were about to move from kitchen to tower when a shadow separated from the top of the gatehouse. Then a second. Then a third. The three huge birds landed side by side, with no sound from feathers or claws, on a window ledge almost exactly halfway up the tower wall.

Vree felt Bannon clutch her arm, fingers digging into flesh. Ravens didn't fly at night.

The ravens had gone from the window when Vree and Bannon reached the commander's room. They'd left two bodies behind them, silently and efficiently dispatched when there'd been no other way to move on. Hiding the bodies had taken more time than the killing.

Commander Jolan's small room had been set up like a command tent, her bed shoved up against one wall, less important than the map table and the strategies planned on it. She slept with one hand thrown up over her head, the paler skin on the underside of her arm defining her place in the dark.

She wasn't alone.

A silent crossing from door to bed side. The edge of Vree's dagger slid through the soft tissue of the throat too quickly for pain, found the spine, slipped between two ridges of bone, and ended it.

The commander's companion was considerably younger, probably Bannon's age. He opened sleep blurred eyes at exactly the wrong time.

Vree tossed a small square of leather stamped with a black starburst onto the bed. The Emperor's first order had been carried out and his point had been made. Treason could not hide from the blades of Jiir.

Now, they had to get to the barbican over the gate with only the soft shadows between moonset and dawn to hide them.

Bannon glanced out the window and grinned. "We take the high road," he said softly.

Measuring the distance between the window and broad top of the fortress' encircling wall, Vree nodded. The only guards were in the barbican. No point in wasting soldiers on a patrol when there was only one possible point of attack.

There was no room on the ledge to stand and jump. There was no room on the ledge for three ravens either but Vree didn't have time to worry about that now. She slid out, feet first, then gripping the ridge of stone, braced her feet against the wall, knees up beside her ears.

One breath, two...

Push off.

Turn in the air.

It had been a long night. She landed hard and too close to the edge. Training threw her weight back before her brain acknowledged the danger and sucking air between her teeth as her elbow slammed into stone, she rolled into the vee of shadow between wall and parapet.

Bannon's landing was messier still but she grabbed his waistband and yanked him down beside her. He pillowed his head between her breasts, mouthed, "Quick nap?" then grinned at her expression.

They'd taken out a target and that always left Bannon a little giddy.

Vree jerked her head toward the gate. The night was nearly over. There were four soldiers on guard.

They weren't expecting an attack from inside the fortress. Vree wondered what they thought when Bannon walked in through the arched door overlooking the courtyard although she supposed the first two died too quickly to think anything. The third had her mouth open to cry warning and the fourth actually got a hand around his sword hilt.

Commander Zayit watched a burning rag drop from the barbican and extinguish itself on the road. "Move them up," she said quietly to the Squad Leader beside her.

The order repeated itself and the company crept forward. She could hear it creaking and rustling like a huge beast rolling over in its sleep.

When the second flame dropped, she stepped out where she could be seen in the pale dawn light and pulled her sword. "Now!"

"They're moving." Bannon announced wiping oil off his fingers.

"Good."

As Vree raised the inner gate, Bannon picked up a discarded crossbow.

A rooster crowed.

Marshal Arnon rode into the fort when it was all over.

The traitor's bodies were stacked on one side of the courtyard, the dead of the Seventh Army on the other. A bloody rag tied around one arm, and a smear of blood not her own over the front of her armor, Commander Zayit walked forward to meet him.

Vree braced the stiffening body of the guard against her shoulder and shuffled it forward. Still hidden behind the edge of the arched doorway, she paused and her fingers tightened on unresisting flesh.

The sun had laid the shadow of the barbican across the courtyard crowned by the impossibly darker shadows of three ravens.

She met Bannon's gaze across the arch and together they looked up.

The marshal's horse stopped at the edge of the ravens' shadow. Shied sideways when he spurred it but wouldn't go further.

In the moment between one heartbeat and the next, the ravens screamed.

Marshal Arnon turned, one hand raised to block the sun from his eyes.

Bannon pulled the trigger on the crossbow.

The marshal jerked in the saddle, and began to fall, a crossbow quarrel buried deep in his left armpit.

Someone yelled, "There!"

An arrow hit the body Vree held.

She shoved it forward.

It hit the stones of the courtyard at the time same as the marshal.

The Emperor's orders had been explicit.

Throats slit in the night. Black starbursts left behind.

So many people never bothered thinking past the obvious.

Commander Zayit barely heard the beating of ravens wings over the pounding of her heart. Then they landed, one, two, three by the marshal's body.

"Commander?"

Without knowing why, she looked up. Past the traitor's body broken on the ground, up to where black shadows moved back out of the light. And she remembered another broken body that had lain like a shadow on the road.

"Commander?"

Some urgency in the question now. The fortress was so quiet, she could hear impact of a heavy beak through flesh.

Marshal Arnon had been right.

The Emperor had taken care of it.

"Let them feed."

People keep asking me if there's going to be another Blood book and I keep saying, "No." No more books, but definitely short stories.

SOMEONE TO SHARE THE NIGHT

YOU WRITE FOR *a living*, Henry reminded himself, staring at the form on the monitor. *A hundred and fifty thousand publishable words a year. How hard can this be?* Red-gold brows drawn in, he began to type.

"Single white male seeks... no..." The cursor danced back. "Single white male, mid-twenties, seeks..." That wasn't exactly his age but he rather suspected that personal ads were like taxes, everybody lied. "Seeks..."

He paused, fingers frozen over the keyboard. *Seeks what?* he wondered staring at the five words that, so far, made up the entire fax. Then he sighed, and removed a word. He had no real interest in spending time with those who used race as a criteria for friendship. Life was too short. Even his.

"Single male, mid-twenties, seeks..." He glanced down at the tabloid page spread out on his desk seeking inspiration. Unfortunately, he found wishful thinking, macho posturing, and, reading between the lines, a quiet desperation that made the hair rise off the back of his neck.

"What am I doing?" Rolling his eyes, he shoved his chair away from the desk. "I could walk out that door and have anyone I wanted."

Which was true.

But it wouldn't *be* what he wanted.

This is not an act of desperation, he reminded himself. Impatient, perhaps. Desperate, no.

"Single male, mid-twenties, not into the bar scene..." The phrase *meat market* was singularly apt in his case. "...seeks..."

What he'd had.

But Vicki was three thousand odd miles away with a man who loved her in spite of changes.

And Tony, freed from a life of mere survival on the streets, had defined himself and moved on.

They'd left a surprising hole in his life. Surprising and painful. Surprisingly painful. He found himself unwilling to wait for time and fate to fill it.

"Single male, mid-twenties, not into the bar scene, out of the habit of being alone, seeks someone strong, intelligent and adaptable."

Frowning, he added, "Must be able to laugh at life." then sent the fax before he could change his mind. The paper would add the electronic mailbox number when they ran it on Thursday.

Late Thursday or early Friday depending how the remaining hours of darkness were to be defined, Henry picked a copy of the paper out of a box on Davie Street and checked his ad. In spite of the horror stories he'd heard to the contrary, they'd not only gotten it right but placed it at the bottom of the first column of Alternative Lifestyles where it had significantly more punch than if it had been buried higher up on the page.

Deadlines kept him from checking the mailbox until Sunday evening. There were thirty-two messages. Thirty-two.

He felt flattered until he actually listened to them, and then, even though no one else knew, he felt embarrassed about feeling flattered.

Twenty, he dismissed out of hand. A couple of the instant rejects had clearly been responding to the wrong mailbox. A few sounded interesting but had a change of heart in the middle of the message and left no actual contact information. The rest seemed to be laughing just a little *too* hard at life.

But at the end of a discouraging half an hour, he still had a dozen messages to chose from; seven women, five men. It wasn't thirty-two, but it wasn't bad.

Eleven of them had left him email addresses.

One had left him a phone number.

He listened again to the last voice in the mailbox, the only one of the twelve who believed he wouldn't abuse the privilege offered by the phone company.

"Hi. My name is Lilah. I'm also in my mid-twenties—although which side of the midpoint I'd rather not say."

Henry could hear the smile in her voice. It was a half smile, a crooked smile, the kind of smile that could appreciate irony. He found himself smiling in response.

"Although I can quite happily be into the bar scene, I do think they're the worst possible place to meet someone for the first time. How about a coffee? I can probably be free any evening this week."

And then she left her phone number.

Still smiling, he called it.

If American troops had invaded Canada during the War of 1812 with half the enthusiasm Starbucks had exhibited when crossing the border, the outcome of the war would have been entirely different. While Henry had nothing actually against the chain of coffee shops, he found their client base to be just a little too broad. In the cafe on Denman that he preferred, there were never any children, rushing junior executives, or spandex shorts. Almost everyone wore black, and in spite of multiple piercings and an overuse of profanity, the younger patrons were clearly imitating their elders.

Their elders were generally the kind of artists and writers who seldom made sales but knew how to look the part. They were among the very few in Vancouver without tans.

Using the condensation on a three dollar bottle of water to make rings on the scarred table top, Henry watched the door and worried about recognizing Lilah when she arrived. Then he worried a bit that she wasn't going to arrive. Then he went back to worrying about recognizing her.

You are way too old for this nonsense, he told himself sternly. *Get a...*

The woman standing in the doorway was short, vaguely Mediterranean with thick dark hair that spilled halfway down her back in ebony ripples. If she'd passed her mid-twenties it wasn't by more than a year or two. She'd clearly ignored the modern notion that a woman should be so thin she looked like an adolescent boy with breasts. Not exactly beautiful, something about her drew the eye. Noting, Henry's regard, she smiled, red lips parting over very white teeth, and it was exactly the expression that Henry had imagined. He stood as she walked to his table, enjoying the sensual way she moved her body across the room and aware that everyone else in the room was enjoying it too.

"Henry?" Her voice was throatier in person, almost a purr.

"Lilah." He gave her name back to her as confirmation.

She raised her head and locked her dark gaze to his.

They blinked in unison.

"Vampire."

Henry Fitzroy, bastard son of Henry VIII, once Duke of Richmond and Somerset, dropped back into his chair with an exhalation halfway between a sigh and a snort. "Succubus."

"So are you saying you *weren't* planning to feed off whoever answered your ad?"

"No, I'm saying it wasn't the primary reason I placed it."

The overt sexual attraction turned off, Lilah swirled a finger through a bit of spilled latte and rolled her eyes. "So you're a better man than I am Gunga Din but I personally don't see the difference between us. You don't kill anymore, I don't kill anymore."

"I don't devour years off my…" He paused and frowned, uncertain of how to go on.

"Victims? Prey? Quarry? Dates?" The succubus sighed. "We've got to come up with a new word for it."

Recognizing she had a point, Henry settled for the lesser of four evils. "I don't devour years off my date's life."

"Oh, please. So they spend less time having their diapers changed by strangers in a nursing home, less time drooling in their pureed mac and cheese. If they knew, they'd thank me. At least I don't violate their structural integrity."

"I hardly think a discrete puncture counts as a violation."

"Hey, you said puncture, not me. But…" She raised a hand to stop his protest. "…I'm willing to let it go."

"Gracious of you."

"Always."

In spite of himself, Henry smiled.

"You know hon, you're very attractive when you do that."

"Do what?"

"When you stop looking so irritated about things not turning out the way you expected. Blind dates *never* turn out the way you expect." Dropping her chin she looked up at him through the thick fringe of her lashes. "Trust me, I've been on a million of them."

"A million?"

"Give or take."

"So you're a pro…"

A sardonic eyebrow rose. "A gentleman wouldn't mention that."

"True." He inclined his head in apology and took the opportunity to glance at his watch. *"Run Lola Run is playing at the Caprice in 90 minutes; did you want to go?"*

For the first time since entering the cafe, Lilah looked startled. "With you?"

A little startled himself, Henry shrugged, offering the only reason that explained the unusually impulsive invitation. "I'd enjoy spending some time just being myself, without all the implicit lies."

Dark brows drew in and she studied him speculatively. "I can understand that."

An almost comfortable silence filled the space between them.

"Well?" Henry asked at last.

"My German's a little rusty. I haven't used it for almost a century."

Henry stood and held out his hand. "There's subtitles."

Shaking her head, she pushed her chair out from the table and laid her hand in his. "Why not."

Sunset. A slow return to awareness. The feel of cotton sheets against his skin. The pulse of the city outside the walls of his sanctuary. The realization he was smiling.

After the movie, they'd walked for hours in a soft mist, talking about the places they'd seen and when they'd seen them. A primal demon, the succubus had been around for millennia but politely restricted her observations to the four and a half centuries Henry could claim. Their nights had been remarkably similar.

When they parted about an hour before dawn, they parted as friends although it would never be a sexual relationship, sex was too tied to feeding for them both.

"World's full of warm bodies," Lilah had pointed out, *"but how many of them saw Mrs. Simmons play Lady MacBeth at Covent Garden Theater on opening night and felt the hand washing scene was way, way over the top?"*

How many indeed, Henry thought, throwing back the covers and swinging his legs out of bed. Rather than deal with the balcony doors in the master suite, he'd sealed the smallest room in the three bedroom condo against the light. He'd done the crypt thing, once, and didn't see the attraction.

After his shower, he wandered into the living room and picked up the remote. With any luck he could catch the end of the news.

He didn't often watch it but last night's…date?…had left him feeling re-connected to the world.

"…when southbound travelers waited up to three hours to cross the border at Peace Arch as US customs officials tightened security checks as a precaution against terrorism."

"Canadian terrorists." Henry frowned as he toweled his hair. "Excuse me while I politely blow up your building?"

"Embarrassed Surrey officials had to shut down the city's Web site after a computer hacker broke into the system and rewrote the greeting, using less-than-flattering language. The hacker remains unknown and unapprehended."

"And in a repeat of our top story, police have identified the body found this morning on Wreck Beach as Taylor Johnston, thirty-two, of Haro Street. They still have no explanation for the condition of the body although an unidentified constable commented that 'it looked like he had his life sucked out of him.'"

"And now to Rajeet Singh with our new product report."

Jabbing at the remote, Henry cut Rajeet off in the middle of an animated description of a battery-operated cappuccino frother. Plastic cracked as his fingers tightened. A man found with the life sucked out of him. He didn't want to believe…

As part of an ongoing criminal investigation, the body was at the City Morgue in the basement of Vancouver General Hospital. The previous time Henry'd made an after hours visit, he'd been searching for information to help identify the victim. This time, he needed to identify the murderer.

He walked silently across the dark room to the drawer labeled Taylor Johnston, pulled it open, and flipped back the sheet. LED's on various pieces of machinery and the exit sign over the door provided more than enough light to see tendons and ligaments standing out in sharp relief under desiccated parchment colored skin. Hands and feet looked like claws, and the features of the skull had overwhelmed the features of the face. The unnamed constable had made an accurate observation; the body did, indeed, look as if all the life had been sucked out of it.

Henry snarled softly and closed the drawer.

"You don't kill anymore, I don't kill anymore…"

He found the dead man's personal effects in a manila envelope in the outer office. A post-it note suggested that the police should have picked the envelope up by six PM. The watch was an imitation Rolex—but not a cheap one. There were eight keys on his key ring. The genuine cowhide wallet held four high end credit cards, eighty-seven dollars in cash, a picture of a golden retriever, and half a dozen receipts. Three were out of bank machines. Two were store receipts. The sixth was for a credit card transaction.

Henry had faxed in both his personal ad and his credit information. It looked as though Taylor Johnston had dropped his off in person.

"Blind dates never turn out the way you expect. Trust me, I've been on a million of them."

In a city the size of Vancouver, a phone number and a first name provided no identification at all. Had Lilah answered when he called, Henry thought he'd be able to control his anger enough to arrange another meeting, but she didn't and when he found himself snarling at her voice mail, he decided not to leave a message.

"Although I can quite happily be into the bar scene..."

She'd told him she liked jazz. It was a place to start.

She wasn't at O'Doul's, although one of the waiters recognized her description. From the strength of his reaction, Henry assumed she'd fed—but not killed. Why kill Johnston and yet leave this victim with only pleasant memories? Henry added it to the list of questions he intended to have answered.

A few moments later, he parked his BMW, illegally, on Abbot Street and walked around the corner to Water Street, heading for The Purple Onion Cabaret. There were very few people on the sidewalks—a couple, closely entwined, a small clump of older teens, and a familiar form just about to enter the club.

Henry could move quickly when he needed to, and he was in no mood for subtlety. He was in front of her before she knew he was behind her.

An ebony brow rose but that was the only movement she made. "What brings you here, hon? I seem to recall you saying that jazz made your head ache."

He snarled softly, not amused.

The brow lowered, slowly. "Are you Hunting me, Nightwalker? Should I scream? Maybe that nice young man down the block will disentangle himself from his lady long enough to save me."

Henry's lips drew up off his teeth. "And who will save him as you add another death to your total?"

Lilah blinked and the formal cadences left her voice. "What the hell are you talking about?"

Demons seldom bothered lying, the truth caused more trouble. She honestly didn't know what he meant.

"You actually saw this body?" When Henry nodded, Lilah took a long swallow of mocha latte, carefully put the cup down on its saucer and said, "Why do you care? I mean, I know why you cared when you thought it was me," she added before he could speak. "You thought I'd lied to you and you didn't like feeling dicked around. I can understand that. But it's not me. So, why do you care?"

Henry let the final mask fall, the one he maintained even for the succubus. "Someone, something, is hunting in my territory."

Across the cafe, a mug slid from nerveless fingers and hit the Italian tile floor, exploding into a hundred shards of primary colored porcelain. There was nervous laughter, scattered applause, and all eyes thankfully left the golden haired man with the night in his voice.

Lilah shrugged. "There's millions of people in the Greater Vancouver area, hon. Enough for all of us.

"It's the principal of the thing," he muttered, a little piqued by her lack of reaction.

"It's not another vampire."

It was almost a question so he answered it. "No. The condition of the corpse was classic succubus."

"Or incubus," she pointed out. "You don't know for certain those men weren't gay and I sincerely doubt that you and I were alone shopping from the personals."

"I wasn't looking to feed," Henry ground out through clenched teeth.

"That's right. You were looking for a victimless relationship and…" Lilah spread her hands, fingernails drawing glistening scarlet lines in the air. "…ta dah, you found me. And if I'm not what you were looking for, then you were clearly planning to feed, if not sooner then later, so you can just stop being so 'more ethical than thou' about it." She half turned in her chair, turning her gesture into a wave at counter staff. "Sweetie, could I have another of these and a chocolate croissant? Thanks."

The cafe didn't actually have table service. Her smile created it. Henry's smile sent the young man scurrying back behind the counter.

"Is there another succubus in the city?" he demanded.

"How should I know? I've never run into one but that just means I've never run into one." The pointed tip of a pink tongue slowly licked foam off her upper lip.

Another mug shattered.

"Incubus?"

She sighed and stopped trying to provoke a reaction from the vampire. "I honestly don't know, Henry. We're not territorial like your lot, we pretty much keep racking up those frequent flyer miles— town to town, party to party..." Eyebrows flicked up then down. "...man to man. If this is your territory, can't *you* tell?"

"No. I can recognize a demon if I see one, regardless of form, but you have no part in the lives I Hunt or the blood I feed from." He shrugged. "A large enough demon might cause some sort of dissonance but..."

"But you haven't felt any such disturbance in the force."

"What?"

"You've got to get out to more movies without subtitles, hon." She pushed her chair out from the table and stood, lowering her voice dramatically. "Since you've been to the morgue there's only one thing left for us to do."

"Us?" Henry interrupted, glancing around with an expression designed to discourage eavesdroppers. "This isn't your problem."

"Sweetie, it became my problem when you showed me your Prince of Darkness face."

He stood as well; she had a point. Since he'd been responsible for involving her, he couldn't then tell her she wasn't involved. "All right, what's left for us to do?"

Her smile suggested that a moonless romp on a deserted beach would be the perfect way to spend the heart of the night. "Why, visit the scene of the crime, of course."

Traffic on the bridge slowed them a little and it was almost two am by the time they got to Wreck Beach. Taylor Johnston's body had been found on the northside of the breakwater at Point Grey. Henry parked the car on one of the remaining sections of Old Marine Drive but didn't look too happy about it.

"Campus security," he replied when Lilah inquired. "This whole area is part of the University of British Columbia's endowment lands and they've really been cracking down on people parking by the side of the road."

"*You're* worried about Campus Security?" The succubus shook her head in disbelief as they walked away from the car. "You know, hon, there are times when you're entirely too human for a vampire."

He supposed he deserved that. "The police have been all over this area, what are we likely to find that they missed?"

"Something they weren't looking for."

"Ghoulies and ghosties and things that go bump in the night?"

"Takes one to know one." She stepped around the tattered end of a piece of yellow police tape. "Or in this case, takes two."

For a moment, Henry had the weirdest sense of deja vu. It could have been Vicki he was following down to the sand, their partnership renewed. Then Lilah half turned, laughingly telling him to hurry and she couldn't have been more different than his tall, blonde ex-lover.

Single male, mid-twenties, seeks someone to share the night.

So what if it was a different someone...

He knew when he stood on the exact spot the body had been found, the stink of the dying man's terror was so distinct that it had clearly been neither a fast nor painless death.

"Not an incubus then," Lilah declared dumping sand out of an expensive Italian pump. "We may like to take our time but no one ever complains about the process."

Henry frowned and turned his face into the breeze coming in off the Pacific. There was no moon and except for the white lines of breakers at the sea wall, the waves were very dark. "Can you smell the rot?"

"Sweetie, there's a great big dead fish not fifteen feet away. I'd have to be in the same shape as Mr. Johnston not to smell it."

"Not the fish." It smelled of the crypt. Of bones left to lie in the dark and damp. "There." He pointed toward the sea wall. "It's in there."

Lilah looked up at Henry's pale face then over at the massive mound of rock jutting out into the sea. "What is?"

"I don't know yet." Half a dozen paces toward the rock, he turned back toward the succubus. "Are you coming?"

"No, just breathing hard."

"Pardon?"

He looked so completely confused, she laughed as she caught up. "You really don't get out much, do you, hon?"

The night was no impediment to either of them but the entrance was well hidden. If it hadn't been for the smell, they'd have never found it.

Dropping to her knees beside him, Lilah handed Henry a lighter. He stretched his arm to its full length under a massive block of stone, the tiny flame shifting all the shadows but one.

"You can take the lighter with you." Lilah rocked back onto her heels, shaking her head. "I, personally, am not going in there."

Henry understood. Succubi were only slightly harder to kill than the humans they resembled. "I don't think it's home," he muttered dropping onto his stomach and inching forward into the black line of the narrow crevasse

Lilah's voice drifted down to him. "Not a problem, hon, but I'd absolutely ruin this dress. Not to mention my manicure."

"Not to mention," Henry repeated, smiling in spite of the conditions. There was an innate honesty in the succubus he liked. A lot.

Twice his body-length under the stone, after creeping through a puddle of salt water at least an inch deep, the way opened up and, although he had to keep turning his shoulders, he could move forward in a crouch. The smell reminded him of the catacombs under St. Mark's Square in Venice where the sea had permeated both the rock and the ancient dead.

Three or four minutes later, he straightened cautiously as the roof rose away and drew Lilah's lighter out of his pocket, expecting to see bones piled in every corner. He saw, instead, a large crab scuttling away, a filthy nest of clothing, and a dark corner where the sucking sound of water moving up and down in a confined space overlaid the omnipresent roar of the sea. A closer inspection showed an almost circular hole down into the rock and about ten or twelve feet away, the moving water of the Pacific Ocean. A line of moisture showed the high tide mark and another large crab peered out of a crevasse just below it. It was obvious where the drained bodies were dumped and what happened to them after dumping.

The scent of death, of rot, hadn't come from the expected cache of corpses, so it had to have come from the creature who laired here.

Which narrows it down considerably, Henry thought grimly as he closed the almost unbearably hot lighter with a snap.

Lilah and a young man were arranging their clothes as he crawled out from under the seawall. The succubus, almost luminescent by starlight, waved when she saw him.

"Hey Sweetie, you might want to hear this."

"Hear what?" The smell of sex and a familiar pungent smoke overlaid the smell of death.

The young man smiled in what Henry could only describe as a satiated way and said, "Like you know the dead guy they found here this morning, eh? I sort of like saw it happen."

Henry snarled. "Saw what?"

"Whoa, like what big teeth you have, grandma. Anyway, I've been crashing on the beach when the weather's good, you know, and like last night I'm asleep and I hear this whimpering sort of noise and I think it's a dog in trouble, eh? But, it's not. It's like two guys. I can't see them too good but I think, hey go for the gusto guys, but one of them seems really pissed 'cause like the tide's really high and I guess he can't go to his regular nooky place in the rocks and he sort of throws himself on the other guy so I stop looking, you know."

"Why didn't you tell this to the police?"

The young man giggled. "Well, some mornings you don't want to talk to the police, you know. And I was like gone before they arrived anyhow. So, like is this your old lady, 'cause she's one prime piece of...OW!"

Henry tightened his grip on the unshaven chin enough to dimple the flesh. He let the Hunter rise and when the dilated pupils finally responded by dilating further, he growled. "Forget you ever saw us."

"Dude..."

"It's a wight," Henry said when they were back in the car. "From the pile of clothing, it looks like it's been there for a while. It probably lives on small animals most of the time but every now and then people like your friend go missing off the beach or students disappear from the campus, but they since they never find a body, no one ever goes looking for a killer.

"Last night, it went hunting a little further from home only to get back and find the tide in and over the doorway. Which answers the question of why it left the body on the beach. It must've had to race the dawn to shelter."

"Wait a minute." Lilah protested, pausing in her dusting of sand from crevasses. "A wight wouldn't care about going through salt water. Salted holy water, yes but not just the sea."

"If it tried to drag it's victim the rest of the way, he'd drown."

"And no more than the rest of us, wights don't feed from the dead," Lilah finished. "And all the pieces but one fall neatly into place. You don't honestly think a wight would pick its victim from the personnel ads do you, hon?"

Unclean creature of darkness seeks life essence to suck.

"I don't honestly think it can read," Henry admitted. "That whole personals thing had to have been a co-incidence."

"And now that we've answered that question, why don't we head for this great after-hours club I know?"

"I don't have time for that Lilah. I have a silver letter opener at home I can use for a weapon."

"Against?"

She sounded so honestly confused he turned to look at her. "Against the wight. I can't let it keep killing."

"Why not? Why should you care? Curiosity is satisfied, move on."

Traffic on 4th Avenue turned his attention back to the road. "Is that the only reason you came tonight? Curiosity?"

"Of course. When a life gets sucked and it's not me doing the sucking, I like to know what is. You're not really…?" He could feel the weight of her gaze as she studied him. "You're not seriously…? You are, aren't you?"

"Yes, I am. It's getting careless."

"Good. Someday, it'll get caught by the dawn, problem solved."

"And when some forensic pathologist does an autopsy on the remains, what then?"

"I'm not a fortune teller, hon. The only future I can predict is who's going to get lucky."

"Modern forensics will find something that shouldn't exist. Most people will deny it, but some will start thinking."

"You do know that they moved the X-Files out of Vancouver?"

Henry kept his eyes locked on the tail lights in front of him. The depth of his disappointment in her reaction surprised him. "Our best defense is that no one believes we exist, so they don't look for us. If they start looking..." His voice trailed off into mobs with torches and laboratory dissection tables.

They drove in silence until they crossed the Burrard Bridge, then Lilah reached over and laid her fingers on Henry's arm. "That's a nice pragmatic reason you've got there," she murmured, "but I don't believe you for a moment. You're going to destroy this thing be-cause it's killing in your territory. But it has nothing to do with the territorial imperatives of a vampire," she added before he could speak. "Your territory. Your people. Your responsibility." She dropped her hand back onto her lap. "Let me out here, hon, I try to keep my distance from the overly ethical."

His fingers tightened on the steering wheel as he guided the BMW to the curb. "You *weren't* what I was looking for when I placed that ad," he said as she opened the door. "But I thought we..." Suddenly at a loss for words, he fell back on the trite. "...had a connection."

Leaning over she kissed his cheek. "We did." Stepping out onto the sidewalk, she smiled back in through the open door. "You'll find your Robin, Batman. It just isn't me."

Henry returned to the beach just before high tide, fairly certain the wight hadn't survived so long by making the same mistake twice. He blocked the entrance to the lair with a silver chain and waited.

The fight didn't last long. Henry felt mildly embarrassed by taking his frustrations out on the pitiful creature, but he'd pretty much gotten over it by the time he fed the desiccated body to the crabs.

He broke a number of traffic laws getting home before dawn. Collapsing inside the door to his sanctuary, he woke at sunset, stiff and sore from a day spent crumbled on a hardwood floor. He tried to call Lilah and tell her it was over, but whatever connection there'd been between them was well and truly broken. Her phone number was no longer in service.

The brief, aborted companionship made it even harder to be alone.

For two nights, he Hunted and fed and wondered if Lilah had been right and he should have been more specific.

Overly ethical creature of the night seeks sidekick.

The thought of who'd answer something like that frightened him the way nothing else had frightened him over the last four and a half centuries.

Finally, he picked up the list of email addresses and started alphabetically.

The man who came in the door of the cafe was tall and dark and muscular. Shoulder length hair had been caught back in a gold clasp. Gold rings flashed on every finger and dangled from both ears. He caught Henry's eye and strode across the cafe toward him, smiling broadly.

Stopped on the other side of the table.

Stopped smiling.

"Henry?"

"Abudla?"

They blinked in unison.

"Vampire."

Henry dropped back into his chair. "Djinn."

Perhaps he ought to have his ad placed somewhere *other* than Alternative Lifestyles.

In 1997 eighteen men sailed a replica of John Cabot's 15ᵗʰ century caravel the Matthew from Bristol (England) to Bonavista (Newfoundland). They spent seven weeks sailing 2,881.9 miles across the north Atlantic in a square rigged ship only twenty meters long.

"*The ocean leaves a mark on everyone's soul.*"   Chris LeGrow, crewmember, Matthew II.

OH GLORIOUS SIGHT

WILL HENNET, FIRST Mate on *The Matthew*, stood at the rail and watched his master cross the dock talking with great animation to the man by his side.

"So the Frenchman goes with you?"

"Aye."

"He a sailor, then?"

"He tells me he's sailed."

"And that man, the Italian?"

"Master Cabot's barber."

The river-pilot spat into the harbor, scoring a direct hit on the floating corpse of a rat, his opinion of traveling with barbers clear. "Good to have clean cheeks when the sirens call you over the edge of the world."

"So they say." Only a sailor who'd never left the confines of the Bristol Channel could still believe the world was flat, but Hennet had no intention of arguing with a man whose expert guidance they needed if they were to reach the anchorage at King's Road on this tide.

"Seems like Master Cabot's taking his time to board."

That, Hennet could agree with wholeheartedly.

"By God's grace, this time tomorrow we'll be on the open sea."

Gaylor Roubaix laughed at the excitement in his friend's voice. "And this time a month hence, we'll be in Cathay sleeping in the arms of sloe-eyed maidens."

"*What* kind of maidens?"

"You aren't the only one to have read the stories of Marco Polo; it isn't my fault if you only remember silk and spice. Slow down," he added with a laugh. "It's unseemly for the master of the ship to run across the docks."

"Slow down?" Zoane Cabatto—now John Cabot by grace of the letters patent granted by the English king—threw open his arms. "How? When the wind brings me the scent of far off lands and I hear..." His voice trailed off and he stopped so suddenly, Roubaix had gone another six steps before he realized he was alone.

"Zoane!"

"*Ascoltare*. Listen." Head down, he charged around a stack of baled wool.

Before Roubaix—who'd heard nothing at all—could follow, angry shouting in both Italian and English rose over the ambient noise of the docks. The shouting stopped, suddenly punctuated by a splash, and the mariner reappeared.

"A dockside tough was beating a child," he said by way of explanation. "I put a stop to it."

Roubaix sighed and closed the distance between them. "Why? It was none of your concern."

"Perhaps, but I leave three sons in God's grace until we return, and it seemed a bad omen to let it continue." He stepped forward and paused again at Roubaix's expression. "What is it?"

In answer, the other man pointed.

Cabot turned.

The boy was small, a little older than a child but undernourished by poverty. Dark hair, matted into filthy clumps, had recently been dusted with ash; purple and green bruises gave the grime on the thin arms some color, and the recent winter, colder than any in living memory, had frozen a toe off one bare foot. An old cut, reopened on his cheek, bled sluggishly.

His eyes were a brilliant blue, a startling color in the thin face, quickly shuttered as he dropped his gaze to the toes of Cabot's boots.

"Go on, boy, you're safe now!"

Roubaix snorted. "Safe until the man who was beating him is out of the water, then he'll take his anger at you out on the boy."

Beginning to regret his impulsive action, Cabot spread his hands. "What can I do?"

"Take him with us."

"Are you mad?"

"There is a saying, the farther from shore, the farther from God. We go a long way from shore, a little charity might convince God to stay longer." Roubaix's shrug held layers of meaning. "Or you can leave him to die. Your choice."

Cabot looked across the docks to the alleys and tenements of dockside, dark in spite of early morning sunlight that danced across the harbor swells and murmured, "Your father was right, Gaylor, you should have been a priest." After a long moment, he turned his attention back to the boy. "What is your name?" he asked, switching to accented English.

"Tam." His voice sounded rusty, unused.

"I am John Cabot, Master of *The Matthew*."

The brilliant blue gaze flicked to the harbor and back with a question.

"*Si.* That ship. We sail today for the new world. If you wish, you sail with us."

He hadn't expected to be noticed. He'd followed only because the man had been kind to him and he'd wanted to hold the feeling a little longer. When the man turned, he nearly bolted. When he was actually spoken to, his heart began beating so hard he could hardly hear his own answer.

And now this.

He knew, for he'd been told it time and time again, that ships were not crewed by such as he, that sailors had legitimate sons to find a place for, that there'd never be a place for some sailor's get off a tuppenny whore.

"Well, boy? Do you come?"

He swallowed hard, and nodded.

"Is Master Cabot actually bringing that boy on board?"

"Seems to be," Hennet answered grimly.

"A Frenchman, a barber, and a piece of dockside trash." The river-pilot spat again. "He'll sail you off the edge of the world, you mark my words."

"Mister Hennet, are we ready to sail?"

"Aye sir." Hennet stepped forward to meet Cabot at the top of the gangplank, the river-pilot by his side. "This is Jack Pyatt. He'll be seeing us safe to King's Road."

"Mister Pyatt." Cabot clapped the man's outstretched hand in both of his in the English style. "I thank you for lending us your skill this day."

"Lending?" The pilot's prominent brows went up. "I'm paid well for this, Master Cabot."

"Yes, of course." Dropping the man's hand, Cabot started toward the fo'c'sle. "If you are ready, the tide does not wait. Mister Hennet, cast off."

"Zoane…"

Brows up, Cabot turned. "Oh yes, the boy. Mister Hennet, this is Tam. Make him a sailor. Happy now," he asked Roubaix pointedly in French.

"Totally," Roubaix replied. "And when you have done making him a sailor," he murmured in English to Hennet as he passed, "you may make a silk purse from a sow's ear."

"Aye sir."

He wanted to follow Master Cabot but the sudden realization that a dozen pairs of eyes had him locked in their sight froze him in place. It wasn't good, it wasn't safe to be the center of attention.

Hennet watched the worship in the strange blue eyes replaced by fear, saw the bony shoulders hunch in on themselves to make a smaller target and looked around to find the source. It took him a moment to realize that nothing more than the curiosity of the crew was evoking such terror.

"Right then!" Fists on his hips, he turned in place. "You heard the master!"

"We're to make him a sailor, then?" Rennie McAlonie called out before anyone could move.

"You're to cast off the lines, you poxy Scots bastard."

"Aye, that's what I thought."

"And you…" The boy cringed and Hennet softened his voice to a growl. "For now, stay out of the way."

He didn't know where out of the way was. After he'd been cursed at twice and cuffed once, the big man the master called Hennet shoved him down beside the chicken coop and told him to stay put. He could see a bit of Master Cabot's leg so he hugged his knees to his chest and chewed on a stalk of wilted greens he'd taken from an indignant hen.

The tenders rowed *The Matthew* down the channel and left her at King's Road, riding at anchor with half a dozen other ships waiting for an east wind to fill the sail.

"Where's the boy?"

"Now that's a right good question, Mister Hennet." Rennie pulled the ratline tight and tested his knot. "Off somewhere dark and safe's my guess."

The mate snorted. "We've ballast enough. Master Cabot wants him taught."

"It'd be like teachin' one of the wee folk. He's here but he's no a part of us. It's like the only other livin' thing he sees is Master Cabot."

"It's right like havin' a stray dog around," offered another of the crew, "the kind what runs off with his tail 'tween his legs when ya tries ta make friends."

Hennet glanced toward the shore. "If he's to be put off it has to be soon, before the wind changes. I'll speak with Master Cabot."

"Come now, it's only been three days." Rope wrapped around his fist, Rennie turned to face the mate. "This is right strange to him. Give the poor scrawny thing a chance."

"You think you can win him?"

"Aye, I do."

The boy's eyes were the same color as the piece of Venetian glass he'd brought back for his mother from his first voyage. Wondering why he remembered that now, Hennet nodded. "All right. You've got one more day."

Master Cabot wanted him to be a sailor, and he tried, he truly did. But he couldn't be a sailor hiding in dark corners, and he couldn't tell when it was safe to come out, and he didn't know any other way to live.

He felt safest after sunset when no one moved around much and it was easier to disappear. Back pressed up against the aftcastle wall, as close to Master Cabot as possible, he settled into a triangle of deep shadow and cupped his hand protectively over the biscuits he'd tied into the tattered edge of his shirt. So far, there'd been food twice a day but who knew how long it would keep coming.

Shivering a little, for the nights were still cold, he closed his eyes.

And opened them again.

What was that sound?

"Ren, look there."

Rennie, who'd replaced the shepherd's pipe with a leather mug of beer, peered over the edge of the mug. Eyes that gleamed as brilliant a blue by moon as by sun, stared back at him.

"He crept up while you was playin'," John Jack murmured, leaning in to his ear. "Play sumptin else."

Without looking aside, Rennie set down the last of his beer, put the pipe between his lips and blew a bit of a jig. Every note drew the boy closer. When he blew the last swirl of notes, the boy was an arm's reach away. He could feel the others holding their breath, could feel the weight of the boy's strange eyes. It was like something out of story had crept out of the shadows. Moving slowly, he held out the pipe.

"Rennie...!"

"Shut up. Go on, boy."

Thin fingers closed around the offered end and tentatively pulled it from his grasp.

He stroked the wood, amazed such sounds could come out of something so plain, then he put it in his mouth the way he'd seen the red-haired man do.

The first noise was breathy, unsure. The second had an unexpected purity of tone.

"Cover and uncover the holes; it makes the tune." Rennie wiggled his fingers, grinned as the boy wiggled his in imitation, and smacked John Jack as he did the same.

He covered each hole in turn, listening. Brows drawn in, he began to put the sounds together.

Toes that hadn't tapped to Rennie's jig, moved of their own accord.

When he ran out of sounds and stopped playing, he nearly bolted at the roar of approval that rose up from the men but he couldn't take the pipe away and he wouldn't leave it behind.

Rennie tapped his front teeth with a fingernail. "You've played before?" he asked at last.

Tam shook his head.

"You played what I played, just from hearing?"

He nodded.

"Do you want to keep the pipe?"

He nodded again, fingers white around the wooden shaft, afraid to breathe in case he shattered.

"If you stay out where you can be seen, be a part of the crew, you can keep it."

"Rennie!"

"Shut-up, John Jack, I've another. And," he jabbed a finger at the boy, "you let us teach you to be a sailor."

Recoiling from the finger, Tam froze. He looked around at the semi-circle of men then down at the pipe. The music made it safe to come out so as long as he had the pipe he was safe. Master Cabot wanted him to be a sailor. When he lifted his head, he saw that the red-haired man still watched him. He nodded a third time.

By the fifth day of waiting, the shrouds and ratlines were done and the crew had been reduced to bitching about the delay, every one of them aware it could last for weeks.

"Hey, you!"

Tam jerked around and nearly fell over as he leapt back from John Jack looming over him.

"You bin up ta crow's nest yet?"

He shook his head.

"Well, get yer arse up there then."

It was higher than it looked and he'd have quit halfway, but Master Cabot was standing in his usual place on the fo'c'sle, not watching but there, so he ignored the trembling in his arms and legs and kept going, finally falling over the rail and collapsing on the small round of planking.

After he got his breath back, he sat up and peered through the slats.

He could see to the ends of the earth but no one could see him. He didn't have words to describe how it made him feel.

Breezes danced around the nest that couldn't be felt down on the deck. They chased each other through the rigging, playing a tune against the ropes.

Tam pulled out his pipe and played the tune back at them.

The breezes blew harder.

"Did you send him up there, McAlonie?"

"No, Mister Hennet, I did not." Head craned back, Rennie grinned. "But still, it's best he does the climb first when we're ridin' steady."

"True." Denying the temptation to stare aloft at nothing, the mate frowned. "That doesn't make the nest his own private minstrel's gallery though. Get him down."

"He's not hurtin' aught and it's right nice to be serenaded like."

"MISTER HENNET!" The master's bellow turned all heads.

"I don't think Master Cabot agrees," Hennet pointed out dryly.

The breezes tried to trip him up by changing direction. Fingers flying, Tam followed.

Although the Frenchman seemed to be enjoying the music, Master Cabot did not. Lips pressed into a thin line, Hennet climbed onto the fo'c'sle.

He barely had his feet under him when Master Cabot pointed toward the nest and opened his mouth.

Another voice filled the space.

"East wind rising, sir!"

Tam's song rose triumphantly from the top of the ship.

"Get him down now, McAlonie!" Hennet bellowed as he raced aft.

"Aye sir!" But Rennie spent another moment listening to the song, and a moment more watching the way the rigging moved in the wind.

Once out of the channel and sailing hard toward the Irish coast, the crew waited expectantly for Tam to show the first signs of seasickness but, with the pipe tied tight in his shirt, the dockside brat clambered up and down the pitching decks like he'd never left land.

Fortunately, Master Cabot's Genoese barber provided amusement enough.

"Merciful Father, why must I wait so for the touch of your Grace on this, your most wretched of children?"

Tam didn't understand the words but he understood the emotion—the man had thrown his guts into the sea both before and after the declaration. Legs crossed, back against the aftcastle wall, he frowned thoughtfully. The shivering little man looked miserable.

"Seasickness won't kill ya," yelled down one of the mast hands, "but you'll be wishing it did."

Tam understood that too. There'd been many times in his life when he'd wished he was dead.

He played to make the barber feel better. He never intended to make him cry.

"What do you mean, you could see Genoa as the boy played?"

The barber feathered the razor along Cabot's jaw. "What I said, patron. The boy played, I saw Genoa. I was sick no more."

"From his twiddling?"

"Yes."

"That is ridiculous. You got your sea legs, nothing more."

"As you say, patron."

"What happened to your head, boy?"

Braced against the rolling of the ship, Tam touched his bare scalp and risked a shrug. "Shaved."

Hennet turned to a snickering John Jack for further explanation.

"Barber did it ta thank him, I reckon. Can't understand his jabbering."

"It's an improvement," the mate allowed. "Or will be when those sores heal."

"That the new world?"

"Don't be daft, boy, 'tis Ireland. We'll be puttin' in to top the water casks."

"We can sail no closer to the wind than we are," Cabot glared up at an overcast sky and then into the shallow bell of the lanteen sail. "It has been blowing from the west since we left Ireland! Columbus had an east wind, but me, I am mocked by God."

Roubaix spread his hands, then grabbed for a rope as the bow dipped unexpectedly deep into a trough. "Columbus sailed in the south."

"*Stupido!* Tell me something I don't know!" Spinning on one heel, balance perfected by years at sea, Cabot stomped across to the ladder and slid down into the waist.

Exchanging a glance with the bow watch that needed no common language, Roubaix followed. At the bottom of the ladder, he nearly tripped over a bare leg. The direction of the sprawl and the heartbroken look still directed at Cabot's back told as much of the story as necessary.

"He is not angry at you, Tam." The intensity of joy that replaced the hurt in the boy's stare gave him pause. He doubted Zoane had any idea how much his dockside brat adored him. "He only pushes you because he can not push the winds around to where he needs them. Do you understand?"

Tam nodded. It was enough to understand that he'd done nothing wrong in the master's sight.

"What's he playing?" Hennet muttered, joining Rennie and John Jack at the bow. "There's no tune to it."

"I figure that depends on who's listenin'," Rennie answered with a grin. He jerked his head toward where Tam was leaning over the rail. "Have a look Mister Hennet."

Brows drawn in, Hennet leaned over by the boy and looked down at the sea.

Seven sleek, gray bodies rode the bow wave.

"He's playing for the dolphins," he said, straightening and turned back toward the two men.

"Aye. And you can't ask for better luck."

The mate sighed. Arms folded, he squinted into the wind. "We could use a bit of luck."

"Master Cabot still in a foul mood is he?"

"Better than he be in a mood for fowl," John Jack cackled. Two days before, a line squall had snapped the mainstay sail halberd belaying pin and dropped the full weight of the sail right on the chicken coop. The surviving hens had been so hysterical, they'd all been killed, cooked, and eaten.

A little surprised John Jack had brains enough for such a play on words, Hennet granted him a snort before answering Rennie. "If the winds don't change..."

There was no need to finish.

Tam had stopped playing at the sound of the master's name and now, pipe tightly clutched, he crossed to Hennet's side. "We needs..." he began then froze when the mate turned toward him.

"We need what?"

He shot a panicked glance at Rennie who nodded encouragingly. He licked salt off his lips and tried again. "We needs ta go north."

"We need to go west, boy."

His heart beat so violently he could feel his ribs shake. Pushing the pipe against his belly to keep from throwing his guts, Tam shook his head. "No. North."

Impressed—in spite of the contradiction—by obvious fear overcome, Hennet snorted again. "And who tells you that, boy?"

Tam pointed over the side.

"The dolphins?" When Tam nodded, Hennet turned on the two crewman, about to demand which of them had been filling the boy's head with nonsense. The look on Rennie's face stopped him. "What?"

"I fished the Iceland banks, Mister Hennet, outa the islands with me da when I were a boy. Current runs west from there and far enough north, the blow's east, northeast."

"You told the boy?"

"Swear to you, not a word."

The three men stared at Tam and then, at a sound from the sea, at each other. The dolphins were laughing.

"North." Cabot glanced down at his charts, shook his head, and was smiling when he looked up again at the mate. "Good work."

Hennet drew in a long breath and let it out slowly. He didn't like taking credit for another's idea but he liked even less the thought of telling the ship's master they were changing course because Tam had played pipes for a pod of dolphins. "Thank you, sir."

"Make the course change."

"Aye, sir." As he turned on his heel to leave the room, he didn't like the way the Frenchman was looking at him.

"He was hiding something, Zoane."

"What?"

"I don't know." Smiling at little at his own suspicion, Roubaix shook his head. "But I'll wager it has to do with the boy. There's something about those eyes."

Cabot paused at the cabin door, astrolabe in hand. "Whose eyes?"

"The boy's."

"What boy?"

"Tam." When no comprehension dawned, he sighed. "The dockside boy you saved from a beating and brought with us... What latitude are we at, Zoane?"

Face brightening, Cabot pointed to the map. "Roughly 48 degrees. Give me a moment to take a reading and I can be more exact. Why?"

"Not important. You'd better go before you lose the sun." Alone in the room, he rubbed his chin and stared down at the charts. "If he was drawn here, you'd remember him, wouldn't you?"

"S'cold."

"We're still north, ain't we; though the current's run us more south than we was." John Jack handed the boy a second mug of beer. "Careful, yer hands'll be sticky."

He'd spent the afternoon tarring the mast to keep the wood from rotting where the yard had rubbed and had almost enjoyed the messy job. Holding both mugs carefully as warned, he joined Rennie at the south rail.

"Ta, lad."

They leaned quietly beside each other for a moment, staring out at a sea so flat and black the stars looked like they continued above and below without a break.

"You done good work today" Rennie said at last, wiping his beard with his free hand. He could feel Tam's pleasure and he smiled. "I'll make you a sailor yet." When he saw the boy turn from the corner of one eye, he turned as well, following his line of sight, squinting up onto the darkness on the fo'c'sle. There could be no mistaking the silhouette of the master. "Give it up, boy," he sighed. "The likes of him don't see the likes of us unless we gets in their way."

Shoulders slumped, Tam turned all the way around, and froze. A moment later, he was racing across the waist and throwing himself against the north rail.

Curious, Rennie followed. "I don't know what he's seen, do I?" he snarled at a question. "I've not asked him yet." He didn't have to ask—the boy's entire body pointed up at the flash of green light in the sky. "'Tis the *Fir Chlis*, the souls of fallen angels God caught before they reached earthly realms. Call 'em also the Merry Dancers—though they ain't dancing much this time of year."

When Tam scrambled up a ratline without either speaking or taking his eyes from the sky, Rennie snorted and returned to the beer barrel. John Jack had just lifted the jug when the first note sounded.

The pipe had been his before it was Tam's but he'd never heard it make that sound. Beer poured unheeded over his wrist as he turned to the north.

The light in the sky was joined by another.

For every note, another light.

When a vast sweep of sky had been lit, the notes began to join each other in a tune.

"I'll be buggered," John Jack breathed. "He's playin' fer the Dancers."

Rennie nodded. "Fast dance brings bad weather, boy!" he called. "Slow dance for fair!"

The tune slowed, the dance with it.

The lights dipped down, touched their reflections in the water and whirled away.

"I ain't never seen them so close."

"I ain't never seen them so..." Although he couldn't think of the right word, Rennie saw it reflected in the awe on every uplifted face. It was like, like watching angels dance.

The sails gleamed green and blue and orange and red.

All at once, the music stopped, cut off in mid note. The dancers lingered for a heartbeat then the sky was dark again, the stars dimmer than they'd been before.

Blinking away the after images, Rennie ran to the north rail only to find another man there before him. As there had been no mistaking the master's silhouette, so there was no mistaking the master.

Tam lay stunned on the deck, yanked down from the ratlines.

Cabot bent and picked up the pipe. Chest heaving, he lifted his fist, the pipe clenched within it, into the air. "I will not have this witchcraft on my ship!"

"Master Cabot..."

He whirled around and jabbed a finger of his free hand toward the mate. "*Tacere!* Did you know of this?!"

Hennet raised both hands but did not back away. "He's just a boy."

"And damned!" Drawing back his upraised arm, he flung the pipe as hard as he could into the night, turned to glare down at Tam…"Play one more note and you will follow it!"…and in the same motion strode off and into his cabin.

Hennet barely managed to stop John Jack's charge.

In the silence that followed, Roubaix stepped forward, looked down at Tam cradled in Rennie's arms then went after Cabot.

"Let me go," John Jack growled.

Hennet started, as though he hadn't even realized he still held the man's shoulders. He opened his hands and knelt by Rennie's side. "How's the boy."

"Did you ever hear the sound of a heart breaking, Mister Hennet?" The Scot's eyes were wet as he shifted the limp weight in his arms. "I heard it tonight, and I pray to God I never hear such a sound again."

Cabot was bent over the charts when Roubaix came into the cabin. The slam of the door jerked him upright and around.

"You are a fool, Zoane!"

"Watch your tongue," Cabot growled. "I am still master here."

Roubaix shook his head, too angry to be cautious. "Master of what?" he demanded. "Timber and canvass and hemp! You ignore the hearts of your men!"

"I save them from damnation. Such witchery will condemn their souls…"

"It was not witchcraft!"

"Then what?" Cabot demanded, eyes narrowed, his fingers clenched into fists by his side.

"I don't know." Roubaix drew in a deep breath and released it slowly. "I do know this," he said quietly, "there is no evil in that boy in spite of a life that should have destroyed him. And, although the loss of his pipe dealt him a blow, that it was by your hand, the hand of the man who took him from darkness, who he adored and only ever wanted to please, that was the greater blow."

"I cannot believe that."

Roubaix stared across the cabin for a long moment, watched the lamp swing once, twice, a third time painting shadows across the other man's face. "Then I am sorry for you," he said at last.

He would have retreated again to dark corners, but he couldn't find them anymore, he'd been too long away. Instead, he wrapped shadows tightly around him, thick enough to hide the memory of the master's face.

"He spoke yet?"

"No." Arms folded, Rennie stared across at the slight figure who sat slumped at the base of the aftcastle wall.

"Ain't like he ever said much," John Jack sighed. "You give 'im yer other pipe?"

"I tried yesterday. He won't take it."

They watched Cabot's barber emerge from below and wrap a blanket around the boy murmuring softly in Italian the whole while.

John Jack snorted. "I'd not be sittin' in Master Cabot's chair when that one has a razor in his hand, though I reckon he hasn't brains to know his danger."

"I don't want to hear any more of that talk."

Both men whirled around to see Hennet standing an armslength away.

"And if ya stopped sneakin' up on folk, ya wouldn't," John Jack sputtered around a coughing fit.

Hennet ignored him. "There's fog coming in and bow watch saw icebergs in the distance. I want you two up the lines, port and starboard."

"Ain't never been near bergs when we couldn't drop anchor and wait 'til we could see."

"Nothing to drop anchor on," the mate reminded them. "Not out here. Now go, before it gets any worse."

It got much worse.

Hennet dropped all the canvass he could and still keep *The Matthew* turned into the swell but they were doing better than two knots when the fog closed in. It crawled over the deck, soaking everything in its path, dripping from the lashes of silent men peering desperately into the night. They couldn't see but over the groans of rope and canvass and timber they could hear waves breaking against the ice.

No one saw the berg that lightly kissed the port side.

The ship shuddered, rolled starboard, and they were by.

"That were too buggerin' close."

Terror wrapped them closer than the fog.

"I hear another! To port!"

"Are you daft? Listen! Ice dead ahead!"

"Be silent! All of you." Cabot's command sank into the fog. "How long to dawn, Mister Hennet?"

Hennet turned to follow the chill and unseen passage of a mountain of ice. "Too long, sir."

"We must have light!"

The first note from the crow's nest backlit the fog with brilliant blue.

Cabot moved to edge of the fo'c'sle and glared down into the waist. "Get him down from there, Mister Hennet."

Hennet folded his arms. "No sir. I won't."

The second note streaked the fog with green.

"I gave you an order!"

"Aye sir."

"Follow it!"

"No sir."

"You!" Cabot pointed up at a crewman straddling the yard. "Get him down."

John Jack snorted. "Won't."

The third note was golden and at its edge, a sliver of night sky.

"Then I'll do it myself!" But when he reached for a line, Roubaix was there before him.

"Leave him alone, Zoane."

"It is witchcraft!"

"No." He switched to English so everyone would understand. "You asked for light, he does this for you."

The dance moved slow and stately across the sky.

Cabot looked around, saw nothing but closed and angry faces. "He sends you to Hell!"

"Better than sending us to the bottom," Rennie told him. "Slow dance brings fair weather. He's piping away the fog."

Tam stopped when he could see the path through glittering green-white palaces of ice. He leaned over, tossed the pipe gently, and watched it drop into Rennie's outstretched hands. Then he stepped up onto the rail, and scanned the upturned faces for the master's. When he found it, he took a deep breath, and jumped out as hard as he was able.

No one spoke. No one so much as shouted a protest or moaned a denial.

The small body arced out, farther than should have been possible, then disappeared in the darkness...

The silence lingered.

"You killed him." Hennet stepped toward Cabot, hands forming fists at his side. "You said if he played another note, he'd follow his pipe. And he did. And you killed him."

Still blinded by the brilliant blue of the boy's eyes, Cabot stepped back. "No..."

John Jack dropped down out of the lines. "Yes."

"No." As all heads turned toward him, Rennie palmed salt off his cheeks. "He didn't hit the water."

"Impossible..."

"Did you hear a splash? Anything?" He swept a burning gaze over the rest of the crew. "Did any of you? No one called man overboard, no one even ran to the rails to look for a body. There is no body. He didn't hit the water. Look."

Slowly, as though on one line, all eyes turned to the north where a brilliant blue wisp of light danced between heaven and earth.

"Fallen angels. He fell a little farther than the rest is all; now he's back with his own."

Then the light went out, and all the sounds of a ship at sea rushed in to fill the silence.

"Mister Hennet, iceberg off the port bow!"

Hennet leapt to the port rail and leaned out. "Helmsman, two degrees starboard! All hands to the mainsail!"

As *The Matthew* began to turn to safety, Roubaix took Cabot's arm and moved him unprotesting out of the way of the crew.

"Gaylor," he whispered. "Do you believe?"

Roubaix looked up at the sky and then down at his friend. "You are a skilled and well traveled mariner, Zoane Cabatto, and an unparalleled cartographer but sometimes you forget that there are things in life you can not map and wonders you will not find on any chart."

The Matthew took thirty-five days to travel from Bristol to the new land Cabot named Bona Vista, glorious sight. It took only fifteen days for her to travel back home again and for every one of those days the sky was a more brilliant blue than any man on board had ever seen and the wind played almost familiar tunes in the rigging.

Given the success of the first X-men movie, putting together an anthology about mutants was pretty much a no brainer. I wanted to do something that didn't involve superheros and was, essentially, scientifically plausible.

SUGAR AND SPICE
AND EVERYTHING NICE

DR. PHILIPS IS an idiot. Oh, she's nice enough in that too-smiley "I want us to be friends" kind of way, but I've been seeing her for almost two years now, ever since the tests showed I'd turned four, and she still hasn't caught on. The thing about child psychologists is that they don't observe you in order to learn about your behavior. See, they've already made up their minds about how you should be acting, so they're actually observing to see that your actions agree with their theories. Once you know what their theories are—piece of cake.

One afternoon, when she was paying less attention than she should have been, I gave myself a nasty paper cut during the building of a large paper mache T-Rex. In spite of anti-cuddling rules, there's really only one way a caring person can respond to a four year old who refuses to stop crying. With my face pressed damply into the curve of Dr. Philips neck, I think I learned as much about her as I did about her thoughts on me. And you know what? By the time you can put a doctor in front of your name, you're way too old to be dotting your i's with little hearts.

Anyway, as long as I answer her questions within the parameters she's established, she's happy.

"I assure you, Mr. and Mrs. Howard, Danielle tests well within the parameters for a gifted child of her age—an exceptionally gifted child of her age."

See what I mean?

"Yeah, well, her age."

A quick glance showed Dad slumped in his chair staring at the scuffed suede toes of his dress shoes. He sounded tired and confused. I didn't blame him, neither of my parents were very bright. Considering they were chickens trying to raise a duck pretending to be a chicken, they were doing a pretty good job and I loved them a lot, but, bottom line, anyone with half a brain would never have accepted procreative help from the Benjamin Avob Basic Biology of Aging Center in the first place. Dad wasn't even my biological father—but since neither of them knew that the other half of my chromosomal mix had come out of a seven year old sperm deposit, I kept the discovery to myself. It wouldn't have made any difference and, besides, they'd have asked how I knew.

From the change in her tone, Dr. Philips had rearranged her smile into its almost patronizing but ever so supportive curve. "I understand that it's been challenging, which is why the Center feels it's time Danielle begin attending that play-group we spoke of earlier."

"One of the main tasks of childhood is to establish friendships with other children both in one-to-one situations and in group situations. Peers play an essential role in the socialization of interpersonal competence and skill acquired in this manner affects the child's long-term development."

Mom does that, parrots back information the doctors have told her, or that she's read on-line, or clipped from one of the half dozen parenting magazines she subscribes to. It's her way of letting them know that she's paying attention.

It always annoys Dr. Philips when she does it. Sometimes, I think that's *why* she does it. I mean, Mom got screwed by this almost as much as I did, although I'm pretty sure I've fixed most of the early, accidental damage.

I couldn't quite suppress a heavy sigh, but by the time the doctor turned to look at me, I was crouched over a model of the International Space Station, rubbing my right ear reflectively against my knee, stretching out the top of one pale pink ankle sock and trying to place a bright blue rectangle intended to represent one of the solar cells on the body of the station. Given the visual evidence, she could only conclude that the noise had come from some sort of construction frustration.

When she closed the file and stood, my parents—trained through dozens of similar meetings—stood as well. "Bring Danielle in on Monday then, at one PM."

"She has French on Monday afternoons," Mom reminded her.

"I think Danielle is as fluent as she's going to get right now. It's not unusual for children to plateau in their language development for a time," Dr. Philips added quickly, "particularly as other areas of growth are occurring." From the way her voice trailed off, she'd just realized she'd given mom another quote. Unable to do anything about it, she continued. "The play group is where Danielle needs to be at this time. If you want to be there for the first introductions, Mr. Howard, I'm sure I can arrange it."

"No. Thank you."

My Dad works as a janitor at the Center. After eighteen years, they call him a Custodial Supervisor, but he's really just head janitor. Good thing he likes the job, because he'll never be able to leave it.

"Dani."

Leaving the Space Station half completed, I crossed to Mom's side and wrapped my hand around hers in a practiced, protective gesture. It was perfectly normal for small children to be overprotective of their mothers. I could almost see the warm glow of satisfaction radiating from Dr. Philips. She just loved the fact that, in spite of everything, I was so normal.

We met Dr. Thorton in the hall. Mom's fingers twitched, and I tightened my grip.

"Mr. and Mrs. Howard, how are you this afternoon." Dr. Thorton's voice filled the broad hall outside Dr. Philips office and would have been enough to stop progress even if his bulk wasn't blocking the way.

"We're all fine, Dr. Thorton."

"Good. Good. And Danielle, how are you?" The broad smile under the button nose folded swooping curves into the generous cheeks.

I muttered something that might have been, "Okay." and then buried my face against the warm curve of Mom's hip.

The doctor leaned closer, and I wondered why he didn't tip over with all that weight balanced so precariously on tiny feet. "Aren't you a little old to be making strange, sweetie? You know me."

Oh, I knew him all right, the sadistic s.o.b.

"She's four." Dad gripped my shoulder protectively.

"Yes. Of course she is." Dr. Thorton's voice rang with fake jolly tones that would have embarrassed a shopping mall Santa. Dr. Thorton sucked at doing jolly. "I'll bet she's really looking forward to play-group."

"Children ages three to six require opportunities to learn cooperation, helping and sharing," Mom told him and we shuffled past.

I had a feeling his mouth was open but I didn't dare check his expression.

Dr. Thorton is a megalomaniacal fool, but he's not an idiot. As Director of Research at the Center, he's one of the few with all the pieces of the puzzle. This is all his fault. I'm *his* failed experiment. I hate him more than you can possibly understand, and I'm going to do him if it takes the rest of my life.

Which is a joke.

With any luck, it's going to take about six months.

Am I looking forward to play group? He can bet his double doctorate I am.

"Danielle, this is Julie Natoobo, Franklin Chin, Sean O'Mara and Betsy Wojtowicz."

Dr. Philips' cheery political correctness was evident in the racial mix. It was like being on the bridge of the original Enterprise without the cheesy special effects. If she hadn't needed an odd number to better study group dynamics, I'm sure there'd have been gender equality as well.

I flashed the quartet of children a brilliant smile and let go of Mom's hand. "Race you to the top of the monkey bars," I called and took off across the grass at top speed. Franklin reached the painted steel a moment after I did, the other three about two paces behind. I won, but by a very small margin. The moment all four were on board, I started talking.

Did you know that conversational skills increase the likelihood that children will become friends with a peer?

I laid it on with a shovel. Wow, could they ever run fast! Gee, look at them climb! I did a little playful teasing. I threw in some interesting gossip—although it was tricky figuring out what gossip even smart four year olds would find interesting.

Children sustain and feel satisfied in friendships where the ratio of positive to negative processes is maximized.

Mom isn't the only one who reads those magazines.

Human beings are hierarchical by nature. Toss a group of them together and one of them will end up the leader, the rest followers. It was essential I become the leader of this particular group. Fortunately, four year olds are fairly easy to impress because no matter how smart they are —and this lot was at least as smart as Dr. Philips thought I was—they're still four years old.

And I'm not.

Physically, I'm no different than my companions. Looking at me, you'd see a normal, healthy, four year old girl—essentially blonde hair, more-or-less blue eyes, dirty knees, the whole package. But according to the experimental data I uncovered by hacking into Dr. Thorton's files through his laughingly inadequate encryption, I'm about fifteen. An exceptionally intelligent fifteen.

Next year, I should be getting my driver's license. I should be starting to date. I should have breasts. I should be menstruating. My incipient woman-hood should be making my father nervous.

Given my intellect, I should be at the stage where I've gained power over my own life—an early high-school graduation, the beginning of advanced degrees, a few inventions, a couple of discoveries, my picture in the papers.

Next year, I'll still be four.

And I'm pretty pissed about it.

Way back when, Dr. Thorton did a little illegal mucking about on the genetic level, re-creating a mutated copy of a gene found in nematode worms that controls aging. Of course it wouldn't have been illegal if he'd stuck with worms but he overheard my Dad telling a fellow custodian how he and Mom were having trouble getting pregnant. Taking advantage of their desperate desire to breed, he offered to help, pumped mom full of fertility drugs, and scrambled her eggs.

His intent was to slow aging *after* maturity.

Oops.

Failures don't get the kind of publicity successes do so I'm the Center's dirty little secret. Mom and Dad were convinced if they told anyone I'd be taken away and dissected. I'm not sure why Dr. Thorton's never gone the "accidental death" and dissection route, but I suspect it's because I'm the closest thing to a success he's ever had. Of the hundreds of other mutated zygotes mentioned in the early files, only three of us attached ourselves to the uterine wall, and only I was carried to term. The other two were selectively terminated when it became clear things were going very wrong. I liked to tell myself that I was going to do Dr. Thorton for my siblings' sakes as well but, bottom line, it was all about me.

By the time I grew out of the eggplant stage, I'd been tested in every way known to science and in a few ways they'd created specially for me. Over time, Dr. Thorton's various reactions taught me what to shut down to make the test results conform to a normal profile. Every anomaly meant more tests. More hours spent strapped down like a large lab mouse.

The more normal I appeared, the more he left me alone.

Most babies wouldn't remember the pain and the terror.

I did.

I needed to get Dr. Thorton alone in a place with no surveillance cameras, and I needed some help getting us both in there at the same time.

Not exactly easy for a four year old.

Thus my manipulation of Dr. Philips who continued to think that the play-group had been her idea.

We met three times a week for ninety minutes—Monday, Wednesday, and Friday—playing outside in the enclosed playground when the weather was good and inside in a redecorated conference room when it wasn't. After the first three weeks—having survived a challenge by Betsy in week two when it was discovered she had 27 teenie babies to my 22—I was the undisputed leader of the group. By week four, I could get them to do anything I wanted.

"I'm bored." Franklin announced, hanging upside down from the top of the monkey bars. He made a grab for Julie's Mr. Sparky and missed. "Bored. Bored. Bored. Stupid. Bored."

I leaned into the tiny triangle uncovered by the cameras—the reason we spent so much time on the monkey bars, well, that and because I was sick of being 37 centimeters tall—and said, "Let go."

You'd be amazed at how high something as essentially fragile as a child can bounce without damage. When, during the hysteria that followed, Franklin never once said, "Dani told me to." I knew it was time to move on.

That afternoon, I started a new game based on a lame Saturday morning cartoon that involved a secret society of dogs saving the world—usually against cats. We did a lot of barking and burying things in the sandbox and arguing over who had to pretend to be the cats. The cats were the bad guys and no one wanted to play them—especially after what we found in the sandbox. We called it Spy Game and the whole thing was pretty much inexplicable to adults which was exactly how I wanted it.

Two days later, when the rain had moved us indoors, I tried to move Spy Game inside. Sean stared at me like I was out of my mind.

"Not *now*, Dani! We *always* play hide-and-seek before snack!"

Four year olds, even smart ones, like schedules. It helps them make sense of a confusing and ever changing world. Don't think for a moment I didn't know that.

There were lots of places to hide in the conference room, thanks to Julie. After an early and unsuccessful game, she'd planted herself in front of Dr. Philip, crossed dimpled arms, and announced indignantly, "We need more stuff. We can't hide without stuff."

"Why don't you play something else?" Dr. Philips had asked in her most condescending way.

Smiling broadly, Julie locked eyes with child psychologist and said, "Let's spend the afternoon watching Barney!"

We got more stuff so fast it made skid marks on the carpeting; big foam shapes, a tent with a tunnel, child-sized bean bag chairs, plastic shelves, multicolored boxes, and all the mess that five active children trapped inside on a rainy day can make.

And we *always* played hide-and-seek before snack.

Snacks came up from the cafeteria kitchen on the same kind of carts they used in the laboratories—stainless steel top and an enclosed bottom with enough space under it for a four year old to hide. After Sean made it all the way down the kitchens and was returned by a snickering security guard with stories of enough fish sticks to reach the moon, the Snack Lady kept the lower doors open and checked the compartment before she left the room.

Adults essentially keep to schedules for the same reason as children. You could set your watch by Snack Lady.

We played Spy Game after hide-and-seek and, with pointed looks at Dr. Philips, developed a secret language capable of expressing astoundingly complex thoughts using bits of four other languages, funny gestures, giggling, and rude noises. Adults didn't get it. Not even when we tried to explain.

"So, Danielle, I hear you kids have a secret language."

The straps kept me from turning my head but, as usual, I could see the reflection of the monitor in Dr. Thorton's glasses. Brain wave activity was text book normal. "Uh huh."

"Tell me about it."

"Can't."

"Why not?"

I rearranged my face into the easily recognizable *grown-ups are so stupid* expression. "'Cause it's a secret."

Okay, I, personally, didn't try very hard.

Spy Game held everyone's attention for two more play-groups and then blew up when Betsy vehemently and vocally protested the unfairness of a game where she *always* had to play cats. Then she pushed Franklin over and sat on him. This was exactly the opening I'd been waiting for.

"I know, I know! We make grown-ups the bad guys."

Well, that's how it translated—I actually hit my forehead twice while spinning around, used the French word for "we", played patty-cakes with myself, stood on my head, coughed up a little German, and meowed. If it's all the same with you, I'll stick with the translation from now on.

The other's were intrigued, especially by the idea of keeping it a secret. Children love secrets. They give the powerless a sense of power. We wouldn't let the "cats" know we were on to them.

The groundwork had been laid, and Dr. Thorton still had no idea I was coming for him.

Part two was going to be trickier, but by the next rainy Wednesday, everyone knew the parts they were to play in the Case of the Big Red Cat with the Neutron Ray Who Was Trying to Rule the World. Franklin made up the name. Julie was so excited she began wetting the bed again.

It all started with Sean. Usually, Sean's nanny picked Franklin up at his mother's condo, drove to the Center, walked both boys up to the conference room, and handed them over to Dr. Philips. On this particular Wednesday, Sean was going to take one for the team. Halfway up the stairs, he'd pull free of his nanny's hand, miss the next step, and bounce back to the bottom before she could say, "The rain in Spain falls mainly on the upper Pyrennes."

Franklin had been upset that he wasn't going to be the one falling, but then Franklin had been upset when he hadn't been the one to get the eraser stuck in his ear.

It had to be Sean.

Sean's father was an actual practicing MD rather than a research scientist. He worked for the Center as the doctor in residence, and I strongly suspected that Dr. Singh's sabbatical and Dr. O'Mara's hiring had been so that Sean could join me in play-group. Because it had been a temporary situation from the beginning, the O'Mara's wouldn't be around long enough to notice anything unusual about the way I aged. Or rather, didn't.

Sean would fall, scream, and be taken to see daddy. Franklin would tag along because, well, he was there.

Dr. O'Mara was a bit of an over-protective father or possibly an all inclusive hypochondriac—the number of preventive supplements Sean took daily lent either conclusion equal weight. With his only son shrieking in his office, neither he nor the woman being accused of allowing the accident to happen would be keeping much of an eye on Franklin.

The Benjamin Avob Basic Biology of Aging Center worked with a number of research subjects in their eighth and ninth decades. If we ignored the way they'd given their permission for the wires and the probing and the tests and I hadn't, the only real difference between us was that my bowels worked fine, thank you very much. In Dr. O'Mara's office, in a cabinet kept unlocked due to frequency of use, were some of the strongest laxatives known to science.

It's amazing what people will repeat in front of a four year old. Maybe they think we're too short to hear them.

Franklin's mission: while Sean's daddy's distracted, grab one of the capsules that looks like a big rootbeer jelly bean.

"And I'll hide it in my belly button!"

"Okay." Who was I to discourage initiative?

Sean won't be actually hurt. Once Dr. O'Mara and the nanny are convinced of this, both boys will continue on to play-group.

Next up, Betsy.

Dr. Wojtowicz was the Center's Chief Administrator, and on Dr. Philip's recommendation, Betsy had lunch with her mother every day we had play-group. Professional parents feel extremely guilty about the time they spend away from their kids, and since they were both at the Center, they might as well put in some quality parental bonding, right?

That bit fell into place without any help from me.

Dr. Wojtowicz's office was down the hall from the conference room we used when the weather was bad.

Usually, when Sean and Franklin passed Dr. Wojtowicz's office, Betsy would join them. On this particular day, there'd be a certain amount of shoving and, during this childish give and take, Franklin would pass Betsy the capsule. Betsy would then run back to kiss her mother and drop the laxative in the coffee pot.

Betsy almost refused to cooperate.

"My mama's not a cat!"

When Franklin sniggered, "Betsy said snot!" she pushed him down and sat on him again. Classic displacement of immature affection into violence according to Dr. Philips who is, as I may have mentioned, an idiot.

"We're protecting your mama from grown-ups who *are* bad guys," Julie explained, glancing over at me for approval.

When I nodded, Betsy reluctantly agreed to do her bit.

Every Wednesday afternoon, Dr. Thorton went to Dr. Wojtowicz's office where they spent approximately ninety minutes arguing about the business of science. They managed to run the Center in only ninety minutes a week by having agreed not to bog each other down with minutia. For example, Dr. Wojtowicz didn't bother telling Dr. Thorton about how she'd saved hundreds of dollars by ordering food for the lab animals in bulk from a Brazilian supplier and Dr. Thorton didn't bother telling Dr. Wojtowicz about me.

I was just the janitor's unexpectedly smart daughter who went to play-group with her Betsy. When Betsy moved on at the end of the year, it wouldn't occur to Betsy's Mommy that I'd be staying behind. She didn't move in the same social set as my parents and it wouldn't be long before she forgot me entirely.

Dr. Wojtowicz drank only herbal tea. Dr. Thorton drank the coffee.

By the time Sean, Franklin, and Betsy joined me in the conference room, I'd nervously chewed the antenna of a plush Teletubby into purple polyester pulp. Waiting to discover if the first part of the plan had been successfully executed had been the longest twenty-seven minutes of an already chronically skewed life.

With all three of them talking at once, high-pitched voices raised to maximum volume as they tried to out-shout each other, there was almost no need for a secret language. Dr. Philips, the only adult present all but covered her ears, and I imagined the audio portion of the surveillance tapes would be unintelligible without some high-tech adjusting.

But why would anyone bother? Of course my friends had exciting things to tell me; Sean had just fallen down the stairs.

When Julie showed up with Mr. Sparky, we synchronized our watches. Winnie the Pooh, a Power Ranger, Barney and two Blues of Blue's Clues all showed essentially the same time—given the various objects rotating as second hands, an exact match wasn't possible.

As usual, we started playing hide and seek just before the Snack Lady was due to arrive. I watched the cart pull up in front of my hiding place and, while the Snack Lady unloaded juice boxes, carrot sticks, and animal crackers, I slid carefully onto the bottom shelf.

The Snack Lady never turned the cart to leave the room, she walked around it and pushed it straight back out. She'd notice the extra weight at the first turn but I wouldn't be with her that long. As we drew near the bathroom door, Franklin announced he had to pee and everyone had to stay hidden until he got back. When he opened the door, I rolled off the shelf and, hidden from the cameras by the cart, crawled into the bathroom.

Franklin was tall for his age. By placing the rubber stool we used to reach the taps onto the toilet seat and then standing on it, he could just reach the cover of the ceiling vent with the plastic screwdriver from the Big Guy Handyman set. One twist pried the cover off and then he boosted me up.

"Find the others really, really slowly," I reminded him as he shoved the vent cover back in place.

Even for a four year old, the air duct was a tight squeeze. I dragged myself along by my elbows following the building plans I'd pulled up out of the maintenance files while a loop of Smileyland music had convinced my parents I'd been enthralled by dancing happy faces.

Dr. Wojtowicz's bathroom was exactly like ours. A quick look through the vent determined it was empty. That wasn't good. There was a limit to how badly even Franklin could play hide and seek. Fortunately, as I was securing my hair ribbon, the door opened.

Dr. Thorton.

I watched enthralled as he hurriedly lowered his trousers but the rolls of fat blocked my view. He dropped to the toilet, it groaned in protest, and I stopped paying attention to exactly what he was doing.

With one hard push, I shoved the vent out. Held by one end of the ribbon, it swung down and hit the wall. Dr. Thorton looked up. Eyes wide, he managed half a sound as I emerged from the duct. Hanging by my knees, a move practiced over and over again on the monkey bars, I grabbed his cheeks.

During the first two years of a child's life, most of the growth of the brain occurs accompanied by the structuring of neural connections. The first "two" years of my life went on for a very long time.

I always knew my how much my mother loved me. As long as we were in physical contact I could hear her thoughts. *Love. Comfort. Safety.* When I got a little older, I could hear the words that went with them. Technically, I was receiving and translating the electric impulses of her brain. Colloquially, I could read minds.

Certain childish desires, vehemently expressed, lead to the discovery I could also edit minds.

Like I said earlier, I was mostly able to fix my mother.

No one was going to be able to fix Dr. Thorton.

Trouble was, I needed physical contact, skin on skin, and I needed to get that physical contact in such a way that no suspicion would fall on me. I had no intention of losing even the limited rights childhood allowed.

I got back to the play-group bathroom just before Winnie the Pooh's right hand—or possibly paw—pointed to the three. Elapsed time, six minutes, most of that spent crawling through duct work. Dangling from the vent, I drooped down onto the toilet and slid off the edge, one of my feet plunging into the bowl ankle deep. Way gross. Fortunately, my shoes and socks were dark and the soaking didn't show.

I shook off as much water as I could and waited just inside the door.

Julie never went anywhere without Mr. Sparky, a ten centimeter tall metal robot her dad had made her out of an antique building set he'd had since he was a boy. At quarter after, safely hidden behind a bean bag chair, holding Mr. Sparky between Snuffy and Bots, my two least favorite teenie babies, she was to stuff his conveniently sized arms into a wall plug.

Winnie the Pooh said quarter after. The lights went out.

I slipped through the smallest opening possible and, by the time the lights came back on not even a moment later, was crawling out from under the computer desk to see what Sean was screaming about. Turns out, Sean's afraid of the dark.

I'd have fixed it for him but he wasn't the only one screaming.

For a woman her age, Betsy's mother managed impressive volume.

It seemed that Dr. Thorton had taken two nice, new number two pencils out of his pocket protector, put the pointed end in each eye and, holding them steady, had taken a hard run, face first into the bathroom wall.

Let's see how *he* likes having things poked into his brain.

No one told the play-group that, of course. Not the sort of thing you'd want four year olds to hear about. I don't know what Betsy's mother told her to explain the screaming but no one told the rest of us anything.

A nearly hysterical lab tech filled Dr. Philips in on the gory details as she stood in the open door, staring down the hall toward the commotion but unable to leave her charges. She was obviously shaken as she closed the door and sank down into the nearest chair.

Sucking a tiny burn on one thumb, Julie walked over and patted her hand. "Are you okay, Doctor?"

"I'm fine," she said, catching up Julie's hand in hers and smiling weakly around at the rest of us. The smile froze as it reached me, and I realized that the pale gray carpet under my wet sneaker had darkened. Dr. Philips looked from the carpet to my face, holding my gaze for a long moment before continuing to smile on each of us. "I'm fine," she repeated with even less conviction.

Maybe Dr. Philips isn't as much of an idiot as I thought.

Not a problem.

I have plenty of time to deal with it.

Bakka Books in Toronto is the oldest science fiction specialty store left in North America. At least I hope it is. By the time this collection comes out "was the oldest science fiction specialty store" might be more accurate. And that's a crying shame. Although I rather like the big box stores—there's just something about so many books all in one place—there's nothing like being able to walk into a small store and ask, "What's new that I'll like?" and know that you'll be handed books you'll enjoy. Since I haven't lived in Toronto for the last 12 years, I have to ask over the phone now, but the result is the same.

Over the years, John Rose, the current—or last—owner of Bakka, has employed a number of people who have gone on to become professional writers. I worked there from 1984 to 1991, and it was the best job I ever had. Not only were the working conditions incredibly supportive (check out John's dedication in Blood Price *for details), but I was surrounded by books I loved and people who read them. Not to mention the people who wrote them. For a while there, we were contemplating advertising for new staff with the phrase: "Work at Bakka. Sell your book."*

I made friendships at Bakka that will last the rest of my life.

In 2002 Bakka Books was thirty years old. To celebrate, John commissioned an anthology, the stories written by ex and current employees. The anthology includes original stories by Michelle Sagara West, Robert J. Sawyer, Fiona Patton, Ed Greenwood, Cory Doctorow, Chris Szego, Tara Tallan, Nalo Hopkinson, and myself.

This is mine. Yes, the book store in it, although not mentioned by name, is Bakka. I think Michelle wrote the review quoted but it could have been me. Actually, now that I think of it, it might have been Naomi.

ANOTHER FINE NEST

THERE WERE THREE other people in the small bookstore. Vicki hesitated to call them customers since in the ten minutes she'd been standing in front of the new releases shelf obstensively reading the staff reviews—her favorite the succinct *Trees died for this?*—none of them had given any indication they were planning to actually buy a book. Two were reading, the third attempting to engage the young woman behind the cash in conversation but succeeding only in monologue.

Without ever having seen him before, Vicki easily identified her contact. Male Caucasian, five eight, dark hair and beard, carrying a good twenty kilos more than was healthy; she could hear his heart pounding as he stared down at the pages of the novel he held. Since he was holding it upside down, it seemed highly unlikely his growing excitement had anything to do with what he wasn't reading. He smelled strongly of garlic.

He was clearly waiting for the other two customers to leave before approaching her. *"They mustn't find out I've called you."*

"Who?"

"Them."

Screw that. Suddenly tired of amateur cloak and dagger theatrics, she walked deeper into the narrow store until she stood directly behind him. Unfortunately, a massive sneeze derailed the impression she'd intended to make. Up close, the smell of garlic was nearly overpowering.

He spun around, dark eyes wide, the heavy gold cross he wore bouncing between the open wings of his jacket.

"Hey." She rummaged in her pocket for a tissue. "Vicki Nelson. You have a job for me?"

Sitting at one of the coffee shop's small tables, Vicki took a drink from her bottle of water and waited for Duncan Travis to pull himself together. His hands, clasped reverently around the paper curves of his triple/triple, were still trembling. She stared at her reflection in the glass, beyond that to the bookstore now across the street, and wished he'd get to the freakin' point.

"I could see your reflection in the glass!"

So could she, but since the glass and her reflection were behind him…

"I checked everyone out as they came into the store."

Oh. Her reflection in the glass at the store. That made a little more sense.

"That's why I didn't know you were you."

"You didn't?"

"No." Duncan detached one hand from the papercup just long enough to sketch a quick emphasis in the air. "I know, you know."

"You know what?"

"About you. What you are."

"I kind of assumed you did, since *you called me.*" Her emphasis on the last three words didn't seem to make the intended impression.

"Not that! People talk you know. And there's stuff, on the web..." Grabbing the base of the cross, he thrust it toward her, the chain biting deep into the folds of his neck.

Vicki sighed. "People say I'm Catholic? Religious? What?"

"Vampire!" He dropped his voice as heads turned. "Nosferatu. A member of the blood sucking undead."

"I knew what you meant." She sighed again. Maybe keeping a lower profile over the last couple of years *would* have been a good idea. "I was just messing with your head. You've got garlic in your pockets, don't you?"

"I am not so desperate that I'd trust you not to drain me and cast my body aside. I have taken precautions." From his expression, Duncan clearly believed his tone sounded threatening. He was wrong.

"Okay." Vicki leaned back in her chair and massaged the bridge of her nose, attempting to forestall a burgeoning headache. "A quick lesson in reality as opposed to the vast amounts of television I suspect you watch. One. Garlic, crosses, holy water—not repelling. Except for maybe the garlic because frankly, you reek. Two. A biological change does not suddenly start reversing the laws of physics. I had a reflection before I changed, I still have one now. Three. If that's a stake in your pocket and, trust me, I'd much prefer it to be a stake 'cause I don't want you that happy to see me, have you considered the actual logistics of using it. You'll be trying to thrust a not very sharp hunk of wood through clothing, skin, muscle, and bone before you get to the meaty bits. I have no idea what you expect I'll be doing while you make the attempt but let me assure you that I'll be doing it faster and more violently than you can imagine. Four. Unless you immediately tell me why you called and said you had a job only I could do—giving me, by the way, your credit card number—not very smart Duncan—I will make you forget you ever saw me." Dropping her hand to the table top, she leaned forward, her eyes silvering slightly. "Eternity is too short for all this screwing around. Start talking."

Duncan swallowed, blinked, and wet his lips. "Wow."

"Thank you. The job?"

"King-tics."

"What?"

"We don't know if they're alien constructs or if they've risen from one of the hell dimensions..."

Oh yeah, way too much "Buffy", Vicki acknowledged silently.

"...but they're infesting the city. Their nest has to be found and taken out."

"Okay. We?"

"My group."

"AD&D?"

"Third edition."

"Right. Nest?"

"They're insectoids. The ones we've seen seem to be sexless workers therefore, they're likely hive based. That means a queen and a nest."

"You guys seem to have a pretty good grasp of the situation, why not take them out yourselves."

Duncan snorted. "In spite of what you seem to think, Ms. Nelson, our grip on reality is fairly firm. Three of us are computer programmers, two work retail, and one is a high school math teacher. We know when we're out of our depth. You turned up on an Internet search—you were local, and certain speculations made us think you'd believe us."

"About King-tics?"

"Yeah."

"So let's say I do. Let's say, hypothetically, I believe there's a new kind of something infesting the city. Why is that a problem? Toronto's already ass deep in cockroaches and conservatives, what's one more lower life form?"

"King-tics are smarter than either. And they drink blood." Confident that he now had her full attention, Duncan stretched out one leg and tugged his pants up from his ankle.

Vicki stared at the dingy gray sweat sock and contemplated beating someone's head—hers, his, she wasn't sure which—against the table. "Try using hot water and adding a little bleach."

"What?" He glanced down and flushed. "Oh."

A quick adjustment later and Vicki found herself studying two half healed puncture wounds just below the curve of Duncan's ankle.

Slightly inflamed and about an inch apart, they were right over a vein that ran close to the surface. "Big bug."

"Yeah. But they move really, really fast. They use the crowds in the subway stations as cover. Bite. Drink. Scuttle away. Who's going to notice a couple of little pricks when we're surrounded by bigger pricks every day of our lives."

"Cynical observation?" Vicki asked the expectant silence.

"Uh, yeah."

"Okay." He'd probably been saving it up too. "You didn't feel the bite?"

"No. I'd have never noticed anything except that my shoe was untied and I knelt to do it up and I..."

Screamed like a little girl?

"...saw this bug. It looked at me, Ms. Nelson. I swear it looked at me..."

She believed him actually. She could hear the before and after in his voice.

"...and then it disappeared. I sort of saw it moving, but it was just so fast. We started looking for them after that, and well, once you know what you're looking for..." He paused then and his gaze skittered off hers but she had to give him credit for trying. "Once you *admit* what you're looking for, it becomes a lot easier to see."

Yeah. Yeah. You know what I am. I got that twenty minutes ago.

"Go on."

"I told the group what had happened and we started looking for the bugs. The King-tics. I mean we spotted them so we figured we should get to name them, right?" When she didn't answer, he sighed, shrugged, and continued. "At first we only saw them at Bloor and Yonge, at the Bloor Station, probably because it's lower. More subterranean. But then, we saw a few on the upper level, you know, the Yonge line. Yesterday, I saw three at Wellsley."

Vicki fought the urge to turn her head. Wellsley Station was a short block south of the coffee shop.

"Thing is," Duncan laughed nervously, "they saw me too. They were watching me from the shadows. First time I'd ever seen them still. Usually you catch a sort of movement out of the corner of one eye but this...It was creepy. Anyway, we talked it over and decided to call you."

"So I can...?"

"I told you. Destroy the nest and the queen. One way or another the subway system hooks up to ever major building in the downtown core. The whole city could become a giant banquet hall for these things."

Vicki sat back in her chair and thought about giant intelligent bloodsucking bugs in the subway for a moment. When Duncan opened his mouth to...well, she didn't know what he was planning to do because she cut him off with a finger raised in silent warning. Giant intelligent bloodsucking bugs in the subway. Feeding off the ankles of Toronto. Another predator—predators—feeding in her territory true but it was somehow hard to get worked up about something called a King-tic.

Giant intelligent bloodsucking bugs in the subway.

She couldn't believe she was even considering taking the job.

Still, that sort of thing always ended badly in the movies, didn't it?

The Wellsley platform was empty except for a clump of teenagers at the far end discussing the appalling news that N'Sync would be on the "Star Wars" Episode Two DVD. On the off chance that the six simultaneous rants would suddenly stop and silence fall, Vicki pitched her voice too low to be overheard. "That's where you saw them?"

Duncan nodded. "Yeah. Right there. In the corner. In the shadows. Three of them. Staring at me."

"If you're talking like a character in a Dasheill Hammett novel on purpose, you should know I find it really annoying."

"Sorry."

"Just don't do it again." Stepping closer, Vicki examined the grey tiled corner for webs or egg casings or marks against the fine patina of subway station grime and came up empty. Sighing, she turned her attention back to Duncan. "What were you doing while the bugs—the King-tics—were staring at you?"

He shrugged. "I stared at them for a while."

"And then?"

"They left." He pointed up the tunnel toward Bloor.

"Right."

His expectant silence took her to the edge of the platform. A train had gone by just before they'd entered the station. She could hear the next one a station, maybe a station and a half a way. Plenty of time. "You wouldn't have an...*artist's conception* of these things would you?"

"Not with me. I could fax it to you when I get home."

"You do that. Go now."

"What are you going to do?"

"What you're paying me to do."

"You're going into the tunnel!"

He sounded so amazed, she turned to look at him. "It's where the bugs are, Duncan. What did you expect me to do?"

"Go into the tunnels," Duncan admitted. "It's just..." He shifted his weight from foot to foot and flashed her an admiring smile. "...well, you're actually doing it. And it's so dangerous."

"Because of the bugs?"

"No. Because of the subway trains."

"Trust me, trains aren't a problem."

Behind the beard, his jaw dropped. "You turn into mist?"

Vicki sighed. "I step out of the way."

There were bugs in the subway tunnels. There were also rats, mice, fast food wrappers, used condoms, and a pair of men's Y-front underwear, extra large. The bugs were not giants, not blood sucking, and although one of the cockroaches gave her what could only be interpreted as a dirty look just before she squashed it flat, not noticeably intelligent. The rats and mice avoided her, but then so did pretty much all mammals except humans and cats. The fast food wrappers and used condoms were the expected debris of the twenty-first century. Vicki didn't waste time speculating about the underwear because she really *really* didn't want to know.

At Yonge and Bloor she crossed the station and slipped down to the lower tracks, easily avoiding the security cameras and the weary curiosity of late commuters.

There were maybe—possibly—fewer rats and mice scrabbling out of her way.

Maybe—possibly—sounds that didn't quite add up to the ambient noise she remembered from other trips.

It depressed her just a little that she'd been down in these tunnels often enough to remember the ambient noise.

When the last train of the night went by, she fought the urge to brace herself against the sides of the workman's niche, rise up to window height, and give any passengers a flickering, strobelike look at what haunted the dark places of the city. *Something about being an immortal undead creature of the night really changes the things you find funny,* she sighed, allowing the rush of wind to hold her in place as the squares of light flashed by.

The maintenance workers traveled in pairs but it wasn't hard to separate the younger of the two from his companion. A crescent of white teeth in the darkness. A flash of silver eyes. A promise of things forbidden in the light.

Like shooting fish in a barrel. Grabbing a fistful of his overall's, Vicki dragged him into a dark corner, stiffened her arm to keep him there, and locked her gaze with his. "Giant intelligent blood sucking bugs."

He looked confused. "Okay."

"Seen any?"

"Down here?"

"Anywhere."

Dark brows drew in. "The cockroaches seem to be getting smarter."

"I noticed that too. Anything else?"

Broad shoulders shrugged. "Sometimes I think I'm hearing things but the other guys say it's just me."

If they're really intelligent and nesting in the tunnels, they wouldn't want the maintenance workers to find them, would they? Even if they did cross over from some television inspired hell dimension, a couple of TTC issue flame-throwers would still take them out. They'd wait, hiding quietly, feeding where it wouldn't be noticed until...

Until what?

Until there were enough of them to... to....

The heat under her hand and the thrum of blood so close wasn't making it any easier to think. Not that she'd ever thought well on an empty stomach.

Later, when she lifted her mouth from an open vein in the crock of a sweaty elbow, she had the strangest feeling of being watched. Watched in an empty section of tunnel with no feel of another life anywhere near.

Watched and weighed.

Mike Celluci was asleep when Vicki got home an hour or so before dawn. He was lying on his back one arm under the covers, one flung out over the empty half of the bed. She slipped in beside him and snuggled up against his shoulder still damp and warm from the shower, knowing this was how she felt the most human—body temperature almost normal, skin flushed. She felt him wake, felt his arm tighten around her.

"So, how'd the job work out?"

"Giant intelligent bloodsucking bugs in the subway." She was beginning to enjoy saying it.

"Seriously?"

"Well, so far I'm pretty much taking the word of my employer. I had a look around the tunnels in question and saw s.f.a., but he truly believes there's something nasty down there and I think he may be right."

"There's a lot of nasty in the tunnels."

Memory called up the underwear. Vicki winced. "Yeah. I know." After a moment, spent pushing back against the large hand stroking her back, she sighed and murmured, "Any rumors going around Toronto's finest about strange shit in the subway?"

"Sweet talker."

"Just answer the question."

"No one's said anything to me but I'll ask around. You should probably talk to TTC security."

"Tomorrow. Well, technically, later today."

"You...hungry?"

Which wasn't really what he was asking her but feeding had gotten so tied up with other things it had become impossible to separate them. They'd tried. It hadn't worked.

"I could eat."

She only took a mouthful or two from him these days. Enough for mutual sensation, not enough to worry about bleeding him dry over time. Every relationship had to make compromises—she never told him that when she got a bite downtown, he didn't die.

Tonight was...different.

Sitting up, sheet folding across her lap, she rolled the taste of his blood around in her mouth.

Sharp. A little bitter.

Like something had been... added?

"S'matter?" he asked sleepily, rubbing the toes of one foot against the ankle of the other.

"Mike, have you been in a subway station lately?" She crawled to the end of the bed.

"Sure."

"Bloor and Yonge?"

"Yeah."

Two half healed puncture wounds under the outside curve of his left ankle.

Her eyes silvered.

The job had just gotten personal.

The sun set at 6:03 PM.

Vicki blinked at the darkness; back in the world between one instant and the next.

The phone rang at 6:04.

Pulling it out of the adapter, she flipped it open and snapped, "What?"

"Ms. Nelson. I saw another one!"

"Duncan?" The reception inside a plywood box wrapped in a blackout curtain inside Mike Celluci's crawl space wasn't the best.

"This one didn't just stare at me, Ms. Nelson. It started walking toward me. It knew who I was!"

"Maybe it remembers how you taste." The words were out of her mouth before she could consider their effect.

"OHGODOHGODOHGOD..."

"Duncan, calm down. Now." A sort of whimper and then ragged breathing. "Where were you when this happened?"

"St. George station. University line. They're spreading, aren't they."

"So it seems."

"What should I *do*?"

"Do?" Vicki paused, half folded around, reaching for the folded pile of clean clothes by her feet. "You should stay out of subway stations." She snagged a pair of socks and began pulling them on. "What blood type are you?"

"What?"

Shimming underwear up over her hips, she repeated the question. "O—positive…"

She cut him off before he could ask why she wanted to know, told him she'd be in touch, and hung up.

Type O blood could be given to anyone because its erythrocytes contained no antigens making it compatible with any plasma. Knowledge from before the change. After, well, blood was blood was blood; hot and sweet and the type, so not relevant.

A lot of people were type O.

Mike Celluci was type O.

The faxed sketch of the King-tic was lying on the kitchen table under an old bank envelope. On the back of the envelope, Celluci's dark scrawl: "If this isn't a joke, TRY to be careful. Better yet, catch one, use it to convince the city they have a problem, and let them deal with the rest. Call me."

Someone in Duncan's group had talent. Drawn on graph paper, the bug was almost three dimensional. Six legs but grouped around a single, spiderlike body. Feathery antennae, like on a moth, two eyes on short stalks, four darker areas against the front of the body that could be more eyes. It had a *face* which was just creepy. Notes under the drawing describe the color as urban camouflage, black and grey, different on every bug they'd seen. The size…

Vicki blinked and looked again.

Giant intelligent bloodsucking bugs.

Still, she hadn't expected them to be so big.

A foot across and another six to eight inches on either side for the legs.

Leaving the sketch on the table, she crossed the kitchen and peered into the cupboard under the sink. Picked up a package of roach motels, put it down again. Grabbed instead for the can of bug spray, guaranteed to work on roaches, earwigs, flies, millipedes, and all other invading insects.

All other?

Probably not, but it never hurt to be prepared.

"Mike? What've you got for me?" Had she still been able to blush, she would have at his response but since she couldn't, she just grinned. "Stop being smutty and answer the question. Because I'm on the subway and do not need that image in my head."

Feeling the weight of regard, Vicki lifted her chin, caught the eye of the very bleached blond young man sitting directly across the train, and let just a little of the Hunger show. He froze, fingernails digging into the red fuzz on the front curve of the seat. When she released him, he ran for the other end of the car.

She really hated eavesdroppers.

"Yeah, I'm listening."

An old woman had collapsed at the Bay Street station and died later in hospital. Police were investigating because according to witnesses she'd cried out in pain just before she fell. According to the medical report she'd died of anaphylactic shock.

"An allergic reaction to something in her blood? What type? Yeah, yeah, I know you told me what type of reaction, what blood type?"

Type O.

"This isn't the actual size, right?"

"Of course not." Vicki smiled down at the TTC security guard and took comfort in the knowledge that she wasn't, in fact, lying. Not her fault if he assumed the bugs were smaller than drawn.

"I'm afraid I can't help you. I mean, Joe Public hasn't complained about anything like this, and none of my people have said anything either." He handed back the sketch, smiling broadly, willing to share the joke. "You've *seen* one of these?"

"Not me. Like I said, I'm working on a case, and my client thinks he's seen one of these."

"And you get paid if they're real or not?"

"Something like that."

"Not a bad gig."

"Pays the bills. What's wrong?"

"What? Oh, just an itchy ankle."

"Let me see." Not a request. No room for refusal. She loved the social shortcuts that came with the whole bloodsucking undead thing.

Two holes. Just below the ankle.

"Do you know your blood type?"

"Uh…A?"

More people knew their astrological sign than their blood type— useful if they were in an accident and the paramedics needed to read their horoscope.

She moved so that her body blocked the view of anyone who might be looking through into the security office—although most of them were trying to see themselves on the monitors. "Give me your hand."

He shuddered slightly as she wrapped cool fingers around heated skin, shuddered a little harder as her teeth met through the dark satin of his wrist. A long swallow for research purposes, another because it was so good, one more just because. A lick against the wound and a moment waiting to be sure the coagulants in her saliva had worked.

Lowering his hand carefully to the arm of his chair, Vicki smiled down into his eyes.

"Thank you for help, Mr. Allan. Is that someone pissing against the wall in the outside stairwell?"

His attention back on the monitors, she slipped out of the room.

There was nothing in his blood, type A blood, that wasn't supposed to be there.

The old woman, type O, had died from an allergic reaction to a foreign substance in her blood.

Mike, type O, had a foreign substance in his blood.

If Duncan Travis also had a foreign substance in his blood then it would safe to assume the King-tics were specifically marking specific blood types. She should check Duncan for markers, find a B and an AB who'd been bitten and...

Screw it. Discovering if they were only marking O's or marking everything but A's wouldn't help her find the bugs any faster. The fact that they were marking at all, and that she couldn't think of a good reason why but could think of several bad reasons, was enough to propel her into the crowd of commuters and down into the Bloor Station.

The fastest way to find something? Go to where it is. National Geographic didn't set up all those cameras around water holes because they liked the way the light reflected off the surface.

If the King-tics fed off subway station crowds then Vicki'd stand in crowded subway stations until she spotted one no matter how much the press of humanity threatened to overwhelm her. At least at the end of the day, they all smelled like meat rather than the nasal cacophony that poured out of the trains every morning.

Oh, great. Now I'm hungry.

Everyone standing within arm's reach shuffled nervously away.
Oops.

Masking the Hunger, she ran through her list of mental appetite
suppressants.

*Homer Simpson, Joan Rivers, Richard Simmons, pretty much anyone who'd
ever appeared on the Jerry Springer show...*

Her mouth flooded with saliva as the rich scent of fresh blood
interrupted her litany. A train screamed into the station. The crowd
surged forward, and Vicki used the Hunger to cut diagonally across
the platform, less aware of the mass of humanity moving around
her than she was of the black and grey shadow scuttling across the
ceiling. With the attention of any possible witnesses locked on the
interior of the subway cars and their chances of actually boarding,
she dropped down off the end of the platform and began to run,
just barely managing to keep the bug in sight.

Duncan was right. For a big bug, the thing could really motor.

Then it turned sideways and was gone.

Gone?

Rocking to a stop, Vicki flung herself back against the tunnel
wall as another train came by, the roar of steel wheels against steel
rails covering some much needed venting. Eleven years on the police force had given her a vocabulary most sailors would envy. She
got through about half of it while the train passed.

In the sudden silence that followed the fading echoes of profanity, she heard the faint skittering sound of six fast moving legs. A
sound that offered its last skitter directly over her head. All she had
to do was look up.

Unlike the King-tic in the drawing, this one had a membranous
sac bulging out from the lower curve of its body. Inside the sac,
about an ounce of blood.

Vicki's snarl was completely involuntary.

Both eyestalks pointing directly at her, the bug brought one
foreleg up and rubbed at its antennae.

Again the feeling of being weighed.

And wanted.

The eyestalks turned and it flattened itself enough to slip through
a crack between the wall and the ceiling.

Easy to find handholds in the concrete since the city had
trouble finding money to repair the infrastructure people could

see. Anything tucked away underground could be left to rot. Pressed as flat as possible against the wall—*What good saving the world if you lose your ass to a passing subway?*—Vicki tucked her head sideways and peered through the crack at what seemed to be another tunnel identical to the one she was in. In the dim glow of the safety lights, it looked as though the shadows were in constant movement.

King-tics.

Lots and lots of them.

Probably nesting in an old emergency access tunnel, she decided as something poked her in the back of the head.

Turning she came eye to eye to eye with another bug. After she got the girly shriek out of the way, she realized it didn't seem upset to find her there, it just wanted her to move. Backing carefully down two handholds, she watched it slide sideways through the crack, briefly flashing its sac of blood.

Hard not to conclude that they were feeding something.

She slid the rest of the way to the tunnel floor, waited for a train to pass, and began working her way carefully up the line. If the bugs were using that crack as their primary access, that suggested the main access had been sealed shut. Twenty paces. Twenty five. And her fingertips caught a difference in the wall.

The TTC had actually gone to the trouble of parging over the false wall, most likely in an attempt to hide it—or more specifically what was behind it—from street people looking for a place to squat. The faint outline of a door suggested they hadn't originally wanted to hide it from themselves. Forcing her fingers through the thin layer of concrete, Vicki hooked them under the nearest edge and pulled, the *crack* hidden in the roar of a passing train.

Under the concrete, plywood and a narrow door nailed shut.

The nails parted faster than the concrete had.

Feeling a little like Sigorny Weaver and a lot like she should have her head examined, Vicki pushed into the second tunnel.

It wasn't very big; a blip in the line between Yonge and University swinging around to the north of the Bay Street station, probably closed because it came too close to any number of expensive stores. Although the third rail was no longer live, it seemed everything else had just been sealed up and forgotten. The place reeked of old blood and sulfur.

Well, they certainly smell like they came from a hell dimension.

Closing the door behind her, Vicki waded carefully toward what seemed to be the quiet center in the mass of seething bugs.

The bugs ignored her.

They can't feed from me, so they ignore me. I've done nothing to harm them, so they ignore me. I also feed on blood so they…Holy shit.

Duncan Travis and his group had been certain there'd be a queen in the nest. They were just a bit off. There were three queens. Well, three great big scary somethings individually wrapped in pulsing gelatinous masses being fed by the returning blood-carrying—no, harvesting—bugs.

You guys haven't missed a cliché, have you?

Sucker bet that the blood being drained down between three frighteningly large pairs of gaping mandibles was type O. The workers could probably feed on any type—since they seemed to be biting across the board—but they needed that specific universal donor thing to create a queen.

Like worker bees feeding a larvae royal jelly.

And Mike laughed at me for watching "The Magic School Bus".

As she shifted her weight forward, a double row of slightly larger King-tics moved into place between her and the queens. Apparently, their tolerance stopped a couple of meters out. Not a problem; Vicki didn't need to get any closer. Didn't actually want to get any closer. Like recognised like and she knew predators when she saw them. The queens would not be taking delicate bites from the city's ankles, they'd be biting the city off at the ankles and feeding on the bodies as they fell.

A sudden desire to whip out the can of bug spray and see just how well it lived up to its advertising promise was hurriedly squashed. As was Mike's idea of grabbing a bug and presenting it to the proper authorities—whoever the hell they were. Somehow it just didn't seem smart—or survivable—to piss them off while she was standing in midst of hundreds of them. Barely lifting her feet from the floor, she shuffled back toward the door, hurrying just a little when she saw that all three queens had turned their eyestalks toward her.

Odds were good they weren't going to be confined by that gelatinous mass much longer.

So. What to do?

Closing the door carefully behind her, she waited, shoulder blades pressed tight against the wood as another train went by. Options? She supposed she could always let the TTC deal with it. It would be as easy for her to convince the right TTC official to come down to the tunnels for a little look as it would be for her to convince him to expose his throat. Not as much fun, but as easy. Unfortunately, years of experience had taught her that the wheels of bureaucracy turned slowly, even having been given a shove, and her instincts—new and old—were telling her they didn't have that kind of time to waste.

Still, given that the King-tics were nesting in the subway system, it seemed only right that the TTC deal with it.

Vicki picked up the garbage train at Sherbourne. There were no security cameras in the control booth and coverage on the platform didn't extend to someone entering the train from the tracks. Tucking silently in behind the driver, Vicki tapped him on the shoulder and dropped her masks.

And sighed at the sudden pervasive smell of urine.

"Your hands! Blood all over your hands!"

"It's not blood," she sighed, scrubbing her palms against the outside of her thighs. "It's rust. Now concentrate, I need you to tell me how to start this thing."

"Union rules…"

Her upper lip curled.

"…have no relevance here. Okay. Sure. Push this."

"And to go faster?"

"This. To stop…"

"Stopping won't be a problem." She leaned forward, fingers gently gripping his jaw, her eyes silver. "Go join your co-workers on the platform. Be surprised when the train starts to move. Don't do *anything* that might stop it or cause it to be stopped. Forget you ever saw me."

"Saw who?"

Mike was watching the news when Vicki came upstairs the next evening. "Here's something you might be interested in. Seems a garbage train went crashing into an access tunnel and blew up— which they're not wont to do—but unfortunately a very hot fire destroyed all the evidence."

"Did you just say *wont?*"

"Maybe. Why?"

"Just wondering." Leaning over the back of his chair, she kissed the top of his head. "Anyone get hurt?"

"No. And, fortunately, the safety protocols activated in time to save the surrounding properties."

"Big words. You quoting?"

"Yes. You crazy?"

She thought about it for a minute but before she could answer, her phone rang. Stepping away from the chair, she flipped it open. "Good evening Duncan."

"How did you know it was me?"

"Call display."

"Oh. Right. But yesterday…?"

"You called before I was up. It's pretty damned dark inside a coffin."

"You sleep in a coffin!?"

"No, I'm messing with your head again. I expect you've seen the news?"

"It's the only thing that's been on all day. You did that didn't you? That was you destroying the nest! Did you get them all?"

"Yes."

"Are you sure?"

"They shit sulfur, Duncan. They were pretty flammable."

"But what if some of them were out, you know, hunting."

"They hunt on crowded subway platforms. No crowds in the wee smalls."

"Oh. Okay. Did you find out where they came from?"

"No. It didn't seem like a good idea to sit down and play twenty questions with them. And besides, they just seemed to be intelligent because they were following pretty specific programming. They were probably no smarter than your average cockroach."

"But giant and bloodsucking?"

"Oh, yeah."

Vicki had no idea what he was thinking about during the long pause that followed; she didn't *want* to know.

"So it's safe for me to go back on the subway?"

"You and three million other people."

"About your bill…"

"We'll talk about it tomorrow in the coffee shop—we should be able to get into the area by then." She looked a question at Mike, now standing and watching her. He nodded reluctantly. "Seven thirty. Good night, Duncan."

Mike shook his head as she powered off the phone and holstered it. "You're actually going to charge him?"

"Well, I'd send a bill to the city but I doubt they'd pay it—given that there's no actual evidence I just saved their collective butts. Again." Demons, mummies, King-tics—it was amazing how fast that sort of thing got old. She followed Mike into the kitchen and watched a little jealously as he poured a cup of coffee. She missed coffee.

"Speaking of no actual evidence; how did you get the garbage train to blow?"

Vicki grinned. "Not that I'm admitting anything, Detective-sergeant, but *if* I wanted to blow up a garbage train in a specific giant bloodsucking bug infested place, I'd probably use a little accelerant and a timer, having first switched the rails and cleared the tunnels of all mammalian life forms."

"You closed down the entire system, Vicki."

"Giant bloodsucking bugs, Mike."

"I'm not saying you didn't have a good reason," he sighed, leaning against the counter. "But don't you think your solution was a little extreme?"

"Not really, no."

"What aren't you telling me?"

Moving into his arms, she bit him lightly on the chin. "I'm not telling you I blew up that garbage train."

"Good point."

"I'm not telling you what I really think of people who watch golf."

"Thank you."

She could feel his smile against the top of her head, his heart beating under her cheek, his life in her hands. Nor was she telling him that people, like him, with type O blood had been tagged so they'd be easier to find. Why bother with random biting when it was possible to go straight to the blood needed to create new queens? Even if they'd been harmless parasites, she'd have blown them up for that alone.

Mike Celluci was hers, and she didn't share.

"Vicki, you going to tell me what you're snarling about?"

"Just thinking of something that really bugs me…"

The idea for the anthology Dracula In London *was that a group of 'vampire writers' would fill in some of Bram Stoker's missing timeline. Of course, this meant I had to read* Dracula *again. I have such a rough life...*

TO EACH HIS OWN KIND

LONDON WAS EVERYTHING the Count had imagined it to be when he'd told Jonathan Harker of how he'd longed to walk "...through the crowded streets...to be in the midst of the whirl and rush of humanity." *Although,* he amended as he waited for a break in the evening traffic that would allow him to cross Picadilly, *a little* less *whirl and rush would be preferable.*

He could see the house he'd purchased across the street, but it might as well have been across the city for all he could reach it. Yes, he'd wanted to move about unnoticed, but this, this was wearing at his patience. And he had never been considered a patient man. Even as a man.

Finally, he'd been delayed for as long as he was willing to endure. Sliding the smoked glasses down his nose, he deliberately met the gaze of an approaching horse. In his homeland, the effect would have been felt between one heartbeat and the next. Terror. Panic. Flight. This London carriage horse, however, seemed to accept his presence almost phlegmatically.

Then the message actually made it through the city's patina to the equine brain.

Better, he thought and strode untouched through the resulting chaos. Ignoring the screams of injured men and horses both, he put the key into the lock and stepped inside.

He'd purchased the house furnished from the estate of Mr. Archibald Winter-Suffield. From the dead, as it were. That amused him.

His belongings were in the dining room at the back of the house.

"The dining room?" He sighed. His orders to the shipping company had only instructed that the precious cases be placed in the house. Apparently, here in this new country, he needed to be more specific. They would have to be moved to a place less conspicuous, but not now, not with London calling to him. He set his leather case upon the table and turned to go.

Stepping around a chair displaced by the boxes of earth, he brushed against the sideboard, smearing dust across his sleeve. Snarling, he brushed at it with his gloved hand but only succeed in smearing it further. The coat was new. He'd sent his measurements to Peter Hawkins before he'd started his journey and had found clothing suitable for an English gentleman at journey's end. It was one of the last commissions Mr. Hawkins had fulfilled for him. One of the last he would fulfill for anyone as it happened. The old man had been useful, but the necessity of frequent correspondence had left him knowing too much.

Opening the case, he pulled out a bundle of deeds—this was not the only house that English dead had provided—and another bundle of note paper, envelopes and pens. As he set them down, he reminded himself to procure ink as soon as possible. He disliked being without it. Written communications allowed a certain degree of distance from those who did his bidding.

Finally, after some further rummaging, he found his clothing brush and removed the dust from his sleeve. Presentable at last, he tossed the brush down on the table and hurried for the street, suddenly impatient to begin savoring this new existence.

"…to share its life, its change, its death, all that makes it what it is."

The crowd outside on Picadilly surprised him, and he stopped at the top of the stairs. The crowds he knew in turn knew better than to gather outside his home. When he realized that the people were taking no notice of him and had, in fact, gathered to watch the dead horse pulled up onto a wagon, he descended to the street.

He thrilled to his anonymity as he made his way among them. To walk through a great mass of Londoners unremarked—it was all he had dreamed it would be. To feel their lives surrounding him, unaware of their danger. To walk as a wolf among the unsuspecting lambs. To know that even should he declare himself, they would not believe. It was a freedom he had never thought to experience again.

Then a boy, no more than eight or ten, broke free of his minder and surged forward to get a clearer look. Crying, "Hey now!" a portly man stepped out of the child's way.

The pressure of the man's foot on his meant less than nothing but he hissed for the mark it made on his new shoes. And for the intrusion into his solitude.

The portly man turned at the sound, ruddy cheeks pale as he scanned the ground.

By the time he looked up, the Count had composed himself. It would not do to give himself away over so minor a thing.

"You aren't going to believe this," the man said without preamble, his accent most definitely not English, "but I could've sworn I heard a rattler." Then he smiled and extended his hand. "I do beg your pardon, sir, for treading on you as I did. Shall we consider my clumsiness an introduction? Charlie March, at your service."

The novelty of the situation prodded him to take the offered hand. "I am…" He paused for an instant and considered. Should he maintain the identity that went with the house? But no. The Count de Ville was a name that meant nothing; he would not surrender his lineage so easily. Straightening to his full height, he began again. "I am Dracula. Count Dracula."

The smile broadened. "A Count? Bless me. You're not from around these parts, are you?"

"No. I am only recently arrived."

"From the continent? I could tell. Your accent, you know. Very old world, very refined. Romania?"

The Count blinked and actually took a step back before he gained control of his reaction.

Charlie laughed. "I did some business with a chap from Romania last year. Bought some breeding stock off me. Lovely manners you lot have, lovely."

"Thank you." It was really the only thing he could think of to say.

"I'm not from around these parts myself." He continued before there was even a chance of a reply. "Me, I'm American. Got a big spread out west, the Double C—the missus' name is Charlotte, you see. She's the reason we came to England. She got tired of spending money in New York and wanted to spend some in London." His gaze flicked up, then down, then paused. "That's one hell of a diamond you've got stuck in your tie, if you don't mind my saying so."

"It has been in my family for a long time." He'd taken it from the finger of a Turk after he'd taken the finger from the Turk.

"Well, there's nothing like old money, that's what I always say." Again the smile, which had never entirely disappeared, broadened. "Unless it's new money. Have you plans for this evening, Count?"

"Plans?" He couldn't remember the last time he'd been so nonplused. In fact, he couldn't remember if he'd ever been so nonplused. "No."

"Then if you're willing, I'd like to make up for treading so impolitely on your foot. I'm heading to a sort of a soiree at a friend's." His eyelids dropped to a conspiratorial level. "You know, the sort of soiree you don't take your missus to. Oh, you needn't worry about the company," he added hurriedly. "They're your kind of people." He leaned a little closer and dropped his voice. "His Royal Highness will be there. You know, the Prince of Wales."

About to decline the most peculiar invitation he'd ever received, the Count paused. The Prince of Wales would be in attendance. The Prince of Wales. His kind of people. "I would be pleased to attend this soiree as your guest," he said. And smiled.

"Damn, but you've got some teeth on you."

"Thank you. They are a...family trait."

The party was being held in a house on St. James Square. Although only a short walk from his own London sanctuary, the buildings were significantly larger and the occupants of the buildings either very well born or very rich. Seldom both, as it happened. It was an area where, by birth and power, he deserved to live, but where it would be impossible for him to remain hidden. Years of experience had taught him that the very rich and the very poor were equals in their thirst for gossip, but the strange and growing English phenomenon of middle class—well researched before he'd left his homeland—seemed willing to keep their attention on business rather than their neighbors.

He followed Charlie March up the stairs and paused at the door, wondering if so general an invitation would allow him to cross the threshold.

Two steps into the foyer, March turned with his perpetual smile. "Well, come in, Count. No need to wait for an engraved invitation."

"No, of course not." He joined the American in removing his hat and coat and gloves, handing them into the care of a liveried footman.

"I expect you'll want to meet his Highness first?"

"It would be proper to pay my immediate respects to the prince."

"Proper to pay your immediate respects," March repeated shaking his head. "Didn't I say you lot have lovely manners. Where would his Highness be then?" he asked the footman.

"The green salon, sir."

"Of course he is, the evening's young. I should have known. This way then." He took hold of the Count's arm to turn him toward the stairs. "Say, there's not a lot of meat on your bones is there? Now me, I think a little stoutness shows a man's place in the world."

"Indeed." He stared down at the fleshy fingers wrapped just above his elbow, too astonished at being so held to be enraged. Fortunately, he was released before the astonishment faded, for it would have been the height of rudeness to kill the man while they were both guests in another's home.

At the top of the stairs, they crossed a broad landing toward an open doorway through which spilled the sounds of men...and women? He paused. He would not be anonymous in this crowd. He would be introduced and be expected to take part in social discourse. While he looked forward to the opportunity of testing his ability to walk unknown and unseen amongst the living, he also found himself strangely afraid. It had been a very, very long time since he had been a member of such a party, and it would have been so much easier had the women not been there.

He had always had a weakness—no, say rather a fondness, for he did not admit weakness—for a pretty face.

"Problem, Count?" March paused in the doorway and beamed back at him.

On the other hand, if this man can move amongst the powerful of London, and they do not see him *for what* he *is...* "No, not at all, Mr. March. Lead on."

There had been little imagination involved in the naming of the green salon, for the walls were covered in a brocaded green wallpaper that would have been overwhelming had it not been covered in turn by dozens of paintings. A few were surprisingly good, most were indifferent, and all had been placed within remarkably ugly frames. The furniture had been upholstered in a variety of green and gold and cream patterns, and underfoot was a carpet predominately consisting of green cabbage roses. Everything that could be gilded, had been. Suppressing a shudder, he was almost overcome by a sudden wave of longing for the bare stone and dark, heavy oak of home.

Small groups of people were clustered about the room, but his eyes were instantly drawn to the pair of facing settees where half a dozen beautiful women sat talking together, creamy shoulders and bare arms rising from silks and satins heavily corseted around impossibly tiny waists. How was it his newspapers had described the women to be found circling around the Prince? Ah yes, as *"a flotilla of white swans, their long necks supporting delicate jeweled heads."* He had thought it excessively fanciful when he read it, but now, now he saw that it was only beautifully accurate.

"We'll introduce you to the ladies later," March murmured, leading the way across the center of the room. "That's his Highness by the window."

Although he would have much preferred to take the less obvious route around the edges, the Count followed. As they passed the ladies, he glanced down. Most were so obviously looking away that they could only have been staring at him the moment before, but one met his gaze. Her eyes widened and her lips parted, but she did not look away. He could see the pulse beating in the soft column of her throat. *Later,* he promised, and moved on.

"Your royal Highness, may I present a recent acquaintance of mine, Count Dracula."

Even before March spoke, he had identified which of the stout, whiskered men smoking cigars by the open window was Edward, the Prince of Wales. Not from the newspaper photographs, for he found it difficult to see the living in such flat black and gray representations, but from the nearly visible aura of power that surrounded him. Like recognized like. Power recognized power. If the reports accompanying the photographs were true, the prince was not allowed much in the way of political power, but he was clearly conscious of himself as a member of the royal caste.

He bowed, in the old way, body rigid, heels coming together. "I am honored to make your acquaintance, your Highness."

The prince's heavy lids dropped slightly. "Count Dracula? This sounds familiar, yah? You are from where?"

"From the Carpathian mountains, Highness," he replied in German. His concerns about sounding foreign had obviously been unnecessary. Edward sounded more like a German prince than an English one. "My family have been *boyers*, princes, there since before we turned back the Turk many centuries ago. Princes still when we threw off the Hungarian yoke. Leaders in every war. But..." He sighed and spread his hands. "...the warlike days are over, and the glories of my great race are as a tale that is told."

"Well said, sir!" the prince exclaimed in the same language. "Although I am certain I have heard your name, I am afraid I do not know that area well— as familiar as I am with most of Europe." He smiled and added. "As related as I am to most of Europe. If you are not married, Dracula, I regret I have no sisters remaining."

The gathered men laughed with the prince, although the Count could see that not all of them—and Mr. March was of that group—spoke German. "I am not married now, your Highness, although I was in the past."

"Death takes so many," Edward agreed solemnly.

The Count bowed again. "My deepest sympathies on the death of your eldest son, Highness." The report of how the Duke of Clarence had unexpectedly died of pneumonia in early 1892 had been in one of the last newspaper bundles he'd received. As far as the Count was concerned, death should be unexpected, but he was perfectly capable of saying what others considered to be the right thing. If it suited his purposes.

"It was a most difficult time," Edward admitted. "And the wound still bleeds. I would have given my life for him." He stared intently at his cigar.

With predator patience, the Count absorbed the silence that followed as everyone but he and the prince shifted uncomfortably in place.

"Shall I tell you how I met the Count, your Highness?" March asked suddenly. "There was a bully smash up on Picadilly."

"A bully smash up?" the prince repeated lifting his head and switching back to English. "Were you in it?"

"No, sir, I wasn't."

"Was the Count?"

"No sir, he wasn't either. But we both saw it, didn't we, Count?"

The Count saw that the prince was amused by the American, so, although he dearly wanted to put the man in his place, he said only, "Yes."

"And you consider this accident to be a *gut* introduction to a Capathian prince?" Edward asked, smiling.

If March had possessed a tail, the Count realized, he'd have been wagging it; he was so obviously pleased that he'd lifted the Prince of Wales' spirits. "Yes, sir, I did. Few things bring men together like disasters. Isn't that true, Count?"

That, he could wholeheartedly agreed with. He was introduced in turn to Lord Nathan Rothschild, Sir Ernest Cassel and Sir Tomas Lipton—current favorites of Prince Edward—and he silently thanked the English newspapers and magazines that had provided facts enough about these men for him to converse intelligently.

He was listening with interest to a discussion of the Greek-Turkish War when he became aware of Mr. March's scrutiny. Turning toward the American, he caught the pudgy man's gaze and held it. "Yes?"

March blinked, and the Count couldn't help thinking that even the horse on Picadilly hadn't taken so long to recognize its danger. It wasn't that March was stupid—it seemed that old terrors had been forgotten in his new land.

"I was just wondering about your glasses, Count. Why do you keep those smoked lenses on inside?"

Because the prince was also listening, he explained. "My eyes are very sensitive to light, and I am not used to so much interior illumination." He gestured at the gas lamps. "This is quite a marvel to me."

Prince Edward beamed. "You will find England at the very front of science and technology. This..." He echoed the Count's gesture trailing smoke from his cigar. "...is nothing. Before not much longer we will see electricity take the place of gas, motor cars take the place of horses, and actors and actresses..." His smile was answered by the most beautiful of the women seated across the room. "...replaced by images on a screen. I, myself have seen these images—have seen them move—right here in London. The British Empire shall lead the way into the new century!"

Those close enough to hear, applauded, and March shouted an enthusiastic "Hurrah!"

The Count bowed a third time. "It is why I have come to London, Highness; to be lead into the new century."

"Gott man." A footman carrying a tray of full wine glasses appeared at the prince's elbow. "Please try the burgundy, it is a very gott wine."

About to admit that he did not drink wine, the Count reconsidered. In order to remain un-noted, he must be seen to do as others did. "Thank you, Highness." It helped that the burgundy was a rich, dark red. While he didn't actually drink it, he appreciated the color.

When the clock on the mantle struck nine, Edward lead the way to the card room, motioning that the Count should fall in beside him. "Have you seen much of my London?" he asked.

"Not yet, Highness. Although I was at the zoo only a few days past."

"The zoo? I have never been there, myself. Animals I am most fond of, I see through my sites." He mimed shooting a rifle, and again his immediate circle, now walking two by two down the hall behind him, laughed.

"And he'd rather see a good race than govern, wouldn't you, Highness?" Directly behind Edward's shoulder, March leaned forward enough to come between the two princes. "Twenty-eight race meetings last year. I heard that's three more visits than he made to his House of Lords."

The Count felt the Prince of Wales stiffen beside him. Before the prince could speak, the Count turned and dipped his head just far enough to spear March over the edge of his glasses. "It is not wise," he said slowly, "to repeat everything one hears."

To his astonishment, March smiled. "I wouldn't repeat it outside this company."

"Don't," Edward advised.

"You betcha," March agreed. "Say, Count, your eyes are kind of red. My missus has some drops she puts in hers. I could find out what they are if you like."

Too taken aback to be angry, the Count shook his head. "No. Thank you."

Murmuring, "Lovely manners," in an approving tone, March stepped forward so that he could open the card room door for the prince.

"He is rough, like many Americans," Edward confided in low German as they entered. "But his heart is good, and, more importantly, his wallet is deep."

"Then for your sake, Highness…"

The game in the card room was bridge, and Prince Edward had a passion for it. After two hours of watching the prince move bits of painted card about, the Count understood the attraction no better than he had in the beginning.

Just after midnight, the prince gave his place to Sir Thomas.

"It was *gut* to meet you, Count Dracula. I hope to see you again."

"You will, Highness."

Caught and held in the red gaze, the prince wet full lips and swallowed heavily.

One last time, the Count bowed and stepped back, breaking his hold.

Breathing heavily, Edward hurried from the room. A woman's laughter met him in the hall.

The Count turned to the table. "If you will excuse me, gentlemen, now that his highness has taken his leave, I will follow. I am certain that I will see you *all* again."

In the foyer, only for the pleasure of watching terror blanche the boy's cheek, he brushed the footman's hand with his as he took back his gloves.

He very nearly made it out the door.

"Say, Count! Hold up and I'll walk with you." March fell into step beside him as he crossed the threshold back into the night. "It's close in those rooms, ain't it? September's a lot warmer here than it is back home. Where are you heading?"

"To the Thames."

"Going across to the fleshpots in Southwark," the American asked archly.

"Fleshpots?" It took him a moment to understand. "No. I will not be crossing the river."

"Just taking a walk on the shore then? Count me in."

They walked in blessed silence for a few moments, along Pall Mall and down Cockspur Street.

"His Highness likes you, Count. I could tell. You have a real presence in a room you know."

"The weight of history, Mr. March."

"Say what?"

He saw a rat watching him from the shadow, rat and shadow both in the midst of wealth and plenty, and he smiled. "It is not necessary you understand."

Silence reigned again until they reached the river bank.

"You seemed to be having a good time tonight, Count." March leaned on the metal railings at the top of the embankment. "Didn't I tell you they were your kind of people?"

"Yes."

"So." A bit of loose stone went over the edge and into the water. "Did you want to go somewhere for a bite."

"That won't be necessary." He removed his glasses and slid them carefully into an inside pocket. "Here is fine."

The body slid down the embankment and was swallowed almost silently by the dark water. Replete, the Count drew the back of one hand over his mouth then stared in annoyance at the dark smear across the back of his glove. These were his favorite gloves; they'd have to be washed.

He turned toward home, then he paused.

Why hurry?

The night was not exactly young, but morning would be hours still.

As he walked along the riverbank toward the distant sounds of voices, he smiled. The late Charlie March had not been entirely correct. The prince and his company were not exactly his kind of people...

...yet.

Growing up, everyone has heroes who are important to them, heroes who help form the way they look at the world. Arthur and his Knights of the Round Table were not among mine. Just so you know.

NIGHTS OF THE ROUND TABLE

THEY MET OUTSIDE the chamber door, the old woman and young. Camelot slept, the night so still and quiet within its walls, they might have been the only two alive.

"Are you ready?"

The girl drew in a deep breath, dark eyes wide, thin cheeks flushed. "I'm, I'm not sure."

"You've no time to be unsure," the old woman snapped. "We do what has to be done."

"What has to be done," the girl repeated as though the words gave her courage.

Lifting her basket in one claw-like hand the old woman laid the other against the iron bound door. "Bring the torch," she said.

The Chamber of the Round Table danced with shadows. Thin bands of moonlight poured through the arrow slits and drew golden lines across polished wood, illuminated the rampant stag carved into a slab of oak, gilded pale blocks of stone.

As the door closed behind them and the shadows wrapped around them both like shrouds, the old woman set her basket down in the rushes, placing a fist on each bony hip. "How the blazes they expect us to clean this place in the dark, I'll never know. They got me comin' in to clean up after 'em once a week since they built this great pile of buggering rock, but does any of 'em think to leave a torch lit. No. My cat's got more brains than the whole sodding lot of 'em."

"But, Gran, it's so romantic."

Her grandmother snorted. "You'll think it's a sight less romantic if you step on one of them morning stars left lying around. Now light us up, Manda, they ain't payin' us to waste time."

Six torches, lit. Seven. The light began to reflect off the pale stone walls filling the room with a soft diffuse glow. Nine. Ten.

Manda carefully extinguished her own small torch. Only one of the shadows, pooled in the depths of a massive chair remained.

"Oh, criminey. Not again."

Manda clutched at her grandmother's homespun sleeve. "Who is it Gran?"

"Sir Gareth, nephew to the king. Used to work in the kitchens with our Sara."

"He what?"

"Long story. You get busy turnin' them rushes now. Any big bits of stuff that ain't supposed to be there, pitch out the window. Unless it looks edible, then tuck it away for later."

"Gran!" Her cheeks were bright pink as she stared across the room at Sir Gareth. "That's one of *the* knights. I can't be doin' cleanin' in front of a knight."

"You can do what you're told, girl, while I goes and has a word with ol' mournful Morris. Odds are good," she added, shaking her arm free of Manda's grip, "he won't even notice you. Servants is invisible to his sort."

"But you're a…" Her grandmother's glare wedged the final word sideways in her throat. "Won't you be invisible?" she rephrased after she stopped coughing.

"No. He knows me." Prominent gray brows drew in and, girded for battle, the old woman stomped around the table. "Well?" she demanded glaring up at the fair young man in the chair who, even sitting, was taller than she was. "Don't you got a home to go to?"

He opened a pair of brilliant blue eyes framed by long lashes. "Is that you, Mother Orlan?"

"No, it's the sodding queen of the fairies."

"Ah fair Tatiana, who doth tempt with silvered words and capricious beauty."

"And I hear she does windows. Spit it out; what was it this time?"

"A raspberry flan."

"Uh huh."

"Fain, but it came to my table with a soggy center and yet the syrup did not reach the edge. Two of the berries maintained still their stems, and others had been crushed beyond recognition. And the cream, well whipped as it was, was nigh to butter. I vow by my faith as a knight, I could have made it better in my sleep."

"You said that?"

He sighed an affirmative. "And my lady has banished me from her chamber."

"We've been through this." Gabbing the front of his tunic, she dragged his head around until she could capture his gaze with hers. "Don't criticize the cooking. Your missus don't like being reminded of that year you spent in the kitchens."

"Two of the berries maintained their stems." The fingers he held up wore a lacework pattern of scars. "Two."

"I heard you the first time."

"And a large fly had been cooked into the syrup."

"Protein. Some of us are thankful to get a fly or two cooked into our flans." Releasing him, Mother Orlan folded her arms and stood quietly for a moment, brow creased in thought. "All right," she said at last, "here's what you're gonna to do. Since you can't keep your mouth shut, we gotta work with what we have. You're gonna go home and clank your knightly way down to the kitchens and you're gonna make that flan the way it's supposed to be made. Then you're gonna take it to your missus and get down on your knees and feed it to her. If you're still as good as our Sara says you used to be, you'll have her eatin' out of your hand."

"But I am a knight of the Round Table," he protested, weakly. "I am a protector of the realm, a slayer of evil, I defeat all those who raise their swords in opposition to Arthur, King of all Briton."

"Trust me, kid, women prefer a man who can cook."

"But you said my lady preferred I not remind her of my time in the kitchens."

"Are you arguing with me?"

"No, ma'am."

"An incredible dessert," Mother Orlan said slowly and distinctly. "Presented to her on your knees. She'll come around. In fact, if'n it's just you and the dessert, she'll come around faster, if you take my meaning."

"Just me and the..." His eyes widened as understanding dawned and his fair cheeks flushed. "I don't know."

"I do. Unless you'd *rather* be sittin' here in the middle of the night moanin' to me when you oughta be home in the sack with your missus."

"No. I wouldn't." The flush vanished as one gray brow rose. "No offense."

"None taken."

"Very well then." Broad shoulders squared, Sir Garth laid both hands against the edge of the table and, with a mighty heave, pushed back his chair. A martial light gleaming amidst the brilliant blue of his eyes, he surged to his feet. "There is no dishonor in a flaky pastry. I will do as you advise, Mother Orlan."

"Atta boy." She watched him stride manfully from the chamber and then returned to her granddaughter. "Lad's a dab hand with a pudding by all accounts"

Tossing an armload of rushes back to the floor, Manda straightened and brushed a lock of hair from her face. "Will it work? What you told him?"

"It'd work on me."

"But Gran..."

"What goes on between a man and his missus is nobody's business; especially where desert toppin's involved."

They finished the rushes in silence.

"Nice to have that done with no unpleasant surprises," Mother Orlan sighed, pulling one of the chairs out from the table and lowering herself carefully into it. "I found half a wvyern's tail in them rushes once. Them boys'll drag the darndest things back from foreign parts."

"Gran! That's the king's chair!"

The older woman made herself more comfortable. "And how do you know that? Every last one of them's the same, and his bum ain't in it now."

Manda pointed with a trembling finger. "That's his name there, in gold."

"And his name makes it his does it? Makes a fiddly bit of polishing if you ask me. Besides, I don't expect he'd begrudge an old woman a chance to rest her weary bones." She dragged her kirtle up so that bare legs the size and coloring of dead twigs swung free. "Ah, that's better that is. Come on then, and I'll show you what's to be done to the table."

The Round Table had been made of a single section of an ancient and venerable oak, carved and polished. Resting on stone pillars the same pale gold as the castle, it ensured that no Knight sat above any other; that all were equal in honor.

"If'n I told 'em once I told 'em a hundred times, if'n you gotta bang on the table take your bloody gauntlets off! Sir Kay's the worst; he's got a temper on him like a weasel in a sack. Look at that gouge. Never thinks he's makin' work for others. Oh no. And there, just look there."

Manda followed her pointing finger and blanched. "Someone's carved their initials."

"Carved something anyways." Mother Orlan squinted down at the marks. "If you can see that's initials, you're doin' better than me. Whole lot of 'em's got bloody awful penmanship." Her remaining teeth gleamed between the curves of a salacious grin. "One of 'em's got some drawin' talent though. And an imagination about the sorts of positions a man and a woman can get themselves into."

"Gran!"

"Oh, I know, it's the…" Both hands waved for emphasis. "…Round Table. You needn't look so horrified. What do you expect when you sits a bunch of men around a wooden table with blades in their hands? They're no different than your brothers. 'Ceptin' they're bigger and they clank," she added after a moment's thought.

"So what do we do?"

"We sands it out, that's what we do."

They'd nearly finished when the chamber door crashed open to show a distraught young knight standing in the doorway. Chest heaving, muddy helm tucked under one equally muddy arm, he swept a near desperate gaze around the room and cried, "Mother Orlan! Mother Orlan!"

She sighed and straightened, one hand in the small of her back. "Stop shoutin' Sir Gawain, I ain't deaf."

He raced around the table and threw himself on his knees at her feet, the force of his landing flinging up a great bow wave of rushes. "Mother Orlan, I pray you will grant me the boon of your wisdom!"

"Stay away from the seafood at an all you can eat buffet."

Golden brows drew in over brilliant blue eyes. "What?"

"Oh. You wanted specific wisdom. What's wrong, kid?"

"Dost thou remember how a year hence, a huge man all of green didst interrupt our feasting? How he did challenge one among our proud company to take his noble axe and strike a blow, having first vowed that twelve months hence that knight would stand and take an equal blow in turn? And dost thou remember how I rose and asked my lord king and noble uncle that the adventure be mine, and when he did full grant me that boon, I took up the axe and cut through flesh and bone beheading the green giant?"

"Remember?" The old woman snorted. "Who do you think had to clean up the mess. Sure, he took his sodding head with him," she explained to Manda who was listening with her fist pressed hard against her mouth, "but first it rolls half way across the room. Oh there's no blood, thanks very much, but we got knights and their ladies throwin' chunks left, right, and center. Had to toss out half the rushes in the bloody room." She turned her attention back to Sir Gawain. "Let me guess. Year's up?"

"The year has passed full swiftly, yes, and..." He glanced over at Manda and back. "Mother Orlan, we are not alone."

"Don't worry, that's my granddaughter, it's her first night. She's learnin' the ropes."

One gauntletted hand clutched at faded homespun. "But this matter is, I fear, of a delicate nature."

"Good. So's she." As Gawain tried to work his way around that, Mother Orlan sighed and prompted: "The year has passed full swiftly..."

His brow unfurled. "...and I rode out to find this Green Knight and keep my vow."

She covered her mouth, turned her head, and coughed. *'Patsy.'*

"Didst thou say..."

"No. Go on. Get to the needing my wisdom bit, we've still got to scrape under the chairs."

"I did not come first to the castle of the Green Knight, but another. The lord of the castle and his lady bade me welcome, fed me well and bid me rest. As night fell, the lord went out to hunt and the lady to my bedchamber came."

"Oh oh."

"Though she was fair and didst long beg for my attention, pleading and throwing herself upon me, pulling the covers from me and laying her hands upon me..."

"Do yourself a favor kid, and get to the point; armor ain't made for those kinds of memories."

Gawain shifted uncomfortably, and nodded. "For the sake of my oath of knighthood, I allowed her but one kiss, and then struck with guilt, leapt from the bed and rode back to Camelot as fast as my horse could run. On the morrow, when the lord of the castle returns, what shall I tell him?"

"You're gonna ride right back?"

"I must, for still my vow to the Green Knight binds me."

"And you don't know if you should tell this fella what's off huntin' that his missus was trying to play hide the sausage with a pretty stranger?"

"Not those words perhaps," Gawain allowed, after a moment's consideration, "but yea."

"Give him what's his."

"But I have naught that does belong to him."

"You gotta kiss from his missus doncha?"

"Give him the kiss?"

Mother Orlan nodded.

"But he's got this beard, and his lips are chapped and..."

"Look, sweetcheeks, I ain't suggestin' you slip him the tongue, but you can't go wrong givin' a fella what's rightly his."

"Give mine host what is rightly his," he murmured, thoughtfully. "I did ask thee for thy advice."

"Yeah, you did."

"So it would fain me to listen to it."

"Yeah, it would."

He stood and, towering over her, smiled a brilliant smile. "Thank you, Mother Orlan."

"Glad to 'blige. And Sir Gawain?"

He paused just outside the chamber and turned.

"Next time, lock your buggering door." When he waved a little sheepishly and clanked away, she turned to Manda. "What the blazes does fain mean?"

"I don't know."

"I thought it might be one of them new fangled words you kids are usin'. Like gadzooks and fizig."

"No, Gran. You know he's got an awfully pretty smile for someone missin' so many teeth."

"You'd be missin' teeth too if'n you spent your hol's sittin' up on a big horse with a big stick while a nuther guy sits up on a nuther big horse with his own stick and you rides full tilt at each other until one of you gets whacked and goes ass over tip."

Manda winced. "Why do they do that?"

"For the glory they reckon."

"Doesn't it hurt?"

"Glory usually does. Now, get your putty knife and take a looksee under them chairs."

"What am I lookin' for, Gran?" she asked, dropping to her knees.

"You'll know it when you sees it." The old woman grinned as the visible bits of her granddaughter stiffened.

"Eww. I didn't even know you could *stick* that to a chair."

"Don't touch anything with your bare hands; half of this lot are dealin' with wizards and the like."

"And the other half?"

"Are also morons."

The torches had burned down over half of their length by the time Manda stood. "Bout time." Her grandmother took her arm and pulled her around the table. "Give us a hand getting up on a chair, I ain't as young as I used to be."

Manda dug in her heels. "If you gotta stand on a chair, Gran, this chair's closer."

Dismissing the offered chair with a disdainful snort, she dragged the girl on by. "I ain't standing on that. That's what they call Siege Perilous."

"Why?"

"I doesn't know bout the siege part but the perilous is plain enough if 'n you ever stand on it. It's got a right dicky leg. This here's good."

"It's Sir Percival's chair."

"Just get me up on it. I ain't as tall as I used to be either, and I can't reach it from the floor."

With one hand tucked in her grandmother's armpit and the other clutching her elbow, Manda heaved. For a skinny old lady, her Gran was a lot heavier than she looked. "What is it you need to reach, Gran?"

"That." Squinting a little, she reached back. "Pass me the can of polish."

Eyes wide, Manda did as she was told.

The cup pulled from the light had been made of plain hammered brass and had clearly seen better days. Holding it firmly in one hand, Mother Orlan rubbed it vigorously with a soft cloth.

"It's the…"

"Oh, aye. Comes in every week regular, just about this time. All the sodding damp round here dulls it down somethin' fierce, but it's gleamin' when I'm done with it, let me tell you."

"But I thought it gleamed because of…"

"Elbow grease. And a bit of polish on an old pair of knickers."

There was no denying that the cup was looking better. Manda cocked her head to one side. "I always thought it'd be, I dunno, more fancy. All over jewels and stuff."

"And does our Shaun have fancy cups all over jewels and stuff?"

"Gran, our Shaun's just a carpen… Oh."

"Exactly; oh." Rubbing the rim against her sleeve, Mother Orlan nodded approvingly. She set the cup back where it had come from, and for a heartbeat the chamber filled with a brilliant light, brighter even than the most beautiful day of summer, and with the light came the sweet scent of roses, and the sound of pounding.

Light and scent faded. The pounding not only continued but grew louder and picked up a metallic ring.

"Gran! What is it!"

"No need to panic, girl. Just help me down and stay away from the door."

Heart pounding, Manda did as she was told. No sooner was her grandmother standing on the rushes, than the door burst open and a knight in dark red armor charged into the room. "Is it here?" he cried, dragging his helm from his head. " The scent of roses led me here and…Mother Orlan." He paused, took a deep breath and looked around the chamber as though suddenly realizing where he was. Broad shoulders sagged, red metal plates whispering secrets against each other. "Did *you* see it, Mother Orlan?" he asked hopefully. "Or you, fair maid."

Manda's mouth opened.

The old woman shifted slightly, her heel coming down hard on her granddaughter's instep. "Sorry, there, Sir Galahad. You was followin' the smell of the rose water I use to freshen the rushes again."

"But I was so sure this time."

"I know, kid, I know.

"But it has been prophesied that I will be the one to find the lost Grail."

"Yeah, well, if you remember where you put these things, you wouldn't lose them." She patted him on the vanbrace in a motherly sort of way. "Off you go now, kid. I got work to finish."

"But I shall never stop searching."

"No one's asking you to, kid." She pushed him toward the door. "You might want to think about oiling your culet though, or it's gonna chaff."

They stood together listening to the thumping and clanking fade as Sir Galahad made his way back down the stairs.

"Why'd you lie to him, Gran?"

"The poor kid's got enough problems, bein' chased and all but never bein' caught. He don't need to know he just missed it again."

Eyes locked on the knot she was twisting into her apron, Manda sighed. "Yeah, I guess."

"Well, *I* know."

"He called me fair lady." A soft smile curved flushed cheeks. "He's dreamy."

"Now don't you be getting mixed up with that lot, girl. Not one of them has what might be called a normal relationship with a woman. Take Sir Percival for example." She smacked his chair. "Stumbles on this castle, spends the night, falls in love, rides off the next day and can't ever find the sodding castle again. Swears he wasn't drinking either. Knights. If you ask me, they all wears their helmets too tight. What you wants is a nice boy who comes home nights instead of buggering off on a quest just when there's work to be done. And speaking of work to be done, check the arrow slits for pigeon bits. Merlin's bloody owl sometimes stuffs them in there. Nothing like the smell of rotting pigeon when you're trying to keep a kingdom together, that's what I always say."

"Nothing there, Gran."

"Good. Then we're done and headin' home."

The door opened again—slowly this time—and a large fair man slouched into the room. His brilliant blue eyes were shadowed and his golden hair looked as though he'd been attempting to pull it from his head. "Oh," he said upon seeing the two women. "You're not done yet, Mother Orlan. I saw Galahad leave and… well it doesn't matter. Never mind me, I just need to sit and…"

His sigh was deep enough to cause two torches to flicker. "...think." Dragging his feet through the rushes, he circled the table, pulled out a chair, and collapsed into it.

"It's Sir Lancelot!"

"You've met?"

"No, Gran, it said so on his chair."

"Said King Arthur and Sir Percival on the chairs I was sittin' in; that don't make me them."

"Oh."

"But, in this case, you're right. It's Sir Lancelot." One hand dove under the edge of her wimple for a contemplative scratch. "He's always been a bit moody."

They stared at him for a while.

"They all look kinda alike, don't they?" Manda said at last.

"'spect it's the all the poundin' they take, beats 'em inta one shape. Well, wait here, I'll go talk to him."

"Let me, Gran."

"Let you what?"

"Talk to him. Give him advice."

"You wants to give advice to Sir Lancelot, a knight unequaled in worldly fame, in beauty, strength, honor, and great deeds?"

"Well, yeah."

Her grandmother shrugged. "Why not. Best you take a crack while I'm still around to fix the mess if'n you screw it up. Well, go on before he sighs again and we're all standin' in the dark."

Rearranging her features into something essentially sympathetic, Manda scuffed through the rushes to the knight's side.

They spoke too softly to be overheard, their conversation illustrated by Lancelot beating his chest and the girl shaking her head. Finally, she grabbed his fist in one small hand and laid the other over her heart. A slow smile spread over the knight's face. He nodded and hurried out of the room, rushing past the older woman as though he'd forgotten she was there.

"So?" Mother Orlan asked when the girl came back to her.

"It's so sad, Gran. But so very romantic." At her grandmother's impatient wave, she picked up her basket of cleaning supplies. "He's been in love with this girl for years, and he's pretty sure she loves him, but he's never said anything and neither has she."

"So, what did you tell him?"

Basket on her arm, Manda relit her small torch off the now sputtering room torches. "That nothing's more important than love and he should follow his heart."

Picking up her own basket, Mother Orlan followed her granddaughter out of the chamber. "Follow his heart," she snorted, glancing back at the round table as she closed the door. "Well, seems harmless enough."

Weirdly, I had lot of trouble writing a fantasy story set in ancient Egypt. While researching it, facts kept getting in the way of the fantasy. Given the beliefs of the time, it is possible to read this story as purely historical fiction.

SUCCESSION

HE RULED OVER an Egypt combined because of her. She had seen him in a vision as though he were the heartspring of the Great River itself, and out of his beginning would stretch a long line of Pharaohs until they ended, finally, in the Great Green Sea. For the sake of this future, she had come to him, offering herself in marriage.

He had been wise enough to know he needed her, to ignore her age which, equal to his own, made it very probable that she would never give him sons. *Other wives may give me sons,* he'd said. *You give me what they can not.*

She had given him the *deshret*, the Red Crown of Lower Egypt. Hers by right. His by marriage. Joined now to the *hedjet*, the White Crown of Upper Egypt. One country, united in them.

He had been wise enough to acknowledge her power, to take her council, to recognize that although he was Pharaoh, Horus incarnate as King, they ruled together.

He had been wise enough to court her friendship. He had even come, a time or two, to her bed and seen to it that the experience was pleasant for them both.

"But now, Menes, you are become a fool," Neithhotep sighed. She had been standing at the window long enough the stone had warmed under her bare feet. The last of the *daheebas* had finally docked, the dowry and the bride unloaded, and the procession readying to wend its way to the palace.

The builders, pulled from their usual tasks, had been working day and night to finish the way of the procession, leaving several other more important parts of Memphis to stand uncompleted. As little as she approved of the Pharaoh's sudden obsession, she had to admit it was pleasant to have some part of this new island city actually finished. She was sick to death of the slam of chisels and the shouts of the overseers.

There. The procession was moving.

Neithhotep stepped away from the window and held out her arms. The two slaves who dressed her hurried forward, one with the nearly translucent over-shift, the other with the heavy collar of onyx and gold that held it in place.

"You have decided to attend, my queen?"

"No, Hemon, I have decided to wear my best so that I may sulk in splendor." The over-shift had been designed to cover her arms while leaving her shoulders bare. Age did not show on a woman's shoulders—and that was very nearly the only place the years had not kissed. Matching gold and onyx cuffs held the billowing sleeves in place, matching sandals, matching band about the short full wig. Her face had already been dusted, kohled and hennaed. A touch of scented oil and she was as ready as she could be. "How do I look?"

"Regal, my queen." The scribe inclined his head. "Gracious."

"Gracious? More than I had hoped for. Let us only hope Methethy is as impressed. I want no more whispered words falling into the ears of the Great Menes."

"The queen is jealous of your new bride, Great Pharaoh. Jealous of her youth and beauty."

Oh please. As though there hadn't been young and beautiful brides before, not to mention concubines and catamites, and she had been jealous of none of them. Well, a little jealous perhaps when Hathor gifted their young bodies with new life and softened their eyes with a mystery she would never know—but that was personal, not political.

The difference today was not with the bride, but rather with the way the girl had been presented. And by whom. The Pharaoh's Vizier thought that by providing a young beauty for the old king to prove his virility upon, it would move him closer to power. That the girl he had procured would be able to influence the Pharaoh to give her a queen's power—Neithhotep's power—which he would then control as he controlled the girl.

"The queen is jealous of your new bride, Great Pharaoh..."

The young were never subtle when they made their play—could his intentions be any more obvious?

Did he honestly think she would allow such a thing? Especially since the only way the Pharaoh could remove her from power without throwing Upper and Lower Egypt into civil war, would be to remove *her*.

The girl could clasp the wrinkled body to her young bosom as often as she could stand it, but it would not bring her one step closer to the throne.

Three attendant slaves, two guards in *her* ceremonial armor, and a boy to carry the large fan of peacock feathers—more of an escort than she would normally require within the grounds of the palace but large enough to please her husband, who would assume she came in state to honor his new bride. Large enough also to remind her husband's Vizier that she had resources of her own, but not so large he could convince anyone she was a threat.

Politics. If it destroyed fewer lives, she would enjoy the game more.

After so many years, Neithhotep knew to the moment when her husband would arrive in the throne room—this time, she subtracted a few moments for desire, arrived earlier than she would normally, and still barely made it to her place before the Great Menes entered, nearly treading on the heels of his guards in his haste. He frowned slightly when he saw her, then smiled and crossed toward with his hands out-stretched, the gold that trimmed his robe whispering secrets against the marble floor.

"Methethy said you would not come."

"Not come?" She smiled as though the matter had never been in doubt, and allowed him to catch up her hands in his. "As your first wife, Great Pharaoh, it is my duty to welcome your newest wife to her home, but it is also my pleasure to be with you to share your joy."

He was honestly pleased, she could see it in his eyes, in the way the tight creases at the corners relaxed under the lines of kohl. His mouth opened—he was about to ask her advice, she knew the expression, had seen it a hundred times and thanked the gods she was seeing it now. If they could just have a chance to speak without his Vizier or his Vizier's spies in attendance...

The gods were not so kind.

The bridal procession had reached the palace.

Menes spun about so quickly, he knocked his wig askew. Neithhotep gently straightened it as she ascended the dais behind him.

Methethy entered first—as she'd known he would—and considerably ahead of the actual procession. He was far too astute to leave so critical a meeting to chance. His eyes flashed when he saw her already in place, the expression gone too quickly to read, but she knew he was not pleased to see her. Hardly surprising as he'd made it quite clear that this new queen would become first in Egypt. Neithhotep could almost see his mind working as he crossed to the double thrones.

"Great Pharaoh, Berner-Ib comes, and she is more than everything she was declared to be."

Berner-Ib. The girl's name meant Sweet-heart. Could the situation become any more cloying? Yes. Merely wait until Egypt's first wife welcomed the newest wife to the family. Neithhotep had every intention of greeting the girl with open arms and overwhelming her with kindness. As she had told the Great Menes, it was her pleasure to share his joy—it was also her intent to remove the Vizier from the equation, to give the girl someone new to rely on.

The Vizier's voice pulled Menes to the edge of the throne. "More beautiful? More graceful?"

"Yes, Great Pharaoh. The most beautiful girl in the length of Egypt, from the First Cataract to the Great Green Sea. The most graceful. The most gracious. And yours."

"Mine."

He was besotted and he hadn't even met the girl. He had heard only Methethy's honeyed words over and over until his desire, his need for this girl had overwhelmed all other senses.

There's no fool like an old fool.

An observation she had no intention of applying to herself.

Berner-Ib would have been told she was her enemy. Which was true.

Beware the first wife; she will poison the Pharaoh's heart against you. You are young, you are beautiful, you should be first not her. She could hear the words as clearly as though she'd been standing beside Methethy as he said them. And she could hear Berner-Ib's words to the Pharaoh even though they had not yet been spoken. *If you want me, Great Pharaoh, you must be rid of her.*

She had to capture the girl's self interest before those words were spoken. Once a man began thinking with his body, intelligent decisions came few and far between.

The bride's dowry entered before her. It wasn't large—Mutardis, the Nubian wife had arrived with twice her weight in gold and ivory, four hunting leopards, a fully trained and outfitted war elephant and a legion of Nubian warriors to add to the Pharaoh's guard. The elephant had made rather a large mess during the festivities. In contrast, Berner-Ib's dowry consisted of two dozen large baskets of grain—symbolic of what would now be sent yearly from her father's lands to Memphis—six pure black hunting dogs, and three burly young men who all bore the marks of stonemasons. A clever dowry Neithhotep granted, in a city still half built the stonemasons alone did much to make up for the lack of gold, but not by any means a Pharaoh's dowry. Her husband was besotted indeed to accept so little.

Berner-Ib entered in a gilded litter, enclosed behind linen draperies imprinted with the Pharaoh's cartoche.

"Shall I bring you your bride, Great Pharaoh?"

Methethy's smile was all gentle deference, but Neithhotep could see his eyes glittering in anticipation of his triumph. She turned her head in time to see the Pharaoh nod. The others would see him incline his head regally; she saw he couldn't trust himself to speak.

The Vizier held his hand at the break in the draperies, and a small hand emerged to lie like a fallen flower petal upon his. A tiny foot in a golden sandal followed and Berner-Ib emerged from her litter like a butterfly emerging from a cocoon.

She was undeniably beautiful, and she moved like a breeze across still water, but she was not the practiced seductress Neithhotep had expected. In fact, if the girl had even had her first blood, she'd be very surprised.

"Is she not everything I promised, Great Pharaoh?"

Neithhotep could hear Menes' heart beating beneath his heavy gold and faience collar.

"She is."

The child flushed. The color touched her cheeks like the kiss of Ra, making her more beautiful still.

"And you have my guarantee, Great Pharaoh, that she will bear you a son."

The guarantee of a son. He had spoken the words to her husband, but he had also thrown them at her like a challenge.

It was much, much worse than Neithhotep had feared.

"I could not get near to her." Neithhotep sank down on a gilded bench, and began to pull off her court finery. "In the one moment that could have been mine, my feet were trapped in shifting sand, and I could only watch mouth agape as my husband and the Vizier swept the child away.

"I don't understand why this child is so much more dangerous than the temptress you expected, my queen."

"Then allow me to gift you with the details, Hemon." She all but threw her collar at the slave waiting to take it. Would have thrown it had she not been so tired and it so heavy. "The child is a pawn in this game, her unfortunate fate to be born with beauty, grace and a *ba* so pure it lights her from within. She is as trusting as an ibis in the reeds. Methethy has probably been searching for one such as she for as long as he has been at the Court of the Pharaoh—one of the right face and form to enchant an old man who needs to be reassured of his physical power and of the right age and innocence to be used in enchantment."

"Magic," the scribe breathed.

The Great Menes believed in science and had constructed his capital around a massive temple to Ptah. His court welcomed doctors and astronomers, artisans and scribes, but there were no wizards.

Until now.

"Magic," Neithhotep agreed, removing wig and band both in one irritated swoop. "He will use her youth and her purity. He will bind it with the first blood of her body, and he will bring our husband to her when the auguries are right, bring her somewhere hidden from the eyes of Hathor and he will give the Great Menes a son."

"Your pardon great queen, but is that such a bad thing?"

She stared at the scribe for a moment then shook her head. "For the Pharaoh to have a son? No."

The Pharaoh had, in point of fact, seven sons—and twenty-two daughters but they were not the issue at this time. All seven of his male children had been born of concubines or slaves, not one of his wives had given him a living son although two had died trying.

"It is the way of the having," Neithhotep continued, pulling an offered shawl around her shoulders. "If we ignore for a moment, the magics; who do you think will control this son when he is born? And when Khepri comes in his own good time to carry the Pharaoh's *ba* to the underworld, who will hold power in this son's place?"

"The Vizier."

"Indeed. The girl will not be able to stand against him. In fact, she will turn to him, for he is all she knows in this strange place. He will wed the son to the mother to gain the sovereignty and will, in point of fact, rule Egypt. Will likely rule in truth the moment child names him heir."

"But for that to happen, he must ensure your death before death takes the Great Menes," Hemon protested, brows drawn down into a deep vee.

"While that is not likely to be a great problem for him, we have more at stake than my life alone."

"Great Queen!"

"What is at stake, Hemon, is the life of Egypt. For we *can not* ignore the magics, not even for a moment. For the son of Osiris made King to allow his divine body to be touched by the dark arts; to place in time upon the throne a Pharaoh born of such darkness..." She shook her head, staring off into the memories of a thousand rituals to honor the gods and keep the land strong.

"The gods will turn away from us?"

The voice of her chief scribe returned her to the present. "We will be fortunate if, in their anger, they only turn away. Too much attention from the gods can be worse than none at all."

"Then you must expose this wizard to the light of Ra!"

"And place myself in opposition to the plans of the Pharaoh? Force the people to chose between the White Crown and the Red? Divide us into two countries again? Place us once more at each other's throat? Is that what you would have me do?"

Her voice had grown sharper with every word, and she spit out the final question with force enough to drive Hemon to his knees.

"No, Great Queen."

Neithhotep watched him for a moment, saw how he trembled, and suddenly sighed, all the anger leaching out of her. "Get up, Hemon. You know how I dislike speaking to the top of your head."

"Yes, Great Queen."

"And you were right, I must do something." This was not the time to be old and tired, even though she was undeniably both. "Methethy's plan rests as this stool does, on three legs. If I can remove one, the plan collapses. There is no point in speaking to the

Vizier, and I am certain he has a thousand perfectly legitimate reasons why I can not see the girl—all of which I could counter in time, but time is on his side." She stared down at the stool, at the three legs ending in gilded copies of the hooves of the sacred bull. Without the bull, there would be no calf. "I will speak with the Pharaoh."

"Your pardon, Great Queen but do you actually think that the Vizier will not have given the Great Menes an answer for everything you might say?"

"I think the Vizier does not know everything I might say."

"Great Queen, the Vizier has said no one is to see the King of Two Lands without his authorization."

Neithhotep lengthened her stride so that, Kenamun, the Pharaoh's chief scribe had to scurry like a fat scarab to keep up. "I am not here to see the King of Two Lands."

She could feel the frown against her back. "But I thought…"

"I am here to see my husband who is in his private quarters. Does the Vizier rule my husband's entire life?"

He did. And they both knew it. But the walls of the palace had ears and the route she'd taken—from the farthest entrance to the Woman's Quarters—lead past many who were listening. Kenamun could no more answer in the affirmative than he could say what he truly thought of her making a eunuch her chief scribe.

"No, Great Queen, but…"

"Has my husband left instructions he was not to be disturbed?"

"No, Great Queen, but…"

"But what, Kenamum?" She stopped at the entrance to the Pharaoh's private quarters and spun around on one heel, spearing the officious little man with a look.

"But…" Kenamum glanced around. Realized the amount of attention their progress had attracted and sighed in surrender. "The King of Two Lands is not expecting you, Great Queen. His slaves will not have prepared a welcome suitable for one of your rank."

It was a pitiful protest, and he was well aware of it.

"I appreciate your concern for my rank," Neithhotep told him, smiling as he shivered slightly. "But the only welcome I desire is from my husband. Stay here." Her attendants bowed and stepped back as she swept regally forward and between the closest pair of guards.

The Vizier has said no one is to see the King of Two Lands…

The changes have been made by the orders of the Vizier…

…as I was instructed by the Vizier, Great Queen.

She frowned as she walked, trying to remember when Methethy had gained so much power. He had been assistant to the old Vizier—she remembered a sleek haired young man who watched and listened and learned. Toward the end, he was doing the Vizier's job and doing it very well. When the old man died suddenly, Menes gave the position to Methethy over the sons of the old Vizier. What had happened to the sons? It bothered her that she didn't remember. And how *suddenly* had the old Vizier died?

Why had no one ever noticed that Methethy was studying the dark arts?

I am becoming old, she sighed, silently. *I had intended only to knock the wind from Methethy's sails by befriending the girl he thought to put in my place. Now, I find myself all that stands between Egypt and the wrath of the gods.*

Next time I will remain sulking in my chambers like the sensible woman I am supposed to be.

"Great Queen, the Pharaoh is not…"

"Expecting me. I know." Neithhotep barely glanced at the slaves as she passed. There had been no priests lingering in the corridors. That was a bad sign.

Menes was sitting in a spill of sunlight, his head propped on one hand, a scroll in his lap he didn't see. He was asleep. Where others might think he was merely thinking deeply, she knew him so well she could see sleep resting on his shoulders. And not only sleep. In softened lines of muscle and in the angle of bone through oiled skin, she could see every one of his sixty-three years.

He had been a great king once. Would it hurt her more to discover he was, like the girl, a pawn in Methethy's plans or that he willingly defied the gods and risked his people?

She stopped far enough away so that he could wake and still deny he'd been sleeping. The conversation they were about to have held pit traps enough, they need not begin with him on the defensive. "Great Menes."

He started. Sleep fled. Clutching the scroll, he turned toward her, his eyes half-hooded. "Methethy said I should not allow you to see me alone."

"That comes as no surprise."

"He says that you are jealous of how I favor him."

"Does he?" Neithhotep snorted, moving around so that she could look the Pharaoh squarely in the eye. "He also says that I am jealous of your new bride. He seems to judge the emotions of others based on his own. I am jealous of neither."

"And yet you clearly labor under strong emotion," Menes murmured, smiling a little.

He knew her well after so many years, and it seemed the time they'd shared had weight enough to pierce the fog Methethy wrapped around the Pharaoh's mind.

"I am concerned," she admitted, beginning to hope.

"That when I have a new wife and son you will fall to nothing in my court?"

Those were Methethy's words. Hope died.

"I am concerned," she snapped, "of the consequences Egypt will suffer if you allow Methethy to use magics to get you a son."

Menes' lip curled. "What consequences?"

He knew. Not a pawn then. To her surprise, she felt relief. Better Great Menes be rash and stupid than helpless.

"The gods will not..."

Fingers white around the ebony arms of his chair, Menes surged to his feet. "I am a god!"

"Then you should know better!" Not the most politic of responses, particularly said in a tone she used when she lost her patience with children and slaves. Still, a retreat here would not help the situation. "Great Pharaoh, I have been a priestess of Hathor in all her many beauties my entire adult life, and there are writings that warn against this, against the *guarantee* of a son or a daughter. Great Hathor is the Mother of all Pharaohs, and children are her gift, not Methethy the Vizier's."

"And the goddess has not gifted me."

"She has gifted you twenty-nine times!"

"But never a son from a queen." He leaned forward his eyes glittering. "There will be a son from this queen—it has been promised me. Methethy gives me the dynasty you foresaw so long ago in your dream."

"Do not bring my dreams into this," she warned. "A son by the dark arts..."

"A son by any means!"

"Will prove you are still vital and strong?" She saw the answer in his eyes and continued before he could realize he'd given so much of himself away. "What of the girl?"

"She is the greatest treasure in my kingdom and once she has had her first blood, she will be mine, the mother of my son, and much exalted. You have no choice but to suffer that!"

"This is not about *me*. Will you allow a Queen of Egypt to be used so? Used as nothing more than a vessel for dark magic?"

He was angry now. "Do not pretend to me you care about the girl."

"I care about Egypt!"

"I will allow a Queen of Egypt to be fed to the crocodiles if it gets me my son," he growled. "Do not doubt me in this, Neithhotep."

They were both breathing heavily.

"I do not doubt you, Great Pharaoh." More was the pity. "Once your mind is made up, the years have taught me that it is futile to attempt to change it."

More than futile, the attempt would only hold him more stubbornly upon his course.

"You have been to see the Pharaoh, Great Queen."

"I am leaving his private chambers am I not?" She should have kept her voice carefully neutral, known better than to give rumor and gossip any fuel at all, but not even she, with years of experience to draw upon, could hide her new dislike of the Pharaoh's Vizier.

Motioning that the Chief Treasurer should go on without him, Methethy fell into step by her side. "It is not fitting that you walk the halls unescorted, Great Queen. Allow me to return you to your attendants."

"Is the Pharaoh not expecting you?"

"The Great Menes will be happy to wait while I do my duty by you, Great Queen."

"The Great Menes will be happy to wait for me, old woman." Neithhotep could hear the words beneath the words.

A crocodile smiled in much the same way.

She slowed her pace, forcing him to shorten his stride as she had earlier forced Kenamun to lengthen his. Petty, but she had asked neither of them to walk with her.

"I hear that you worry about Egypt, Great Queen."

"Your ears are fleet of foot if they had time to tell you that," Neithhotep snorted.

"My ears…? Ah, yes, my ears. The Pharaoh's security is my concern."

"Because I can not get to you unless I go through him?"

This new smile had honest amusement about it. No, not honest, but Methethy was definitely amused. "Plain speaking, Great Queen. I will gift you with the same—as you can not go through him, you can not get to me."

The backs of the Pharaoh's ceremonial guard were an armslength away. Beyond them, her attendants and the constant, ever-changing crowd of nobles, merchants, artisans and slaves. They must not know, must not be forced to chose sides. The Red Crown could not be seen in disagreement with the White. The union of Upper and Lower Egypt was too fragile still; war still too possible.

She turned and saw this knowledge reflected on Methethy's smiling face.

"I am tired," she sighed. "You may gloat tomorrow."

He bowed deeply and murmured for her ears alone. "I am sorry you take this so personally Great Queen, but you can not stop me."

"If he had said nothing in the throne room, if he had never mentioned a son—no, if he had left me out of this altogether, never started that stupid, 'the old queen is jealous of the new' I wouldn't have been in the throne room." Rubbing her temples, Neithhotep dropped down onto the bull-legged stool. "He wanted me there. He goaded me into going so that I would see the girl and he could let me know exactly what he is doing."

Frowning Hemon froze, a scroll half unrolled. "But why, Great Queen?"

"Methethy is not the type to hide his lamp under a basket— what is the point of orchestrating such a clever coup if no one knows? He needs someone to appreciate the full magnitude of what he does—but not just anyone. It must be someone worthy of knowing."

"So your life is not in immediate danger."

She thought about that for a moment. "No, I suppose it isn't." Her lips twisted into a self-mocking smile. "A little joy in every life it seems."

"He must have known you would try to stop him."

"He is young, he is powerful—he doesn't think I can. The Great Menes will not listen to reason; the people can not be made to chose between us, and both the Vizier and the girl are in a circle of the Pharaoh's guard, six guards deep. Not literally, Hemon," she added catching sight of the scribe's expression. "I merely mean they are so well protected by the Pharaoh that I can not prevent this insult to the gods without causing the very war I am trying to avoid."

"You can not reach the Pharaoh, the Vizier or the girl, Great Queen."

About to snarl that he tell her something she did not already know, her mouth closed with a snap as he did.

"You *can* reach the gods."

Although Hathor had a temple within the city large enough for all of Memphis to attend her many festivals, Neithhotep preferred the small wooden temple within the palace complex. As First Queen and High Priestess, she had spent half her life in this quiet sanctuary. Built to her exact specifications, it matched the temple her mother and her mother's mother had served the goddess in. She waved away the attentions of a lesser priestess, and walked slowly toward the enclosed sanctuary, the painted eyes of the goddess' many faces following her.

On the back wall of the sanctuary was a painting of Hathor as the Great Mother, her cow body stretched across the sky, Horus suckling at her teats, Ra held in safety between the spread of her horns.

You can reach the gods.

She should have thought of that herself.

But what to say?

Perhaps, she thought, laying the lotus blossoms she'd brought as an offering down before the Goddess, *this is when I should listen.*

But the Goddess stared out at her with wide eyes and remained silent.

Sighing, Neithhotep stepped back to the bench her age had granted her, and sat. Behind her, in the main part of the temple, she could hear a priestess—who was also a wife of the Pharaoh although she couldn't at the moment recall her name—casting auguries over a child.

I am old, Great Mother. She glanced down at her hands, at the way the skin wrapped loosely around the bone, at the marks of age across the wrinkled backs. *And I am used to knowing what to do. This wizard seeks to twist a child from your son, Horus made King, to raise up not your child as Pharaoh but his. If I stop him, I break apart the unity I have lived my life for. If I do not stop him, how can my country survive the just retribution of the gods so denied?*

Again, the Goddess remained silent.

Neithhotep felt her mind begin to drift. She had always found this aspect of Hathor comforting. The Great Cow, the Mother of all Pharaohs... Her thoughts slid over the little distance from the Great Cow to the Sacred Bull and from the bull itself to how she had thought of Menes as the Sacred Bull and from there to a memory of the first time she'd given Hathor's blessing as a priest collected the sacred seed into a clay cylinder corked tightly in its narrow end.

She snapped out of memory so quickly she couldn't catch her breath and had to sit, one hand clutching her chest while possibilities tumbled around in her head.

"As a Queen of Egypt, Berner-Ib becomes a priestess of Hathor the moment she finishes her first blood."

The Pharaoh flicked his fingernails against the arm of the throne. "She has not *had* her first blood."

The Great Menes was sounding sulky, tired of being denied. Good, that could only make him more susceptible. "Then—in Hathor's name—I must know when she begins so that the preparations for her ritual may be properly timed."

Lip curled, Methethy leaned forward to capture the Pharaoh's ear. "Great Menes, did this "ritual" occur with your other wives?"

"As Great Menes is aware," Neithhotep answered before the Pharaoh could, "his other wives were older. The ritual occurred but there was no need to know of the queen's blood or to have you involved."

"Then why am I now involved?" Menes demanded.

Neithhotep bowed as gracefully as her back would allow. "Your concern for your new queen's safety has made it difficult for me to deal with her directly."

If Berner-Ib does not have this ritual, then she may not be perceived as truly a queen. That could disrupt the smooth transfer of power later on.

No need to read the Vizier's thoughts, she could see them flowing like the Nile in flood across his face.

You are up to something old woman.

He was not much of a wizard, or he would have used the dark arts to scry her purpose. She had begun to suspect he was merely an ambitious man who stumbled upon one spell in his studies and now looked to use it to his advantage.

Momentarily startled by the rude gesture she made, hidden from the rest of the court by the wide sleeve of her overdress, Methethy recovered quickly and smiled. "I suggest, Great Pharaoh, that one of your new queen's women gift Queen Neithhotep with the information she desires when it occurs. I also suggest that Queen Neithhotep be granted access to the new queen for the duration of the ritual only, and that it be held in the small temple in the palace—so that she be from your side for the least amount of time."

"Let it be so."

"They appear to be slender vases."

"They are." The cork was well hidden within the narrow end. It hadn't been difficult to find artisans able to create what she needed—a potter for the narrow cylinders, a metal worker for the stands that held them erect and hid their true function. She had him create two dozen only to confuse the Vizier's spies. "The girl has begun to bleed, have you found the next night the stars will align as Methethy needs?"

"It was not easy, Great Queen. The magical texts are complex and with no wizard to guide me…"

"Do you have the night?"

"I believe so, Great Queen."

"You believe so?" When he nodded, his eyes miserable, she spared him a comforting smile. "Do not worry, Hemon. We deal with the gods. Belief is everything."

Neithhotep saw Methethy's eyes widen as he took in the Pharaoh's wives and daughters behind her. It was one thing to know their number, it was another entirely to see them gathered together in a small temple—all wearing robes identical to girl he escorted. He would have more trouble keeping her in view than he had anticipated. The wives and daughters were a smoke screen only.

Neithhotep had told none of them what she intended, allowing their curiosity about the new, isolated queen to draw them from the Women's Quarters.

She had made the Vizier wait outside the temple, a lesser priestess purifying both the new queen and her escort with lotus blossoms dipped in scented oil and droning out the longest blessing in the history of the Two Lands. When Neithhotep saw his patience reach the breaking point, she stepped forward and held out her hands for the girl.

Berner-Ib was as lovely up close as she had been from a distance. Neithhotep could almost understand how an old man could risk so much so foolishly for one melting glance from her dark eyes...her eyes...She glared at the Vizier. The girl's eyes were clouded and dull.

"I am taking no chances, Great Queen," he murmured as he placed the chill hand on hers. "If you had planned to appeal to her directly, I'm afraid you'll get nothing but placid agreement and mindless cooperation."

"She has been drugged."

"Relaxed," he corrected mildly. A hand waved back at the Pharaoh's guard suddenly surrounding the temple. "The Great Menes wishes for nothing to disturb your ritual and has sent guards to keep the curious from all your doors. He requests that you return his queen to me the moment the ritual is complete. And I will examine her," he added, "to ensure there has been no barrier placed in my way." Bowing mockingly, he stepping back through the temple door and stood, arms folded, at the edge of Hathor's domain.

By the time two of the Pharaoh's daughters lead Berner-Ib unresisting into the sanctuary, Neithhotep was as heartily tired of the whole thing as the waiting Methethy had to be and was becoming concerned that the drug would wear off too soon. She was prepared with drugs of her own but would rather not have to use them.

Finally, as she was beginning to despair, a warm, damp yeilding packet was pressed into her hand. Turning, she met the gleaming onyx eyes of Menes' youngest concubine.

The concubines had a good sideline going selling the Pharaoh's seed to the better apocotharies to be used in charms against impotence. Neithhotep refused to speculate on what the lesser apocotharies

used. Concubines not high in the Pharaoh's favor lived as good a
life as the first wife allowed, and today she had called in the debt.

"The goddess intercedes directly?"

*"Perhaps she fears that time is running out and the new queen is his last
chance—I do not question the will of the goddess."*

*Pouting a little, the girl twisted a shining strand of hair around her
fingers. "Great Menes has not called me to him since the new queen arrived."*

*"Neither has he been to the new queen," Neithhotep said pointedly. The
old woman and the young exchanged a speaking glance. "You must go to
him—I would not presume to instruct you on how to proceed from there, but it
is vital you lie with him. So, if I may, I suggest you convince him that you fear
he is no longer strong or vital enough to please you, and then let him prove you
wrong."*

"The Vizier..."

*"Will be escorting the new queen to the temple. You must begin the
moment he leaves the Pharaoh's side and use him as an excuse to leave quickly
when it is done."*

Neithhotep had wasted no strength on worrying whether the concubine could slip past the Pharaoh's guard into the temple—after all,
the girl had been trained to wrap men about her tiniest finger. Now,
as she slipped into the sanctuary, she pulled the slender clay tube
from under her robes. Warmed by her body heat, it would not chill
the prize poured into it.

The girl lay on the bench staring up at Hathor's gentle eyes.

"I miss my mother," she said suddenly.

"I know child." Neithhotep folded dimpled knees to make
room and sat as well, replacing the girl's legs across her lap. "There
are days I miss mine."

In three months there were rumors the new queen would bear the
Pharaoh's son. By five months the rumors were celebrated as truth—
all the auguries in every temple said the baby was a boy. The cel-
ebrations lasted for days. Great Menes was like a man reborn. He
worked the words "my son, Djer," into every speech. He forgot
aches and pains. He ate and drank like a young man.

The apocotharies did a growing business in impotence charms.

He even took up hunting again.

The ruling of the country was left to the Vizier as the Pharaoh rediscovered his youth—which was not a situation Neithhotep had anticipated, but it came as no real surprise.

She knew she lived only so Methethy could gloat.

Great Menes' protection continued to surround him like an army.

Berner-ib came to Hathor's temple when ritual demanded. Heavy with the Pharaoh's son, she was strong and healthy and willingly joined the prayers to Taurt, the hippopotamus Hathor wore as the protector of pregnant women and infants. As she prayed, Neithhotep prayed beside her.

They were together in the temple, the old queen and the young, walking slowly to the door where Methethy waited, when a young guardsman covered in mud stumbled toward them, wet sandals slipping against the polished floor.

Pushing past the Vizier, he dropped to his knees, gasping for breath. "Great Queen, the Pharaoh..."

"To me!" Methethy snapped, yanking him around. "Talk to me!"

"...something went wrong during the hunt, Great Lord! Great Menes has been killed by a hippopotamus."

As one, the two queens turned to stare at the statue of Taurt.

"Killed?"

"Carried off, Great Lord. But we retrieved the body."

Neithhotep turned again, and met the Vizier's eyes.

Methethy stiffened, suddenly realizing no army surrounded him now. Leaping forward, he grabbed the young queen by the arm.

To his surprise, she screamed.

Did she scream because he hurt her? Or because the news of the Pharaoh's death had at that moment penetrated the fog of her pregnancy? Neithhotep neither knew nor cared.

"He tries to injure the Pharaoh's son! Stop him!"

She wore the *deshret*. She could command when she had to.

Menes had been a great king once. And her husband.

But she could not get to the Vizier unless she went through him.

Although she had kept Egypt from the consequences, he had willingly dishonored the gods and they had turned their faces from him. Or toward him. Too much attention from the gods can be worse than none at all.

Pushing the girl into the arms of a priestess and waving the half circle of guardsmen back, she lowered herself carefully to one knee beside the bleeding body of the Vizier. Mortally wounded, he was not yet dead. "I told the Great Menes not to hunt the hippopotamus. I told him I knew his age as well as my own and he should leave this foolishness for younger men. I told him that a son would not return to him the strength and speed of his youth. I told him *not* to hunt the hippopotamus." Others would hear her words as mourning, but she saw that Methethy understood and leaned closer still. "You were wrong," she told him softly. "It wasn't personal; it was always politics."

She ruled over an Egypt combined because of him. Honored the man he had been and ruled as the Pharaoh Iti, crowned with the Red and the White in one crown in the name of his son, Djer, the second in a long line of Pharaohs destined to end finally in the Great Green Sea.

For the sake of this future, she had gone to him.

I'm very fond of Old Oreen. I can see the city laid out in my head.

Because I no longer write stories on spec, I had the idea for this story in my head for years before a market appeared and I actually wrote it down.

SWAN'S BRAID

HORSES. TERIZAN COCKED her head to one side and sifted the sounds of the city. A lot of horses. And no one rode in Old Oreen, although in the newer areas the laws had been changed. The sound of horses, therefore, could mean only one thing.

"Swan's back! The Wing has returned!"

Terizan grinned. Obviously, she wasn't the only one who realized what the sound meant.

Buzzing like a hive of excited bees, the crowd began to push back against the shops and stalls, treading both on merchandise too slowly snatched to safety and each other. Terizan saw a number of small children being lifted to better viewpoints and decided the idea had merit.

Slipping sideways into a narrow alley, she leapt for a cistern pipe, touched toe to window-ledge, and awning pole, and swung up onto the sandal maker's flat roof. Settling down beside a large clay pot of hot peppers like she belonged there—few people stopped to question first impressions—Terizan lifted a hand to block the late afternoon sun just as Swan's Wing rode into view.

The crowd didn't so much cheer as scream its appreciation.

Helmless, her short hair glinting like a cap of mountain gold, Swan rode in front, flanked a half length back by her second, the man they called Slice, and her standard bearer, a girl no older than Terizan who bore a bloody bandage around one eye as proudly as she bore the banner. There were a lot of bloody bandages, Terizan noticed. It seemed that Hyrantaz's bandits had not been defeated without cost.

But, in spite of the popular belief that it couldn't be done, they *had* been defeated. Slice carried Hyrantaz's head on a pike, the jaw bobbing up and down to his horse's rhythm.

They'll be going to the Crescent, Terizan thought, eyes locked on Swan as she passed, the red gold of her life-braid lying like a narrow line of fire against the dusty grey of her backplate. Terizan's heart pounded harder and faster than usual. *If I hurry, I can be there first.*

It seemed that half the city was already in the Crescent when Terizan arrived. She saw a number of people she knew, ignored most of them, and pushed her way in beside a friend in the front row. He turned languidly, and when he saw who it was, his heavily kohled eyes widened in mock horror. "You're sweating."

Breathing a little heavily, Terizan wiped her forehead on her sleeve. "I beg your pardon, Poli. I forgot that you don't."

Poli smiled and patted her cheek. "Not without cash up front." His smile was his greatest asset; he had a way of using it that convinced the recipient that no other living being had ever been smiled at in such a way. Terizan wasn't at all surprised that he'd been able to make his way through the crowd to a place beside the Congress' steps where he could not only see, but hear all.

The distant cheering grew louder and then spilled over into the surrounding crowd. Terizan wanted to leap up and down on the spot as others around them were doing, trying for their first look at the Wing, but she took her cue from Poli and somehow managed to stay calm.

"SWAN! SWAN! SWAN!" The chant became a roar as Swan reached the Congress' steps and reined in her horse. The Wing spread out behind her.

Terizan counted, and then counted again. There were only a dozen riders and two pack horses plus the standard bearer, Slice, and Swan herself. The twelve had seemed like a hoard in the close confines of the old city, but here, in a single line, they were frighteningly few. "That *can't* be all that survived."

"The rest are camped outside the city boundary," Poli said calmly, not so much to her as to the air. "Not in the same place they were camped when they made their kind offer to rid the trade road of Hyrantaz's pack of hyenas, but close enough."

"How do you know?"

Poli raised an elegant brow. "Do you honestly think I *wouldn't* know where a great many mercenaries who have just returned from a dangerous campaign, will no doubt wish to celebrate their survival and are soon to have a great of money are camping?"

"Sorry." She wondered briefly how he'd managed the entire statement in one breath, and then lost all further interest in Poli, the crowd, and the rest of the Wing as Swan raised a gauntleted hand.

"You're drooling," Poli murmured, his voice amused.

"Am not." But she wiped her mouth anyway. Just in case.

When the noise of the crowd finally faded in answer to Swan's command, the huge double doors of the Congress building swung open, and the council that ran the city-state of Oreen, stepped out. All seven were present and all in full robes of state; but then, they'd had plenty of warning, Terizan reflected, for the runner who brought the news of Hyrantaz's defeat had arrived at dawn, his shouted news jerking the city out of sleep.

"We have done what we were hired to do," Swan declared before any of the councilors could speak. Terizan shivered as the other woman's clear voice lifted the hair on the back of her neck. "We have come for payment."

Reluctantly dragging her gaze from Swan, Terizan could see how agitated some of the councilors were—constant small and jerky movements betrayed them. *They didn't think she'd win; the idiots.*

Councilor Saladaz, who'd recently been appointed to his sixth straight cycle as head of the Congress, stepped forward and cleared his throat. "There was the matter of proof," he said.

At a gesture from Swan the two pack horses were led forward and the bulky oilskin bundles heaved off to lie at the councilor's feet. "It was…inconvenient to bring the bodies," the mercenary captain told him dryly as ropes were untied. "These will have to do instead."

Saladaz leapt backward as the battered heads rolled out onto the Congress steps, and the crowd roared with laughter. Out of the corner of one eye, Terizan saw Poli raise a scented cloth to his nose, even though the smell was no worse than a great many parts of the city in high summer.

"They will have to be identified," Saladaz declared at his most pompous, struggling to regain his dignity.

"I'm sure there are those about who would be happy to help." From all around the Crescent came cries of agreement. Caravans that surrendered without a fight, Hyrantaz had stripped bare of everything save lives—it amused him to see a line of naked, helpless people stagger off towards the city, not all of them surviving to reach safety. "I'll take a third of what we're owed now and the rest at the end of the week."

Councilor Aleezan, who most considered to be the best brain in the Congress, stepped forward, laid a slender hand on Saladaz' shoulder and murmured something in his ear. Too far away to hear what was said, Terizan saw Saladaz nod. He didn't look happy.

"It will take a moment to count the coin," he said, tucking his hands into the heavy embroidered cuffs of his robe and scowling up at Swan. "If we can have it sent to you later today..."

"By noon," Swan suggested, in no way making it sound like the ultimatum everyone knew it was. "We'll be headquartering at The Lion."

"By noon," Saladaz agreed.

At a nod from his captain, Slice whipped his pike forward, and with a moist thud, Hyrantaz's head joined the pile on the Congress steps.

Terizan felt her knees go weak as Swan smiled. "To complete the set," she said and pulled her horse's head around.

"SWAN! SWAN! SWAN!" The cheers that followed the Wing from the Crescent echoed off the Congress, battering the councilors from two directions.

"She's so..."

"Barbaric?" Poli offered. That at least one of Swan's immediate ancestors was a Kerber—a loose confederacy of warring tribes that kept the west in constant turmoil—was obvious.

"Beautiful," Terizan snapped.

Poli laughed. "Well, you do know where she's staying. You could always wander in and..." He winked. "...introduce yourself." He laughed again as she paled. "Never mind, dear. I suppose you're still young enough for unrequited lust to have a certain masochistic fascination." Gathering up her hand, he tucked it in the crook of his arm. "I'm sure that with your skills you'll be able to get close enough to watch her without her ever suspecting you're there."

"I can't." Terizan pulled her hand free, suddenly remembering what the Wing's return—*What Swan*, she corrected—had pushed out of her head. "I'm going to the Guild today."

Poli looked at her for a long moment. When he spoke his voice was softer and less affected than she'd ever heard it. "That fall really spooked you didn't it?"

She nodded, trying not to think about the carving crumbling under her foot, about the long drop, about the landing. "If I'd broken something..."

"But you didn't."

"I'm not fool enough to think it'll never happen again." She spread her hands. "The Guild takes care of you. You know that, Poli. The whores had one of the first Guilds in the city."

"Granted. But somehow I just can't see you meekly accepting a Guild's control over your life." His features fell into the nearest thing to a frown she'd ever seen him wear. "You don't even take advice well."

When she shrugged she could still feel the ache in bruised bone and the terror of lying in the darkness and wondering what would become of her if her strength and agility had been destroyed. "I've made up my mind, Poli."

He shook his head. "And you're not likely to change it, are you?" Sighing, he leaned forward and lightly kissed her cheek. "Be careful, sweetling." Then, just in case he should be accused of sentiment, added archly, "Friends who don't expect freebies are rare."

The Thieves Guild believed that anyone who couldn't find them and gain access had no business applying for membership. The yellow stone building built into the inside curve of the old city wall showed no outward indication of what went on inside but Terizan had heard the stories about it most of her life.

"Getting into the house is just the beginning. You have to take a thieves' path to the Sanctum deep underground."

She didn't believe all the stories about the traps set along that path—wizards were too rare and far too expensive to use for such mundane purposes—but she believed enough to approach with caution. The roof would be guarded, likewise the windows that were even remotely accessible. Which left her with two choices; an inaccessible window, or the front door.

While there was a certain in-your-face kind of charm to walking in through the front door, Terizan decided not to risk it, as that was very likely the kind of attitude the Guild could do without. Besides, for a good thief, no window was truly inaccessible.

A hair shorter and a half a hair wider, she mused, squatting silently under the tiny window tucked into the eaves, *and I wouldn't have made it*. As it was she'd very nearly had to dislocate a shoulder and slice the curve off both hips to get through. Strapping her pack to her chest—no point in carrying equipment if it couldn't be reached quickly—Terizan started looking for a path into the heart of the Guild house.

Some considerable time later, she sat down on the floor of a grey-tiled hall and thought seriously about going out the way she'd come in. She'd dealt with all the locks, all the traps, and a dog—who'd been incredibly surprised to have a live and very angry rat tossed at him—but was no closer to finding the Sanctum than she'd been. Her stomach growled and she sagged against the wall, about at the end of her resources, personal and otherwise. Her pack was almost empty and the tiny lantern, now closed and dark at her side, was nearly out of oil.

And then she heard the voices.

Someone was making loud, angry accusations. Someone else was making equally loud, angry denials. Terizan sank lower and lower until her ear pressed against the floor. She still couldn't make out the words but she didn't need to. Smiling in spite of her exhaustion, she traced the edge of the tile next to the one she was sitting on and felt a pair of hinges and a wire.

Movement of the wire would very likely ring bells or the equivalent to announce the immanent arrival of company. Resisting the urge to hum, she twisted it up so that the trap door no longer affected it and carefully applied pressure to the tile. Underneath, was the traditional narrow chute. Bracing herself against the sides, she chimney-walked down, pausing only long enough to close the trap.

The voices were much louder.

"...pay for results!"

It was a man's voice but it made her think of Swan, dumping the heads in front of the councilors and demanding payment. Hardly surprising, as lately everything made her think of the mercenary captain. Earlier the tiny beam of light from her lantern had made her think of Swan's lifebraid gleaming against her armor. Sternly, she told herself to get her mind back on the business at hand.

"...received exactly what you paid for. If the end result was not what you desired that is not the fault of this Guild."

Her fingertips touched the bottom trap door. She could see the thin lines of light around three sides and knew this had to be the end of the line. The voices were directly below her.

"You haven't heard the end of this." The growled warning carried more force than all the shouting. A door slammed.

Muscles straining against the stone, Terizan turned herself around and gently pushed the trap door open a crack. She could see the edge of a scarred wooden table, piled high with junk.

"Although we fulfilled the terms of the agreement, he could cause trouble later," a new voice muttered.

A third voice sighed and admitted, "He could."

"Don't be ridiculous. He has no desire to have his association with us made public. Still, although I hate to do it, I suppose it wouldn't hurt to make some small attempt to mollify him." A woman's hand with long, narrow, ringless fingers reached into Terizan's limited field of vision and picked up a parchment scroll. It took her a moment to realize she was seeing it through a lattice work of rope. A net. Obviously, she was intended to go flying into it whereupon half the supports would break away, leaving her dangling helplessly in mid air.

Her blood singing, she opened the door a little further, grabbed the edges and swung back with it. At the far end of the swing, she let go. Momentum carried her curled body past the edge of the net. She uncurled just before she hit the floor, landing heavier than she would've liked.

She could feel astonishment wash over her like a wave as she straightened.

A half a dozen lanterns banished all shadow from the small room. Two of the walls were covered, floor to ceiling in racks of scrolls, one in a detailed map of the city, the fourth held a pair of doors. Spread out over the floor was a costly, though stained, carpet. A man, a woman, and a person who could have been either or both, sat behind the table and stared at her, open-mouthed. No one knew their names, but they called themselves the Thieves' Guild Tribunal.

Terizan bowed, conscious only of how exhausted she was. "I'd like to apply to the Guild," she said and stepped forward pulling out the last two items in her pack. "I took this dagger from the Captain of the City Guard, you may have heard it was missing, and this is Hyrantaz's earring—I took it this afternoon."

"From his head?" The man leaned towards her, his bulk suggesting he no longer actively indulged in the Guild's business. "You took it from his head in the Crescent?"

Terizan shrugged. There'd been so many people crowding around it had been embarrassingly easy—but if they didn't know that, she wasn't going to mention it.

As the fat man started to laugh, the woman looked speculatively up at the trap door.

"You brought the rat in with you," the third person said all at once, as though they'd come to a sudden illuminating realization. "It distracted the dog long enough for you to get away and then convinced the dog's handler that he was only after the rat. That's brilliant! But what would you have done if there'd been two dogs?"

Terizan shrugged again. "Gone looking for another rat?"

The fat man was now laughing so hard tears were running down his cheeks. "Took it from his head," he kept repeating.

The woman sighed audibly and came around the table. "I think it's safe to assume the Guild is interested in admitting you. Your arrival here was very...impressive."

"I thought I was *supposed* to make my way to the sanctum."

The older woman nodded. "You were. But no one's ever done it before."

"No one?"

"We'd previously considered it a major accomplishment if someone got safely into the lower levels of the building." As Terizan glanced up at the trap door and the net, she added, "Of course, a good thief is prepared for every possibility."

Terizan heard the silent warning that she not get cocky about her accomplishment, and so merely said, "I agree..." and then had no idea of how to refer to any of the other three people in the room.

"You may call me Tribune One." The woman half turned, waving a hand at first the androgyne and then the fat man. "These are Two and Three. You realize you must still complete an assignment of our choosing?" At Terizan's nod she turned her towards the door on the left, opened it, and pushed her gently through. "Balzador, get our candidate here some nourishment."

The thieves playing cards in the antechamber looked up in astonishment, and Balzador leapt to his feet with such energy that a Queen of Destiny fell from his sleeve and fluttered to the table. "Candidate?" he squeaked.

The tribune smiled. "Yes. She's just dropped in, and as we'd like to discuss her...test, I leave her in your capable hands."

As the door to the sanctum closed, Terizan heard Tribune One murmur, "You've got to admit, she's very clever." Then the latch clicked, and the iron-bound, oak planks cut off Three's reply.

The card players continued to stare. "Just dropped in?" Balzador said at last.

"All things considered," One murmured over her steepled fingers, "there's really no need for you to prove yourself to us. However, formalities must be observed."

Terizan, who'd been fed, feted, and won six monkeys in a quick game of caravan, bowed slightly.

"We have, therefore," One continued, "decided to make your test showy but not especially difficult. You have five days to bring us Swan's braid."

It might have been only because of the blood roaring in her ears, but the acoustics in the room suddenly changed. "Swan's what?" Terizan managed to stammer.

"Braid. In five days bring us Swan's life-braid."

By thieves' standards, The Lion was not in what could be termed a profitable part of the city. Three story sandstone tenements surrounded it, some with tiny shops on the first floor, the rest divided into small suites or single rooms. Almost all had external stairs, a few had roof gardens. Terizan lived in nearly an identical neighborhood—although closer to the center of Old Oreen—and knew exactly what the area had that would be worth stealing. Nothing much.

Except that Swan was at The Lion.

"In five days bring us Swan's life-braid."

She'd been too astounded to protest and had submitted without comment to being blindfolded and lead by Balzador up to a concealed door in an alley near the Guild house. *"When you come back,"* he'd told her. *"Come here. Someone will meet you and guide you down."*

When she came back. With Swan's braid.

She couldn't do it. Couldn't offer that kind of an insult to the most beautiful, desirable woman she'd ever seen. *Face it, Terizan,* she sighed to herself as she watched The Lion from the shadows across the street, *if you got close enough to actually touch the braid, your heavy breathing would give you away.*

The large louvered panels in the inn's front wall had been folded back, and the celebration in the common room had spilled out onto the small terrace. A number of the celebrants wore the red swan on their tunics, but Swan herself remained inside.

Wondering just what exactly she thought she was doing, Terizan crossed the street and entered the inn. No one noticed her, but then, not being noticed was one of the things she did best. With a mug of ale in her hand, she became just another of the townsfolk who wanted to get close to the heroes of the day.

Swan, holding court in the center of the common room, had been drinking. Her eyes were bright—*Like jewels,* Terizan thought.,—and her cheeks were flushed. In one hand she cradled an immense flagon and in the other a slender young woman who, as Terizan watched, leaned forward so that ebony curls fell over her face and whispered something in the mercenary captain's ear.

"You think so?" The flagon emptied, Swan stood, kicked her chair back out of her way, and tightened her grip around the young woman's waist. Red-gold brows waggled suggestively. "Prove it."

"Here?"

The Wing roared with laughter at the matter-of-fact tone, and a couple began clearing bottles and tankards off the table.

Swan cuffed the nearest one on the back of the head and then turned the motion into a courtly gesture towards the stairs. "I think not," she declared. "This lot has a hard enough time keeping up to me without my setting yet another impossibly high standard."

As the two women made for the stairs, amidst renewed laughter and advice, Terizan slipped back into the shadows.

The next night, she watched a nearly identical scene. *Nearly* identical in that while the young woman was again dark and slender, it was a different young woman. By the time Swan elbowed open the door to her room—both her hands being occupied—Terizan was on the tiny balcony of the building next door. By the time Swan began testing the strength of the bed, she was outside the window.

She'd spent the day thinking about the Guild. Without intending to, she'd found herself outside the building she'd fallen from, picking a bit of plaster off the ground. It couldn't have fallen when she had, but it could easily have been from the same disintegrating carving. She'd turned it over and over and finally crushed it, wiping the grey powder off on the edge of someone else's tunic.

Dying didn't frighten her as much as an injury that would put her out on the street to starve.

The Guild took care of their own.

When they were finished, and the sweat-slicked bodies lay tangled and sleeping, Terizan measured the distance from the window to the bed, judged the risk, and decided it was twice as high as it needed to be. After all, Swan had a preference for slender, dark-haired women.

"…a good thief is prepared for every possibility."

Including, it seemed, the possibility of stealing Swan's braid.

"Poli, I need you to make me noticeable."

One delicately plucked brow rose as Poli turned from his mirror to face her. "I beg your pardon?"

"I've decided to take your advice."

"Which bit of advice, sweetling?"

Terizan felt her cheeks grow hot and wished he wouldn't look at her like he was looking inside her. "Your advice about Swan," she growled.

"Did I give you advice about Swan?" He absently stroked cosmetic into his neck. "I don't remember, but then you've never taken my advice before, so I admit I'm at a loss."

"You said that since I knew where she was staying, I should wander in and…and…" Unable to finish as memories of Swan and the dark-haired young woman got in the way of her voice, she waved her hands and assumed Poli would understand.

His smile seemed to indicate he did. "How noticeable?"

"Do I really look like this?" Staring into Poli's mirror, Terizan found it difficult to recognize the person staring back at her.

"No, dear, I created this out of whole cloth." When she went to brush a feathering of hair off her face, Poli gently caught her hand. "Don't touch. That's not for you to mess up." He twitched at the silk tunic he'd insisted she borrow and smiled proudly at her reflection. "I merely emphasized features you usually keep hidden," he told her, touching her temples lightly with scent. "And if we add my small contribution to your natural grace—try not to move quite so much like a cat on the hunt, sweetling—you should be impossible for our mercenary captain to resist."

Her heart beginning to race, Terizan managed a strangled, "Thank you."

She felt Swan's eyes on her when she walked into The Lion and only the thought of lying in that alley with broken bones kept her moving forward. Tossing her hair back out of her eyes—why Poli thought being half blind was attractive she had no idea—she hooked a stool out from under the end of a trestle table and sat down. When a server appeared she ordered a flagon of the house white, mostly because she'd heard the landlord watered it. While she had to drink, she couldn't risk slowing her reflexes.

After a couple of long swallows, she looked up, met Swan's eyes, and allowed her lips to curve into the barest beginning of a smile. Then she looked down again and tried to stop her hands from shaking.

"Move."

"Ah, come on, Captain…"

"Zaydor, how would you like to stand fourth watch all the way to the coast?"

Terizan heard the man beside her laugh, obviously not taking the threat at all seriously. "Wouldn't like it at all, Captain."

Swan sighed. "How would you like me to buy you another pitcher of beer?"

"Like that a lot, Captain."

"How would you like to drink it on the other side of the room?"

Zaydor laughed again, and Terizan heard his stool scrape back. He murmured something as he stood, but all Terizan could hear was the sudden roar of her pulse in her ears. When Swan sat beside her, knee brushing hers under the table, she had to remind herself to breathe.

Although even Poli had long since given up trying to teach her to flirt, Terizan found her inability was no handicap as the mercenary captain needed little encouragement. She listened, she nodded, and she let her completely besotted admiration show. That was more than enough.

"Shall we?"

It took a moment before she realized that Swan was standing and holding out her hand. *I don't have to decide about the braid now*, she thought, allowing the other woman to draw her to her feet. Desire weakened her knees but she made it to the stairs. *I can wait until after.*

After.

Terizan stroked one finger down the narrow, red-gold braid lying across the pillow and tried to force herself to think. It wasn't easy as her brains appeared to have melted during the last couple of heated hours and dribbled out her ears.

Swan sighed in her sleep and shifted slightly, brushing damp curls against Terizan's hip.

If I'm going to do it, I should do it now. Do it and get it before she wakes. As she tensed to slip from the bed, she realized that she'd decided, at some point, to take the braid. It may have been when a particularly energetic bit of sex had pulled at joint still bruised from the fall; she didn't know, and it didn't matter.

She dressed quickly, quietly, slipping her sandals under her borrowed sash—there'd be climbing when she left the inn. Picking up Swan's dagger, she bent over the bed and lifted the braid.

A hand slapped around her wrist like an iron shackle and she found herself flat on her back, Swan crouched on her chest, and Swan's dagger back in Swan's hand.

"And with my own dagger." Gone was the cheerful lechery of the common room, gone too the surprisingly considerate lover—this was the mercenary captain who'd delivered Hyrantaz's head to the council. "Were you planning on making it look like a suicide?"

Terizan swallowed and managed to squeak out, "Suicide?"

"Or perhaps," Swan continued, her thoughtful tones in direct and frightening contrast to her expression, "you'd planned on making it look like an accident. Was I to have become entangled with my blade at the height of passion? I doubt you could make that sound believable, but then, *I'd* be dead so *I* wouldn't have to be convinced."

"Dead?" Incredulity gave her voice some force. "I had no intention of *killing* you!"

"Which is why I caught you with a knife at my throat?"

"It wasn't at your throat," Terizan snapped, temper beginning to overcome fear. "If you must know, I was going to steal your braid!"

"My braid?" Frowning, Swan sat back. Her weight continued to pin Terizan to the bed, but the dagger was no longer an immediate threat. One hand rose to stroke the narrow, red-gold plait hanging forward over a bare shoulder. "Why?"

"To prove that I could."

Swan stared down at her in confusion. "That's all?"

"Of course…"

"*…I suppose we should make an attempt to mollify him.*"

Her eyes widened as she suddenly realized who the Guild had decided to mollify. Councilor Saladaz had hired the Guild, had not been entirely satisfied, and Councilor Saladaz was a powerful man who could be a powerful enemy. If Swan's braid was stolen the mercenary captain would be humiliated and apparently that would make the councilor happy. The thief sighed as deeply as she was able considering that the larger woman still sat on her chest. The thought of Swan's humiliation didn't make her happy at all—although she supposed she should've thought of that before she tried to steal the braid.

Terizan stared up at the mercenary captain and weighed her loyalties. Adding the knowledge that she was at Swan's mercy to the scale—and ignoring the spreading heat that realization brought—she came to a decision. "I'm pretty sure the Thieves' Guild sent me to steal your braid in order to humiliate you."

"What?"

"They're sucking up to Councilor Saladaz. He wasn't entirely happy with something they had done for him."

Swan's eyes narrowed. "Why would Saladaz hire a thief?"

"To steal something?" Terizan bit her lip. *Oh great. Now on top of everything else she'll think I'm an idiot.*

To her surprise, Swan repeated, "To steal something," as though it were a brilliant observation. "Could a thief," she demanded, "be sent to *steal* through a mercenary troop and warn a bandit leader of an attack?"

"Someone warned Hyrantaz that the Wing was coming?"

"Someone, yes. One of my pickets said he thought he saw a slender, dark-haired woman slip through our lines. Moved like a thief in the night, he said. We found no trace of her, and we've had trouble with dryads before, but Hyrantaz *was* warned and now you tell me that Councilor Saladaz..." The name came off her lips like a curse. "...has been dealing with the Thieves' Guild." She leaned forward and laid her blade back under Terizan's ear. "Could Saladaz have hired a thief to warn Hyrantaz?"

Terizan sifted through every commission that she'd ever heard the Guild was willing perform. "Yes. It's possible."

"It wasn't you, was it?"

Her mouth gone completely dry, Terizan had never heard so deadly a threat spoken so quietly. Mutely, she shook her head.

Swan nodded. "Good." Then in a movement almost too fast to follow, she was off the bed and reaching for her clothes.

Terizan drew her legs up under her, ready to spring for the window but unable to leave. "You've been waiting for the dark-haired woman haven't you? That's why you've been..."

"Taking dark-haired women to bed?" Swan yanked the laces on her breeches tight. "I thought she might come back to finish the job so I made myself available."

She should've known that there'd be a reason, and she should've known that the reason had nothing to do with her. She tried to keep from sounding wistful. "Why do you believe me when I say I'm not the woman you're looking for?"

Swan twisted around and, just for an instant, so quickly that Terizan couldn't be certain she actually saw it, her expression softened. "Maybe because I don't want you to be." Then she bent and scooped her sword belt off the floor.

"Where are you going now?"

"To separate Saladaz's head from his shoulders."

"You're just going to march into the Congress and slaughter a councilor?"

"Not slaughter, execute." Her lips drew back off her teeth. "I lost a lot of good people out there, and that asshole is going to pay."

"And then?"

Hands on her hips, Swan turned to face the bed. "And then what?"

"And then what happens?" Terizan slid her feet into her sandals and stood. "I'll tell you. You'll be arrested because you have no proof Saladaz did anything and then a lot more good people will get killed when the Wing tries to get you out of jail."

"So what do you suggest?"

Terizan ignored the sarcasm. "I suggest we get proof."

Both red-gold brows rose.

"We?"

"Yeah, we. I, uh, I mean I owe you for not killing me when you had the chance."

One corner of Swan's generous mouth quirked up in the beginning of a smile. "Not to mention, for not turning you over to the city constables."

"Not to mention." She spread her hands. "The most obvious reason for Saladaz to want to warn Hyrantaz is that he wanted to keep him in business, and he could only want to keep him in business if he was taking a percentage of the profits."

Swan nodded, slowly. "That makes sense."

"The councilor has a reputation for admiring beautiful things so just suppose some of his payment was not in plain coin but in the best of the merchandise taken from the caravans."

"Suppose it was."

"Well, if someone should go into his town-house, they could likely find that merchandise."

"And how would this person know what merchandise to look for?"

"Easy; every fence and constable in Oreen has a list."

Swan looked surprised. "They can read?"

"Well, no, but scholars are cheap."

"All right." The mercenary captain folded her arms across her chest. "What does this person do once she's found the merchandise in the councilor's house? It won't prove anything if you steal it."

"We could take it to one of the other councilors."

"We don't know that the other councilors weren't in on this deal as well."

Terizan smiled; if only for the moment Swan had referred to them as *we*. "Then we take it to the people."

"Are you sure you're good enough for this?" Swan hissed, scowling at the iron spikes set into the top of the wall surrounding Councilor Saladaz's townhouse.

"If you hadn't been expecting a dark-haired woman to try something, I'd have had your braid."

"You think." She shook her head. "I don't like this. It's too dangerous. I don't like sending someone into a danger I won't face myself."

Terizan flexed fingers and toes, preparing for the climb. "First of all, you're too good a captain not to delegate when you have to and secondly, you're not sending me. It was my idea; I'm going on my own."

"Why?"

Because I'd cheerfully roll naked on a hill of fire ants for you. Something of the thought must have shown on her face, because Swan reached out for her. Terizan stepped back. That kind of a distraction she didn't need right now. "We settled that already. Because I owe you for not killing me."

"So you're going to kill yourself?"

She wanted to say it was perfectly safe, but she didn't think she could make it sound believable. "Just make sure there's a constable or two ready when I come back over the wall. Are your people in place?"

"Everyone's ready."

"Good."

Terizan had spent the early part of the day investigating the councilor's security arrangements while Swan readied her Wing for the evening's work. If it was to be done at all, it had to be done before full dark. The wall wasn't much of a problem. That it hid nearly everything behind it, was.

She'd heard dogs in the garden so she planned to avoid the garden entirely. Saladaz probably thought that the jump from the top of the wall to the twisted wrought iron of a second floor balcony was impossibly far. He was almost right. Two fingers on each hand hooked around the railing, and Terizan just barely got her feet forward in time to stop her body from slamming into the house.

The tall louvered shutters were closed but not locked, and before anyone could come to investigate the sound of her landing, she was moving silently down an upper hallway.

They won't be in the public rooms; they'll be someplace private, but not locked away. He'll want to enjoy them, gloat over them, or there'd be no point in taking the risk of owning them.

She passed a door that gave access into a room overlooking the inner courtyard, and all the hair on her body lifted. Unlike the Thieves' Guild, the councilor had obviously considered it worth the expense of having a wizard magically lock at least one of his doors.

Terizan smiled and kept moving. *Might as well hang out a sign...* She had no intention of trying to get around the spell and pick lock. Thieves who held exaggerated ideas of their skills quickly became decorations on the spikes of the Crescent, and a sensitivity to magic kept her safely away from things she couldn't handle.

At the next door, she sped though a bed chamber—in use, but given the hour, empty—went out the window, and onto the inner wall. There were servants working in the courtyard, but her long-sleeved tunic and trousers were close to the same shade as the brick, the short, corn-colored wig she wore was only a bit lighter, and, as good thieves learned early in their careers, people seldom looked up.

Fingers and toes splayed into nearly invisible cracks, Terizan inched across the wall. For one heart stopping moment, she thought there was a spell on the window as well, but then realized she was reacting to the distant feel of the door lock. The window had no lock, but then, why should it? The window looked over a private courtyard.

The room behind the window was a study. It held a massive table with a slanted writing surface, racks and racks of scrolls, a number of very expensive glass lamps—had she been on personal business the lamps alone would've brought a tidy profit—and a cushioned lounger with a small round table drawn up beside it. There were beautiful ornaments on display all over the room. The three she recognized immediately, Terizan slipped into her pack. A quick search of the scrolls discovered two sets of ebony handles chased with silver from the merchants' list of stolen goods. She took one and left the second. After all, something had to remain for the constables to discover. A malachite inkwell was far too heavy, so she contented herself with removing the set of matching brushes.

Even without the inkwell, the extra weight made the trip back along the courtyard wall much more interesting than the initial journey had been. A handhold, barely half a fingerwidth, began to crumble. She shifted her weight and threw herself forward; stretching, stretching. Her toes clutched at safety, and she started breathing again.

Down below, the servants continued doing whatever it was that servants did, oblivious of the drama being played out over their heads.

Bedchamber and halls were crossed without incident. Chewing the corner of her lip, Terizan measured the distance from the balcony back to the wall. Logic said it had to be the same distance going out as coming in, but logic didn't have to contend with a row of iron spikes and a weighted pack. *If I jump a little short, I can catch myself on the base of the spikes and listen for Swan. Once I hear her, I can pull myself up to the top.* She flexed her knees and tried not to think about what would happen if she jumped a little *too* short.

Then her hands were wrapped around the spikes. She bit back a curse as one knee slammed into the bricks and held her breath listening for the dogs.

"I'm telling you, Constable, I saw someone climb over this wall."

They were directly opposite her. Gathering her strength, Terizan heaved herself up onto the top and began to run, bow-legged, for the far end, her heels touching down between every fourth spike.

"There! Up there! Stop thief!"

Heart in her throat, Terizan threw herself up into a young sycamore tree and down onto the roof of a long, two story building. She had to get to the center of the city. At the end of the building, she danced along a narrow ledge, spun round a flag pole, bounced up an awning and onto the top of another wall. Behind her, the hue and cry grew as more and more people took up the chase.

"There he is! Don't let him get away!"

She touched ground, raced through a tangle of back streets—peripherally aware of the occasional large body that delayed pursuit—crossed the High Street with what seemed like half of Oreen after her, darted between two buildings and shrugged out of her pack. An ancient addition had crumbled, leaving a dangerous stairway to the rooftops. Terizan skimmed up it, hanging the pack on a projection near the bottom, and threw herself flat behind the lip of the roof just as the chase reached the alley.

"Look! There's his pack!"

Wincing a little as the thieves' stair crumbled under purposefully heavy footsteps, Terizan stripped off her trousers and turned them inside out to expose the striped fabric they'd been lined with. The sleeves came off the tunic and were stuffed into her breast band, significantly changing her silhouette. The wig she added to a pigeons' nest and couldn't see much difference between them.

With all the attention on the alley and her pack, it was an easy matter to flip over the far side of the building and into a window before anyone reached the roof by more conventional methods. It helped that two very large mercenaries were having a shoving match on the stairs.

By the time she reached the street, the mob had turned and was heading back to Councilor Saladaz's townhouse. Out in front ran a pair of merchants who'd lost everything to Hyrantaz's bandits.

"Your left tit is lopsided."

Terizan slipped a hand inside her tunic and shoved at the crumpled sleeve. "Better?"

"Much." Swan grinned and stepped out of the shadow of the doorway. She linked her arm through the shorter woman's and they began to walk back to The Lion. "Everything worked out just like you said it would. When the constable pulled the drawstring on the pack, everything in it fell out at his feet. He stared open-mouthed and a number of my louder officers stirred up the crowd, demanding to see each piece. When he held up the scroll ends, I thought the merchant they'd been taken from was going to spit fire. I've never seen anyone so angry. One of my people bellowed that the thief came out of Councilor Saladaz's house and that was all it took. The councilor is not a very popular man right now."

They could hear the roar of the crowd in the distance. If anything, it appeared to be growing both louder angrier as it moved away from them.

"I left plenty for them to find," Terizan murmured. "And I expect when they're done with Saladaz it'll occur to someone that perhaps the other councilors ought to be checked out as well."

"You're quite the strategist."

Terizan's face flushed at the emphatic admiration in Swan's voice. She mumbled something non-committal and kept her eyes on her feet.

"Given that what you do is illegal and the odds *have* to catch up to you sooner or later—which would be an incredible waste—have you ever considered taking up another profession?"

"Like what?"

"Oh...mercenary perhaps."

Terizan stopped dead and turned to stare up at the taller woman. Although her night sight was very good, the shifting shadows of dusk made it difficult to read Swan's expression. "Do you mean..."

"Thanks to that son of a leprous baboon..." She cocked her head as the background sounds of the crowd rose momentarily to a foreground scream of victory. "...who is even now being taken care of—I have a few openings."

"But I don't, I mean, I can't..." Terizan took a deep breath and tried again. "That is, I won't kill anyone."

Swan shrugged. "I can always get plenty of swords; brains are harder to come by. Besides," her voice softened and one hand rose to cup Terizan's face, "you're smart, you're beautiful, you're amazingly flexible; I think I'd like to get to know you better."

The thief felt her jaw drop, and the evening suddenly grew much warmer.

"There's no need to decide right away," Swan continued, her grin suggesting she could feel the heat of Terizan's reaction. "I'm not taking the Wing anywhere until we're paid, so we've got another two nights to see if we'll suit."

"SWAN! SWAN! SWAN!"

The people of Oreen screamed their approval as Swan and twelve members of the Wing rode into the Crescent. Although all seven members of the council waited on the steps of the Congress, only four were actually standing. Councilor Saladaz and two others stared out at the crowd with sightless eyes, their heads having joined Hyrantaz and his bandits.

"So is it love?"

Eyes locked on Swan, Terizan shrugged. "I don't know."

Poli shook his head and sighed. "So are you going to accept her offer?"

"I don't know."

"Does she know that you're responsible for all this renewed adoration?"

"Don't be ridiculous."

"I am never ridiculous. But I do recall being asked to spread a rumor that Swan was behind the discovery of Saladaz and his little business arrangements." He smoothed down his tunic and smiled. "I guess he should have paid her right away and got her out of town."

Terizan grinned as Councilor Aleezan handed over the rest of the Wing's payment and the crowd went wild. Then the grin faded. "Poli, what should I do?"

He had to place his mouth almost on her ear to be heard over the noise. "What do you want to do?"

What *did* she want to do? Swan was exciting, exotic, exhausting, and not an easy person to live with. The Wing would accept her initially for Swan's sake and in time for her own, but would she ever accept the Wing? They were as good at killing people as she was at stealing from them and she'd never really approved of slaughter for a living.

His manicured nails digging into her shoulders, Poli shook her. "Terizan, you have to make a decision. What do you want to do?"

"I want…" She didn't want to worry about injury or sickness or age. She didn't want to leave the city. And as much as she desired her, adored her, maybe even loved her, she didn't want to spend the rest of her life trying to keep up to Swan. Not to mention that she strongly suspected she'd hate sleeping in a tent. "I want to join the Thieves' Guild."

Poli released her and gracefully spread his hands, the gesture clearing asking, "So?"

"SWAN! SWAN! SWAN!"

Terizan watched the Wing, and Swan, ride out of the Crescent on a wave of adulation. She'd agreed to meet them at the Lion and give the mercenary captain her decision. Fortunately, she thought Swan would understand. Unfortunately, if she wanted to join the Thieves' Guild, she had a small problem.

"SWAN! SWAN! SWAN!"

The life-braid gleamed like a line of fire down the back of Swan's armor. Terizan chewed on a corner of her lip and suddenly smiled.

Maybe not.

"Uh, Tribunes…" His eyes wide, Balzador peered into the Sanctum. "Uh, Terizan is back."

One looked up from a detailed plan of the Congress and frowned at his expression. "Did you forget to use the blindfold again?"

"N...no. I used the blindfold but..."

"Good." Two cut him off. "Remember, she isn't a member of the Guild until she fulfills our commission. Although," he added in an undertone, "all things considered, we no longer really need to mollify our late client."

"Y...yes, I know but..."

Tribune Three sighed and turned from racking an armload of scrolls. "Well, if she's back, where is she?"

"Right here." Terizan pushed past the stammering Balzador and into the Sanctum.

One glanced up at the trap door in the ceiling, then smiled. "And did you bring us Swan's braid?"

"I did." Reaching behind her, she pushed the door the rest of the way open.

Swan swept off her blindfold, and bowed, eyes gleaming.

The tribunal stared, open mouthed, fully aware that if anything happened to their Captain, the Wing would tear the city apart.

"What is the meaning of this," One demanded at last.

Terizan echoed Swan's bow. "You never specified that I had to remove the braid from Swan."

"We, we," Two sputtered, then Three began to laugh.

"We never did," he chuckled, slapping meaty thighs. "We never did. We said bring us Swan's braid and she most assuredly has done that."

Two's narrow lips began to twitch.

Finally, One sighed and spread her hands in surrender. "Welcome to the Guild, Terizan." Almost in spite of herself, she smiled. "We'll remember to be more specific in the future."

"I'm almost relieved you didn't take me up on my offer." When Terizan looked hurt, Swan cupped her chin with one hand. "You'd steal the company out from under me in a month."

"I don't think so," Terizan began, but Swan cut her off.

"I do. I've seen you operate. Next time I'm back this way, you'll be running that Guild."

Terizan frowned. There *were* a number of things she'd like to change. Most of them ran out her ears as Swan bent and kissed her good-bye, but she was sure she'd think of them again. Just as soon as she could start thinking again. She swayed a little as Swan released her.

Swan swung up into the saddle and flicked her braid back over her shoulder. "You've stolen my heart, you know."

"Come back and visit it."

"I will."

Terizan raised a hand in farewell as Swan rode out of the stable yard then climbed to the top of the tallest building in the neighborhood to watch the Wing ride out of Oreen.

"Next time I'm back this way, you'll be running that Guild."

She dropped onto a balcony railing and danced along it to a narrow ledge. The day was fading and she had a lot to do. Plans to make. She grinned and touched her hip. Safe in the bottom of a deep pocket, sewn into a tiny, silk pouch, was a long red-gold hair, rippled down its length from the weave of the braid.

This entire story was generated by a line from the musical "Once Upon a Mattress":

"And look at Snow White; she had seven men working for her day and night. Oh sure, they were short but there were seven of them."

Then the tale grew, as they do, in the telling.

IN MYSTERIOUS WAYS

"YOU WANT ME to steal *what?*"

"The Eye of Keydi-azda."

Terizan stared at the Tribunal in disbelief. Her question had been rhetorical; she'd heard them the first time. "Keydi-azda is a god."

"One of the so-called small gods." Tribune One cocked her head and raised a slender brow. "Do you have a problem with that?"

"Actually, yes. People who steal from gods spend the rest of their very short lives in uncomfortable circumstances; then they endure a painful eternity of having their livers eaten by cockroaches."

Tribune Three snickered.

One ignored him so pointedly his cheeks reddened. "You're saying you don't think you can do it?"

"No. I'm not saying that." Terizan spread her hands in what she hoped was a placating manner—the last thing she wanted was to irritate the Tribunal. Actually, the last thing she wanted was to steal the Eye of Keydi-azda, but not irritating the Tribunal came a close second. They weren't particularly fond of her as it was. "I'd just rather not."

Tribune Two's pale eyes narrowed and thin lips opened to make a protest. A sharp gesture from One closed them again.

"Very well. As you don't seem to *approve* of this job…"

Terizan winced, realizing that the Tribune's choice of words had not been accidental and reflecting that she really had to learn to keep her opinions to herself.

"…you may go."

A little surprised it had been that easy, Terizan bowed gratefully. She had her fingers around the heavy iron latch that secured the door to the Sanctum when One added, "Send in Balzador, would you?"

"Balzador?" She whirled around and swept an incredulous glance over the three who ran the Thieves' Guild. "You're going to send Balzador to steal the Eye? There's no way he's up to something like that."

"Then who is?" One asked, steepling long, ringless fingers and examining Terizan over the apex. "If you are unwilling, who do you suggest we send to the Temple of Keydi-azda in your place?"

Who indeed. Mere days before she'd joined the guild, Terizan had found herself on a narrow ledge that lead no where. To go back meant almost certain discovery and her head adorning a spike in the Crescent. To go on meant trusting her weight to an ancient frieze of fruiting vines carved into the side of the building. That feeling of having no choice but a bad one had been remarkably similar to what she felt now.

The only sound in the Sanctum was the quiet rustle of fabric as Three shifted his bulk into a more comfortable position. Even the lamps seemed to have stopped flickering while they waited for her reply.

Either she became responsible for the thief they sent, or they sent Balzador, who didn't stand a chance.

She lived again through the moment when the carving crumbled under her foot and she plummeted two stories down, only luck keeping her from finishing the fall as a crippled beggar.

The guild took care of their own, but at a price.

"You've already accepted the contract?" she said at last.

"We have."

"To steal the Eye of Keydi-azda?"

"Yes."

"I'm going to need more information than that."

Three picked up a narrow scroll from among the junk piled high in front of him and began unrolling it. "We assumed as much."

"You assumed rather a lot," Terizan muttered sinking cross-legged down onto a stack of recently acquired carpets.

One smiled, her austere expression growing no warmer. "Yes," she said, "but then, we can."

Terizan walked slowly down the Street of Prayers, grinding her teeth. She hated being backed into a corner, and she really hated the smug, self-satisfied way Tribune One had done it. When an orange-robed follower of Hezzna stepped into her path and attempted to hand her a drooping palm frond, she glared up at the veiled face and growled, "I wouldn't."

Behind the orange haze, the kohled edges of the acolyte's eyes widened. Holding the frond between them like a flaccid green sword, he stepped back out of her way.

Feeling a little better, Terizan quickened her pace. Traffic picked up in the late afternoon, and she didn't want to waste the anonymity the crowds provided. At the top of the street, junior priests, robed in pale blue, stood on the four balconies of the Temple of the Light and sang out the call to the sunset service. At the bottom of the street, junior priests, wearing identical robes of dark grey, stood on the balconies of the Temple of the Night and did the same. Up and down the Street of Prayers, the people of Old Oreen hurried to complete the day's business. Very few of them were heading to either service. As far as Terizan could see, none of them were praying.

According to the Tribunal, Keydi-azda's Temple shared a wall on one side with the imposing bulk of the Temple of the Forge and on the other with the building where the Fermentation Brotherhood held their weekly meetings. Two stories high but only one room wide, its fronting built of the same smoke-blackened yellow brick that made up most of the rest of the city, it was an easy temple to overlook. A weather worn eye carved into the keystone over the arched door gave the only indication of what waited inside.

The door lead to a short hall and another door. Drawing in a deep breath and reminding herself that she was only scouting the job, Terizan stepped over the threshold.

It was quiet, dim, and smelled of sandalwood.

At one end of the rectangular room, shelves rose from tiled floor to painted ceiling. Petitioners could either leave an offering or remove an item they felt they needed. The shelves were half empty. At the other end of the room, stood a small altar where a cone of incense burned in a copper dish.

Above the altar was a second carving of an eye. More ornately carved than the exterior eye, it also boasted an iris of lapis lazuli centered by an onyx pupil.

Keydi-azda was the god of comfort. After a meal, fat men would loosen their belts and sigh, "Bless Keydi-azda." Terizan had murmured the blessing herself on occasion when a good night allowed her to pay for more than bare necessities. Everyone knew the name of Keydi-azda.

Not many, it seemed, came to the temple.

Terizan sang The Drunken Baker quietly to herself. Twelve verses later, she was still alone.

"The priest is old," Tribune Two had said, *"and sleeps soundly."*

"Must be napping now," Terizan muttered, walking silently toward the altar, another hair rising off the back of her neck with every step. She'd just have a closer look and be gone before anyone noticed she was there.

The Eye sat loosely within its collar of stone.

If I slid a blade behind it, it'd just pop off into my…

"…hand."

Surprise, as much as the unexpected weight, nearly sent the disc crashing to the floor. Although barely larger than her palm, it curved out two fingers thick in the center of the onyx and was heavier than it looked.

Heart beating so loudly an army could've marched through the temple without her hearing it, Terizan slipped the Eye under her clothes and sashed the flat side tight against her belly. Braced for contact with cold stone, she found it unexpectedly warm.

Then she turned and walked out.

No one tried to stop her. Feeling slightly separated from the world as she knew it, she made her way back to the Thieves Guild and handed the Eye of Keydi-azda over to a grinning Tribune Three.

It was as simple as that.

Even Balzador could've done it.

A triple knock jerked Terizan up off her pallet, heart in her throat, and propelled her halfway out the narrow window before her brain began working.

Constables didn't knock.

"Get a grip," she told herself firmly, drawing her leg back over the sill and rubbing at the place where her knee had cracked against the edge of the sandstone block. "It's probably just Poli wondering if you want to go to the dumpling maker's with him." The sun suggested it was past noon, late enough for Poli to be up and thinking of his first meal of the day.

Tugging the worst creases out of her tunic, she limped to the door, drew the bolt, and swung it open.

One artificially arched brow arched even higher as Poli's critical gaze swept over her and around the tiny room. "You're sleeping late. Busy night?"

Terizan ignored the implication. "Bad dreams." She stepped aside to give him room to enter. "I must've woken up a hundred times."

"Guilty conscience." Removing a pile of clothing from the only chair, he sat and smiled beneficently. "Nothing a little food won't cure. Do try to wear something that won't embarrass me."

"Like there's a lot of choice," she muttered dragging her only clean pair of trousers down off a hook. Shoving one foot into a wide leg, she caught her toe in the thieves' pocket above the cuff, bounced sideways, tripped over the tangled blanket, and fell to the sound of ripping cloth, missing a landing on the pallet by inches.

As she swore and rubbed her elbow, Poli surveyed the split seam and shook his head. "You've got to start shopping off a better quality of laundry line, sweetling. Wear the dirty ones before we starve to death."

"The worst of it is," Terizan sighed, doing as he suggested, "I didn't steal them. I bought them from old man Ezakedid, and he told me they were only second hand." She shoved her feet into her sandals and bent to pull the straps tight. Without straightening she looked from the piece of broken strap in her left hand, to Poli. "This is not starting out to be a very good day."

The dumpling maker had sold out of cheese dumplings so Terizan rolled her eyes, ordered lamb, and bit through her tongue while trying to chew a chunk of gristle soft enough to swallow. She spit out a mouthful of blood and picked up her cup.

"There's a dead fly in my water."

"Not so loud," Poli advised, wiping his fingers on the square of scented cloth he was never without, "or everyone will want one."

Leaning forward, he lowered his voice. "Do you see the young lady in the yellow scarf? There by the awning pole? I think she's trying to catch your eye."

Terizan refused to look. "The way my luck's been going today, she's probably an off duty constable."

"I don't think so."

"Poli, I'm not interested." She shifted in place and slipped a hand up under her tunic to scratch at her stomach.

"You're never interested, sweetling."

"That's not true."

"No? If everyone in the city had your libido, I'd starve. You're not harboring a broken heart are you? I told you not to pursue a relationship with a mercenary."

"What are you talking about? You practically threw me into her bed."

"Nonsense." His lazy tone sharpened. "Can I trust that the itch you're chasing is not caused by some sort of insect infestation?"

"I have no idea, but its driving me crazy." Fleas would be just what she needed.

"Let me look."

Figuring that the little Poli didn't know about skin could be inscribed on a grape with room left over for the entire Book of the Light, Terizan leaned away from the table and lifted her tunic a couple of inches.

"It's just a rash," he announced after a moment's examination. "Most likely caused by something you've leaned against—something circular from the look of it. I don't think it's dangerous, merely uncomfortable."

Something circular.

Through the sudden buzzing in her ears Terizan heard her voice tell the Tribunal, *"People who steal from gods spend the rest of their short lives in uncomfortable circumstances."* She hadn't meant *uncomfortable* literally but why not; Keydi-azda was the god of comfort after all. And it certainly explained the way her day had been going.

"All right, sweetling. What have you done?"

She shook herself and pulled down her tunic. A quick look around the dumpling maker's cantina showed no one sitting close enough to overhear. "I did a job for the guild..."

By the time she finished, Poli had paled beneath his cosmetics. "You stole the Eye of Keydi-azda?" he hissed. "Are you out of your mind?"

"I can't see as I had much choice."

"They gave you a chance to send someone else. Any other thief would've taken it."

She laid both hands flat on the scarred table top and leaned forward until their noses were almost touching. "I'm *not* any other thief."

Poli closed his eyes for a moment, then he sighed. "No, you're not, are you. Well, there's only one thing to do. You've got to put it back."

"I can't. I gave it to the Tribunal. I don't know who has it now."

"Can't you find out?"

"Sure, I mean the guild always insists on a written contract for blackmail purposes. All I'd have to do is break into the Sanctum and steal it."

Poli ignored the sarcasm. "Good."

Terizan opened her mouth to protest then closed it again. *People who steal from gods spend the rest of their short lives in uncomfortable circumstances.* A short, uncomfortable life. She'd planned on a long life. She had too much to do to die young. "Oh bugger," she sighed. Although she'd certainly intended to challenge the Tribunal's authority, she'd expected to have a little more time to strengthen her position in the guild. Fighting the urge to scratch, she dipped her finger in her cup and traced a circle within a circle on the table—driving a splinter in under the skin far enough to draw blood. "All right, you win. I'll find out who has it and I'll steal it back."

"Your guild encourages free-lance work," Poli reminded her.

"I doubt this is what they had in mind," she muttered around her injured finger.

He waved a dismissive hand. "Then they should have been more specific."

"You're not helping, Poli. First problem, there's always at least one member of the Tribunal in the Sanctum."

"Don't they trust you?"

"We're thieves, of course they don't trust us." Eyes narrowed, she stared down at rapidly evaporating sketch. "I think I can get rid of the Tribune, at least for a few minutes…"

The herbalist Terizan decided to use had a small shop facing the cramped confines of Greenmarket Square. As it wasn't an area she frequented, personally or professionally, she hoped she'd be neither recognized nor remembered. Ignoring sales pitches as wilted as the vegetables, she made her way around the edges of the square and, just outside her destination, stepped on something soft that compacted under her sandal.

It turned out *not* to be a rotting bit of melon rind.

The dim interior of the shop smelled of orange peel and bergamot. Bundles of dried herbs hung from hooks in the ceiling and were packed into stacks of loosely woven baskets. Bottles and boxes crammed the shelves along one wall. In one corner, a large terra cotta jar sweated oil. Dust motes danced thickly in the single beam of light that managed to penetrate the clutter.

As Terizan entered, stained fingers parted the beaded curtain in the back wall and an ancient man shuffled through the opening. "How may I help you?" he wheezed. "Love potions? Women's problems? A soothing balm to ease the pain of inflamed eyes?"

"Cazcara zagrada powder."

"Ah, constipation." He squinted in Terizan's general direction. "I should have known from the smell."

"That's on my shoe!"

"Of course it is. Two doses, one monkey."

"I need four."

"Four?" Shaking his head, he lifted a stained basswood box onto the counter, opened it, and spooned the coarse brown powder onto a piece of fabric with an amazingly steady hand. "Be careful," he told her as he twisted the corners up and tied them off with a bit of string. "I don't care how backed up you are, just one dose of this will put you in the privy blessing Keydi-azda. And that's no laughing matter, young woman!"

"Trust me, I'm not laughing." Wiping the snarl off her face, Terizan handed over the two copper coins.

The large antechamber outside the Sanctum smelled strongly of onions. Peppers would've been better but onions would have to do. Terizan traded jests with a group of thieves playing caravan then made her way across to the pair of kettles steaming over small charcoal fires, the four doses of cazcara zagrada palmed and ready. "Is it done yet?"

"Is it ever done before sunset?" Yazdamidor growled. He'd been a thief until a spelled lock cost him the use of one arm. Now, he cooked for the Guild.

"Look, Yaz, I'm in a hurry..."

"Got a job, does you?" He snorted, not waiting for her answer. "Course you do, smart one like you." Scooping a bowl of barley mush out of the first kettle, he thrust it at her. "There's always someone what can't wait. Go ahead, just don't blame me if it ain't cooked through."

She doctored the stew as she scooped it onto her mush, stirring in the powder with the ladle and hoping that she'd got as little of it as possible into her own food. Unfortunately, the way things had been going, she expected an uncomfortable evening. The meat *was* cooked through but, since the goat had probably died of old age, she couldn't see as it made much difference.

She finished before anyone else started. As the caravan players filled bowls and moved to join her, she clutched her stomach, muttered a curse, and hurriedly left the room. Racing up the stairs, only partially faking, she heard Yazdamidor laugh and shout, "Told you so!"

Now, it was all a matter of timing.

Most thefts were, patterns being easier to break into than locks.

In order to join the guild, thieves were expected to make their way through the guild house to the inner Sanctum. The rumors that reached the city of deadly traps and complicated protections were exaggerated but not by much. Terizan was the first thief to have ever made it all the way. Since no one had done it since, it was safe to say she was also the only thief to have made all the way.

As a member of the guild, her access to the House had improved since that afternoon and, this time, it wasn't necessary to enter through an attic window. Even avoiding the dogs, she only had to cover half the distance. Disconnecting the wire set to ring warning bells inside the Sanctum, she pried up a tile and laid an iron bar—removed from a trap she'd disabled a few moments earlier—across the opening. The rope tied to the middle of the bar she uncoiled as she chimney-walked down the narrow chute to the trap door at the bottom. Easing it open a fingerwidth, she listened.

Nothing.

The Sanctum was...

Then she heard the scraping of a horn spoon against the side of a wooden bowl and hurriedly rebraced her feet. Regrettably, since she'd already begun to move, the angle was bad and she wouldn't be able to hold her position for long. As the muscles in her lower back began to cramp, she wondered if the Tribune about to be so abruptly visited would believe she was just reliving past glories. Probably not.

It didn't help that her stomach felt as though fire ants were nesting just below the surface of her skin. She squirmed to ease the itch and her left shoulder slipped.

Oh crap...

As she fell, she grabbed the edge of the trap door and used it to swing out past the net waiting to scoop up those who entered without proper planning. A summersault in midair and she landed facing the Tribune's table.

The empty room echoed to the sound of footsteps pounding up the long flight of stairs used to bring clients unseen into the Sanctum. It was the only direct route into the heart of the guild house and the upper end was both trapped and guarded. It was also the most direct route to the privies.

Silently thanking whatever gods she hadn't pissed off, Terizan wiped sweaty palms on her thighs, vaulted the table, and jerked to a stop in front of the shelves of scrolls. There were a lot more than she'd noticed from the other side of the room.

Think, Terizan, think. They have to have a system or they'd never find anything themselves. There appeared to be three sections. *One for each Tribune? Why not.* She moved to left. Tribune One had given her the job. *Okay. This happened yesterday, it's got to be right on top.*

It wasn't.

Terizan couldn't read but she figured she'd recognize the hieroglyph for the Eye. Nothing looked familiar on any of the scrolls she opened.

I don't believe this...

"...eats anything. It's no wonder he's made himself sick." Tribune One's unsympathetic observation drifted down the stairs.

If the Tribunes caught her in the Sanctum, they wouldn't just throw her out of the guild, they'd throw her out in little bleeding pieces.

Heart pounding Terizan leapt up onto the table and jumped for the hook that supported the near end of the net. Something moved under her foot and she almost didn't make it. Glancing back, she saw she'd crushed the middle of a scroll as big around as her fist.

Bugger, bugger, bugger...

Blood roaring in her ears, she dropped back onto the table, scooped up the scroll, stuffed it down one trouser leg, and jumped again.

"Look at that, he's left the door open."

Her fingers closed around the end of the rope she'd left hanging and, knees tucked up against her chest to avoid the net, she transferred her weight. Her swing forward reopened the trap door. She scrambled into the ceiling, braced herself against the sides of the chute and flicked the rope up out of the way so the springs could close the door again.

"What was that?"

One snorted. "Probably rats."

"Four legged or two?"

High overhead, pulling herself out into the corridor, Terizan missed the answer.

She couldn't take the scroll back to her room—if the information it contained was important enough the Tribunal would hire a wizard to search for it—so she took it to the only safe place she could think of.

Although there were three lamps lit, the temple of Keydi-azda was deserted—no petitioners, no priest. A linen cloth hung over the empty socket that should have held the Eye. Fully intending to leave the scroll on one of the shelves, Terizan leaned against the wall under a lamp and unrolled it. If it came to a confrontation with the Tribunal, any information she could glean might help to keep her head on her shoulders.

Within the outer sheathing, a number of parchment pages were attached to the upper handle. Nothing on the first page looked familiar.

"I've got to learn to read," she muttered. Centered in the top of the next page, the Eye of Keydi-azda stared out at her. "I'll be fried..." Remembering the near fall that had ensured she pick up this particular scroll, she glanced toward the altar and added a quiet,

"Bless Keydi-azda." Just in case. She couldn't make out who'd paid for the job so she turned another page.

"The Staff of Hamtazia?"

And another page.

"Amalza's Stone?"

Altogether, since the last dark of the moon, seven icons had been stolen, all from small gods. Two days ago, Terizan wouldn't have much cared but she was beginning to realize it was the small things that made life worth living.

The hieroglyph on the bottom of the last page had to represent the people who'd hired the Guild for all seven thefts. Unfortunately, it was a incomprehensible squiggle as far as Terizan was concerned.

"May I help you, child?"

She hadn't heard the priest approach. His quiet question provoked a startled gasp and a few moments of coughing and choking on her own spit. When she finally got her breath back, she wiped streaming eyes with the palm of one hand and glared at him.

"Oh my, that didn't look to be very comfortable at all," he murmured sympathetically.

All things considered, Terizan bit off a rude reply and shoved the scroll under his nose. "Do you recognize this?"

"Oh yes. It was made by one of the priests of Cot'Dazur. See the three points and the dots below…"

"Who?"

The priest sighed and folded his hands over a comfortable curve of belly. "One of the new gods. There's a huge temple in the new town, all painted plaster and lattice work. Very stylish but not much substance, I'm afraid."

Scratching thoughtfully, Terizan frowned and wrestled these new pieces into place. "How does a god *get* substance?"

"Time." He smiled a little sadly. "Those who believe build it up, over time."

"Suppose you didn't want to wait?"

"You wouldn't have a choice, child. It isn't something you can suddenly acquire." Over their heads, the lamp sputtered and went out. "Oh my, I'd best get more oil." He patted her arm with one soft hand and waddled off toward the altar.

Uncertain of how to address him, Terizan took a step forward and called, "Your worship?"

"Yes, child?"

"I've heard that the Eye of Keydi-azda is missing." Together they glanced over at the linen drapery.

"Yes, I'm afraid it is."

"You don't seem very upset."

"I have been assured it will be returned."

"Assured? By who?"

"Why by Keydi-azda, of course."

Terizan sighed. "Of course," she repeated, laid the scroll on one of the shelves beside a small clay cup, left the temple, and ran into half a dozen of the Fermentation Brotherhood just leaving a meeting. As they attempted to stagger out of her way, one of them puked on her foot.

Cot'Dazur turned out to be the god of nothing in particular, although there seemed to be a divine finger stuck in a great many pies.

"Is your business not what it could be? Are you suffering from a broken heart? Do you want to impress an employer? A certain someone?" Colored flames from half a dozen flickering torches throwing bands of green and blue and gold across her face, the priest leaned forward and pointed an emphatic finger at a plump young man. "Would you like to have an application considered by the governing council?" She leaned back and spread her arms, her voice rising, her volume impressive. "Why run about to a half a dozen different temples when your problems can be dealt with under one roof." As music started up inside the building, she stepped aside and gestured through the open door. "Come. Petition Cot'Dazur."

It was a catchy tune, and Terizan, hidden in the crowd pouring up the steps, found herself moving in time to the beat—until she stubbed her toe and the pain distracted her.

Inside, lamps burning scented oil fought futilely against the smell of fresh paint mixed with half a hundred unwashed bodies. Had the ceiling not arced better than two full stories high with a row of open windows running below both sides of the peak, the combination would have quickly overpowered even the most ardent supplicant.

Painted into the plaster over the door was a representation of Cot'Dazur with features so bland they seemed designed to appeal to just about everyone. From where Terizan stood, the paint looked wet. *When the priest of Keydi-azda said this was a new god, he wasn't kidding.*

Pushed up against a stucco wall, she scowled and brushed fresh plaster off her shoulder. A good thief avoided stucco—it not only crumbled easily, it also marked those who came in contact with it. Tonight it looked like she wasn't going to have a choice.

Most of the crowd had broken into smaller groups, each clustered around a red robed priest. Somehow, even though the music continued in the background, the noise never quite rose to unbearable levels.

"Would you like some sweet-dough?"

Terizan eyed the tray of deep fried dough and her lip curled. "No, thanks." Grease and stucco combined would be just what she needed.

"A cinnamon tea?"

"No. I'm, uh, fasting."

The acolyte smiled down at her. "This is your first time, isn't it?"

Since he didn't seem to expect an answer, Terizan didn't bother giving him one. Something about him set her teeth on edge. It wasn't his height, most people were taller than she was. It wasn't the blinding glory of his smile, or the cleft in his square jaw, or the breadth of his shoulders under his robe. It wasn't any single feature—it was the way they combined that she disliked. While she might've responded better to a woman, she doubted it. Glancing around the temple, she saw that all the acolytes, men and women, shared a similar bland prettiness—they were young and cheerful and completely interchangeable. The priests, who had to be at least a little older, seemed much the same. In fact, they all looked rather remarkably like the painting of their god.

"How much does all this cost?" she asked as a trio of dancers began preforming on a small raised dais.

"Nothing at all to you," the acolyte assured her. "But donations are gratefully accepted."

Which explained the empty copper pot in the middle of the tray of sweet-dough. And the rosewood boxes carved with the hieroglyph of Cot'Dazur scattered strategically about.

"Gee, too bad I haven't got a monkey on me." She almost admired the way his smile never wavered as he disengaged and

moved on. When his attention seemed fully occupied by a peti-
tioner with a little more coin, she worked her way toward the front
of the temple.

Compared to the quiet, contemplative temple of Keydi-azda,
all the *rah, rah Cot'Dazur* set her teeth on edge—although she had
to admit as she paused a moment to listen to an impassioned
prayer for the speedy recovery of a sick camel that involved
some very realistic spitting, it was the more entertaining way to
spend an evening.

The Guild of Thespians could take lessons from these guys...

There was the expected small door beside the altar. Terizan
waited until a particularly athletic solicitation drew most eyes then
slipped through it.

The sudden quiet made her ears ring.

It took time for a god to gain substance, and first impressions
suggested this lot wouldn't care to wait. If they planned to use the
stolen icons as a shortcut to achieving divine power then all seven
would have to be grouped together at a focal point somewhere in
the temple. Inside the altar was the most obvious spot, but not even
the best thief in Oreen could get to them until after the crowd ate its
fill of sweet-dough and went home.

A short flight of dark stairs lead to a narrow room lit by a single
lamp. Street clothes hung neatly on hooks over polished wooden
benches, and a large wicker basket probably waited for dirty robes.
Terizan squirmed into the darkness below a bench and settled down
to wait.

Laughing voices woke her.

Feet flickered past her hiding place, shadowed shapes against
the shadows by the floor. Most of the conversation seemed to
center on how full the collection boxes had been and on how much
sweet-dough had been eaten. Since Terizan had always believed that
priests were people just like any other people, she couldn't understand why it bothered her so much to be right. The smell of fresh
varnish made her want to sneeze, but that, at least, was a discomfort
she was used to.

When the laughing voices left, she thought she could hear two,
maybe three people moving quietly about the room.

"How much longer?"

"Patience, Habazan, patience."

Terizan recognized the voice of the priest who had drawn the crowd into the temple. She had an unmistakable way of pronouncing every word as if it came straight from her god.

"But we have the icons."

"Granted, but even small gods will be able to hold their power for a while."

"I thought if we took the symbol of their power we took their power."

"We did. The small gods and their icons have become one and the same in most people's minds. With the icon gone, the people assume that the god is gone and will stop believing. When enough of them stop, the gods will end, and their power—through the icons—will be ours."

"Will be Cot'Dazur's."

"Of course. That's what I meant."

"But how much longer?"

"Not very."

Not very, Terizan repeated to herself as the priest and her companion took the lamp and left the robing room. *Not very long before the small gods end.* She lay where she was and scratched at the rash on her stomach. She didn't have to do this, didn't have to risk anything to return the Eye of Keydi-azda. If the priest of Cot'Dazur was right, in not very much longer Keydi-azda would be unable to effect her life. All she had to do was endure a few discomforts and soon it would end.

Keydi-azda would end.

Terizan sighed and slid out from under the bench. Any other thief would let it go. Wouldn't risk it. But as she'd told Poli, she wasn't any other thief. *I've never killed anyone, and I'm not about to start now.*

Slipping on one of the dirty robes, she started down the stairs and cracked her forehead on the edge of a metal lamp bracket.

...which doesn't mean I'm not tempted.

The altar had been carved from a solid piece of the local sandstone. It might have been hollow underneath, but Terizan's instincts said otherwise. There was always the possibility that the priests had hired a wizard to sink the icons into the stone, but from what Terizan had overheard, she didn't think that had happened.

So they had to be hidden somewhere else.

Somewhere in the temple.

Somewhere that could be used to focus the power from the seven gods onto Cot'Dazur.

Hugging the shadows at the base of the walls, Terizan made her way toward the doors. In the combination of moon and starlight that spilled through the open windows, she could just barely make out the painting of the god.

Wet paint.

Cot'Dazur couldn't possibly be *that* new.

The collection boxes were lighter than she expected. She only hoped they'd hold her weight. When she had them stacked as high as her head, she made a bag out of the robe, tucked her sandals under her sash and climbed carefully to the top of the pile. From there, she stepped onto the lintel of the door.

The plaster was still wet enough to cut with her longest lockpick. She sliced out a careful square, slipped it into the bag, and reached into the hole. Her fingers brushed the familiar cold curve of the Eye of Keydi-azda. Some of the other pieces were a little harder to find, and by the time she'd finished, she'd destroyed most of the painting.

She was just about to step back onto the boxes, bag tied to her back, the Staff of Hamtazia shoved awkwardly through the knots, when she heard voices approaching from outside.

"I'm sure I left it up in the robing room. I'll only be a minute."

Oh crap. When they opened the door, the boxes would go flying. Balanced on the lintel, Terizan measured the distance to the closest window and realized she had no choice but to attempt it. If she couldn't go down...

Stretching her left arm out and up as far as she could, she drove her longest pick into the wall, swung out on it, kicked holes in the plaster, changed hands and did it again with her second longest pick. The Dagger of Sharidan, Guardian of the Fifth Gate, would have worked better but she couldn't take the time to dig it out. As she crab-climbed up and over toward the window, the returning acolytes pushed open the door.

The sound of collection boxes crashing to the floor, some of them bouncing, some of them smashing against the tile, covered her involuntary curse as the second longest pick proved too short and began to pull out of the wall. Desperately scrabbling for a toe hold, she ignored the shouting from below as the astonished acolytes stumbled over bits of broken wood demanding that somebody bring them a lamp.

Her fingertips caught the bottom edge of the window.

A new voice shouted from deep inside the temple.

Shit! I should've known there was caretaker! She'd been incredibly lucky so far but unless she got out the window before the caretaker came with a light that wouldn't mean much. Under better circumstances, she'd have used her grip on the window as an anchor and moved carefully around the corner onto the side wall. Under these particular circumstances, she jumped.

Her right hand gripped the ledge safely but lost its grip on the pick. As the steel spike began to fall, Terizan jerked her head forward and caught it in her mouth, somehow managing to hang on in spite of a split lip. Anything left behind could lead a wizard right to her.

Muscles straining, she got the upper half of her body over the window sill, wrestled the Staff of Hamtazia out the opening, and lowered herself onto the steeply angled roof. *If I can make it to the ground before they figure out which way I went,* she reasoned as she began to slide, *they'll never catch me.* Most roofs in Oreen were flat or domed—it wasn't until she noticed how fast the edge was approaching that she realized her danger.

That's a story and a half drop! Flipping over onto her stomach she dug in fingers and toes but the clay tiles overlapped so smoothly there was nothing to grab. Then her legs were in the air. Her body began to tip while she tried grab a handful of roof.

Her hip hit a protrusion of some kind. Then the knotted robe slammed up under her chin and her left arm pit and she found herself hanging between two of the decorative wooden things that stuck out from under the edge of the roof, dangling half throttled from the jammed Staff of Hamtazia.

It's about time something went my way…

Since her hands were free, she quickly returned both picks to the seams of her trousers, pulled herself up enough to free the Staff, then dropped. By the time the hue and cry began, she'd lost herself in the shadows.

In the temple of Keydi-azda, the same three lamps burned unattended. Although Terizan half expected something to go wrong, the Eye fit back into the stone socket as easily as it had come out. The other six stolen icons, she set carefully onto the shelves where they'd be found by those who needed them. Then she knelt, folded back the robe, and pulled out the last item it held. The first square of damp plaster she'd cut out of the wall—the face of Cot'Dazur, miraculously in one piece in spite of everything.

"I'm a thief," she told the watching Eye of Keydi-azda. "I'm not a judge, and I'm not an executioner. I've never killed anyone and I'm not about to start. If the priests of Cot'Dazur need their icon back, they can find it here with the rest."

The silence was absolute but Terizan hadn't expected an answer. She didn't need a god to tell her when she was doing the right thing. Brushing bits of plaster dust from her clothes, she left the Eye to keep watch alone.

"So what did the Tribunal say?"

"What could they say?" Terizan bit into a cheese dumpling and sighed in contentment. "The priests of Cot'Dazur complained that the stolen icons had been stolen back, and the Tribunal pointed out that they'd fulfilled their part of the contract, and what happened to the icons after they were handed over was not their problem."

"But they don't have the contract."

"The priests don't know that. If they did, they'd cause trouble. So, as much as they'd like to come down on the thief with both feet, the Tribunal is not going to do anything that may push whoever took the contract into telling the priests that it no longer exists. Although they *have* nailed shut the trap door in the ceiling of the Sanctum."

Poli studied her from under darkened lashes. "So they suspect it was you?"

"They've never liked me much. They think I'm ambitious." Her grin pulled to one side by her swollen lip, her expression seemed more disdainful than amused. "You know, Poli, this whole thing was a set up from the start. The Tribunal had no reason to send me after the Eye, anyone could have done the job. But, even pinched and prodded by the god, no one else could have stolen the contract out of the Sanctum or have got the icons back from Cot'Dazur."

Equal to the announcement, Poli nodded calmly. "Of course, the Tribunal planned on double crossing Cot'Dazur all the time."

"No, I don't think so. Had any other thief stolen the Eye, Cot'Dazur would, this minute, be absorbing the power of the small gods. I think I was *their* solution."

"You think you were the gods solution?" Poli reached across the table and patted her arm. "Think highly of yourself, don't you, sweetling."

"Actually, yes. But it's also the only explanation that makes sense. The way I work it out, seven gods owe me a favor. Eight if you consider that I didn't destroy that pretty picture of Cot'Dazur when I had the chance."

Poli sat back looking a little stunned. "Eight gods," he said at last. "All owing you a favor." He blinked twice then managed to recover his poise. "Well, I suppose that it's a good thing they're small gods."

Terizan flashed him a triumphant smile. The rash was gone, her bruises were healing, and the immediate future looked bright. "But there are eight of them."

"Should I be worried?"

"You? No" She took her time eating another dumpling, savoring the moment. As Tribune One had implied, there were a number of things about the guild that had never met with her approval. They were small things, for the most part, but it was, after all, the small things that made life worth living.

Bless Keydi-azda.

I can't think of a single thing to say about this story. Not a word. Nothing. Nada. I'm drawing a complete blank.

Tell you what, in the interest of making this collection interactive we'll leave a space and after you've read "The Lions Of Al'Kalamir", you write something here.

THE LIONS OF AL'KALAMIR

"IS IT JUST me or are there more Kerbers in the city lately?"

"More Kerbers?" Terizan popped the last bit of bulgar laden flatbread into her mouth and leaned back as she chewed. "I hadn't noticed."

Poli made a small moue of distaste. "Chew or talk, sweetling, not both at the same time."

"Sorry." She swallowed before continuing. "I only notice people who have something that might be worth stealing. Kerbers have nothing that's worth the risk."

"What about their weapons? I thought the Kerber's blades were the best."

"They are, but I don't think so highly of my skills that I'd try to take a weapon from a Kerber." As one of Poli's delicately arched brows arched even higher, Terizan grinned across the table at him. "Okay, maybe I do think that highly of my skills, but I'm not completely crazy."

"So it's safe to assume that the Kerber advancing across the cantina toward us is not on vendetta?"

Terizan turned so quickly the bench rocked, and the hulking figure sitting alone on the far end growled a wordless warning. Wrapped completely in voluminous, sand colored robes the advancing Kerber noted her attention with a nod and began moving a little faster.

"I don't like the way the robes hide their gender," Poli murmured.

"Since when does that matter?"

"It matters in the approach, sweetling. I know you don't get out much, but men and women are *not* the same."

Terizan's response got lost in the Kerber's arrival.

"I have a message for you." The voice was a sexless whisper, barely emerging from behind the veils.

"For me?"

A gloved hand opened and a swan's feather dropped onto the table.

A message from Swan, the mercenary captain who'd helped Terizan get the better of the Thieves' Guild Tribunal. A message from Swan, who'd offered a thief a place in her company. A message from Swan, who'd... Terizan swallowed and managed to keep her voice nearly normal as she asked, "Should we go someplace private?"

"Someplace less likely to be overheard."

"My place?" Poli offered politely. When both heads turned toward him, he spread his hands. "Well, you clearly want to keep whatever it is you're doing under wraps. If you leave with Terizan people will assume you want her to steal something. If you leave with us both and we go to my rooms, people's assumptions will be confused."

The Kerber nodded. "Confused would be good."

"Confused will be an understatement," Terizan muttered as she stood.

Two of the three brothels that had given the Street of Pleasures its name had moved out to the new city along with many of the independents. In remaining faithful to old Oreen, Poli was able to afford a pair of attractive rooms up on the third floor over a wig maker's shop.

"Good idea," Terizan said, gesturing toward the folds of colored gauze over the two tall windows in the sitting room. "A thief'd get tangled up in those."

"Well, yes," Poli admitted, "but that's not why I did it. It softens that harsh afternoon light, spreads the shadows, makes everyone look more beautiful. Beautiful people tip better." He turned to the Kerber and smiled. "Can I get you anything?"

"This isn't a social call, Poli." Turning to the Kerber, Terizan folded her arms. "I'd like to hear Swan's message now. What does she want?"

"You." A deft twist dropped the robes to one side and Terizan found herself caught up in a familiar embrace.

"That certainly looks like a social call to me," Poli commented dryly. "No wait, it's beginning to look like something I'd charge for."

Disengaging enough to catch her breath, Swan grinned down at the woman in her arms. "Actually, I have a job for you."

"My point exactly."

"Poli, shut up."

"I need the services of the best thief in Oreen to end a civil war."

"Prince Hasan al'Kalamir is dead. His two surviving sons are fighting over who should inherit. Essien, the elder by some seven minutes hired the Wing."

"They're twins?"

Swan shook her head, the brilliant red-gold of her life braid swaying almost hypnotically with the motion. "No, different mothers. The Prince, may he rot in the Netherhells, raised both Essien and his half-brother Jameel to consider themselves the heir." One corner of her expressive mouth quirked upwards. "They can't stand each other, but that's nothing to how they feel about him. Anyway, with the Wing's help, Essien defeated his brother—although didn't manage to actually kill him—and took the Palace."

"That sounds like the civil war is over," Terizan pointed out. She'd had to fight to hear Swan's story over the multitude of voices in her head calling out the mercenary captain's name—and one or two other more explicit suggestions.

"It would be over except for one small problem. The people of Kalazmir won't accept Essien as their Prince unless he has the regalia which is locked in a secret treasure room somewhere in the catacombs under the Palace. Unfortunately, Essien was a little quick to kill his father's old vizier who was the only other person—besides dear, dead, daddy—who knew where in the catacombs that treasure room was. Is."

"He's got an army he's not using now, why doesn't he send them down to look for it?"

"Because after the first one died, the rest wouldn't go. He tried sending captives, promising them a long and happy life if they bring out the regalia, but they keep dying too. The old prince was rather remarkably paranoid, and this place has traps up the ass."

"How painful," Poli murmured. "More beer?"

"Thanks. Anyway, the natives are getting restless and Essien's decided he has no time to waste. When he asked if I had any ideas, I immediately thought of you. You *are* the only supplicant to have ever made it all the way to the inner sanctum of the Thieves' Guild."

"True," Terizan acknowledged, slowly. "But while I'd do anything for you, I really prefer that *anything* didn't involve dying. Most of the traps in the guild house were non lethal."

Swan snorted. "I imagine that most of the traps in the catacombs are usually non lethal as well. The lot Essien's been sending below ground couldn't figure out how to dig a field latrine with detailed instructions. First one down sprang a pit trap you could see from the entrance."

That did seem to raise the odds a bit, Terizan thought. Then Swan smiled at her, and she stopped thinking at all.

"Please, Terizan. I know you can do it."

Lost in Swan's smile, she heard Poli sigh.

"And I really want to get the Wing out of Kalazmir before the rains start," the mercenary captain continued.

"So the two of you will be leaving immediately?" Poli wondered.

Shooting him an exasperated glare—in spite of what Poli seemed to think, she wasn't quite ready to surrender to the inevitable—Terizan leaned forward and pinned Swan with her most businesslike expression. "Wouldn't it be simpler if this Essien just had the regalia copied?"

"He can't, it's god-touched. Even if he could afford to have it copied, the priests would immediately know it's a fake."

"All right, if I bring out this regalia; what's in it for me?"

"Anything else you can bring out of the treasure room."

She felt her jaw drop. "Anything?"

"Anything," Essien agreed. Stroking his narrow mustache, he stared darkly down into the catacombs. "You have my word as al'Kalamir."

"Thank you." Although he wouldn't actually *be* al'Kalamir until she came out with the regalia, Terizan decided to let that slide. There were enough of the Wing around to see that he kept his word regardless of what he chose to call himself.

"Two things I can tell you for certain to beware of ," Essien continued. "One, my father, may he rot in the Netherhells, paid a wizard for three spells, but what the spells do, I have no idea. Two,

beware the lions of al'Kalamir." As Swan stepped forward, frowning, he raised a ringed hand. "Given the conditions down there, I
doubt they're real lions, Captain. It is merely something the vizier
was fond of saying." Dark brows drew thoughtfully in. "In fact, it
was the last thing vizier said; beware the lions of al'Ka..." The last
word trailed off into a fair impersonation of a man choking on his
own blood. A number of the soldiers standing around laughed, but
Terizan rolled her eyes. A little less killing and a little more questioning would have been a little more helpful from where she stood.

Settling her pack more comfortably on her shoulders, she moved
to the top of the long flight of stone stairs. A slight smell of putre-
faction wafted up from below.

"We can also tell you with some certainty that there's a pit trap
under that first big blue tile," Swan said dryly passing over a lantern.
"Pressure on the middle of the bottom step releases the support
and..." Her gesture made the result quite clear. "It sounded deep,"
she added, somewhat unnecessarily in Terizan's opinion. Bending
forward, the mercenary captain lightly kissed the top of the thief's
head. "Be careful."

"I'm always careful," Terizan told her. Careless thieves ended
up with their heads adorning the spikes of the Crescent—or more
specifically in this case, smashed open like a melon at the bottom
of a pit.

"So much for the easy part of the trip," Terizan murmured thoughtfully as she ducked under the trigger mechanism that would set a
course of counterweighted blades swinging, their positions having
been given away by the diced bits of body scattered down the corridor. The chopped bits of robe surprised her a little as Kerbers
seldom got involved in anything but inter-tribal warfare, mostly because they were usually so pre-occupied with inter-tribal warfare.
She wondered if Swan—who got her coloring and her right to
wear the robes from a Kerber grandfather—had felt as though she'd
been fighting on the wrong side. Probably not. Swan and her Wing
were mercenaries, and the right side was always and only the side
paying the bills.

Like the other four traps set off by the unfortunate soldiers
who'd gone into the catacombs, this one had automatically reset
after having been sprung. She had to give the old prince credit, he'd

been willing to pay for the best. Five soldiers, five traps. From this point on, there'd be no corpses to warn her.

"Which ought to improve the air quality, if nothing else."

So far there'd been no sign of the three spells, although a faint feeling of unease had been licking up and down her spine ever since she'd stepped over that first, trapped tile. The sensitivity to magic that usually kept her from blundering into things she couldn't handle seemed to be reacting non-specifically to the entire place—which could mean any number of unpleasant things, but since none of them were particularly helpful, Terizan ignored the feeling as much as she could and got on with it.

The next trap involved a large, and probably heavy, section of the ceiling. Terizan had no idea how it could possibly be reset but wasn't curious enough about it to risk being flattened. Another pit trap and the ubiquitous spring-loaded spears later, she reached a short corridor that seemed, at first inspection, to be trap free.

As a second inspection turned up the same result, she moved slowly forward, came to a T-junction, and paused. Not enough time had passed since the building of the catacombs for the correct path to have been worn into the stone, and the webs of the few, small spiders who'd chosen to live in the dark seemed to show no preference. Lifting her lamp, she watched the flame flicker one way and then the other, the strangely equal breezes causing it to smoke slightly as it bent.

"All right, the odds are good the vizier, the old prince, and who-ever actually designed the route to the treasure room were all right handed. Nine times out of ten, when given a simple choice between one direction and the other, right-handed people turn to the right."

When she reached her first dead end after three corners and two cross corridors, she retraced her way to back the T-junction.

"All right, so this is that one time out of ten they don't go to the right."

Except that heading left took her into an identical maze.

"Which isn't really surprising from a prince who raised both of his sons to think of themselves as heir," she muttered, scowling at nothing in particular.

About to retrace her steps yet again, she heard a sound that froze her in place. The prince's warning to beware the lions of al'Kalamir ringing in her ears, she'd actually taken two steps back when she realized that lions seldom seldom sang and certainly weren't in the habit of adding new and salacious verses to *Long-Legged Hazrah* in a better than average baritone. When Hazrah stopped inspiring, the voice started in on *The King's Menagerie*. Although the echoes made it difficult to tell for certain, Terizan didn't think the singer had moved while she'd been listening.

Sighing, she pulled a monkey from her pocket and deftly flipped the coin up into the air. "Heads, I find him and make sure he isn't a threat. Tails, I ignore him and get on with the..."

Heads.

It took her longer to find him than she'd expected. He'd been standing at a dead end, probably inspecting the wall for secret passageways when the floor underneath him had given way, slanting suddenly downward. Her lamp resting on the lip, Terizan squatted and stared down a slope too slick and too steep to climb but angled with just enough false promise that anyone caught would die trying.

The man in the hole had been silent since her light had spilled into his prison.

"I can't pull you out," she said, setting her grappling iron into the gap where the slope joined the floor and dropping fifty feet of silk rope down into the hole, "so I hope you can climb."

Her only answer was a tightening of the rope.

"Fine, be that way," she muttered. Pulling her dagger, she laid the blade against the knot. If she didn't like what she saw, she could always send him back into the pit and have one of Essien's people retrieve him later. That he could only be a fellow thief was not particularly reassuring—in her experience thieves were not always the pleasantest of people.

She could hear him breathing heavily—even with the rope the climb wasn't an easy one. She heard him curse, heard something, probably a knee, slam into the wall as he slipped, then finally saw a hand come up into the light. A second hand took a higher grip.

Not a thief. At least not a professional, the hands and arms were far too large. And not a soldier, no soldier ever wore that much jewelry—that much *good* jewelry, Terizan amended, rapidly calculating the street value of each piece. A heavy gold thumb ring set with a star sapphire flanked by diamonds would buy her a few months security even after the Guild's commission. *All right, not a thief, not a soldier...*

The top of his head came into the lantern light, and Terizan sucked air through her teeth. In this part of the world, hair a brilliant red-gold meant only one thing. Kerber. But Kerbers tended not to wear jewelry. So, like Swan, he hadn't been raised in the tribes.

For Swan's sake, or maybe just for Swan's resemblance, she couldn't send him back into the pit so, keeping her dagger ready, she moved out of his way.

Concentrating on the climb, he didn't look up or speak until he was lying face down on the floor. He turned his head toward her, life braid sliding across his bare back, and wiped the sweat from his eyes with one shaking hand. "Who in the Netherhells are you?"

"You're welcome." Terizan shoved his leg aside and began to pull up her rope.

After a startled moment, he grinned and propped himself up on an elbow. "I do beg your pardon. Being down in a pit for two days does tend to wear at a man's manners. I am, indeed, most grateful for your rescue. And," he added, as a small bundle appeared wrapped in the last twenty-five feet or so of rope, "for retrieving my pitiful possessions. I left the robes down in the pit; after two days I'm sure you can understand why."

The bundle consisted of a flaccid waterskin and a pair of expensive sandals wrapped in a vest. Although plain, the vest's fabric had the heavy, fluid feel of high resale value. She tossed it to him and while he dressed, used the time to refill her lamp. When half the oil she carried was gone, she was leaving whether she'd found the treasure room or not.

"I don't suppose you're carrying food and water?" he asked at last.

"I might be." Although he sounded hopeful, not dangerous, she kept her gaze locked on his face, repacking rope and oilskin by touch. "But there's both waiting at the entrance."

"For you, perhaps, but not for me. If I show myself…"

"…your brother will kill you?"

One red-gold eyebrow rose and he smiled charmingly at her. "Have we met?"

Terizan ignored the charm and answered the question. "No, but there's only two people who want the regalia. I know you're not Essien, so you have to be Jameel. Besides, you sound much the same when you talk. I expect that's why you didn't say anything until you were out of the pit."

"And you'd be right," Jameel admitted. "Although you must grant that I have the better singing voice."

"I wouldn't know," Terizan told him dryly. "I haven't heard your brother sing." He wore two long daggers in his belt. Probably Kerber steel although the bad light made it difficult to tell for certain.

Jameel tracked her gaze and spread both hands. "I'm not going to fight you for your supplies— that would be boorish in the extreme, considering you just saved my life."

"True."

"But as I'm not giving up my search for the treasure room nor going back down into that pit, it might be best if we work together."

He sounded so reasonable, she almost agreed. Then she remembered. "I'm working for your brother."

"It's a funny old world isn't it? So am I."

Terizan snorted and stood.

"I tell you no lie, little thief." Jameel mirrored her action. "My brother has an army in the city, has secured the palace, and has hired the best mercenary troupe in the region. My army is scattered. I doubt I could even get my mother's family to fight for me again, and it's only a matter of time until I'm found and executed. It seemed to me that my only chance of survival is to be the one who presents the regalia to Essien."

"A peace offering?"

"Exactly."

It made sense. Terizan didn't care about the regalia, it was the treasure room's other contents she had plans for. "You'll swear you couldn't have done it without me? So I get paid?"

Jameel bowed, his life braid falling forward and lying like a line of fire along the crease of his neck. "I'll swear that I'd have died without you."

"Just remember that when we get out," Terizan muttered. She didn't trust him, but it was hard not to like him, although, besides the superficial resemblance he bore to Swan, she wasn't quite sure why. As he straightened, she threw him one of her waterskins. It made no sense to have saved him from the pit only to have him die of thirst. "The name's Terizan. And that's all the water you get," she warned him. "Ration yourself."

"My thanks, Terizan, for your generosity." He drank thirstily and, with an effort, recorked the skin. Slinging it over his shoulder, he used the gesture to jauntily flick his life-braid back. "Now what?"

A good question. Considering where she'd found him, it was a good bet the prince knew as little about the true path through the maze as she did. "It—or rather they—can't be classical mazes," she murmured, "too many thieves know the patterns. And yet it can't be too complex or no one would be able to remember the key."

"Only my father, may he rot in the Netherhells, and the grand vizier knew the key."

"Exactly…" Thinking of how long it had taken her to come this far, Terizan suddenly smiled. "We're going back."

"Back?"

"To the corridor leading to the maze entrances." She waved a hand toward the dead end. "Do you honestly think your father would put up with this sort of shit in order to get to something that belonged to him? The mazes are a distraction. There's another way."

"Brilliant."

"Thank you." Holding the lamp up to shoulder height at the first corner, she peered at the stone. "I've marked the…"

"Wall?" Jameel asked. His tone suggested this wasn't unexpected. "My father, may he rot in the Netherhells, had a wizard spell the maze," he explained as she whirled around to face him. "You can make as many marks as you want but the moment you stop looking at them, they disappear."

"So if I don't remember the way out?"

"Well, let's just say we're both going to get a lot thinner. And speaking of thinner," he added, gesturing at her pack. "You wouldn't have anything to eat in there would you?"

He looked so hopeful, she sighed and tossed him a bag of dates as they started down the corridor. "I don't suppose you know what the other two spells were?" she asked taking the first right.

"How do you know there's two more?"

"Essien told me there were three, but he didn't know what they were."

"I know of one other besides the wall thing. My father, may he rot in the Netherhells, had a tapestry that had been magically woven to represent the catacombs. If a thief managed to get in, he could watch their progress. Watch them die."

"Lovely man."

"None lovelier." He licked his fingers clean and the red-gold brow rose again. "Are you sure this is the right way?"

Terizan turned left. "Yes. Where's the tapestry now?"

"The grand vizier used it as his shroud. It was wrapped around him when they lit the pyre."

"And the third spell?"

"I have no idea. I don't like to argue with a professional, Terizan, but I really think we need to go right here."

Terizan turned left again. "Why didn't your brother tell me about the walls and the tapestry?"

"I doubt he knew. He was always off learning to be a statesman or a swordsman, hoping our father, may he rot in the Netherhells, would approve of him."

"While you did what?

"I hung around and sucked up, big time. Are you sure we're…"

"Yes." She turned right. "What about the lions of al'Kalamir?"

"Lions?" He had a pleasant laugh—or would have had, Terizan decided, had he not been laughing at her. "How could there be lions down here? It's too dark, and there's nothing for them to eat. Present company excepted, of course."

"Of cour…shit on a stick!" They'd reached another dead end.

"You know, I did think that we should have turned right back there."

Spinning around, Terizan found her flat, unfriendly stare swamped by a *well-I-did-mention-it-before* sort of a smile. "Do you remember this part of the pattern from the tapestry?" she sighed.

Jameel spread his hands, rings winking in the lamplight. "I might."

Two rights, a left, and another dead end later, he added, as though no time had passed, "Or it might have been a lucky guess."

Terizan took a deep breath and exhaled slowly. Then she frowned and did it again, head lifted and turned back the way they'd come. "Here." She thrust the lamp into his hands. "Take this and stay here."

"Why?"

"Because I need to smell something other than lamp oil and you." She was out of the light by the time she reached the last corner. Eyes closed, she pivoted first to her left and then to her right. Now that she was taking the time to notice, she could smell, very faintly, the not entirely unpleasant aroma of rot.

"How fortunate for us my brother didn't decide to hire you immediately."

"Not very fortunate for those soldiers," Terizan pointed out as they stepped out into the corridor connecting the two mazes.

"I expect they were mine, not his." He paused as they reached the t-junction and stared up toward the entrance to the catacombs. The angle hid the last body from view, but all five were making their presence felt on the slight breeze. "I'll have to see what I can do about getting them out of here and burying them with full rights."

Bring a bucket, was Terizan's initial reaction, but Jameel sounded so distressed she kept it, and other pertinent comments, to herself.

Now she knew what she was looking for, it took her no time at all to find the outline of the door in the stone wall. A few moments more and she uncovered the keyhole.

"I imagine you don't need the key?"

"That's right." Rummaging around in her pack, she brought out a package of dried figs. A strangled noise from Jameel made her look up.

"You're going to pick the lock with dried figs?"

"No." She handed him half. "We're going to eat while I refill the lamp."

He really did have a pleasant laugh.

Behind the door, a flight of stairs lead down into a darkness too thick for Terizan's small light to make much of an impression. A dozen steps and the door closed behind them with a small, snick.

For a prince, Jameel knew a number of very creative profanities.

"Don't worry." Not even bothering to turn, Terizan took another two steps, wishing she could see just a little further than her own feet. "There's a latch on this side, I noticed it when we came through."

"You're sure?"

"Trust me. Neither your father nor the Grand Vizier had any more intention than I do of being trapped down here."

The stairs broadened as they descended. Level ground was a six foot wide corridor, tile not stone and judging from the small section they could see, probably beautiful.

"No turns," Terizan murmured.

"How can you tell?"

"The way the sound travels. Stay close." She'd counted forty-nine paces when something up ahead reflected back a glimmer of light. "Gold."

"That's it then." As Jameel surged past her, she heard a tiny click.

Sweeping his feet out from under him, she got him flat on the floor just in time.

They laid there for a few moments longer, staring up into the darkness. They could see neither the huge metal spike nor the mechanism that had swung it down out of the ceiling but it was a dominating presence never-the-less.

"Well." Jameel's voice bounced back off the ceiling. "It seems I owe you my life a second time."

Taking what seemed like her first breath in hours, Terizan turned her head toward him. "A third time. I also got us out of the maze."

Smiling, he shrugged as well as he was able given his position. "Sorry, you know what they say about the memories of princes."

Terizan snorted and rolled over onto her stomach. "Actually I do." Inching forward, pushing the lamp ahead, she pointed toward a slightly raised floor tile. "Look here. If you survived the way in, that one'll get you on the way back. Swan's right, your father was a very paranoid man."

"You have no idea."

"I'm beginning to."

A pair of shims jammed the trigger mechanisms, although thief and prince both carefully stepped over the actual tile. It took them longer to cover the next eleven paces than it had to cover the first forty-nine, but there were no more traps.

The double doors to the treasure room had been covered in beaten gold, and the handles hung from the mouths of two beautifully crafted golden lions' heads.

"The lions of al'Kalamir."

"Don't touch them," Terizan warned. "They're probably the trigger to the third spell."

His fingertips a hair's breadth from the left lion, Jameel froze and slowly let his hand drop back to his side. "So what do we do?"

"*You* stand back while *I* pick the lock, then we stuff something in the hole and use it to open the door."

"Very clever."

"Thank you." Pulling her two largest lockpicks from her trouser seams, she knelt, stared into the keyhole and shook her head. "The key must've been huge. I wonder where it is."

"I expect it went to the pyre with my father, may he rot in the Netherhells."

"Don't take this personally or anything, but the vizier didn't seem to want either you or your brother to get hold of the regalia.

"Well, he didn't like us much." When pacing took him too quickly out of the light, he rocked back and forth, heel to toe. "You're an incredible person, you know that?"

"Why?" Terizan asked absently, most of her attention on the lock.

"Look what you've done. You've defeated my father, may he rot in the Netherhells, walked through his traps as though they weren't there, solved the puzzle of his maze, and saved me two— no, three—times."

Feeling slightly embarrassed by his enthusiasm, she pulled the last fig from her pocket, took a bite and chewed while she worked. "That doesn't make me an incredible person," she said at last and, using the larger of her two lockpicks, pulled the door open a few inches. "It merely makes me an incredible thief." Before she stood, she took a quick look at the mechanism. "Be careful, there's no latch on the inside of this, if the door closes while we're inside, we're stuck."

"So we'll be careful." He waited until she was standing beside him then flashed her a quick smile. "Shall we?"

The door was so perfectly balanced, it took almost no effort to swing it wide. From where they stood, the lamplight barely spilled over the threshold, but that little bit refracted into a hundred sparkling stars. As they moved closer, the hundred stars became one until, blinking away afterimages, they stared down at the regalia of al'Kalamir. The crown rested in the circle of the pectoral, the two rings within the circle of the crown. Each section of the pectoral and both of the rings bore a piece of quartz the size of Terizan's thumbnail. Another piece over an inch across was centered in the front of the crown. Only the settings, a heavy red-gold almost the color of a Kerber life-braid, had any intrinsic value.

There was nothing else in the treasure room.

Taking a deep breath, Terizan set the lamp on the pedestal by the regalia. "Your brother is a pile of leprous baboon shit," she snarled.

"Granted," Jameel agreed, reaching out to touch the crown with a single finger. "Any particular reason you bring it up now?"

"I was to take my payment from the other items in the treasure room."

"And you think he knew there was nothing else in here?"

Mouth open to say just exactly what she thought, Terizan paused. It hadn't even occurred to her that he wouldn't have known.

"And you'd be right," Jameel continued. "We both knew. Father, may he rot in the Netherhells, made no secret of it."

"*I* didn't know," Terizan growled, "and he knew I didn't... What are you doing?"

Sapphire thumb ring tossed onto the pedestal, Jameel slid one of the regalia rings into its place. "Just trying things on. After all, this is my heritage as much as Essien's, and this'll be my only chance." The second ring slid onto his other thumb. He laid the pectoral on around his neck without fastening the catch and settled the crown on his head. "Well, what do you think? Does it suit me?"

Even through her anger, she had to admit that it did. The gold of the crown almost disappeared in his hair so that the large piece of quartz seemed to float above his brow refracting far more light than it should have—more light, she suspected than was actually in the room. Had she not seen the regalia off Jameel, she'd have thought he was wearing a king's ransom in diamonds.

"It's the whole god-touched thing," he told her when she said as much, "but it only works when all the pieces are together and on a prince of Kalamir."

"You look better than Essien will," she muttered.

He laughed then suddenly sobered. "I'm sorry, Terizan."

"Why, because your brother is such a shit?"

"For that too."

It wasn't so much a blow as a hard shove into the back wall of the treasure room. Her head hit stone, and, seeing stars, she slid to the floor. Jameel grabbed the lamp and stepped out into the corridor.

"I'm sorry," he said again, and closed the door.

All at once more tired than angry, Terizan got slowly to her feet, careful not to leave the definition of the wall. The darkness was so complete, touch would be her only useable sense, and she had no time to get lost, even in such small room. One hand against the back wall, she moved into a corner and halfway along the side. Jamming her left foot into the angle of floor and wall, she leaned out as far as she could and scooped Jameel's forgotten ring off the pedestal.

At least the trip isn't a total loss...

Straightening, she finished the side wall and reached the doors, pushing gently on the nearest. It swung silently open a handspan and she lightly touched the piece of dried fig she'd jammed into the mechanism. Getting in was only part of the problem, a good thief always made sure there was a way out.

She could see the lamp and realized Jameel had almost reached the stairs. There *was* a latch on the inside of that door but it wouldn't be easy to find. Still, it wouldn't hurt to slow him just a little bit more.

Not long before, she had stolen the Eye of Keydi-azda and ended up ensuring the continuing existance of eight small gods. Six of them still owed her for it. One of them had been Yallamaya, the Zephyr That Blows Trouble From the World. An emphatic prayer reminding Blessed Yallmaya of the debt—gods having much the same memory as princes—drew a gentle breeze past her cheek that grew to a gust wind by the time it reached the other end of the corridor.

Terizan heard Jameel swear.

The lamp blew out.

His footsteps echoed in the corridor as he bounded up the stairs and under cover of the noise, Terizan walked eleven paces and squatted to check the trigger tiles. He'd taken the time to remove the shims. Clearly, he'd inherited some of his father's paranoia.

By the time she'd worked her way past the trap, Jameel was pounding on the inside of the door, not even searching for the latch, just trying to beat his way out. By the time she'd covered half of the forty-nine paces, his rising panic was beginning to make her regret blowing out the lamp. He'd spent two days, trapped in the dark, waiting to die, and she'd thrown him right back there again. His terror made it hard to remember that he'd left *her* to die in the treasure room.

By the time she reached the bottom of the stairs, she could hear only the sound of labored breathing from the top.

"You didn't pass the dead soldiers on the way in," she said softly, "or you'd have known they were yours. Two of them were Kerbers. You know another way into the catacombs, and you'll use that to get out. You have no intention of taking the regalia to your brother, and you never did."

"I locked you in." It was a token protest. It sounded more like he was saying, *you're not really here.* And saying it like he'd said it a hundred times before. Two days in complete darkness. Complete silence. Waiting to die.

"You thought you did."

"I reset the traps."

"So?"

Jameel laughed, a shaky sound but free of panic. "Oh yes, I forgot. You're very good at what you do. So, what happens now."

He recovered quickly, but she'd seen that before. He also moved very quietly for large man—but not quietly enough.

"You go back up those two stairs," Terizan told him. "And we'll keep talking. You don't, I leave you alone in the dark.."

"You can't get by me."

"Not as long as you stay by the door," she agreed. When she heard him return to the top of the stairs, she added, "We need each other to get out." Which wasn't entirely true. She could taunt him until he charged, then easily slip by and have him bargain for his freedom with the regalia, but she had as little intention of creating a powerful enemy as she did of leaving him in the catacombs to die. Thieves who never learned that the paths between people were as precarious as those along the edges of buildings, took fatal falls. "I suggest we go back to your original plan; you give the regalia to your brother in return for your life."

"No. I have as much right to rule as he does."

"Except that he's out there, and you're in here, and I was hired to get him that regalia."

"What do you care? Essien screwed you out of your payment!"

"Technically, no." In spite of everything, Terizan couldn't prevent a smile. After all, a similar technicality had gotten her into the Thieves' Guild. "Essien never said there was anything else *in* the treasure room. He's not responsible for my assumptions."

After a moment, Jameel sighed. "You're taking this rather well."

"Getting angry," she told him flatly, "doesn't change things. Now, are we going to stay here, in the dark, and argue about this or are we leaving?"

She heard him sigh again. "We're leaving."

"My way?"

"I can't stay down here."

"I know."

The third and final sigh had a reluctant smile shaping it. "Your way."

Each piece of the regalia flared as Essien stroked it lightly with a reverent fingertip. Lifting his hand, he turned to the priests and curled his lip in what might have been a smile. "Satisfied?"

"We are satisfied, al'Kalamir." The priests looked so relieved Terizan had to wonder what would have happened to them had the regalia not been genuine. Removing the priests would certainly have removed any protests.

"Good." Continuing the turn so that the regalia was at his back, he allowed the smile to become genuine. "The coronation will be this afternoon. You'll all stay of course."

Terizan looked to Swan who shrugged and nodded.

"Good," Essien said again. "And afterwards, I'd be happy to have you witness the execution of my brother."

Jameel began to move, but the guards who'd been flanking him grabbed his arms before he took his third step and forced him to his knees.

"My last bit of unfinished business," Essien murmured patting his brother's cheek.

Ignoring instincts that told her not to get involved, Terizan's fingers clenched into fists. "He brought you the regalia!"

"There are two answers to that, little thief. The first is that, for reasons of your own which I do not need to know, you allowed him to carry the regalia out of the catacombs. Jameel may have handed it to me, but only through your efforts. The second response is a little more succinct." He spread his hands. "So?"

And that second response was impossible to argue with. One part of her mind watched Jameel struggle—his life-braid, so like Swan's whipping back and forth as though it would be free on its own—and the other part tried to think of something, anything she could do. She felt Swan's hand close around her shoulder, but she shrugged it off and stepped forward.

"What about my payment?"

Essien's dark brows rose. "I thought you said the treasure room was empty of everything but the regalia?"

"It was, but you said I could have anything I brought out." She nodded toward the struggling prince. "I want him."

Jameel stopped struggling.

"By your own words, I brought him out so by your word as al'Kalamir, he's mine."

"My word as al'Kalamir," Essien repeated. He walked around the small table so he could stare at his brother and the thief over the regalia.

The silence stretched and lengthened. Terizan could hear nothing from Swan and those of the Wing who were behind her. The Wing would take their cue from Swan and Swan seemed willing to let her play this out.

"My word as al'Kalamir," Essien repeated again. Glancing down at the regalia he frowned thoughtfully. "And you have made me al'Kalamir." When he glanced up again, he'd clearly come to a decision. "Very well, he's yours. But the next time I catch him..."

"He's on his own."

"That's four times you saved my life."

"It won't happen again," Terizan reassured him. "You're going back to your mother's people. And I'm going home."

One hand holding the flapping end of his veil, Jameel grinned down at her from the saddle. "Maybe I'll find myself a wife and settle down. Put all this behind me."

Terizan snorted. "Good luck."

"So, what happened between you and Jameel down in those catacombs?"

Had Swan not been so well armed, Terizan might have attempted to exploit that suspicious tone with a little teasing. As it was... "I saved his life three times, and the pile of leprous baboon shit tried to lock me into the treasure room."

"So you saved his life a fourth time?" The mercenary captain snorted.

"It seemed like the thing to do." She'd managed to block out most of her memories of their ride from Oreen to Kalamir. Everything except the nights with Swan had been hot, sandy, and painful. Horses were too far off the ground, saddles were not made for comfort, and Swan, while a suprisingly considerate lover, was a less than patient riding instructor. Now, once more in the saddle, it was all coming back to her. "He kept reminding me of you."

"Why?" Suspicion had made its move into jealousy.

"The life-braid. You have one just like it."

"Oh."

Terizan smiled at the tone and tried not to fall off her horse.

"So, did you ever find out about the lions?"

"Find out? I put one in charge and saved the other's life. The lions of al'Kalamir," she prodded when Swan looked blank. "al'Kalamir is the prince's title. Jameel and Essien were the lions."

"But why beware...."

"Jameel said the vizier didn't like them much. Since Essien killed him, his dislike seems to have been well founded."

"I'm sorry I got you into this."

"Why?"

Swan shrugged. "Beware the lions of al'Kalamir and all that. One of them cheated you and one of them tried to kill you after you saved his life four times."

"Only three times at the time."

"Still. I'd have been furious. In fact, I was furious for you."

Clinging to the saddle with both hands, Terizan smiled. "I don't get angry. Instead, I stole one of the regalia rings, and I slipped it into Jameel's pocket when I said good-bye."

The mercenary captain sucked air throw her teeth. "Essien's going to know it was you. You've left a powerful enemy back there."

"No. Jameel forgot a thumb ring in the treasure room. I grabbed it and left it in the missing ring's place."

"Essien will think Jameel took it."

"Uh huh."

"And I thought I brought you from Oreen to end a civil war."

"The war's over. They had to bring in mercenaries and Kerbers to fight this one. You were paid off when Essien got the regalia and the Kerbers have lost interest. Now, it's personal. Essien will never feel secure on the throne as long as a piece of the regalia is missing, and Jameel will never feel secure knowing Essien's people will be coming after him."

They rode in companionable silence for a few minutes, wrapped in the noises of the Wing on the move.

"You know," Swan mused, "they could have lived happily ever after if you hadn't done this."

Terizan smiled over at her lover. "One of them cheated me and one of them tried to kill me after I saved his life four times."

"Three." Swan pointed out.

"Still..."

"Do you know what I think?"

"That beer is better than wine. That everything tastes better with enough dried chilies to kill a normal woman. That sex in a tent with a couple of dozen mercenaries listening in is perfectly normal. And..." Terizan winced as her horse changed his gait, rubbing her inner thigh against a buckle. "...that in spite of evidence to contrary, saddles are not instruments of torture."

"No...well, yes, but also that the lions of al'Kalamir should have been told to beware of you."

Even perched as precariously as she was, it was difficult not to look smug. "Oh yeah. That too."

The thing about being the best is that people keep making you prove it.

SOMETIMES, JUST BECAUSE

"WAS IT SOMETHING I said?"

Tribune Two paused, pale eyes narrowing, one hand raised to indicate the target on the map of Oreen.

Tribune Three snickered in what could, in no way, be considered a reassuring manner, amusement sending oily drops of sweat dancing down the smooth rolls of his neck.

Tribune One lifted a sardonic brow; as much, it seemed at her companions as at the thief facing them. "Why do you ask?"

"First you want me to steal from gods; now wizards." Terizan scratched at a flea bite on her forearm. "If I didn't know better, I'd think you were trying to get rid of me."

"Get rid of you?" One asked, eyebrows moving from sardonic to exaggerated shock. "The only thief to ever make it all the way to the Sanctuary?"

"The thief who can bring Swan and her Wing of mercenaries to heel?" Two added.

Three rolled his eyes heavenward. "The thief who dares to steal from the gods themselves and in such a way she benefits from the theft?"

"The thief who holds the debt of the al'Kalamir for bringing his regalia out of a trapped and enchanted treasure room?"

"The thief whose current investments with the Guild have reached close to record levels in a record amount of time?"

"Why would you think the Guild would want to get rid of you?"

Terizan shrugged, the movement causing a dribble of moisture to run down her sides, making her cotton tunic less comfortable and even more fragrant. "Just a feeling."

"Besides," One amended with an aristocratic snort, "it's only *one* wizard."

"Right."

"And even were you not the best we have, your sensitivity to magic would make you the logical choice."

"Uh huh. Usually, my sensitivity allows me to *avoid* magic. Breaking into a wizard's tower and stealing a curse…"

"A curse anchor," Three offered helpfully when she paused.

Terizan nodded her thanks. "…is not avoiding. It's st…" Suddenly realizing that the Thieves Guild Tribunal might think she was calling them stupid instead of the concept and fully aware that the consequences of such a misunderstanding would likely not be in her favor, she forced her tongue around a different combination of letters. "…range. Strange to think I could even get into a wizard's tower."

"Strange but not impossible," One replied, the twist in her lips a fair indication she'd actually heard the original word but was content to ignore it for now. "The Council has given us full plans of not only the grounds around the wizard's tower but of the interior of the tower itself with all known spells and enchantments marked."

"The wizard's servant was most forthcoming," Three added, smiling broadly.

"Tortured?" Terizan asked.

"Bribed." From the tone, she assumed Tribune Two would have preferred the former. "The woman came to the Council when it became clear that this recent heat was the wizard's doing."

"Gee, since she's frying too I'm surprised she didn't offer the information from the goodness of her heart." Raising a hand between her and the three nearly identical expressions facing her, Terizan sighed. "Sorry. Kidding. Go on."

"Besides your percentage of the rather sizable fee the Council is paying us to steal this anchor, you will of course be able to remove anything else that takes your fancy."

Take anything else she fancied from a wizard's tower? They really *were* trying to get rid of her.

Something of the thought must have shown on her face as Two leaned forward, map crinkling under damp palms. "Of course, if you refuse the job, we'll only have to send someone else."

Someone less likely to succeed.

One and Three looked at her and smiled.

Someone less likely to survive.

It was a bitch being the best.

"Okay. Let me see if I got this straight." Balthazar leaned against the doorjamb, arms folded, brow furrowed. "The wizard's pissed at Council for telling him to cut down that big thorny hedge so he makes it hot. His servant goes to Council, tells them the wizard is making it hot, and for a price, she'll tell how to stop it. Council comes here and tells the Tribunal they'll pay them to steal the thing the wizard's using to make it hot. The Tribunal gives you the job so you're going to steal an anchor from the wizard?"

"Essentially, yes." Terizan tested the grip of a grappling hook, tossed it back in the basket, and pulled out another.

"Ain't anchors kinda big?"

"It's not that kind of an anchor. It's just a small item the wizard is using to focus the curse."

"Oh." He stuffed his hand into his armpit and scratched vigorously. "You get *all* the good jobs."

"Balthazar, do you remember what wizards do to thieves they catch?" Crossing the storeroom, she ran questing fingertips over the ropes sorted onto a row of brass hooks by length and weight.

"Sure. They turn them into mice then set the cat on them."

"I don't want to be a mouse."

"I wouldn't mind."

As she turned toward him, an eyebrow rose in a conscious imitation of Tribune One.

"Right." Bare feet shuffled against the tile. "But you won't get caught, you're the best."

Right. And that was working out so well for her. Gods. Wizards...

"You *never* get caught," he added mournfully.

He'd been caught twice. Once more and the guild would ground him—Magistrates were expensive in Oreen, and the guild wouldn't pay out indefinitely.

It was, if possible, hotter in the storeroom than it had been in the Inner Sanctum. Hotter and dustier. Wiping her face on her tunic left a grey/brown smear across the fabric. One more thing and she could head for the relative cool of the streets.

"What happened to *your* stuff?" the older thief wondered as she sorted through the lock picks for a set that felt right in her hand.

"Nothing."

"Then what's with the shopping spree?"

"Items you use frequently become imprinted with your...essence."

"Scent?"

"Close enough." Terizan tossed the set of picks that felt the least wrong into her pack. "I'm not taking anything into that tower that might tell the wizard who I am."

"Sweetling, wizards are not exactly in my line of work. They're reclusive, every last one of them. They have no interest in the pleasures of the flesh, they're only interested in the pursuit of obscure knowledge, and their only indulgence is arcane ritual." Poli frowned at her in the mirror, a minimalist expression that wouldn't disturb his cosmetics. "What?"

Grinning, Terizan waved a hand at the bottle, jars, and brushes. "Arcane ritual?"

"Don't be ridiculous; this is skill, not magic." A touch of oil on his lower lip and he turned to face her, looking stylized and beautiful.

"Looks like magic to me," she told him fondly. Poli in cosmetics looked more like himself. If she'd tried to apply an equivalent amount of paint and powder, she'd have looked like one of the priests of Busoo, the God of Laughter. "So if you have no first hand knowledge…" She handed him his robe as he stood. "…have you heard anything?"

Eventually, the whores heard everything.

"Sweetling, you're not listening—wizards don't use the services of my guild."

"People who work for wizards do. Don't they?"

"No." He narrowed kohled eyes and sighed. "Terizan, have you agreed to steal something from the wizard's tower?"

"You know I can't answer that."

"Wonderful. So, sharing your bed with an insane mercenary captain isn't enough to satisfy this sudden death wish of yours? Now, you want to be turned into cat food?"

"One." Terizan flicked a calloused finger into the air. "Swan isn't insane, she's just really, *really* good at what she does which happens, incidentally, to be mayhem. Two." A second finger followed the first. "I don't have a death wish. I have a reputation as the best thief in the city, and that brings with it certain unavoidable responsibilities, but I have every intention of surviving the experience. And three." She folded the first finger down.

"You can't afford me, Sweetling."

The oldest of the storytellers throwing words into the air on the Street of Tales insisted there were once three wizard towers in Old Oreen. A non-descript neighborhood of middle-class shops and houses had grown up over the ruin of one, the squalid hovels and tenements of the Sink covered another, and the third stood alone. Had stood alone for as long as anyone could remember.

According to the storyteller, that middle-class neighborhood produced more than its share of priests and artists and the totally insane. And the Sink—well, every city had a cesspool, the Sink was the cesspool of Old Oreen.

"Do the stories say how those two towers were destroyed?"

"They do." The storyteller sucked her teeth and waited, right arm raised so she wore her cupped hand like a hat, the bowl of her palm facing the sky. Or at least the awning over her square of pavement.

Terizan sighed and dropped a monkey into the old woman's hand. She waited patiently while the brass coin vanished into the folds of a grimy robe and a little less patiently as a small leather bottle was consulted.

"It was a dark and stormy night," the storyteller began at last, adding, as Terizan's brows rose, "No, really, it was. A dark and stormy night…" She cleared her throat. "…thunder, lightening, hail. A night that cleared the streets of all the good citizens of Oreen—as few as they were within the walls in those dark days. When the ground beneath the city shook and the air filled with the scent of burning hair and the screams of tormented souls rode on the backs of howling winds, no one dared to turn an eye to the cause. No one but one small boy," she added hurriedly as Terizan opened her mouth to protest. "A small boy who swore he saw ribbons of red spiraling from one tower, ribbons of blue from another, and bands of white around the third. In the morning there was but one tower remaining and blasted, empty, cursed ground where the other two had stood."

"Two of them fought, the third shielded himself."

"So it seems." Her hand rose once more to lie against her head and Terizan sighed.

"That wasn't worth another monkey. What was said of the remaining wizard?"

"Ah, young one, the stories I could tell you…"

Terizan twirled the coin between her fingers. "Give me the high points without embellishing and this is yours."

"Embellishing." Rheumy eyes narrowed. "A large word for one in your profession."

A second coin joined the first. "A large fee for one in yours."

"True enough, times being what they are."

Terizan didn't ask how times were. It would only lead to more stories and a higher expected payment.

"They say that the wizard remains in that tower to this day, extending his life by fell magics. That he is secretive, even for a wizard. That young women enter his tower and emerge as old women a lifetime later with no memory of their service. They say he lives on moonlight and dew. That those who try to breach his solitude meet a grisly doom." She snatched the tossed coins out of the air with the ease of long practice. "You know about the whole thief-mouse-cat thing?" When Terizan nodded, her face refolded itself into a new pattern of contemplative wrinkles. "Your guild must value your talents highly."

"Yeah, that's what they keep telling me…"

Although space was at a premium in Old Oreen, no one had attempted to build up against the wall that defined the triangular grounds surrounding the wizard's tower—which was more than a little annoying since it meant Terizan would have to cross a broad, open street in full view of the tower's upper windows no matter which part of the wall she approached. On the bright side, the neighboring houses had turned their backs to the wizard, presenting no windows and therefore no likelihood that she'd be seen and the Guard called.

"Because there's nothing like worrying about being arrested when you should be worried about becoming a mouse," Terizan muttered. Torches in iron brackets jutted from the top of the wall not quite close enough together to prevent narrow bands of shadow between them—thieves' paths. The trick would be reaching one.

Hidden in the darkness where the back of one house joined another, she ticked off items on her mental copy of the servant's list.

The gate and the path from the gate to the tower are heavily warded. Step on it and my master will know everything there is to know about you.

No problem. She hadn't planned on taking either the gate or the path.

"The thorn hedge that grows around the inside of the wall is not magical but it is deadly. You must move slowly, methodically to defeat it."

Defeat it? Terizan had no intention of fighting with it.

"The only safe way to enter the tower is from above. My master keeps pigeons and has no desire to know everything there is to know about them, but they will act as an alarm if you're not careful."

Pigeons. Flying rats. The thief who didn't plan for their presence on every rooftop in Old Oreen had a short career.

"I'll leave the trapdoor unbarred."

Once inside the tower things got...complicated but she'd worry about that later.

The crescent moon slid behind a cloud.

Wiping sweaty palms against her thighs, Terizan took a deep breath, locked her gaze on the path she planned to use, and raced forward. Time had worn a handy ladder of hand and foot holds in the wall. At the top, her body pressed against the capstones, the sandstone still warm from the heat of the day, she turned in place, and slowly—very, very slowly—began to climb down between the thorns and the wall.

Fortunately, the thorns were attached to big bushes rather than any kind of clinging vine, and the space between bushes and wall, although not exactly generous, was almost wide enough to slide through unscathed. As long as she kept herself from snatching punctured body parts away, she was reasonably sure she could avoid attracting further attention from the bush.

Attracting attention from a bush. This is why I hate stealing from wizards.

One of the reasons anyway. That whole thief/mouse/cat thing didn't thrill her.

When her feet touched the ground, she shuffled them sideways until she lay in the angle between earth and wall staring out between twisted trunks as big around as her arm at a grassy lawn. Two body lengths, maybe two and a half, and she'd be in the clear. Crawling forward on fingers and toes, she tried to ignore the debris mixed into the leaf litter and the heated, heavy smell of rot. Things impaled on the thorns eventually fell. Instincts very nearly had her claim a heavy gold ring, but a hint of brass changed her mind. Moving on, she left it—and the finger bone that wore it—where it lay.

Should the wizard happen to look out the right windows, he'd
see her on the lawn. All the hair lifting off the back of her neck,
Terizan unhooked the crossbow from across her chest and fired the
grappling hooks toward the roof, fully intending to be *off* the lawn
as quickly as possible. A faint hiss of metal against stone and two of
the padded edges caught.

By the time she reached the roof, any pigeons startled by the
appearance of the grapple had gone back to sleep. Shadow silent,
Terizan coiled her rope, replaced the grapple in her pack and slipped
past the coop.

The trap door was locked.

It wasn't *supposed* to be locked.

Isn't it fortunate I have trust issues. She hadn't become the best by
leaving things to chance. Or disgruntled servants. After screwing
a hook into the center of the wooden door, she carefully slid a
metal tube from the thieves pocket in the wide seam of her trousers, ran a fingernail through the wax seal, unscrewed the metal
stopper, and outlined a rough square out about two inches from
the edge of the door. She had no idea what the liquid was but the
alchemist had assured her it would get rid of problem tree stumps.
He'd also warned her that it was highly illegal to use on anything
but problem tree stumps and had winked broadly while pocketing
his extremely high fee.

The wood dissolved.

Terizan lifted out the square and found herself staring down
into the emerald gaze of a plump calico cat sitting on the top-
most landing of a spiral staircase.

Tossing a cotton square stuffed with dried catmint down
the stairs—thief/mouse/cat implied there would *be* a cat somewhere in the tower—she dropped quickly to the landing as the
cat disappeared.

The room she wanted was on the next landing down.

There was a wizard globe outside the door. She waited until her
eyes adjusted to the light, checked for traps, and pushed open the
door finger-tips touching only the random pattern of wood not
imprinted with magic.

The wizard's workroom looked exactly the way Terizan expected
a wizard's workroom to look, crowded with books and scrolls and
a confused jumble of a hundred arcane objects—although she hadn't

expected the wizard's servant to be pacing back and forth in front of a full length mirror. The two women stared at each other for a long moment.

"The trap door was barred," the servant said at last, crossing her arms over a plump bosom.

Terizan shrugged. "I noticed."

"A final test." She nodded toward the room's only window. As far as Terizan could tell from her position by the door, it looked out on the darker, less exposed side of the tower. "I was watching for you."

"I came up the other side."

"But that side…"

"Wasn't being watched," Terizan pointed out. Good thieves learned early on that the way less traveled usually had more guards on it. "As long as you're here, where's the anchor?"

Nothing stood out. If she had to find it on her own in this mess, she'd be here for hours.

"The what?"

"The thing the wizard's anchoring the heat to!"

"Oh, that."

"Oh that?" For someone who'd allegedly gone to the Council, with the information —who'd been paid a great deal of money *for* the information—she sounded as if this was the first she'd heard of either anchor or, for that matter, heat. The general, all purpose, what-kind-of-an-idiot-steals-from-a-wizard bad feeling Terizan had had since her meeting with the Tribunal, began to grow more specific.

A sound on the landing outside the workroom took her from stool, to table's edge, to bookshelf, to balanced on the top of the thick, open door. When the wizard—Who else would be on the landing in a wizard's tower outside a wizard's workroom?—came into the room, she'd drop down behind him and make a run for it.

Thief/mouse/cat. Not going to happen.

Glaring down at the wizard's servant, she laid a silencing finger against her mouth just as the calico cat stalked into the room.

"My master isn't here," the servant sighed. "That's why you are."

"What?"

"He's been stolen."

"What?"

"I need you to steal him back."

Terizan opened her mouth and closed it again. Carefully avoiding the cat—all things considered, staying on the cat's good side seemed smart—she jumped down off the top of the door. "The wizard's been stolen?"

"Yes."

"Don't you mean kidnapped?"

"No, stolen. Turned into a doll, and then stolen right from this room."

"By who?"

She glanced over her shoulder at her reflection. "Something from the mirror."

Some*thing*? That didn't sound good. "Another wizard?"

"I don't know. The mirror showed me what happened but not the form of my master's enemy."

Terizan glanced at the mirror but saw only the reflected servant and workroom. "And you want me to steal him back?"

"Yes."

"From the something in the mirror?"

"Yes."

"Go into the mirror, and steal him back?"

"Yes."

"Are you nuts?"

"No."

She sounded so matter-of-fact that Terizan frowned. "Is there some sort of spell on this place that kicks in if he's not back by a certain time? Something that would destroy the city?"

"Goodness, no!"

"Then why would I agree to steal him back from something inside a mirror?"

"Because you're the best."

"Oh for…" Throwing up her hands, Terizan pivoted on one heel, took two steps out onto the landing, pivoted again and took two steps back. "First, how do you know that?"

"You're here."

Okay. Terizan had to admit that was fairly solid evidence.

"The Council went to the Tribunal," the wizard's servant continued, "and the Tribunal chose you. They wouldn't have chosen anyone but their best—that's why I went to them, why I told them the story I did. I couldn't risk not having the best."

"So the wizard isn't causing the heat?"

"It's summer. It's always hot in the summer, and people always seem to forget that."

"It's hotter than usual. And for longer."

The servant shook her head. "No, it isn't. What was your second point?"

"My what?"

"You said *first*. That implies a second."

Wondering why she didn't just walk away, Terizan reversed the conversation far enough to remember what her second point had been. "What does my being the best have to do with agreeing to steal the wizard back? Wouldn't you assume that, as the best, I'd be too smart to do something so stupid?"

"I assumed that, as the best, you would rise to the challenge."

Terizan found the urge to slap the smug smile off the older woman's face almost impossible to resist. The only thing that stopped her was the knowledge that she'd heard the plan, that nothing was preventing her from leaving, and she was still standing in the wizard's workroom. "What's in it for me? And if you're about to say, *the challenge...*" Arms folded, Terizan curled a lip and put on her best street tough expression. "...think again. I'm a thief, not a hero."

"When he is safely returned to his tower, my master will reward you. My master has many, many treasures. Gold. Jewels."

"Your master is a doll."

"Not once you return him here and I put this around his neck." The bronze amulet dangling from the servant's hand wouldn't have been worth more than a monkey on the street, maybe another monkey for the chain. "This protects him from magical attack. Had he been wearing it at the time, he would never have been changed and taken."

"Why wasn't he?"

"It turns his neck green." Sighing deeply, she dropped it into her apron pocket. "Every now and then, he takes it off to bathe."

"Right."

Gold.

Jewels.

No other thief in the guild could claim to have stolen a wizard back from inside a magic mirror.

Oh no. Don't even think that. You are not... Terizan caught sight of the expression on the servant's face and sighed. *Oh crap. Yes, you are and she knows it too.* "All right, you win. What do I have to do?"

"Just walk into the mirror."

"And he'll be right there?"

"If I expected it to be that easy," the older woman sighed, "would I need the services of the best thief in Oreen?"

Good point.

Her gaze locked on her reflection—which didn't look happy—Terizan crossed the workroom, tripped over a box of scrolls, and only just managed to stop herself from hitting the floor by grabbing a handful of apron.

"You're not filling me with confidence, here." She slapped Terizan's hands away from the bunched fabric and straightened it herself.

"You want confident?" Terizan muttered stepping forward. "How's this: if this is a trick and I find myself with my nose mashed against the glass and you laughing, I'll kick your..."

"...ass."

Her body sizzling in reaction, she found herself standing alone in a reflected version of the wizard's workroom. Heart pounding, she spun around to face the mirror and discovered her reflection had not crossed over with her. A hand against the glass found only that—glass.

It seemed that she needed the wizard in order to get home.

"Oh goody." The words echoed slightly. "Incentive."

A quick search determined that the doll-wizard was not in the tower. In fact there were no magical items of any kind—every thing was show without substance. *And speaking of show...*Terizan walked to the window and looked out over a city that was almost but not quite Oreen. Like the workroom, like the tower, everything had been reversed—mirror imaged—but that wasn't the most disturbing change. Oreen never slept. The streets were never empty of people. The air was never still and quiet.

This Oreen looked and sounded abandoned.

No. Never lived in.

It was nearly midnight on the other side of the mirror, a dark night with a cloud covered crescent of moon. A thieves' night. On this side, a cold grey sky shed a cold grey light and a thief would have to be very good indeed to move through the city un-remarked.

According to the storyteller, there had once been three towers in Old Oreen.

If she had to search Oreen for the wizard doll, the logical place to start would on the site of one of those two towers. Which tower, though? Which of the defeated wizards seemed the most pissed off about it? On the ruins of one—a middle class neighborhood. On the ruins of the other—the Sink.

Personal prejudices suggested she should head towards the middle class neighborhood. Fortunately, she was merely prejudiced, not delusional.

One problem: this was not the Oreen the towers had disappeared from, this was her Oreen, a copy of the city on the other side of the mirror, and in her Oreen there was only one tower. She could see the Sink. She couldn't see the tower.

Maybe when she was closer.

How do you get to the Sink?

You slide in on shit of your own making.

Street wisdom aside, there were a number of ways into the Sink.

Taking the direct route, she could walk down the middle of the street unimpeded by people or dogs or mountebanks or constables or priests. It would be the fastest and the simplest route, it would shorten the length of time she'd have to spend inside the mirror— definitely a plus—and, as she'd told the wizard's servant, those were the routes that were seldom watched.

Seldom. Not never.

The hair lifting off the back of her neck convinced her to stay out of sight.

By the time she reached the Street of Tears—a road that had once lead between a long demolished jail and the executioner's block in the Crescent and that now marked the edge of the Sink—she knew she wasn't alone even though she'd seen and heard nothing. As a rule, her instincts were good, and she was willing to give them the benefit of the doubt.

Might have been nice if they'd stopped me from walking into the mirror in the first place, though. Or if they'd made some noise during that whole 'here's a challenge you can't resist' thing.

If she knew the 'something' was there, then the odds were good the 'something' knew she was there as well even if didn't know exactly where. Slipping into the Sink, she worked harder to stay hidden.

"But you won't get caught, you're the best."

Her gut told her this would be the worst possible time to disprove Balthazar's statement. Caught on this side of the mirror, there'd be no guild to buy her freedom.

The air was so still she could feel it move past her, and the silence left her no masking noises to hide behind. On the bright side, the filth and decay that usually choked the Sink's narrow streets had form but no substance. On the other hand, she was beginning to see teeth in the shadows.

Given a choice, she'd have taken the filth and decay no matter how hard it was on the sandals.

About a third of the way in, she could feel the tower although the way its presence danced against her skin like a thousand invisible ants kept her from being really happy about it. She still couldn't see it though, and that would make breaking into it just a little more difficult than usual.

Crouched on a roof between a crumbling chimney and a pile of debris, Terizan peered at the space she knew the tower filled and wondered what in the names of the small Gods was she supposed to do now. How did a thief, even the best of thieves, break into a feel...

She froze. Held her breath. Tried to stop her heart from beating so loudly inside her chest. She wasn't alone on the roof.

It was behind her. Whether it was tracking her or had merely found her was irrelevant—it was there. And coming closer. Hunting her.

What does a good thief do when the situation can't be salvaged?

They steal away.

All things considered, not very helpful.

Running like all seven Hell's however, that sounded like an option.

Breaking cover, Terizan sprinted for the edge of the roof and flung herself across the gap between the buildings. She'd leapt greater distances a hundred times—one of the nice things about the Sink was how close together the buildings were. And one of the unfortunate things was how structurally unsound those buildings were.

Under normal circumstances, she'd have never jumped without being certain of where she was going to land.

Not normal circumstances.

The Hunter landed in the space she'd just vacated sending a frisson of terror through blood and bone. It was close enough now for her to feel more than just 'something'.

Hunger.

As her feet slammed down on the ancient yellow bricks, they began to crumble. Throwing herself forward did little good with nothing solid underfoot to push off from.

Terizan had originally joined the thieves' guild because a cornice had crumbled and she'd fallen a story and a half to the ground. Fingers scrabbling for purchase on disintegrating brick, she realized through the building panic that this fall was going to be a whole lot worse. The last time, there'd been nothing waiting for her when she hit the ground.

Closing her eyes, she silently cursed all wizards, their servants, and their stupid invisible towers!

Thick sod cushioned her impact with the ground, leaving her winded but essentially unharmed.

Sod? Her eyes snapped open. She'd been expecting cracked cobblestones, a cracked skull, and rending teeth, not the well manicured lawn surrounding what had to be the second wizard's tower. A quick roll tucked her under the cover of a garden bench. She lay there unmoving, counting her heartbeats, until it became clear no one had seen her.

Or they *had* seen her and were waiting for her to further commit herself.

I should be *committed.* Looking on the bright side, the Hunter hadn't followed her over the wall. *It probably knows that I'm in enough trouble without it.* Although, considerate invisible monsters were of dubious comfort right now.

Crawling forward on elbows and toes, Terizan peered out of her sanctuary. Living in the middle of an empty city, this wizard had no need for thorn bushes to discourage visitors. Even in the real Oreen, being invisible would probably be defense enough—although she knew a number of people it wouldn't discourage.

The second tower looked a lot like the first. The biggest difference was in the number and design of the windows—there were more of them, and they all boasted decorative stonework on lintels and sills creating a thieves stair right to the roof. The whole place pulsed with magic. The last thing Terizan wanted to do was spend more time than she had to inside, but if the wizard's workshop was in the same place, and the wizard wasn't *in* the workshop, she could be in and out the open window in two shakes of a cat's tail.

And what if the wizard *was* in the workshop?

What if the doll-wizard wasn't?

Telling herself firmly to stop borrowing trouble, Terizan started her climb.

At least I don't have to worry about being spotted by someone outside the tower grounds. Did outside the tower grounds even exist? High enough to see over the wall, she balanced securely on top of a protruding lintel, jammed her fingers into the space between two bricks, twisted her gaze back over her shoulder, and nearly fell. The city both did and didn't exist—rippling in and out of sight like a desert mirage behind a curtain of heat.

More wizardry!

Stifling a snort, she started to climb again. At this point in the game there wasn't going to be *less* wizardry.

Below the edge of the uppermost window, she paused, and listened. The silence was so overwhelming she feared for a moment that she'd gone deaf and lightly rubbed her fingers against the ledge of dressed stone just to hear the soft *shrk shrk*.

Not deaf then. Good.

Her breathing shallow and as quiet as she could make it, Terizan adjusted her grip and peered over the edge of the window ledge.

The workshop looked so much like the one she'd first broken into that she wasted half a heartbeat wondering if she'd gotten turned around and was at the wrong tower. Then she started noticing the differences. No mirror—magic or otherwise—dominated an inside wall. More scrolls were piled haphazardly than shelved. And in a space hurriedly cleared by shoving a jumble of odds and ends aside—where one of the odds was an emerald as big Terizan's thumbnail and one of the ends a string of tiny gold skulls—stood an eleven inch doll wearing not particularly well-carved wizard's robes.

No sign of the second wizard.

Unless it had been the wizard chasing her through the city…

Do not go there!

Because if it *had* been the wizard, there was no way this could end well.

She pulled herself up and into the room, pausing for a moment crouched under the window to make sure her entry had gone unnoticed. No point in moving away from an exit she might have to suddenly use.

When no alarms sounded and no magical flares went off, she hurried across the room to the doll. It didn't look like much. It certainly didn't look it had once been alive. It looked…well, it looked kind of skinny and ineffectual, if truth be told.

Now she'd found what she'd been sent for, time was of the essence. Terizan didn't know where the other wizard was—in bed, in the kitchen, in the privy—and it didn't matter, she had to be back on the other side of the mirror before the wizard returned to the work room and noticed the doll was missing.

Grappling hooks pulled out of chest pack, doll shoved in, hooks set, rope dropped out the window, and a quick slide to the ground. She shook down her gear, sprinted across the lawn, climbed to the top of the wall and…

Oreen continued to pulse in and out of sight. Sprawled along the capstone, she fought the urge to puke as she closed her eyes and rolled off the wall. Considering how she'd gotten into the tower grounds, there seemed to be only one logical way to get out.

Ow!

Cobblestones.

Her shoulder blades were hard against the nearest building before her eyes were fully open. Bruises could be inventoried later; right now it was more important to get out of sight. The Hunter could be…

Something between a sound and a feeling drew her gaze upward. She could see only crumbling yellow brick and above it a pale grey sky, but she knew the Hunter was perched on the roof of the building directly above her, staring down at her. Terizan froze, expecting it to pounce, knowing she couldn't move fast enough to avoid it.

No pounce.

It seemed to be moving back from the edge.

Heading for the stairs…

A terrifying supernatural hunter that had to take the stairs? That cranked the terrifying down a notch or two, releasing her from her paralysis and lending speed to her feet. Maybe it hadn't followed her over the tower wall because it couldn't make the jump between the buildings, not because of magics designed to keep it out. If she took the high road across the city, the thieves' path that used the spaces between the buildings as much as the buildings themselves, maybe it wouldn't be able to follow her.

If she could just reach the other tower—the first tower— she'd be safe.

Unfortunately, as she dropped down into the angle where the back of one house joined another, the copy of the hiding place she'd used to study the wizard's wall back when the night was new, she felt the Hunter's presence in front of her. It had apparently *also* realized that if she reached the first tower she'd be safe.

Muscles trembling, joints aching, Terizan slumped to the ground and fought to keep her labored breathing from giving her away. Her chosen craft tended toward intense moments of specific exercise rather than marathon exertions. Between the climbing of two towers and the crossing and re-crossing of half of Oreen, she was exhausted. She had no energy left to fight the Hunter even if she'd had any idea of *how* to fight it.

And the next time someone feeds you a line of crap about how you're the only thief good enough to steal an enchanted wizard back from inside a mirror, what are you going to say?

Terizan, you're an idiot.

Harsh, but true.

The doll looked no worse for its trip across the city. Reaching deep into her thieves' pocket, Terizan pulled out the brass amulet the servant had said would return the wizard to his human form. She'd stolen it from the servant's apron during her bit of pre-mirror stumbling. A good thief realized that getting in was usually the lesser part of the job—getting out again with the goods, that was the tricky bit and it sometimes helped to have a little leverage.

The Hunter brushed against the edge of her senses.

Of course, it also helped to be alive.

Amulet poised to drop over the doll's head, Terizan hesitated.

If she brought the wizard back here, in the angle with her, he'd demand an explanation. Before she'd have a chance to give one, the Hunter would be upon them, and with the wizard's attention on her, they'd be doomed. So he had to come back with his full attention on the Hunter.

Setting the doll so that it faced the broad street between the houses and the tower, Terizan threw herself up the narrow end of the angle until she perched between the two walls a long body-length from the ground. All she had to do now was drop the amulet over the doll's head.

Which would be a lot easier if her hands would stop shaking.

Okay on three.

One.

She could feel the Hunter approaching, moving fast and with the kind of purpose that suggested it knew exactly where she was.

Oh screw it.

She dropped the amulet.

No flash of light, no colored smoke—just a doll one moment and a wizard the next. And the moment after that...

"Oh dear!"

Which, as an initial observation concerning the Hunter, didn't sound very martial. Or very wizard-like for that matter. Terizan had to admit she'd been expecting something more along the lines of "Be gone foul fiend!" Or maybe an instant flare of eldritch fire.

Cowering. That can't be good!

Fortunately, the eldritch fire came an instant *after* the cowering and, as the after images faded, Terizan realized she could no longer feel the Hunter. Skinny, the wizard definitely was. Ineffectual, apparently not.

Body language suggesting confusion more than victory, he began to turn when a poof of displaced air announced the arrival of the second wizard. Appearing in the alcove behind his former captive, he was clearly counting on the element of surprise. As his hands came up and the air began to crackle, Terizan adjusted her grip on a protruding brick, briefly considered the Guild's position on non-violence, and kicked him in the head.

He dropped like a rock.

She lifted her gaze from the crumpled body to find the first wizard, the doll-wizard, staring up at her.

"Do I know you?"

"No." How much should she tell him? How much would it be safe to tell him? How safe would it be to lie to him considering that even if she could get the amulet off him, he wouldn't become a doll and she needed him to get back through the mirror? "I'm the thief your servant hired to steal you back."

The wizard blinked; the movement slow and deliberate enough that Terizan tensed for magic. "Ahmalayz hired a thief?"

No magic. Just a puzzled question. "It's a long story."

"I'm sure it must be. I wasn't aware you could hire thieves. The same way you hire a...a gardener?"

Her fingers were starting to cramp. "Something like that."

"Oh." He glanced down at the other wizard then back up at her. "You're very thorough."

"Yeah, well..." She shrugged as much as her position allowed. "I'm the best."

"I see. I guess you'd have to be, though, wouldn't you?" They stared at each other for a long moment then the wizard gestured toward his tower. "We'd better be going before Zafran wakes up."

"You're not going to turn him into something unpleasant?"

Pale grey eyes blinked again. "Should I?"

"He turned you into a doll."

"Yes, well I sent him..." Another gesture, this one taking in their immediate surroundings. "...here. Things even out don't they?" Without waiting for an answer, he turned started along the road toward the gate.

Figuring that Zafran still had a way to go before he settled the score, Terizan dropped to the ground and hurried to catch up.

"So, this is what Oreen looks like." His tone was conversational, mildly curious; they might have been walking home from the market.

"You live in Oreen."

"I don't get out much."

According to the stories, he didn't go out at all. "How did that other wizard..."

"Zafran?"

"Yeah, him." Terizan might be fool enough to think she could steal a wizard-doll from inside a magic mirror but she wasn't fool enough to make free with a wizard's name. Names had power. "If he's been here for so long, how does he know how Oreen looks?"

"He doesn't. Zafran's landscaping runs to nothingness and fog. This seeming of the city came from your mind."

"My mind?" Suppressing a shudder, she glanced around at the reflection of home and protested, "My mind doesn't like an empty Oreen."

"Oh, this place can't do people. People have substance."

"But the Hunter…"

"The thing I destroyed?" He smiled down at her. "The Hunter, that's a good name for it." His voice did everything but pat her on the head. Terizan found herself wanting to slap him which was probably not a good idea all things considered. "The Hunter was created over the years from Zafran's anger. He'll be glad it's gone." A soft, condescending clucking of his tongue. "He always did have trouble controlling his anger."

They were at the gate, almost to safety. Terizan glanced back over her shoulder and nearly tread on the edge of the wizard's robe as she followed him through the gap in the wall. "What about the third wizard? What happened to him?"

"Her." His expression contained only gentle admonishment. "You're very curious. You do know what curiosity killed?"

"Yeah, but I thought you liked cats."

Thief-mouse-cat.

"That's right, I do."

They stepped through the mirror together.

Ahmalayz clutched at her apron pocket with one hand and jabbed an indignant finger toward Terizan with the other. "You stole the amulet!"

Terizan shrugged. It seemed pointless to deny it with the proof draped around the wizard's neck.

"You stole my amulet?"

Stealing from wizards. Not a good thing. Getting caught stealing from wizards. A worse thing. She walked over to the window, trying to look as though the possibility of going out it hadn't even begun to cross her mind. "If I hadn't stolen the amulet, we wouldn't have made it back. The Hunger would have taken me and…the other guy would have re-taken you."

"But your intent…"

"Was to get us both out of the mirror in one piece."

"You're not lying to me." He sounded pleasantly surprised. "All right then. How much do I owe you for…stealing me from Zafran."

She stared out the window, comforted by the sounds rising up from the city. "You don't. I did it for the challenge."

"She's the best thief in Oreen." Ahmalayz had a sneer in her voice, but the wizard only nodded.

"Then because debts are an uncomfortable thing to have hanging about, let me give you a bit of advice in exchange for your rescue. My rescue. The rescue."

With one last look at the cloud cover between her and the stars, Terizan turned to find the pale grey eyes locked on hers. The sweat running suddenly down her sides had nothing to do with the oppressive heat.

"Zafran was believed to be the best wizard in Oreen."

"You didn't get it? I thought you were the best?" Two sneered.

Terizan shrugged.

"Council won't pay for your failure!" Three snapped. "We'll have to send someone else to get the anchor."

About to point out that no one else stood even half a chance at success—or she'd have never gone in the first place—Terizan found her words drowned out by a sudden crash of thunder. It echoed down the long, narrow stairs that connected the inner Sanctum with the world above. It vibrated in the shelves of scrolls, and it brought with it a cool breeze and the sound of rain.

One steepled her fingers and frowned. "It seems the spell has been removed regardless."

"We could tell them our thief was successful, thus the rain."

Terizan frowned. Did Tribune Three just say thus?

"No." Jowls wobbling, he continued, negating his own suggestion. "The Council wanted the artifact themselves. They have a minor spell caster on staff; she was going to test it."

"Then we could..."

Terizan left them to their arguing. In the end they'd tell the council that they'd been unable to complete the job because, in the end, thieves couldn't also be liars or the whole system fell apart.

It wouldn't be long before the rest of the guild knew she'd failed. She hadn't been caught but neither had she stolen the item she'd been sent to steal.

That the item didn't exist was irrelevant; only two people knew that and Ahmalayze wasn't going to tell or the wizard would find out that she'd laid out his tower defenses. For the same reason, the servant wouldn't tell that she'd broken into the tower. The wizard didn't get out much. He had no idea how Oreen worked.

Terizan could have asked for something from the wizard's work-room, something the Council would have believed was the anchor but then the Council would have assumed things *could* be stolen from the wizard and the next time they thought he was interfering they'd come to the Guild again. And the guild would come to her.

Now they wouldn't because they knew it couldn't be done.

From the speculative glances that followed her across the common room, the whispers of her failure had already begun.

After a nap, she'd console herself with some shopping having stopped on her way back to the Guild House and fenced the string of gold skulls for tidy sum. By now, the skulls had been melted down. By tonight they'd just be part of some jeweler's inventory on the Street of Glass.

"Zafran was believed to be the best wizard in Oreen."

And look where he ended up.

Sometimes, Terizan stole to make a point.

Sometimes to right a wrong.

Sometimes because she really hated to be dicked around.

And sometimes just because she was the best thief in Oreen.

Even if only she and Zafran knew it.

Come check out our web site for details on these Meisha Merlin authors!

Kevin J. Anderson

Robert Asprin

Robin Wayne Bailey

Edo van Belkom

Janet Berliner

Storm Constantine

John F. Conn

Diane Duane

Sylvia Engdahl

Phyllis Eisenstein

Rain Graves

Jim Grimsley

George Guthridge

Keith Hartman

Beth Hilgartner

P. C. Hodgell

Tanya Huff

Janet Kagan

Caitlin R. Kiernan

Lee Killough

Jacqueline Lichtenberg

Jean Lorrah
George R. R. Martin
Lee Martindale
Jack McDevitt
Mark McLaughlin
Sharon Lee & Steve Miller
James A. Moore
John Morressy
Adam Niswander
Andre Norton
Jody Lynn Nye
Selina Rosen
Kristine Kathryn Rusch
Pamela Sargent
Michael Scott
William Mark Simmons
S. P. Somtow
Allen Steele
Mark Tiedemann
Freda Warrington
David Niall Wilson

www.MeishaMerlin.com